The Ambassador's Daughter

A Novel Out of Africa

Samantha Ford

******

Also by Samantha Ford

The Zanzibar Affair

The House Called Mbabati

A Gathering of Dust

Amazon Reviews

*"This is simply the best book I've read in a very long time.
This talented lady brings Africa alive.
Wilbur Smith you have some competition…"*

"A cracking good story with a totally unexpected twist at the end!"
John Gordon Davis – author of Hold My Hand I'm Dying

"Having read all Wilbur Smith's books, this author ranks up with the best of them. Best read I've had for years!" Peter C. Morgan

Acknowledgements

Special thanks to the following for their input.

Mark Baldwin for yet another unforgettable and truly atmospheric cover. - mark@creativemix.co.za

My editor Michael Pilgrim who is a joy to work with.
- pilgrimist@outlook.com

Brian Stephens for guiding me through the whole process of formatting and getting the book up on Amazon both as a paperback and an eBook.
- www.moulinwebsitedesign.com

Most importantly to all the people who have bought my books and given such wonderful reviews on Amazon. I thank you. To be compared to John Gordon Davis – one of Southern Africa's most loved authors, and Wilbur Smith is, indeed, a huge compliment.

Disclaimers

I am well aware of the fact there is no British Embassy in Cape Town, only the British Consulate General.

The Lord Nelson bar, at the Mount Nelson Hotel, no longer exists.

All the characters are fictitious but I have taken the liberty of distorting some characters history and geographical locations to fit the story.

She whispers through your dreams at night.

Like the cry of a Guinea Fowl she calls to you. "Come back, come back."

From far away you hear her voice, seducing you with a beauty you can never forget. The sounds of her, the smell of her, the essence of her, as she waits.

The grasses whisper, the colour of a lion's mane, then sigh with the longing for you to come home where you belong.

The sudden stillness, the silence and the strange light, the bleached whiteness of the wings of birds against an indigo sky. In the distance, the ground shakes with booming thunder, as the lightening spits across the sky, the clouds heavy with promise. The leaves quivering, then still again.

Then when the storm is over, the chorus of frogs croaking in discordant harmony, the birds returning as a joyous choir, and the sound of the hollow monotonous drips on the banana leaves. The mists of the rain covering the hills like a widow's veil.

The Guinea Fowl cries once more. "Come back, come back."

And your heart breaks for this place you remember.

*This place called **Africa.***

Chapter One
The Shepherd

The bleating of the sheep, grazing on the tinder dry grass, carried across the hot African bush. The shepherd dozed under a tree, finding some respite from the punishing heat of the sun. He opened his eyes as the first rumble of thunder heralded an approaching storm. Struggling to his feet he reached for his thick walking stick, adjusting the knot of the cloth over his torso. Shrugging his cloak over his shoulders he whistled to the herd of animals, rounding them up for the long trek back to his village.

Large drops of rain spattered on the dirt path beneath his feet kicking up puffs of grey dust, covering them. He heard the bleating of one of his sheep in the distance, near the slow-moving river. He frowned. No, his herd were all accounted for, he knew of no other goat or sheep herders in the area.

Puzzled he turned towards the direction of the river, his eyes searching for the animal, his ears tuning and tracking the pitiful bleating.

There was silence apart from the occasional rustle of water as the river meandered on its way to an unknown destination. Eza hunkered down on the riverbank, no sign of any goat or sheep, no sound of it.

Then he heard it. Not the bleat of a goat or sheep, but another plaintive sound. He looked swiftly left and right and out across the wide river. The water was thick and sluggish, its banks crowded with barely penetrable reeds and hidden outcrops of slippery rocks. Rotting detritus of dead trees caught and tangled in the reeds, a flash of faded colour from a plastic bag snagged on an outstretched slimy branch.

Something was caught in the reeds on the opposite side. It would be impossible to cross the river from here; it was deep and he could not swim. But he knew further up he could cross on the flat rocks and make his way over, to where the river narrowed briefly before gathering speed and plunging over the ravine.

Moving swiftly, he rounded the bend of the river and found the rocks nestling amongst a shallower part of it. His herd of sheep stopped and looked around, their yellow eyes unblinking, their chins moving rhythmically, as they bent their heads and started to graze.

Eza made his way back, as nimble as a goat, listening for the bleating of the lost animal, willing it to cry again so he would have some kind of beacon to work towards. He would have to be quick before the relentless river gathered speed and rounded the bend.

There it was again. With care he used his stick to part the long reeds on the river bank, his feet sinking into the wet mud.

The child was lying on its back, its dark hair clinging wetly to its scalp, its eyes tightly closed, the tiny chest heaving with spent tears, a toy of some sort wrapped around its arm. The river growled as it passed, hissing through the reeds on either side.

Eza touched the child gently, murmuring to it. "It is alright little one, I am here. Eza will not hurt you. Eza will take you back to the village, you will be taken care of. Shhhh… do not cry anymore. You are safe now."

He wrapped his soft rabbit hide cloak around the whimpering child, shielding it from the heavy rain now falling, before he tucked it under his armpit then hastily moved it to the crook of his arm as the baby once more started to cry lustily.

Eza looked back down the river – how could it be this child was in the river? There were no villages for miles around, only his own, which was far away.

He crossed back over the river and re-joined his herd. The child still crying against his chest. With care he laid it down under the shelter of a small bush. Untying a tin from his belt he searched for his female sheep with her lamb. He knelt at her side and filled the tin with her warm milk and headed back towards the child. With little success he tried to feed it, but he was clumsy and the child, so obviously hungry, screamed even louder, as the milk slopped onto the ground.

Eza looked wildly around for any other options, he slapped the heel of his hand against his head. The mother of the young sheep would have to feed the child, there was no other way. Tying the female to a sturdy branch of a bush he placed the baby beneath her. Holding it up he watched the child nuzzle against the teat, then latch on, drinking greedily. The mother bleated softly, her yellow eyes staring ahead, her mouth moving rhythmically, unperturbed at this strange creature clinging to her.

2

The exhausted child's eyes closed, as it fell asleep in Eza's arms, the milk dribbling from its mouth, diluting with the tears on its cheeks. He carefully took the strange looking inflated doll from around the child's arm and inspected it. It was made of soft plastic and full of air, with arms held in front almost in a circle. Its eyes were large and black, the mouth a red circle of surprise. Around its waist a skirt of short yellow strips, not unlike the short skirts worn by the young girls of his own people. Its arms held around in a permanent gesture of a hug. Gingerly he attached it to his leg, where it clung.

His eyebrows crawled up his forehead in puzzlement. Taking it off he studied it, finding it unattractive and odd. This then, he thought, this strange creature had saved the child's life, keeping the baby afloat as it made its hapless way down the dangerous river.

Wrapping the baby up again, he held it against his warm chest, crooning softly, rocking back and forth to soothe the traumatised child.

The Chief of his clan would know what to do.

But where did this child come from with its bright, but swollen eyes?

He lifted his head and sniffed the air, his gaze washing over the land in front and around him.

The wind was picking up, curling the edges of his cloak. With haste he stood up, holding the child close. He urged his animals over the rocks anxious to reach higher ground. He would shelter in the cave high up in the hills, they would be safe there, away from the storm which would surely come, and soon.

He adjusted the pouch of goat skin across his chest to accommodate the child. The pouch contained all he needed; his bow and arrows, herbs and leaves which would soothe the cuts and bruises on the child's body. Once inside the cave he would build a fire using his sticks, to keep the baby warm. There were many rabbits near the cave, he would spear one and cook it over the fire. Perhaps the little one would need more than milk when it woke up.

Fleet of foot he loped towards the higher ground, his soles hard and deeply cracked from running barefoot in the bush since he was a small child himself, oblivious to the sharp stones, burrs, thorns and biting ants beneath them.

In his haste to reach higher ground he was unaware the strange looking toy had fallen from the child's grasp. It bounced down the hill before being picked up by the strong winds, tumbling towards the river where the now swift currents carried it away.

Eza reached the cave, wrestling his soft cloak from his shoulders he laid the sleeping child down, using his pouch as a pillow, his cloak as a blanket. Kneeling he started the fire, blowing gently on the tentative puffs of smoke.

Satisfied, he collected thorn tree branches and stacked them up against the entrance of the cave to keep the animals safe from any predators.

He returned to the child, lifting it gingerly into his arms. Hunkering down he reached into his leather pouch and drew out a stick of dried meat and placed it in the child's open mouth. It sucked greedily, gurgled and smiled at him, a tiny hand reaching out and clutching his finger, holding tight.

Eza felt an ancient connection for this little creature with its green eyes and high cheekbones. Something unexpected inside of him took flight. He, as a nomadic herder, a shepherd, had never taken a wife, he was too poor to pay the bride price. But now he felt a deep connection to another human being, someone he could love without having to pay, or ask for anything in return.

He looked down at the now sleeping child and smiled. Tomorrow he would find the rabbit and hope someone as small as this would be able to share it with him after he had cooked it over the evening fire.

Somewhere on the baby's journey down the river one of its shoes had been lost. Eza carefully removed the other one, for what use was one shoe if you had two feet? He opened his pouch and placed the shoe inside, covering it with his special leaves, medicinal herbs and potions.

Perhaps, he pondered, if the Elders agreed he might be allowed to be the honorary father, or perhaps uncle, of the foundling?

Eza knew there was now a bond between the child and himself, and in the ways of his culture, he knew he would protect it for as long as he would be allowed.

"*Eish!* The God's were good to reward him with this child, but it would be for the Chief to decide its fate.

*****

Eza's rescue of the baby had not gone unnoticed. The eyes downstream, hidden in the foliage of a tall tree, had followed his every move.

The watcher melted into the thick undergrowth planning his escape route. He would travel under the cover of darkness and make his way back to the farm.

He calculated he would be there before the sun rose; it was unlikely he would have been missed.

The police would be coming to search for the child, he would have to move quickly. But he knew they would never find him.

That which remains unspoken can never be known.

Chapter Two

Two days later Eza saw his village up ahead. The Chief had chosen the spot for his people well. Each dwelling was set amongst numerous bushes, giving the residents some natural privacy from each other. Eza's simple shepherd's hut nestled at the end of a dirt track. He put the sheep in their pen and made his way through the back of the village, the child carefully hidden, until he came to the Chief's round house, set back away from the others, the privacy deserving of his status. A spiral of smoke came from another small dwelling close by, where the Chief's daughter, Mirium, lived.

The Chief would know what to do, and would take wise counselling from the other two Elders, the Chief's brothers.

The Chief was sitting outside, under a tree, on his intricately carved three-legged chair, puffing on his home-made pipe as he watched Eza approach.

Eza bowed, carefully unknotting the cloth holding the baby. With both hands he held the child out to the Chief.

"I found this child in the river, I thought it was dead, but not dead, much hungry. I took milk from my mother sheep to feed it. I have brought it to the village because I did not know what should be done."

The Chief sucked in his breath his eyes lingering on the face of the child now lying in his lap. "What you have done is the right thing Eza, the child will be safe here with us. But it will not be easy." Once again, he studied the face of the sleeping child intently.

"But what of the parents of the child, Chief," Eza asked anxiously. "Will they not look for it? Will the Police not be looking for this child when it is missing?"

The Chief was silent for a few moments, considering this possibility. "Perhaps, Eza, the parents had no money to feed the small mouth."

Eza frowned. "Could it not be, Chief, the child fell into the river? Could this not be possible?"

The old Chief shook his head. "A mother stays close to her child if there is water nearby. But it is also possible it was taken from the town and then down to the river. Maybe the child was stolen."

He looked at Eza. "But the Gods have sent it to us. Take this child to Mirium, she must take care of it now. I will speak to the Elders and see if we are all agreed this is the right thing to do."

Eza lifted the child and walked down the short path to the home of Mirium, calling her name as he entered the gloomy coolness inside her home.

"Mirium, it is I, Eza. The Gods have sent a gift to you to replace the child you lost to the fever."

Mirium looked down curiously at the child Eza was holding out to her, tears filling her eyes. She took the child, with shaking hands, and held it close to her breast. Then she sat and unwrapped the cloth from the child's body. "A small child, I am thinking, not even two rainy seasons maybe."

Mirium shook her head. "*Eish*, there will be trouble with this baby, but we must protect it." The child began to cry and the moment was lost.

"I will thank the Chief for the gift of this child from the Gods," she turned away from Eza, crooning softly, "but now I must feed this little one, it will be hungry. I will take care of it. Go now Eza."

Eza backed out of the hut, thankful the child was now in the safe loving arms of the Chief's daughter Mirium; his own arms feeling the sudden absence of the baby.

*****

The Chief looked around at his two brother Elders, normally no villagers were allowed to attend such meetings, but the Chief wanted Eza present to tell his story of finding the child in the river.

When Eza had finished his story, the Elders discussed in detail what should be done. What story should be told, not only to the village people but also to the police who would surely come in their search for the child.

The Chief did not want any trouble with the police and, in his experience, it was always trouble with the police.

One of the Elders cleared his throat noisily. The Chief nodded to him to speak. "Your daughter, Mirium, lost her only child to the fever. The child is buried high in the hills of the sleeping lions. When the police come to look for this unwanted child, they will only see Mirium with her own child. The little one will be safer here than anywhere else. If we tell them the child was found in the river, they will take it from us. The mother will not claim it is hers if they find her, for this will mean big trouble for her. The police will put it in the place for unwanted children, this place they are calling an orphanage, where there is not enough love for all the small ones".

The Chief nodded and sucked on his pipe. "Only you my brothers, Eza and Mirium know the child is here – it is better this way. We will not tell the people of the village. This way when the police come, our people will tell the truth that they know nothing of a lost child."

He tapped his pipe on the side of his chair and stood up. "I, the Chief, have spoken and this will be done. Now, I must go and see again my new grandchild."

He turned to Eza. "You must not be troubled by this decision Eza. We the Elders are proud of you for rescuing the child. For bringing it to us. This child belongs to us now and will be safe here with our family. As is our tradition the one who saves a life becomes part of that life. Therefore, you will be the honorary uncle as is our way. When decisions are made for the little one as it grows up, you will be included in such decisions, for the child is yours as well."

The Chief paused and frowned. "No. There is another way, a safer way. No one in the village must see Mirium with the child. You will take Mirium as your wife. You must both leave with haste when the darkness comes which will be soon now. Take the child with you. Travel as far away as the days will take you. This you must do.

"When you return any troubles with the police will be over. I will send a message for you with my brother." He nodded at his youngest brother. He is our finest tracker and will be able to follow your journey. He will tell you when it is safe to return. He will bring you back along the old path of our ancestors; the ancient path of the elephants. He is the only one in the village who knows this way.

"My brother will take your sheep and goats and mix them with his own. The village people will know nothing of this plan."

Eza's chest swelled with pride as he tried to stem the unexpected tears in his eyes. Now he had something he could truly call his own. A child, a wife, eight sheep and four goats.

8

Chapter Three
The Mother

With her career now over and the mother of six-year old Ben, Sara had decided to stay on in the country she had grown to love. Away from the prying eyes of the media and the scandal which had blown her life apart. She had fled to the Eastern Cape and the safety of her father's small cottage.

Her father, Sir Miles Courtney, had retired on his return to England and now lived, quite alone, on the family estate in Dorset. Her mother had died shortly after their return from Cape Town.

Determined to make a life for herself and her son, Sara began to design small pieces of jewellery using silver and colourful beads. With the Trust Fund left to her by her mother she had no financial worries.

Her unexpected brief affair with Adrien, who was working at one of the lodges, had resulted in the birth of baby Charlie.

Now, sitting on the veranda of her African cottage in a sagging cane chair, she listened to the rain hammering on the tin roof, drowning out any other noise. Sara watched it sweep over the polished red stone floor, bloated drops landing briefly on the table then bouncing into oblivion. The vicious howling wind screamed through the trees bending and breaking them as easily as a matchstick. The ominous rumble and crack of thunder and the blinding, streaking lightening, allowed her a brief glimpse of the landscape before plunging it into darkness again. Charlie, unafraid, curled on her lap covered with a baby blanket.

She watched the fat raindrops dancing off the stone steps. Not the soft, pale cold rain of England; rain that seeped into the walls of your house and deep into your bones.

Here in Africa the wind and rain were its heartbeat, the thunder its ageless voice, the lightening its spiteful and unpredictable anger.

Tomorrow the skies would be the sapphire blue of Africa, and she would feel the blush of warm sun on her arms and face.

The back of the small cottage was protected by a high bank of rocky outcrops surrounded by thick impenetrable green bush. Sara had never seen any animals up there. In the distance, the wide flowing river made its endless journey to the rapids then plunged over the rocky shelf before continuing on its way.

Sara sighed with contentment, yes, she was alone, but rarely felt lonely. She didn't live in a bubble of loneliness wondering what had gone wrong, and yes things had gone wrong in Cape Town. Her joy came from the beauty around her, her laughter from the company of her children.

She looked down at the sleeping baby, running her finger lightly down Charlie's golden cheek, the tiny hand with its perfect nails, like miniature pearls, clinging to her own grown up, war worn, and worldly hand. No, she was never lonely.

She loved the country and the people. The Africans seemed to have a huge capacity for living life in the moment, rich or poor, seeming to squeeze the life out of it. Even if there were strikes, or riots, or political demonstrations, they still chanted, laughed and danced their way through the chaos.

They were a noisy people, without doubt, with their wide smiles and beautiful teeth, shouting cheerfully at each other, their conversation sounding like a ferocious verbal duel, their laughter peeling across the busy streets in the cities and towns she had visited.

She remembered nursing a glass of wine at an outside café in Cape Town. At the next table were six African women celebrating a baby shower, without any prompting they started to sing. Their voices rose as one, in perfect harmony as they sang their haunting welcome to the coming child. She had felt the tears prickling her eyes, and understood.

Sara smiled. You might leave Africa, but Africa never lets go of you. She was like a lover you can never possess, only love and remember over the passing of time – and long for with all your heart, a place of unimaginable staggering beauty, and relentless hope.

Sara loved the two-hour drive to the lodge where she sold her hand made jewellery. Determined to protect her children from the outside world she left them behind with Beauty, the nanny.

Passing small villages with their round thatched conical roofed homes, gathered together in a *kraal*. In the distance the soft slopes of rolling green undulating hills. The small children running bare foot in the dust as they waved, calling out to her and smiling as she drove past, swamping them with dust. Chickens leaping away from the sides of the road, clucking indignantly and attempting an ungainly flight, small feathers coming adrift and floating away.

In this world of slender Griqua people, their skin the colour of strong tea, their high cheekbones and wide nostrils; the woman with the golden hair and pale delicate features stood out in sharp contrast.

She would look back on this time in her life, and all the challenges life had thrown at her before coming here. But be totally ill equipped for the greatest challenge of her life. Like a lion seeking out a vulnerable impala in a herd; the whisper of death stealthily moving towards her.

Her thoughts came back to her children, the focal point of her life.

At first Sara had been worried about how Ben would react when his sibling was born. Fearing he might feel displaced by the arrival of another child. But her worries were allayed when she saw how protective of Charlie he was.

Sara home schooled Ben and when Charlie arrived, she hired Beauty to help her with the children. The African sun had caressed their bodies turning them golden brown. She smiled, here was the most wonderful place to bring up children, unfettered by layers of clothes, they could run wild and free.

*****

One day Charlie had come back to the house, wearing a tee shirt covered in blood. Horrified, Beauty had swept the child up in her arms. A deep gash down Charlie's arm was the source of the blood. Sara, hearing the crying, came rushing into the kitchen.

"What happened, darling, did you fall?"

Beauty peeled off the child's top and showed Sara the split skin. "Oh baby, that must hurt. Here, Mommy will make it better for you."

Once cleaned up and bandaged Sara returned to the kitchen with the child snuffling in her arms. "Let's make Charlie's favourite supper, Beauty, sausages and chips. Okay, Charlie, would you like that – a special treat just for you?"

Charlie nodded, but didn't smile.

Shaking her head, Beauty went back to preparing dinner. In her mind Ben should be at a proper school, a boarding school, in Port Elizabeth. He was running wild out here with no supervision, no father in his life to reprimand him and teach him some manners.

Sensing something behind her she turned. Ben was standing there watching her.

"What happened to Charlie, Ben?" she scolded him.

Ben helped himself to a freshly baked biscuit, cooling on a tray. "Charlie was following me then tripped over a rock, a big sharp rock. That's what happened, honest!"

"*Eish*! Ben, I hope you are not telling lies to Beauty," she hissed at him, as she wiped her hands on her apron.

Beauty looked at the tee shirt. She would attend to it tomorrow. Miss Sara had looked upset. She would make her some strong tea. Opening the fridge door, she took out the sealed container of sugar.

Eish, the ants were bad this year. Everything had to be kept in the fridge. In the mornings her sink was full of scurrying activity, perhaps the rains might come soon. A large rain spider, high up in the beams of the kitchen, promised nothing.

*****

As Sara sipped the hot sweet tea Beauty had brought her, she recalled another time she had heard Charlie screaming and crying out in the garden, alarmed she had run outside shouting his name. "What's wrong Ben?"

She'd sucked in her breath. "What have you done to Charlie's hair?"

Ben had turned, his face red, the scissors hidden behind his back. "There was a burr stuck in it. I was trying to pull it out and Charlie hit me, so I hit back. Not hard Mommy, but I was only trying to help?"

He had bent to put his arms around the child, but Charlie backed away, looking at him with eyes full of mistrust.

Ben held out his hand. "Come on Charlie, I'm sorry I hurt you, let's go down to the tree house. I found a bird's nest down there, with eggs – I'll show you?"

Charlie took his hand, the moment instantly forgotten.

Chapter Four

Now the hot berg winds were blowing in from the desert, the air was thick and unforgiving. Sara hated the berg winds which often brought fire to the surrounding areas. The children seemed unaware of the change in the weather.

The birds were silent, as though holding their breath waiting for something. The stillness of the bush unnerving, the heat from the winds drying the skin on her face and making her eyes feel gritty.

Feeling unsettled she stood up and wandered around the garden. Everything felt strange and she shivered despite the humidity. Her garden roses were wilting, the grass pale and brittle beneath her feet.

The rains were late this year, but they would come when they were ready. Nothing to be done about nature. It followed its own path oblivious to what was going on in the world around it.

Sara sat back down on the steps of the veranda waving a magazine to and fro in front of her face, trying to cool down. In the distance a jagged split of lightening lit up the darkening sky, followed by a deep rumble of thunder. The old palm tree in front of the house stood silent. Sara used it as her barometer for the wind. It clattered and whispered and told her which way the wind would blow, its old trunk creaking like an old bath chair in need of lubrication.

She called out to the children. "I think you guys should come inside now, there's a storm coming. I don't want you playing outside."

Ben took the toddlers hand. "Come on Charlie, Mom's right, we'll be safer inside. We can play your favourite game?"

Sara rubbed her eyes, feeling the familiar tightening at the back of her neck heralding the arrival of another headache, made worse by the closeness of the impending storm. "I'm going to lie down for a while, Ben. See if I can get rid of my headache. With Beauty away, I want both of you stay inside until the storm has passed."

"You go and have a sleep Mom. I'll look after Charlie. We're going to play hide and seek."

Two hours later Sara sat up groggily on her bed, massaging the back of her neck. The headache had gone but she felt thick headed with sleeping so heavily. Glancing at the clock next to her bed she realised the children would be hungry.

She looked out of the window. The storm had passed and left only a fine drizzle of rain through which a glorious rainbow had appeared. She watched it briefly fade, then went to find the children.

"Ben? Charlie? Where are you? Come on guys, no hiding. You know I don't like it when you hide."

Only silence greeted her. Frowning she walked from room to room, then out onto the veranda, scanning the garden and surrounding bush. Nothing. In the distance she could hear the growl of the now fast-moving river.

The first slither of fear moved through her stomach. Taking a deep breath, she steadied herself. "Ben! Charlie! Where are you?"

There was silence except for the monotonous dripping of raindrops on the leaf of the banana tree to her left, as she stepped down into the garden. A cloud passed over blotting out the sun, the sky turning grey again. Her foot nudged something and she leapt back, always fearing the snakes that sometimes appeared in the garden. She bent down and picked up Charlie's much-loved stuffed rabbit, sodden with rain and covered with mud.

The wind was picking up again and with it, fine veils of soft rain, like fast moving clouds, sweeping in from the hills. Sara ran back inside, throwing a light jumper over her dress.

"Mom?" Sara turned, her breath shuddering in her throat with relief.

"Ben! Where have you been? I told you not to go outside, you were both to stay inside." She bent down and hugged him tightly, until he squealed and wriggled free of her arms.

"Now go and get Charlie. It's raining again and getting cold."

"Mom?"

She knelt down again and held him at arm's length. "What is it Ben?"

His eyes were skittish with fear. "I can't find Charlie Mom? We were playing the counting game and then hide and seek. It was my turn to hide so I counted to ten and then went to look, like I always do."

He was crying hard now. His voice hiccupping. He wiped his nose on his arm, leaving a smear on his cheek. "I looked everywhere. I know you said not to go outside, so I looked around the house, but not anywhere else. I'm scared, because I can't find Charlie. I only called in a little voice, because I didn't want to wake you up with your head hurting so much."

Sara could hardly breathe as she felt a wave of panic wash over her. "We'll look together Ben," she said firmly. "Go and put on something warmer. I'll get an umbrella."

Ben ran back to her pulling a jumper over his head. Biting back her apprehension she held his hand tightly as they set off to search the garden and the surrounding bush.

"Charlie *must* have come outside, Ben. Look, I found the bunny? Do you remember when you last saw it?"

Ben gave a little frightened laugh through his tears. "Charlie never went anywhere without the bunny Mom."

Sara tried to get her scattered thoughts together, overridden by a terrible fear for Charlie. Half an hour later they had exhausted all the possibilities of where the child might be. Picking up on her fear Ben couldn't stop crying.

"Ben, we need to get some help, I'm going to phone the game lodge and ask them to send some staff to help us, before it gets dark." She closed her eyes briefly. Charlie was out there somewhere, all alone, and when night fell, would be terrified. She had to find her baby.

Running back inside she dialled the lodge. They had trackers and rangers; they would know where to look.

"Everyone is out on game drives, Miss Sara, the receptionist told her cheerfully. "Yes, even in this weather!"

Sara stifled the desire to scream. "My child has gone missing. We've looked everywhere. Please, I'm desperate! Is there no-one at the lodge who could come and help us?"

"Hold on for me Miss Sara, I'll speak to the lodge manager."

Sara tapped her foot in terror, every minute that passed took her child further away. "Yes, yes, I'm still here – can anyone help?"

"Mr Paul, the lodge manager, will come with some of the kitchen staff and when the rangers come back, they'll join him at your house. He'll be with you in an hour or so. Please give me the directions?"

Sara put her arm around Ben. "Help is coming, Ben, we'll find Charlie!"

Paul Weston drove as quickly as possible over the rutted dirt roads, glancing out of the window at the relentless rain, trying to imagine what might be going through Sara's mind as she waited for them to arrive. In an hour's time it would be dusk and a search would be difficult. He checked the directions he had been given and drove faster.

He had never met either of her children. He had first met Sara when she had arrived at his lodge, wanting to know if the lodge shop would stock some of the jewellery and beadwork she made.

Her work was impressive and local jewellery was always of interest to his well-heeled guests. Sara had re-stocked the shop four times in that year and although they had shared lunch on each occasion, he knew little about her.

Although he was intrigued with this rather attractive woman, with her choppy blonde hair, he sensed there were hidden boundaries and he respected this, and didn't breach them. Instinct told him, having dealt with hundreds of guests over the years, there was a much bigger story behind this softly spoken woman with the English accent.

In the distance he could see the lights of her house, the first time he had ever been here. In the back of the vehicle his five members of staff, all equipped with strong torches, clung to the sides of the vehicle, the rain pattering on their rain hooded capes. Two rangers would join them as soon as they returned from the game drives, the others would have to stay with the guests. But with this heavy rain, and darkening skies, they would be hard pushed to find any spoor.

*****

Two hours later, two hours of relentless searching, and calling the child's name, Paul his rangers and kitchen staff, returned to Sara's house, she was outside waiting for them

Paul took off his cap and shook the rain from it. His cape was shiny with rain. "I'm sorry Sara. There's no sign or trace of Charlie. The weather's not helping, and now it's just too dark."

He put his arms around the distraught woman and led her to a chair on the veranda. The little boy called Ben, huddled next to her, his eyes swollen with tears, he looked exhausted and frightened, his face white and pinched.

16

Squatting down in front of her he placed his hands over hers, the muddy rabbit still clutched in her clenched fists. Her hands felt frigid between the warmth of his.

"Sara, we'll have to report this to the local police in Willow Drift. They have far better resources than we do to do a thorough search. They should be able to arrange something with the City police in Port Elizabeth. They have more man power, helicopters, vehicles, sniffer dogs. Every hour counts now, okay?"

Sara nodded, her eyes darting unceasingly, searching the garden and the bush, as they had done for the past two hours, her voice hoarse from calling the child's name.

"I'm going to ask Zeb to stay here with you until the police arrive." He nodded at the ranger standing next to him, who looked at him with worried eyes. "This is no time to be alone – okay?"

He stood up and went inside to find the phone. Moments later he returned, rubbing the back of his neck with frustration.

"Bloody hopeless! The local police station in Willow Drift has only two members of staff at the moment and can't help us until the morning. They promised to contact Port Elizabeth, but said it would take some time before they could assemble a search party with the necessary paperwork, vehicles, dogs and possibly a helicopter."

He knelt in front of her again, careful not to wake the little boy now sleeping next to her. He took both her hands in his. "I'll bring my rangers back at first light tomorrow and we'll conduct our own search of the area, and wait for the police…they're bringing a tracker with them, one of their best apparently. His name's Sipo. Bit of a legend in these parts. A Detective Joubert will be heading up the search party."

Sara slumped forward in the chair burying her face in her hands. "Oh God, oh, God, my child is out there in the dark, in this terrible weather, terrified. We must keep looking!" Her voice was raw with emotion.

"I'm sorry Sara, it'll be impossible to keep searching now. We'll find Charlie, I promise you. But not tonight."

"We need an accurate description of the child. A photograph, do you have one taken recently?"

She shook her head. "No, I don't have any photographs of either of the children. I don't like them having their photographs taken, not since we came to live here."

"Mom can draw a picture of Charlie? She's good at drawing pictures of boys. She draws lots of things!"

They both turned to look at the boy who was sleepily watching them both.

Paul turned to Sara. "You need to do this; the search party will need to know what Charlie looks like. Can you have something for us to work with by first thing tomorrow?"

"Yes, I'll try Paul. I'll do my best," she said distractedly. Her eyes traversing the garden and the bush beyond.

Paul stepped off the veranda and joined his staff at the vehicle, before Sara could see the hopelessness he knew was showing in his eyes.

Chapter Five
The Tracker

At first light the following morning, Paul was back, as promised, with four rangers. The two local police constables from the small town of Willow Drift, and the detective were not far behind him, with their tracker, Sipo.

Sara had produced a sketch of Charlie, as promised. Paul plugged in the copying machine he had brought from the lodge, and printed off a dozen copies and handed them around.

They spread out and started their search again for the missing baby. The heavy rains from the night before made their task almost impossible. They found imprints of the children's feet everywhere near the property but this told them nothing, they expected to find them where the children lived.

The police had set up road blocks on the main Willow Drift road, and questioned drivers and passengers, asking if they had seen the missing child, showing them the rough sketch. So far no-one had.

Returning to the house the police, the tracker and the rangers, agreed they would have to widen their search with the help of the police in Port Elizabeth, a two-hour drive away.

*****

The young Afrikaans police detective from Willow Drift, Piet Joubert, met with Paul Western, the lodge manager. Paul brought him up to date on events so far.

Then Joubert interviewed Sara at her cottage, and questioned her at length on the circumstances leading up to Charlie's disappearance. He listened to her, his shrewd blue eyes missing nothing.

Piet Joubert was an ordinary looking man, his dark hair cut short, his body tanned, lean and strong. But his deep blue eyes were startling in their clarity, rimmed with long dark eyelashes. On his right wrist he wore a three-strand black bracelet made of elephant hair.

Ben clung to his distraught mother saying nothing. Detective Joubert asked permission from Sara to question the young boy as to what he thought might have happened, as he was the last person to see the child before it disappeared.

When questioned, the boy repeated what he had told his mother. They were playing hide and seek and then Charlie was gone.

After the interview, Paul insisted Sara and Ben return with him to the game lodge, where she would at least have people around her.

Taking his leave Piet Joubert gathered up his notes. "I'd like to set up a command post at your lodge Mr Weston. Would that be convenient?"

Paul nodded. "Yes, of course. But I must insist the guests are not intruded upon by your presence there. Hardly what they would expect on their safari of a lifetime. You may use my office, but I trust you will be discreet?"

The detective put his hat on and left, looking back briefly at Sara and her son.

Paul now turned to Sara. "We have a guest staying with us, a doctor, I think she should take a look at you, perhaps prescribe something to help, until we find Charlie?"

The ever-present tears filled her panic-stricken eyes again. "I can't leave here! What if Charlie comes back and there's no-one here? I can't do that, I can't!"

"You must, Sara, I insist. Charlie is not nearby," he paused, choosing his words carefully. "You have to let the Port Elizabeth police widen the search using their resources. We need that helicopter, the tracker dogs and more manpower. You must let them do their job and not have them distracted by your presence here. They'll want to search the house and grounds and," he hesitated briefly, "along the river banks."

"No, I can't leave here, I can't."

Sighing, Paul realized there was only one way he would be able to persuade this hysterical woman to come with him, and that was by getting angry.

"Sara, I have a lodge to run, guests to look after. Zeb, my trackers and rangers are employed by me to look after them. They pay a lot of money for their safari. You have to co-operate, which you're not doing at the moment. Do what's best for your child, not what you think is best for you."

Sara closed her eyes, then stood up slowly, holding onto the chair for support. "Alright Paul, I can't think straight anymore. I can't think of anything except Charlie. Give me a few minutes to pack a few things."

Twenty minutes later she emerged from the cottage, lifting up her son she clambered into the vehicle with Paul and the other men. The child struggled in her arms, insisting they had to take Charlie's other favourite toy with them, so when Charlie was found he could give it back.

He scampered back into the house and disappeared. A few moments later he was back, a little rucksack bouncing on his back.

The vehicle turned out of the drive and sped back to the game lodge.

*****

Sipo clung to the side of the safari vehicle as it bounced and slid over the wet bush track, his mind quickly going through the search for the child. His keen eyes, and uncanny knack for seeing things others may have missed, had not let him down.

Hunkering down at the side of the river he had wiped the rivulets of water sliding from his hair and into his eyes, then studied the rutted mud and the grasses. Many animals had been to drink over three or maybe four days, he had carefully pushed aside the tangled reeds with his spear and leaned closer.

The shepherd, had been here recently.

Sipo sat back on his haunches and scratched the stubble of his beard.

No, this was not possible. He would have been on the other side of the river as he always was with his livestock.

Sipo stood up and looked at the wind wrinkled river, the sun turning its grey muddy colour into a river of shimmering gold.

The shepherd was a good man, decent and honest – he would never hurt any creature, human or otherwise. Sipo, using his spear, carefully obliterated any trace of the shepherd's recent presence and stood up.

He loped back the way he had come, his splayed toes seeping into the mud.

The shepherd had been carrying something heavier when he left the river bank. It would explain the deeper footprints in the mud.

There could be only one reason for this. The shepherd had found one of his herd, he had taken it and buried it somewhere, away from any prowling predators.

This could be the only explanation.

Chapter Six
The Tracker

The day after the child disappeared the Port Elizabeth police arrived by road and helicopter. Again more road blocks were set up, the police fanned out covering a much wider area, as the helicopter swooped low over the dense bush. The two sniffer dogs set to work, having picked up the scent of the child from the little stuffed rabbit.

*****

Despite an extensive search of the bush, the river banks and the road blocks, there was no sign of the child. The police and trackers returned to the lodge where Detective Joubert had set up his command post in Paul's office. When everyone had been introduced, he addressed them.

"I'll be heading up this case and I want to thank you for your assistance in our search." He brought them up to date on the circumstances surrounding the child.

Joubert looked at the faces of the men and women in uniform and decided on his next move. Running his fingers through his short-cropped hair he addressed his team.

"The chances of finding this child alive now, are slim. But we're not going to give up.

"We need to extend the search. I want you to visit all the villages in the surrounding area." He turned to the map pinned to the game lodge manager's wall. Using his cane, he pointed to four different locations.

"Don't be heavy handed. We need to work with these people not against them. I don't want, or need, any trouble if they think we're accusing them of something. In the present political climate, anything can happen."

One of the officers raised his hand. Joubert nodded at him. "Yes, Mike?"

"Sir, might I respectfully suggest we officers take a back seat on this one?"

Detective Joubert scowled at him, knowing what was coming. "Take a back-seat Mike? What exactly are you suggesting?" His anger was palpable in the cold tone of his voice.

Mike drummed his fingers on the table, looking embarrassed at being in the spotlight which he had turned on himself. "Well sir, with the current situation, and the new government still in transition, it might be, er, more diplomatic to send our fellow African officers into the villages. The sight of a white officer might evoke anger and suspicion as to our motives…"

His voice trailed off as he saw the fury in Joubert's face. "I don't give a fuck about politics Mike, and I don't give a fuck about the colour of a police officer's skin! Get out there and do the job. There is a child missing and I want it found and I don't care who finds it. We are police officers not bloody politicians. We do our job and we do it together, as we always have done."

He slammed his cane down on the table, breathing heavily. Lifting his head, he looked around the table until he found the face he was looking for.

"Sipo. You're the best tracker in our unit. I want you to select three of your best men, preferably ones who speak the language of the people of the four villages we will search. Mike, you will choose your men, I want two uniforms for each village."

He shuffled through the untidy papers on the desk. "Here are the search warrants should they be required. I trust this won't be necessary, but you need the correct documents should the situation call for it.

"Be courteous and respectful. See if you can get them to assemble their people in each village, so you can address them together. Ask permission to search their individual homes. They won't like it but it has to be done. We must do everything possible to locate Mrs Saunders child, yes?"

The police officers nodded warily. The local villagers had a healthy respect for the police but a deep distrust of their motives. There could be trouble if the situation in each village was not handled with great care and diplomacy.

"Find out the name of the Chiefs in all four villages. Request a meeting with them. Don't go in with any aggression. Sit with the Chief,

24

talk about the crops, the animals, the weather, the welfare of his people, how he feels about the politics in the country now. Win him over, then respectfully request to meet all his people both young and old. Every single one of them. I want a head count of everyone in each village."

Joubert looked back at the map then turned to the attentive faces in front of him. "I would suggest the officer in charge take a small gift as a token of friendship and respect, perhaps a goat? I would also suggest the sergeant does the talking and not the officer, unless the situation requires otherwise.

"Now. Collect your vehicles, get out there. Find out what happened to Charlie Saunders."

*****

Whilst the police doggedly searched, Detective Piet Joubert, from the Willow Drift police station, once more interviewed Sara at the lodge.

Although heavily sedated from the drugs the doctor, a guest at the lodge, had given her, her answers were lucid as she once again recalled as much as she could from the day her child disappeared.

Frequently breaking down, Sara did what she could. Ben always at her side. Joubert could see she was close to a complete breakdown. He would be as gentle as he could with his questions.

Joubert looked down at his notes and frowned. "Is there any possibility Charlie's father might have kidnapped the child? Or anyone for that matter. Did you notice any strangers hanging around in the past couple of days, any vehicles you hadn't seen before?"

"No. Absolutely not. Charlie's father has no idea where we live, so that's impossible. He lives in France. No, I didn't notice anything unusual in the way of cars or strangers. Oh God, I can't do this! I want my child back." She buried her face in her hands and gave into her grief, her body shuddering, the tears leaking through her fingers. Ben buried his head in her lap and sobbed.

Detective Joubert made some more notes, then looked up at her, his expression completely impassive. "I need the name of the father of the child Mrs Saunders?"

He watched her closely as she lifted her head from her hands and wiped her wet cheeks. Her eyes darted down to her son. The boy had lifted his head and was watching his mother intently.

"Mrs Saunders?" he prompted.

25

Sara looked at Ben's frightened face. "Ben, mommy is going to be a long time talking to the police. Maybe one of the staff could look after you whilst you have a swim?"

Ben shook his head vehemently. "No! I want to stay with you. I want to be with you when they find Charlie, please Mom?"

"No, Ben," her voice hardened. "I need to be alone with Detective Joubert for a while. Do as you're told!"

Sara stood up and took his hand. In one swift move Ben kicked her hard on the leg before bursting into tears. "I want Beauty, she'll know where Charlie is, she'll find Charlie!"

Detective Joubert watched them leave the room. Something was amiss here. Mrs Saunders was making no attempt to comfort her distraught son. Beauty would probably be the nanny. He needed to bring her in for questioning too.

A few moments later Sara returned, looking visibly shaken, a small bruise already appearing on her leg where Ben had kicked her.

"I'm sorry about that Detective Joubert. He's normally a placid child but obviously overwrought about Charlie."

Detective Joubert nodded and picked up his notebook. "Yes, I expect he is, a natural reaction. Now, I have some more questions for you, Mrs Saunders. Can you describe what Charlie was wearing?"

Sara clasped her upper arms and frowned. "I'm not sure, shorts and a top I think?"

Joubert looked up. "Colour?"

"I'm sorry Detective Joubert, I can't think straight at the moment. I can't remember."

He frowned and scribbled in his notebook. "This Beauty, Ben mentioned. She was the nanny?"

Sara nodded. "Yes, Beauty has worked for me for some years now."

"Where is she Mrs Saunders?"

"She went back to her family in Swaziland for a few days, she said her mother was unwell."

Joubert turned to a fresh page in his notebook. "And when was this? When did she leave?"

Sara put her hands to her face. "She left the day before Charlie went missing."

Joubert looked at her pensively. "You saw her leave then?"

"Well, no, I didn't. She said she was meeting a friend at the bus stop, not far from here."

"Is it possible, Mrs Saunders, that she didn't leave? Stayed in her quarters and then waited for an opportunity to take the child? Perhaps when the children were playing their game of hide and seek? Charlie would have gone with her with no fear.

"Is it not possible she took the child then handed it over to Charlie's father? Perhaps for a great deal of money and that's why she has not returned? Could it be that the friend at the bus stop was the child's father?"

Sara stared at him astounded. "Beauty would never do anything like that! She loves Charlie. She wouldn't do anything like that to me either?"

Joubert ran his fingers through his hair and continued. "I have to explore all possibilities. I need her full name and her identity number as a matter of urgency, plus a description of her."

"That's not going to be possible. You see Beauty was not in the country legally. Her name is Beauty Dlamini... She doesn't have an identity number, it's not necessary in Swaziland."

She shook her head firmly. "No, Inspector Joubert. Beauty would never take Charlie from me. You'll be wasting precious time trying to find her. Please keep searching. I want my child back! If Charlie is with Beauty, I would be more than happy, because she would never hurt the child. But Charlie is not with her!"

There was a rapid knocking on the door.

Detective Joubert stood up, smoothing down his jacket, he glanced at Sara, opened the door then closed it softly behind him.

*****

Sara stood up and paced the room, something was happening. Had they found Charlie? Please God let them have found Charlie. Was it possible Beauty had taken the child?

She bit her lip, tasting blood. Charlie would have gone with her, with no fear.

If Charlie had been found she would have no choice but to tell the truth. But, God, oh God, if Charlie was never found she would have to live with a terrible secret for the rest of her life.

Chapter Seven

Mike and Sipo clambered into their vehicle and set off for the last village on the list. Sipo had suggested this particular one.

"I was brought up near this village sir, it could be some members of the community here might remember me. I speak their language. I know their ways."

Mike had agreed, and as they sped through the bush leaving clouds of red dust in their wake, he wound up his window, glancing at Sipo.

"What are the chances, my friend, of finding this child alive?" he asked softly.

Sipo stared through the windscreen into the distance. "The chances are not good, it is true. A small child walking alone in the bush is in danger from the animals. The river can be looking safe, but with a storm coming," he shrugged, "beneath lie strong currents. The river is not caring what it is carrying. A small child would be swept away and when the river is getting angry it will drop this small child over the thundering falls. Should a small child survive this, which the river would not like, when the river slows down there are many crocodiles."

He turned to look at Mike, his light eyes creased with sadness and regret. He shook his head. "It is my thinking this child is gone."

Mike slammed his fist on the steering wheel, then sighed heavily. "We have to keep searching no matter what the outcome is. The thing bothering me Sipo, is this. The river is a twenty-minute walk from the cottage, the baby could never have walked that far alone. Therefore, it is my belief that the child was carried there, if indeed this is what happened. With our extensive search we would have found it by now, right?"

Sipo nodded. "This is so, but there are many predators in the bush, hungry for food," he finished lamely.

Mike shook his head. "The dogs would have found the remains Sipo, you know that."

"Sir, the hyena leaves nothing after a kill, no bones."

"Also, Sipo, I'm not buying into the theory that the nanny was involved, someone would have seen her carrying the child."

In the distance Sipo could see the conical thatched roofs of the village he knew well.

"Here is the village, Sir."

Chapter Eight
The Shepherd

Eza looked up, shading his eyes from the searing sun. In the distance he could hear the thwack, thwack, thwack of a helicopter. Quickly he pulled his wife and child into the deep shadows of a coral tree beyond the gaze of the policeman's flying dragon.

He watched as the pilot swooped down, flying low over the thick tangled bush, the rotor blades sending billowing clouds of dry dust, coating trees and bushes left in its path. Guinea fowl squawked and fled in terror. The birds seething beneath the branches of the great tree, exploded into flight shrieking into the endless skies

The pilot did not see the small family huddled there. With one final sweep he lifted his craft and moved on.

Eza turned to his wife as she rocked the agitated child in her arms. "We must wait Mirium, to be sure they have gone and do not return. Then we will find a secret place in the hills. We will be hidden there. The Chief will send a message when it is safe for us to return to our village."

An hour later they emerged from the safety of the tree and made their way swiftly into the hills. Away from prying eyes and the noisy machine in the skies with the wings of a dragon fly.

Hidden in the cave, Mirium nursed the fretful baby, crooning and rocking it. Eza blew on the smouldering fire, the skinned rabbit lay on a rock ready to be cooked. Pulling the two ostrich eggs out of his pouch he handed one to Mirium and drank deeply from the other, the cool water filling his mouth.

"Tomorrow I will return to the stream and fill the eggs again. The little one will need water for washing."

Mirium nodded and clapped her hands softly, thanking him.

Eza stood up and went to the entrance of the cave and scanned the rolling hills and bush. He smelled the fire before he saw the wisps of

30

smoke dissipating into the cloudless sky, painting white airstreams reminding him of the inside bones of his ancestors.

"A fire is coming Mirium. The hot winds from the desert will make this fire very big." He narrowed his eyes following the trail of smoke now beginning to billow into the sky. "It is many miles from our village, but close to this place where the foreigners come from over the sea to see our animals from their trucks. But we will be safe enough."

Mirium looked up from the child. "Perhaps, Eza, the police will not come to look for the child with all this fire you are seeing?"

"Perhaps this will be so. Much will be burnt and much will not be there after the fires have taken their share of the land."

Mirium turned back to the small bowl in front of her and stirred the contents, as her father, the Chief, had instructed her.

Satisfied with the temperature of the liquid she turned back to the child.

Chapter Nine
The Tracker

Mike and Sipo drove slowly through the village, careful not to churn up too much dust and cover the curious faces of the villagers. Mike parked under the shade of a small tree and adjusted his cap and jacket before alighting from the vehicle. He removed his sunglasses and wiped away the half-moon crescents of dust under his eyes before sliding them into his pocket. Eye contact would be absolutely necessary when meeting the Chief and his people.

*****

Outside one of the bigger thatched huts, set a little back from the rest, a tall man stood straight, pulling his soft cape around his shoulders to cover the slight chill coursing through his body.

The police. The Chief knew they would come to search for the child.

Not moving he watched the man with the shiny buttons approach, with his assistant. The white man removed his cap and introduced himself. The Chief stared at his companion – this he had not expected. Eza's childhood friend Sipo. Here was trouble already.

Carefully lowering himself onto his carved chair he gestured for the policeman and his tracker to sit on the two hastily provided stools.

Sipo, as was customary and respectful, asked after the Chief's family, his children, how the crops and animals were doing, what harvest was expected after the rains. His thoughts on the new President, Nelson Mandela.

The Chief replied, ignoring the officer of whom he was much afraid, even though he was the Chief of his people and the white man a mere policeman. Of Sipo he was now also afraid.

After the exchange of the gift of a goat, Sipo cleared his throat and looked at Mike. Mike nodded.

In the language of the Griqua people Sipo explained the reason for their visit. A child had gone missing and despite extensive searches by the police no body had been found – no child had been found. Would it be possible, he asked, for the Chief to gather all the people in the village and ask if anyone had seen a small child? Would it be possible also for them to search the dwellings of the people of the village to assure the authorities they had carried out their orders, as required by law?

The Chief rose from his chair. He spoke angrily, in broken English. "I will call the people from my village. I will ask them. Do you not think I, as the Chief, would know of a strange child here? How could this child hide in a village such as ours?"

"Ask him how many people live in this village Sipo? I think he would be more comfortable speaking in his own language. English seems to make him angry." Mike murmured as he made notes.

The villagers congregated outside the Chief's house; their eyes wide with curiosity. Many had never seen a white man with such strange clothes before and they were afraid.

When the Chief's people had been counted, Mike made another note in his book. Out of the thirty-two inhabitants, two were missing.

"Ask the Chief where two of his people are Sipo. We must account for everyone."

Sipo translated this question.

The Chief had not looked at the police officer since the introduction and he didn't now. Once more in broken English he replied.

"One of our own is lying awaiting burial, you may go and see him if you wish, his wife is with him. It is the place with the black feathers. These are the two of my people you seek."

The Chief stood up indicating the meeting was over. "If it be your wish to search the huts of innocent people then this must be done as ordered by the police."

His body rigid with anger he lifted the rattan matting from his door and disappeared into the gloomy depths.

Mike and Sipo entered the huts and made a cursory search, they avoided the hut with the black feathers containing the dead man and his wife.

Sipo headed back towards the Chief's hut. "I will thank him, Sir, for allowing us to perform our duties."

Mike scribbled in his notebook without looking up and nodded. He reached for his hat and made his way back to the police vehicle.

"Chief?"

Silence emanated from the Chief's hut. Sipo called again, this time more loudly. The Chief commanded Sipo to enter but did not offer him a place to sit.

"You have finished your task then? You have finished looking for that which is not there? My people are angry. You should go now."

Sipo murmured his apologies. "We will not trouble you again Chief, but this had to be done."

The Chief lifted his head and stared at Sipo, his eyes as hard as pebbles. "And where does your heart lie Sipo?"

Sipo looked straight back at him. "I am working with the police, this is true. But my heart lies with my people. They will always come first, as it has always been. The Griqua people would never harm anyone, only the animals they need to eat, and this they do with prayer and thanksgiving."

The Chief and the tracker stared at each other, their gazes locked. The unspoken name on both their lips.

The Chief turned his head away and stared through the door at the rolling hills in the distance. "It is better you do not come here to the village again. It will only bring trouble to you."

Sipo left the hut and went to join his partner in the police vehicle. "Our work here is done, Sir, no trace of the child. These people are not involved. It is hoped the other officers have more news then we have."

Mike put his sunglasses on, started the vehicle and turned to leave the village. He scratched his head with his pen then rammed his hat back on his head. "I'll never understand these people Sipo, with all their secret ways. Come on let's get back. I need a long cold glass of beer and a good night's sleep." He peered through the dusty windscreen, screwing up his eyes. "Looks like a bush fire has started. That's not going to help. Especially if the wind changes direction."

Sipo stared straight ahead for the journey back to the police headquarters, saying nothing.

Chapter Ten

The berg winds whipped the flames into a frenzy of rolling fire balls consuming the parched earth and everything in its path. Thick clouds of smoke covered the bush for miles around.

The bush fire hungrily devoured everything in its way, sweeping through the bush and licking up the trunks of hundred-year-old trees. The hot desert winds blew fiercely, fanning the flames, the sky and the sun red from the intense heat.

Houses, shacks, vehicles and farmsteads were burnt to the ground. Miles and miles of farmland burned and died with the roaring flames and heat.

The authorities fought the flames with every means at their disposal. Police, farmers, volunteers and fireman toiled relentlessly to bring the fires under control. Helicopters hovered overhead with their water loads, trying to gain some control of the inferno.

Animals frantic to escape the deadly flames died in its path, too exhausted to outrun nature. Maddened cattle bellowing, quivering with shock, blood dripping off their peeled flanks. Trees and telegraph poles, sheep, goats and donkeys lay in smouldering heaps.

The flames swept invincibly onwards, roaring and hissing as the fires reached the river. The river normally placid and clear, now black with ash and the smouldering detritus of trees, bushes and dead animals.

Then two days later the wind dropped and dark clouds formed on the horizon. Firemen and their volunteers breathed a prayer of relief as they wiped their sweaty faces with exhaustion.

Then the long-awaited rains came, hitting the ground like stair rods, thundering through the bush, breaking and bending plants and flowers, the wind whipping the trees into a frenzy, snapping off heavy branches and tossing them into the air like unwanted toys. Trees lay strewn across the ground, felled by the fury of the storm.

Wild animals huddled under trees, their coats darkened by the onslaught of the rain. Monkeys took shelter high up in the trees, clinging to each other as the branches swayed and bent, their fur clumped together, their eyes fluttering against the rain.

Deep throaty thunder roared and boomed in the distance, lightening dazzled and spat through the dark sky. The smell of the parched earth greedily colliding with the wetness, the hiss and wisps of mist as it hit the scorching dirt roads.

Africa at its angriest was a beautiful sight to behold. The scent of the rain impossible to capture.

Chapter Eleven

The body of Charlie was never found.

The media, hungry for the story about Sir Miles Courtney, the ex-British Ambassador's reclusive daughter, made their way to the Eastern Cape. Swamping the papers day after day with lurid headlines as to what might have happened. The Press pack recalled the scandal in Cape Town concerning Sara Courtney Saunders, and her ex-husband Simon, and threw this into the mix to ramp up the headlines. When the woman had taken off for her hiding place in the bush, she had only one child. So, who was the father of this second child, the one who had gone missing? The body never found.

They hunted down the surviving mother and child, Sara and Ben. Ignoring the guard at the entrance of the game lodge, untouched by the fire, the journalists swarmed into the lodge, ignoring the astonished looks from guests, enjoying their lunch.

Paul Weston stormed out of his office. Outraged at the invasion of the media and their intrusive cameras and microphones.

"This is private property!" he bellowed at them, "Get out, get off the property immediately."

"We think Mrs Saunders and her son, Ben, are maybe staying here, sir?" one of the journalists, Ted Ford, questioned. "All we ask is for a statement from the mother?"

"Have you no pity at all, any of you? The woman is grieving dammit, and her home lost to the fire. She's in no condition to speak to anyone about anything. Now get off the property. Get out!"

Muttering they left. The Australian journalist, Ted Ford, renowned for his hard-nosed approach to anything and everything, angrily left the lodge.

"Who wants to put some money on the fact there won't be a picture of Charlie to be found?" He muttered to his fellow journalists. "I bet any she had of him went up in flames like the house did. No evidence the boy ever existed, I checked. Not even a birth certificate. Just a half assed drawing of the kid done by its mother.

"So, who was he? Where did he come from? What was the mother hiding?"

His fellow journalist shrugged. "Must have adopted him maybe? We'll probably never know as those papers would have gone up in flames as well."

The disgruntled and frustrated press pack headed back to Cape Town.

Chapter Twelve
The Mother

The gate to the small cottage wobbled back, bent and buckled. On either side the fence poles smouldered, pale grey smoke reaching upwards, the safari vehicle from the lodge already spotted with white ash.

Sipo, the tracker, stayed in the vehicle looking straight ahead at nothing in particular as was his way, although his eyes missed nothing. Sara alighted from the vehicle, glancing at him briefly, then stood in front of the cottage and stared around at the now alien landscape.

Where once there were green leafy trees and bushes, only black skeletons remained, the trees eerie, naked and charred, making a wailing sound as the wind whispered through them, their burnt branches pointing accusingly at an innocent blue sky above.

A determined tree, seemingly untouched by the fire, still grew unscathed through the crack of a great boulder, crafted by the wind and rain over hundreds of years.

Even the birds had disappeared leaving only the crackle of burnt grass beneath her shoes, puffing up small clouds of black ash, covering her feet and ankles in seconds. Cremated birds as brittle as the scorched earth disintegrated beneath her feet. The hosepipe blackened, curled and twisted like a petrified snake.

Beauty's round house was still standing, wisps of grey smoke rose lazily from what little thatch was left.

Four Hadeda birds suddenly erupted from Beauty's roof, their ungainly flight peppered with their raucous screeching cries, making Sara jump with fright. She had always disliked them, finding them as ugly as vultures, but noisier.

Sara sucked in her breath, as she entered what was left of her father's cottage, then coughed as her throat tightened and her eyes streamed. Ash was everywhere, penetrating every crevice, a grey coat covering everything. Even the buckled silver rose bowl on the skeleton of the burnt dining room table was shrouded with it.

The pale cream curtains were gone the walls peppered with dark soot, going from room to room in a daze Sara knew she would find nothing. In the kitchen the old stove and 'fridge now reduced to dull burnt metal. Broken crockery littered the black floor.

She wandered into Charlie's burnt out bedroom. Like Charlie, there was absolutely nothing left at all. Ben's bedroom told the same story. Her own room was shrouded in ash. In the sitting room, her once crowded desk full of personal papers, books and photographs had perished.

Her legs buckled beneath her as she slid down the soot covered walls and put her head in her hands, her anxious fractured mind finally stilled.

All gone. Their personal belongings, clothes, shoes – everything.

And Charlie, her beloved Charlie. Gone.

She didn't notice Sipo coming into what used to be her bedroom, only felt the slight pressure on her shoulder. "Missus? There is nothing left here for you now. We should go back to the lodge."

She roughly pushed away his hand. "Leave me alone. I don't want to go anywhere. Leave me here. I have nothing left to go to."

He knelt in front of her. "But Missus what of your son, who will need you now more than before? You must go to him and comfort him. Come."

Helping her up, he steered her unsteady legs back outside and helped her into the vehicle. Getting behind the wheel he turned the key and the engine burst into life. Then unexpectedly he turned it off. A frown marking his placid face.

"Missus?"

Sara didn't look up, just stared at her hands as though she had never seen them before.

Sipo cleared his throat. "Your child has gone to a better place, a safer place. It was not meant to be to live with you when you are old. It was written the child should be taken from you."

"Oh God! What do you know of love and loss!" Sara bent over, an ancient keening noise Sipo had heard many times when death came calling, coming from the depths of her being.

He turned the engine on again and whispered to her. "I am sorry, Missus, very sorry."

He drove slowly back to the lodge, his knuckles white on the steering wheel. His duty had been to tell the truth. But how could this be done now? The Chief had banned him from returning to the village. The Police would arrest him for withholding vital evidence, for not telling them what he had seen down on the banks of the river.

The shepherd. His childhood friend's muddy footprints.

Insects blundered against the windscreen, their fat bodies exploding on impact leaving splashes of blood, then turning into arcs of white smears as he turned on the wipers to clear the windscreen. The thorns of trees and bush scraped the sides of the vehicle like living nails trying to make their way inside. But Sipo's thoughts were far away.

His people feared the police. There had been no trace of the missing child in the village they had searched, his old village. A child such as this, would draw much attention. It would not be possible to hide this child.

Sipo dropped Sara at the lodge and made his way back to the station, alone with his troubled thoughts.

*****

Through the window of the office, Detective Joubert watched Sipo drive off and went out to the reception area. Sara was walking slowly past the check in desk, looking as though she had aged ten years in only a few days.

"Mrs Saunders?"

She looked up. "Detective Joubert? I thought the police had all gone back to the station."

"Mrs Saunders, I need you to come to the manager's office with me please?"

He saw the hope flare briefly in her eyes, then the look of fear which crossed her face.

He stood aside and followed her to the office. "Please sit Mrs Saunders."

She sat abruptly. "Did your men find anything. Any sign of Charlie, Detective Joubert?"

Without answering her, he snapped thin latex gloves over his hands and unzipped a plastic evidence packet in front of him, holding up the contents.

"We did a search of the lodge and all the rooms, including yours, whilst you were at your house with Sipo."

He brandished the small garment, with its pale brown marks, in front of her. "Have you seen this before Mrs Saunders?"

Sara stared at the stained garment. "I'm not sure, it's possible. Where did you find it?"

"It belongs to a child, Mrs Saunders. We have reason to believe it belonged to Charlie."

Sara looked at him and he saw the terror in her eyes.

"Mrs Saunders, this garment was found hidden under the mattress in your room here at the lodge. Can you explain this to me? How did it get there? Did you hide this evidence?" His words as sharp and as deadly as a snake preparing to strike.

She shook her head mutely. He watched the colour drain from her already pale face.

"You see, Mrs Saunders there was a witness. This witness watched you carry Charlie down to the river. When you came back, you came back alone."

He stood up and came around the side of the desk. A police sergeant entered quietly and stood with his back to the door.

"Mrs Saunders I am placing you under arrest for the alleged murder of your child Charlie Saunders. You are, of course, entitled to a lawyer. Meanwhile," he nodded to the sergeant who unclipped the handcuffs from his belt, "you will be taken to the Willow Drift police station to be formally charged, and remain there until such time as correct procedure can be followed."

Sara stared down at her manacled hands a look of disbelief on her face. "This is all a terrible mistake. Where is my son? I need to see my son?"

"Not possible Mrs Saunders. Due to the new evidence against you, it has been decided that your son will be safer in the care of one of our police woman. Then he will be taken into care until such time as the courts decide on his future."

Sara stared at him. Then straightened her back and sucked in her breath. "How dare you do this to me. How dare you! I don't want a lawyer Inspector. I insist you contact the British Embassy in Cape Town and speak to the Ambassador, Sir Christopher Lincoln. My father was the Ambassador before Sir Christopher.

"Please call him and explain the situation. I will take my guidance from him and not you!"

42

Detective Joubert looked at the haughty woman sitting in front of him, and sighed, his expression completely impassive. The situation would now become even more complicated.

Diplomats and Politicians thrown into the mix was something he didn't need at this point in the investigation. He knew full well, from his background check of her, who her father was.

*****

Sara held up her hands, the cold metal of the handcuffs chafing her delicate wrists. She had no fear of handcuffs, she'd been cuffed before, but under different circumstances. "Take these off immediately. I'm not going anywhere until you have spoken to Sir Christopher!"

Detective Joubert had no choice but to make the call. He left a message with the Ambassador's secretary, stating the matter was extremely urgent and he would appreciate a return call as soon as possible. Briefly he explained the situation.

He put the phone down and looked at the furious woman sitting in front of him. "I trust you are not going to try for diplomatic immunity Mrs Saunders? In a case like this, it won't wash. But let me talk to this Sir Christopher…"

He broke off and picked up the chirping phone. "*Goeimore. Dit is speurder Joubert hier. Warmee kan ek u vandag help.*" He smiled into the phone at his private joke. The war between the Boers and the English might well be long over, well before his time, but the Afrikaner has a long and bitter memory.

"Detective Joubert? I trust you speak English?" Sir Christopher's voice barked down the phone.

"*Ja,* Sir Christopher. When it is necessary."

"Well, it is. There seems to be a serious incident concerning Mrs Saunders? I understand you have her in custody. Kindly explain the exact circumstances to me. I want the hard facts from you personally, not the speculation from the media."

Detective Joubert picked up his notes and left the room. Outside on the deck he found a quiet corner and brought Sir Christopher up to date with the situation.

There was a short silence, then a more subdued voice at the end of the phone. "Detective Joubert, Mrs Saunders is a British citizen. I shall do everything in my considerable power to protect her. She has a right to a lawyer, which we will provide for her. Meanwhile, until I have more information, I insist the Embassy take responsibility for her. She will be returned to Cape Town where the Embassy shall provide a safe haven for her until the situation has been clarified with her legal team. Do you understand Detective Joubert?"

Joubert sighed audibly. "Sir Christopher the law must take its course. *Ja*, of course she is entitled to a lawyer. Mrs Saunders must appear in front of the local Magistrate in Willow Drift, and be charged with the alleged murder of her child, based on the evidence we have against her. A witness has come forward who cannot be named at this moment in time."

He held the phone away from his ear as Sir Christopher bellowed down the phone. "Mrs Saunders has no criminal past Detective; she is the daughter of the former British Ambassador. I understand, from you, all her personal papers, including her passport, were destroyed in the fire of her home. Therefore, Detective, she is not a flight risk. The Embassy will guarantee her bail, whatever it might be.

"Our own South African lawyer will be at the Magistrate's Court with Mrs Saunders tomorrow morning. I need to know where she will be held, her lawyer will wish to consult with her when he arrives this afternoon, he's already on his way to Port Elizabeth."

Joubert closed his notebook. "Very good Sir Christopher. I will furnish your lawyer with the details he will require, as to where Mrs Saunders is going to be held. Please ask him to call me on this number."

Sir Christopher continued. "Give me the name of your Police Chief, I will speak to him directly. I will also speak to the South African Foreign Affairs Minister. Neither your Government, nor mine, wish for this to escalate into an international incident, Detective Joubert, there are enough problems in the political arena already and I'm sure you would not wish to add more to them. Once the Press get hold of this it will be a circus."

Sir Christopher cleared his throat and continued, Joubert could hear him trying to keep his anger at bay. "Perhaps you are unaware that Mrs Saunders, before she came to live in South Africa, was a high-profile reporter in the UK? The UK was a huge supporter of Mr Mandela. Sara Saunders, as a top journalist, was very vocal with her support of Mandela's release. Our people protested for years outside your Embassy in London for his release. I think a little consideration is called for here in the best interests of Mrs Saunders."

Joubert shook his head and stared out of the window, watching the lodge guests enjoying their sundowners, wishing he was sitting there

44

with them. "I'm afraid, Sir Christopher, it is a little late for that. The Press have already tried to get into the lodge where Mrs Saunders was staying during our extensive search. They will be filing their stories ready for the morning papers. They didn't get near Mrs Saunders, but, well *ja,* you know what the Press are like, making it up as they go along."

His voice hardened. "But this is my case, Sir Christopher. Your lawyer will need to speak to me when he arrives. The Police Chief will tell you the same. I'm afraid politics will not come into this. A crime has been committed and is therefore outside the gambit of any politician."

"The Press! Damn vultures, that's what they are, feeding off of misery!" He harnessed his anger again, and lowered his voice. "Thank you for your time Detective Joubert. I appreciate your co-operation. My secretary will revert to you with the Foreign Minister's reaction. Regardless of your opinion, I shall be speaking to him. Now, if you will, I would like a word with Mrs Saunders?"

Joubert returned to the office and handed Sara the phone, then sat back in his chair, watching her.

"Now listen to me, Sara. It all looks extremely serious at this stage. I am going to call your father and inform him of the situation, he may have some constructive suggestions. Hold yourself together as best you can. I'll see what can be done there."

With tears running down her cheeks she whispered her thanks and handed the phone back to the detective with her shackled hands.

Detective Joubert stood up, pushing his chair back. He came around the desk and helped her to her feet. Surprising himself in the process.

"Mrs Saunders," he said softly, "I don't believe you are a flight risk; you have been through something no mother should have to endure. But I have a job to do." He unlocked the handcuffs. "Your lawyer will be here this afternoon. Our small jail in Willow Drift is already full. I will drive you to town where you will be placed in safe custody at a house we use in these circumstances. A policeman will remain outside the front door and escort you and your lawyer to the Magistrate's Court first thing in the morning."

Sara stared at the floor, speechless with shock.

Chapter Thirteen
The Ambassador

Sir Miles Courtney shook his newspaper irritably before throwing it down on the table next to him.

He levered himself up from his favourite chair, with the help of his walking stick, and stared out of the window. His faithful golden Labrador, Maggie, never far from his side. Sensing her owner was troubled she nuzzled his hand.

Miles looked down and stroked the dog's head. "Ah, Maggie, much easier to have a dog than raise a rebellious child, eh?"

His eyes traversed the gardens of his country estate. The sweeping driveway lined with elderly copper beech trees. As a child, an only child, he had loved the seasons of England. The first Spring daffodils and bluebells shooting up under the trees in the dell. The pink blossom of the trees, softening the hard lines of the high walls around the estate.

*****

Then the hard, brittle ground of winter beneath his heavy boots as he walked around his property, Maggie at his heels. The dark mornings, swathed in grey, or sweeping soft rains, the days short, the nights long. The ancient outlines of his family home silhouetted against the dark skies.

He fondled Maggie's head. His dreams of filling the big house with grandchildren and their friends, had come to naught. Only an old man wandering around the empty rooms with just Maggie for company.

There were times when his memories of the many postings he had had, his time in Africa especially, cut through him like a knife. The frantic social life of a Diplomat abroad now only a distant memory. He missed his life. Mother Theresa had once said that in the future the new pandemic for human beings would be loneliness. He was beginning to think she may well have been right.

His relationship with his daughter had always been tempestuous. Despite her mood swings as a child she had been a loving daughter. Yes, she shouted at him, argued with him, was impatient with him over the last few years.

Two years ago, they had had a blistering argument over the phone about Ben and his education. Miles didn't approve of Sara home schooling the boy out there in the bush. He felt Ben would be better off in a boarding school where he would have a more disciplined life, with children of the same age. Running wild in the bush was not conducive to good manners and acceptable behaviour. Not in his book anyway.

Sara, predictably had lost her temper with him. Telling him to mind his own business. She would bring Ben up the way she wanted.

She hadn't spoken to him or been in touch, apart from an annual Birthday and Christmas card, ever since.

Sara. Sara. Sara. Why could she never keep herself out of trouble? He sighed and rubbed his forehead. The world of television had suited her well as a profession. Always chasing trouble for a story and finding it in some God-forsaken country most of the world had never heard of. But he had to admit she'd been good at it.

After the scandal with Sara's husband, Simon, and his hasty departure from South Africa, Sir Miles had tried to protect her from the media by persuading her to stay in his bush home where she would be hidden from prying eyes.

Some years ago, he had taken a wrong turning on one of his many trips around the South African countryside and stumbled across the empty house, almost hidden in the dense bush. Intrigued he had stopped and walked around the property. Walking up the short ramp he had peered through the dust covered windows. Clearly no-one had lived there for some years, the outline of what was once a garden had been taken over by nature, the bush claiming it back inch by greedy inch.

He had tracked down the owners of the cottage and put in an offer to buy it.

Once he had purchased the cottage, he had made a courtesy call on the village closest to the modest cottage, meeting the people and the Elders. The Chief would sometimes make his way to the house, cycling shakily on the rutted roads, taking a short cut through the bush.

He and the Ambassador would sit contentedly outside on the patio, learning each other's ways and thoughts, although the Chief sometimes struggled with his English words. It amused the Ambassador when the Chief referred to him as "The Chief of the White people from over the water."

Sir Miles would treasure his memories of fishing in the river, the solitude, far away from the relentless bustle of Cape Town. The evenings spent under the stars, a small fire crackling and hissing as he cooked his dinner. The wonderful smell of chops and sausages sizzling over the fire, a potato nestling in the bed of embers. The sounds of nocturnal birds and animals the only company he needed.

When Sir Miles tenure came to an end, he came to tell the old Chief from the village.

After discussing the crops, the weather, the politics and members of the Chief's family, as was the custom, Sir Miles cleared his throat.

"This land and this house built upon it, belongs to your people, not to us, old man. I wish to make a gift of it to you, for your friendship over the years. There will be trouble in this country and to possess land is a good thing. It will give you something of your own in the future, something no-one can take away from you. You'll have the legal papers to show the new Government it is yours."

The old Chief was overwhelmed with this most generous of offers and clapped his hands softly together in acknowledgement of this unexpected gift.

"I will look after this place and this land, but my people, and I myself, are happy in our small village. Although this place is a long bicycle ride away from there, this house will be safe with us and we will watch over it for you."

Sir Miles had smiled at him. "Alright, old man, then so it shall be. I have the deeds to this house and land here in this envelope. You must keep the papers safe. I have left instructions in my Will and when the time comes you will become the rightful owner. If you don't want to live in it, and I would understand your reasons, you can sell it."

They had shaken hands on it and the old Chief had returned to his village, holding his prized envelope carefully, puzzled but happy with the generous gift to him and his people.

He would remember the English Chief from across the water.

When the scandal broke in Cape Town, Sir Miles had sent a message from England, to the Chief, to say his daughter, and her son, would be living in the house for an unknown length of time and it was her wish to live alone, without visitors.

The old Chief was puzzled. Surely the daughter would need help in caring for his newly acquired home and the land it was upon?

He would get his youngest son, Joseph, to keep a watchful eye on the White Chief's daughter, Sara, and his pending new property.

.

Chapter Fourteen

Sir Miles had been shattered to hear the news his daughter was now under house arrest in Cape Town and his grandson taken into care. The South African government now greedy to show the world a privileged white woman, going on trial for murder, would not be shown any favours, despite all the diplomatic strings the Embassy had tried to pull.

The British Ambassador to South Africa, Sir Christopher Lincoln had broken the news to him, explaining the circumstances as to why Sara had been arrested.

"I'm sorry Miles, but I'm afraid the South African government is going to make a sacrificial lamb out of her. The highest court in the land has now insisted she be held like anyone else due to go on trial. With the new Government now in power they're not going to do your daughter any favours.

"Sara will be treated like any other person, black or white, who is accused of the crime of murder.

"Many of the old cadre of ANC comrades think it is fitting that Mandela has finally been released, and a white woman with a diplomatic background will be going to the same jail he was released from. Poetic justice they seem to think."

"Did you try the diplomatic immunity route Christopher?"

"Yes, of course. As far as the new Government is concerned, she is a British Subject, like thousands of others here and she has no rights in that regard. However, with the overcrowded prisons we were lucky to be able to persuade the Magistrate to allow Sara to stay with a staff member here at the Embassy, under house arrest of course, until her trial."

A week later he called Miles back to bring him up to date.

"I've assembled the best legal team I can. There's a bright young chap, an African, an Advocate with more degrees than you and I put together. He's deadly in court and if anyone can persuade the jury of her innocence it will be Nicholas Gabene.

"I've spoken to Nicholas and he's willing to represent your daughter. He's been briefed by another top attorney the Embassy has used before, Sam Curtis. Sam was the attorney who was with Sara when she appeared before the Magistrate. He brought her back here to Cape Town.

"Bail has been set at R500,000. The Magistrate instructed Sara to hand in her passport but, of course, it was destroyed in the fire. However, we will issue a new one and hand it in as requested.

"What I would advise, Miles, is you don't come over for the trial. You're well known here and the media will go wild. Nicholas agrees the less we give those hyenas the better.

"Things have changed a lot Miles, since you left. The country is still in a state of chaos. I will give Sara all the support she needs. I must insist the less publicity this trial gets the better it will be for her."

"Alright Christopher. I'm sorry, I'm finding it nearly impossible to take all this in."

Sir Miles heard the noon day gun go off, a daily occurrence in Cape Town, and imagined he could hear the panicked flapping of the pigeon's wings as they rose in fright. He tuned back into the conversation.

"We'll do our best, of course. Nicholas fought like a tiger to keep her out of jail awaiting trial. I'm sorry to tell you she is in a desperate state, so much so Nicholas is going to try and get her off on medical grounds. After all Charlie's body was never found and that's always tricky for the prosecution."

Christopher paused briefly. "When I say get her off, I'm afraid it doesn't mean she won't spend some time in a secure psychiatric facility, this is the route Nicholas wants to take."

Miles rubbed his cheek, feeling desperately tired. "What is the situation with Ben?"

Christopher cleared his throat noisily. "Ben is obviously traumatised. Meanwhile he's in a safe foster home where the media can't get hold of him. Nicholas will try for a private meeting with the Judge in Chambers. He feels Ben won't hold up in a courtroom, and I agree with him, after all he's only eleven. But the Judge will want to speak to him."

Miles closed his eyes at the horror of it all, and gripped his cane. "Have you spoken to him?"

Christopher's voice softened. "I have. He doesn't say much at all, which is understandable when he has lost his sibling and also his mother in many ways. He is under psychiatric care; he sees the doctor every week. Our main concern now is that we get the best outcome from the trial for Sara, and take it from there.

"We have a trial date, six weeks from now. I can't promise anything, I'm sorry." He cleared his throat. "The Embassy has guaranteed the R500,000 bail request but perhaps you would be kind enough to transfer the amount through to our account?"

"Of course, I'll instruct my bank this morning. I appreciate all you are doing Christopher. As you can imagine the media over here in the UK has gone into a frenzy. Sara was well known here, a familiar face on television, they're camped down at the end of the drive with their confounded microphones and cameras. I feel like a prisoner in my own home. Can't even get up to London for a few nights at my club. The damn story is all over the newspapers and television. It's a bloody disgrace!"

Miles slowly put the phone down and, leaning heavily on his cane, lowered himself into his chair which creaked in protest. His heart was beating uncomfortably in his chest.

What shocked him more than anything was the fact Sara had not told him she had had another child, something he would never be able to admit to anyone. Another thing he could not, would not admit, was the fact that he had failed to bond with his grandson Ben. Yes, he had an obligation to the child, but that was all.

Charlie, a child he would never meet. A child his daughter had allegedly killed. A child he would never know, as he didn't know, or understand, Ben.

Maggie put her head on Miles' thigh, her big sad eyes matching those of her shattered owner.

*****

Christopher put down the 'phone and leaned back in his chair. Even though he had procured one of the best lawyers in the land, he had his doubts if a woman who lived alone out in the bush, practically hiding her children from everyone, known to be reclusive, and who was now mentally in a precarious state, would stand up to the rigours of a murder trial which was being covered by all the newspapers in South Africa.

The bloodied garment she had allegedly hidden under the mattress in her room at the lodge, the fire which had burnt her house to the ground destroying any other possible evidence. The fact there was not a single photograph of Charlie Saunders to splash across the front pages, only a poorly drawn sketch, and her refusal to name the father of the child. Well, everything was stacked against her, including the witness who had come forward. The witness who was being given the full protection of the law.

He reached inside the top drawer of his desk, extracted a glass and a bottle and poured himself a large whisky.

He doubted even Nicholas would be able to keep her out of prison.

The international media had swiftly picked up on the story of the daughter of Sir Miles Courtney, they waded in, taking no prisoners, now the whole world knew about Sara Courtney-Saunders, her private life was private no more and the press bayed unceasingly for her blood.

Sara Courtney-Saunders who had killed her own child. Sara Courtney- Saunders who had not uttered one word since her arrest and had had her son taken away from her, for his own safety.

In a catatonic state, traumatised by what she had been accused of, her feelings must have calcified.

Christopher took a large mouthful of his drink. Sometimes the mind blocks things out, a defence mechanism, like amnesia where memories can't be detached from emotions. Perhaps this was the case with Sara now.

No, Christopher would not tell Sara's father she had not uttered a single word since her arrest. He thought Miles had sounded rather odd on the phone. Probably the shock he surmised, glad for once he himself did not have children and never intended having any.

Sara's Advocate, Nicholas Gabene, and her lawyer, Sam Curtis would have their work cut out for them trying to defend their client.

His private phone chirped on his desk.

"Sir Christopher? Nicholas Gabene here."

"Ah, Nicholas, good to hear from you – I hope?"

The Advocate cleared his throat and got straight to the point. "I've been through all the files, all the evidence, and I've spoken to Detective Joubert who handled the investigation in the Eastern Cape. It appears Sara was on medication, prescribed by a guest, who was a doctor, staying at the lodge. Some sort of tranquilizer which is understandable considering the situation. However, when her room at the lodge was searched the police found other prescriptive drugs. Pain killers for migraine headaches, and, wait for it, a bottle of Rohypnol pills."

"Rohypnol?"

"Yes. It's a powerful drug, a tranquiliser, which helps you sleep. However, the downside is when a person takes it, they can behave in a normal manner, talk in a coherent way, in other words can appear to be quite normal. But, and this is a big but, it is also a hypnotic. A person can behave in a perfectly normal way but have absolutely no recollection of what they are doing, or, more to the point, what they have done."

Christopher rubbed the back of his neck, knowing what was coming next.

"So, what are you saying here Nicholas?"

"The afternoon Charlie went missing Sara had told her son she had a headache and was going to take a nap. It's possible she took a Rohypnol, by mistake and not a pain killer. If this was the case, she would have no recollection of what happened next - taking Charlie down to the river, and, well, committing the alleged crime. With absolutely no knowledge of her actions."

Christopher reached for his bottle of whisky and poured another generous helping. "Dear God…"

Nicholas continued. "I went to see Sara and put it to her this might have been what happened. As you know she's not speaking at all. But this evoked a reaction from her. She stared at me, shaking her head.

"The life in her eyes seemed to close down, difficult to explain really. Like turning off a life support machine. Then she finally spoke."

"It's possible then? I killed my own child?"

"Thing is Christopher, this could well be so. If it is, I think I have a strong case. I'm not saying I can get her off but there are exceptional circumstances here. Sara, if this is true, would have no recollection of killing her child. Therefore, it wasn't premeditated murder."

"Did she say anything else Nicholas?"

"Nothing. Dealing with her own demons. I don't think she will utter another word. I think I can understand that. I don't think she intentionally murdered her own child, although it's not unheard of. But if she thinks she might have it will be nearly impossible for her to deal with."

"So, what next?"

54

"I'll give it everything I can. I have extenuating circumstances and a client who won't talk. I doubt she will walk free, but perhaps an institution for a few years. Maybe we can get a reduced sentence on the premise the crime was committed whilst the accused was not of sound mind.

"Sara can't be forced to testify by the prosecutors, she can be called only if she wants to testify – and as she won't talk… it's not going to happen."

He could hear Nicolas shuffling papers around on his desk. "In a situation like this the Judge may well take into account if Sara was not criminally responsible, or alleged to be mentally ill, that she be evaluated by a couple of psychiatrists and a psychologist. The principal being, an altered state of mind can excuse a crime – it's built into the legal system here. I'm hopeful Sir Christopher, very hopeful. Prisons all over the country are absolutely crammed to capacity, so this might also be in our favour."

"Thank you, Nicholas. I don't think Sir Miles needs to know about this yet. He's taking the whole situation badly, he's not in good health, as you know. Thanks for the call and bringing me up to date."

Sir Christopher drummed his fingers on the desk top then took a gulp of his drink.

Next week, as the British Ambassador to South Africa, he was due to present his credentials from the Queen to the new President, Nelson Mandela. He had no doubt the President was well aware of the Sara Courtney-Saunders situation. But it would not be correct protocol to bring the subject up, unless Mr Mandela did.

Sir Christopher had the greatest respect and admiration for the new President of the country. A wise and forgiving man who, with a stroke of genius, had brought his country together in spectacular fashion.

Rugby had always been a symbol of deep racial divide between the Afrikaner and the black man. A symbol of their pride and identity. On the day of the World Cup final in Johannesburg, he had captured the heart of the entire nation when he walked out onto the pitch wearing the green and gold jersey of the Springboks, greeting each player by name.

On that glorious day the Springboks had won the World Cup.

Christopher smiled as he remembered. He had never seen anything like it in his life. The entire nation had erupted with pride and happiness for their national team. South Africans whether they lived in a ten bedroomed house or a shack in a township united in their pride and joy. It seemed for one glorious day the infamous past of the country had been forgotten. For a brief moment in time, South Africa was a nation united.

It was the first major step forward for the vision of the new President and all his people. The man had performed a miracle. Even the most embittered Afrikaner had hope in his heart for the future of his country, and their place in it.

A miracle indeed.

A miracle was what Sara Courtney-Saunders needed now. He would present his credentials to the President and if the subject didn't come up, he would seek another private audience with the great man as soon as possible afterwards.

*****

A week before the trial was due to start, Sir Christopher once again sat opposite the President in his office at the Union Buildings in Pretoria. After formalities had been exchanged, they briefly discussed the Springboks being the greatest players in the world, then Sir Christopher settled down to the business in hand.

Before he could begin, Mr Mandela held up his hand.

"Sir Christopher," he said gently, in a voice which was now famous around the globe. "I know why you are here. Mrs Courtney-Saunders?"

The Ambassador nodded.

"I'm sorry. I would help if I could, but this is a fledgling new country with its own Constitutional Court. The law must be followed. I cannot be seen to take sides with anyone who has been arrested for an alleged murder.

"I have the greatest respect for your country and I ask you show the same respect now, to mine. Mrs Saunders will get a fair trial and be sentenced accordingly.

"I know the horror of prison, as you well know. I know the judge personally who will preside over the court in this particular case. Judge Mary Engels is fair and compassionate. You have chosen an excellent Advocate in Nicholas Gabene."

Sir Christopher looked at him in surprise, he was well briefed on the case after all.

The President stood up and held out his hand. "The case is not watertight. The child's body was never found. It's difficult to sentence

56

a person to life imprisonment when there is no body. The mother, Sara, has a severe mental condition, is catatonic, if I understand correctly?"

He led Sir Christopher to the door of his office. "I have great admiration for your country, Sir Christopher, and your Queen. Your people were vocal for many years outside our Embassy in London, keeping my name in the headlines and demanding my freedom."

He shook the Ambassador's hand firmly and smiled at him. "I will be following the court case closely. I thank you for your call this morning."

Sir Christopher slid into the back seat of his staff car more perplexed than he had been when he stood outside the President's office door. Had there been a slight hint, despite Mr Mandela's insistence the law must take its course. Was it possible he might be able to assist in some way?

As a man not given to praying and asking for help, Sir Christopher bowed his head briefly as the car, the Union Jack fluttering off the pennant staff, drove slowly under a canopy of heavy Jacaranda trees, bowing and nodding heavily, their fallen flowers creating a magical purple carpet of beauty before the moving car.

A prison in an African country, for a white woman, didn't bear thinking about.

Chapter Fifteen
The Mother

The day of the trial of Sara Courtney-Saunders had arrived. Dressed in a simple black dress, she was brought up into the courtroom.

She sat down next to her Advocate, Nicholas Gabene, on one side, and Sam Curtis her Attorney, flanking her left.

Having been briefed on the state of the accused's mental health, Judge Engels had banned the media and their cameras from her courtroom.

The prosecutor clambered to his feet and read out the charges to the Judge.

"Please rise Mrs Courtney-Saunders? How do you plead?"

Sara rose unsteadily to her feet looking bewildered and frightened. She said nothing. A woman, the Judge observed, perilously close to a complete mental and physical breakdown.

Nicholas rose to his feet. "My Lady, my client has not uttered a word since the day she was arrested. As you can imagine this has made it difficult to represent her, which is her legal right. She will however nod her head if asked a direct question."

Judge Engels made some notes and looked up. Above her the South African coat of arms shimmered with dust motes from a shaft of sunlight angling through the high window. "Mrs Courtney-Saunders do you plead guilty?"

Sara shook her head – no.

"Mrs Courtney-Saunders you are therefore pleading not guilty?"

Sara shook her head – yes.

The Prosecutor spent the next hour putting forward all the evidence to prove Sara had killed her own child, including the bloodied garment found under her mattress in the lodge where she had stayed after the fire had burnt her house to the ground.

Using his considerable deadly skills in the courtroom Nicholas argued against the prosecution. There was no proof the child had been murdered, after all the body had never been found.

At the end of the fifth day of the trial the Judge ordered that Ben Saunders be brought to her. She would meet with him in her chambers and interview him herself.

Judge Engels looked at the boy seated opposite her; she had removed her robes to make Ben feel more comfortable in her presence.

An hour later she rang the buzzer on her desk and a court attendant led the boy away.

Judge Engels looked down at the notes she had made. She found it inconceivable that a mother could do this. Sara was an educated woman, the daughter of a distinguished British Ambassador. The boy had kicked his shoes against the chair until she had admonished him. His young face full of grief and anger. She would not allow the boy into the Court Room under any circumstances.

On the final day of the trial Nicholas Gabene played his trump card. The Rohypnol tablets the police had found in Sara's room. His closing argument was strong. If Sara Courtney-Saunders had committed the crime she was accused of, despite no body being found, then having taken one of these tablets in error, she would have been in a hypnotic state and incapable of knowing what she was doing. Therefore, he argued, she could not be held responsible for her actions.

The trial was over. The Judge ruled that the evidence against Sara was inconclusive. The accused had not been of sound mind at the time of the murder and, therefore, in her considered opinion, and those of the two psychiatrists and a phycologist who had interviewed Sara over the past few weeks, Sara Courtney-Seymour, was so traumatised since her child disappeared, there was no proof beyond reasonable doubt she had committed the crime of murder.

The Judge ruled out a prison sentence for the accused, but sentenced her to eight years in a secure psychiatric facility, or longer if this was considered necessary by doctors at the facility. The child Ben would be taken into care by Social Services until such time as other suitable arrangements could be made.

The trial was over and Sara was led away.

Advocate Nicholas Gabene collected all his files, pushing them into an already bulging briefcase. He shook hands with Sam Curtis, the attorney he had worked with.

"Good outcome Sam. I had hoped for better, but I knew it was going to be a difficult trial. However, we've kept Sara out of prison. The sentence the Judge handed down was fair."

He shrugged off his gown and draped it across his arm before picking up his briefcase. "Now to face the Press waiting outside. I've prepared a statement. I'll give them the bare bones of the outcome. Hopefully they will then disappear and chase some other story, some other unfortunate victim."

"Don't count your chickens Nicholas," Sam said as he accompanied him out of the court room. "A child who disappears, will always be the subject of intense speculation. It might go away for months, then some other reporter with some space to fill in his newspaper will bring the whole subject up again, about what might have happened, and it will rear its ugly head once more!"

They shook hands. "Thanks Sam. I'll call at the Embassy after the press conference and brief Sir Christopher, although he has been following events closely himself. Then he'll have to break the news to Sara's father. It's going to be a tough call."

Chapter Sixteen
The Ambassador

Sir Christopher braced himself before picking up the phone and calling Sara's father.

"It was the best outcome we could hope for Miles. Nicholas did a splendid job. The prosecution was no match for him. I know you've been following the story on Sky, and no doubt watched the press conference Nicholas gave.

"Sara will be well looked after. The main thing now is to get her the best medical care available. She'll have her own cell of course, with around the clock surveillance, we can't rule out suicide. Sara is in a precarious state as you can imagine. But in time we must hope she recovers."

Miles sighed deeply. "I was planning to fly to South Africa as soon as possible. I want, and need, to see my daughter. However, my doctor has warned against it, and I must heed his advice. Perhaps in time my health will improve enough for me to make the trip."

"Sound advice, I think. Let's give some time for the dust to settle. Sara, given time, may wish to talk, not now of course. We need to give Ben some time to come to terms with things as well. Perhaps sometime in the future you might want to consider having custody of him? For now, he is in a good foster home. I think we should leave things as they are, I doubt another upheaval in his young life will help."

Miles could hear the doves calling from the Embassy's lush gardens and he smiled sadly. It all seemed so long ago now.

"Yes, yes of course. Ben must be given time to adjust. I would be like a stranger to him now. Let's see how he gets on then reassess the situation."

Christopher continued, trying to lighten his tone in a bid to give Miles some hope for the future. "There's another private psychiatric facility in the Western Cape. I'm going to give it a few months, then work with Nicholas to see if we can get Sara transferred there. Where she is now is very much an institution, has the feel of it, the smell of it.

"The Haven is more like a private hospital. The house used to belong to a Greek tycoon who lived here. It's situated about an hour from Cape Town in the Winelands.

"If Sara doesn't cause any problems, be the model prisoner in fact, I think it can be done. I'll do my best. I'll keep in touch with her medical doctor and psychiatrist."

"You're a good man Christopher, a good friend," Miles said, his voice breaking slightly, overcome with the past few week's events.

The line went dead.

Sir Miles, leaned on his cane, feeling all of his seventy years. Slowly he walked through to the kitchen where he seemed to spend most of his time lately. Here he had his favourite chair next to the fireplace, a cheerful fire was keeping the room warm.

Nursing a glass of brandy, he watched the bare leaves of the trees in the garden. The day was bereft of colour and although it was only three in the afternoon, the sky was already growing dark.

Maggie was sleeping in front of the fire, her mouth and paws twitching as she dreamed of things far more pleasant than Miles had done recently. Christmas carols played softly in the background. He looked around the ancient old room, not a single Christmas decoration indicated the time of year.

There were Christmas cards propped up on the mantelpiece atop the fireplace, but what he yearned for more than anything was the sound of laughter, the shouting and the talking, any noise, the clattering of plates as food was prepared, the aroma of a turkey cooking slowly in the oven, the vegetables scraped and cleaned waiting their turn, a full bar spread out on the side table, crystal glasses winking in the light from the fire and candles.

But more than anything he thought of his daughter, now spending Christmas locked up in an institution in Africa. Of his only grandchild, confused and alone, surrounded by complete strangers.

He refilled his glass and sat down heavily in his chair, propping his cane against the table.

Maggie roused herself at the sound of the cane banging the table, and clattering to the floor. She shook herself awake, releasing a shower of unwanted golden fur. The dog had hair to spare and shared it with everyone and anyone. Picking up a soft toy she gently laid it on Miles' knee, her tail whirring like a windmill.

"Ah, Maggie. What would I do without you girl?"

He picked a few golden hairs off his pullover and, feeling the warmth of the brandy coursing through his bloodstream, picked up his book and disappeared into a kinder world than the one he seemed to have inherited over the past months.

A few moments later he laid the book down, and stared out of the window again, watching the rain slithering down the glass, at intervals the wind picked up and the rain hit the windows as if a handful of gravel had been thrown.

He would write to Sara and send the letter via the diplomatic pouch. Sir Christopher would make sure it reached his daughter. Even if she wouldn't speak, it was possible she might write to him.

Chapter Seventeen
The Shepherd's Wife

The first few weeks after the child was found it cried constantly for its mother, pushing Mirium away. Patiently Mirium waited until the child fell back into her arms exhausted by sorrow and tears.

Then, some months later, the tracker came with news. It was safe to return. The nomadic couple and the child returned to the village. This child, they told the curious villagers, they had found next to its dead mother deep in the bush, they had buried the mother and brought it home and made it their own.

Small children peeped through the door of the hut to see this newcomer; their eyes wide with wonder. Mirium encouraged them to come inside and play with the withdrawn child.

"What is the name of this little one?" one of the small boys asked.

"The name of the little one is not known. To call it a name it does not know would cause much sorrow for the child. It is decided we shall call it Bibi, until such time as the little one comes to understand we are family now. Then we shall give our chosen name. Bibi is a gift from God and sent here to be amongst us, to be safe and cared for now it has no mother of its own."

*****

Mirium now watched the children as they tried to coax Bibi to come and play with them. One of the young boys squatted down and stared at the child.

"But this Bibi does not speak the language of the Griqua people, our people, this Bibi has no words? Only small sounds?" He frowned.

"What are the words this Bibi is saying?"

Mirium shook her head. "I do not know these few words, my child, but Bibi will soon learn our ways and our language. We must give the little one time."

"Come Bibi," the boy held out his hand. "I will take you to see the new baby goat."

The toddler looked at his outstretched hand then spun around screaming with terror and into Mirium's open arms.

"Hush, little one, you have nothing to fear with us. I will come with you to see the baby goat. Come."

All this, of course, was said in the curious language of the Griqua people. A language, soft and lilting, peppered with clicks and strange sounds only they could understand.

In the months that followed, Bibi, like any other small child, became curious and started to venture outside to play with the other children in the dry dust, chasing the chickens with the best of them, collecting their feathers and making shapes on the dusty floor of Mirium's hut and drawing stick figures with the sharp ends of the feathers, engrossed with childish games.

The Griqua were originally from the desert, descendants of the San people. A secret, mystical, people who could find water and food where others could not, who heard and knew of things before others. They were a pastoral, nomadic tribe, healing themselves with the herbs and leaves they carried in their small leather pouches. Across their backs the men carried bows and arrows for hunting, their secret poisons, from plants and snakes, a deadly weapon to bring down an animal in flight.

They were a proud people, their faces different from other tribes with their coffee-coloured skin, pale eyes and slight wiry bodies. Some built simple conical huts with thatched roofs, and settled there, younger ones moved to the bigger cities, hungry for knowledge of life outside their clan, in the new South Africa where Mandela and the Government had promised jobs and money, a bright future, which they were eager to embrace. With empty promises from the past, empty stomachs, empty hopes and dreams, they moved to the big towns and cities looking for that hope and promise.

The tribe shrank leaving only small pockets of them scattered to the wind living in small villages, unwilling to change the simple way of life they had always known. It was so with Eza's village.

*****

From the moment of Bibi's arrival, the child was embraced with warmth, and love by these softly spoken people. The child responded to them with trust and after the initial bumpy start, adapted to the new environment with cautious ease.

Sometimes, in the evening, Mirium would watch Bibi staring into the fire, the soft blanket of animal skin draped around slender shoulders, the child's lips moving silently, with thoughts somewhere far away.

"What is it little one, what is it my Bibi?"

The child's head would lift, eyes swimming with tears. "*Lot*, Mama, *Lot*," creeping into the safety of Mirium's arms, Bibi would weep until exhausted. Mirium would pull the soft cloak tighter around the little one, trying to give the comfort so desperately needed. But for all her fierce tender love and concern, she knew the child was thinking of its birth mother and had not forgotten her.

Perhaps, she thought, as she rocked the sleeping child, perhaps the Chief had been wrong after all. But, oh, she loved this strange child and would never give it up.

She reached for the small bowl and carefully applied the mixture to the sleeping child's skin.

Chapter Eighteen
The Tracker

Sipo, Eza's childhood friend, heard the news of the outcome of Sara Courtney-Saunders trial from Detective Piet Joubert.

"So, Sipo, justice has been done. Mrs Sara Courtney-Saunders will spend a minimum of eight years in a secure psychiatric facility in the Western Cape. Longer if necessary, this will depend on the medical staff who will be looking after her."

Sipo looked at his feet, taking this news in, then looked up at the Detective. "What sort of place will this be Sir, like a hospital perhaps?"

"Well it can hardly be called a hospital Sipo. It's a place where Mrs Courtney-Saunders will be guarded like all the other inmates incarcerated there. It's like a prison, but for convicts who are greatly disturbed mentally."

"But what of her son sir? What will happen to him?"

"The boy will be handed over to Social Services and they will place him in a safe foster home. He will undergo regular meetings by a psychiatrist who will monitor his progress and take care of him."

"He will see his mother then? Be able to visit her in this place?"

Detective Joubert pinched the bridge of his nose. "No, this will not be allowed."

"*Eish.* We do not have this in our culture. The Chief decides such things for his people."

"So, Sipo, you came to see me to ask for some leave to visit your family?"

"Yes sir, there are family affairs I must attend to."

Detective Joubert signed off the leave application and handed it to Sipo.

Sipo saluted, then turned and left the room. Feeling the detective's eyes boring into his back.

Detective Joubert screwed the top back on his pen and leaned back in his chair.

He shook his head with frustration. These people with all their secrets, sometimes he felt they only told him what they wanted him to hear.

*****

Sipo did have family affairs to attend to. He had already sent a message to Eza, but as his boyhood friend, and not a police tracker. He was going to meet him by the large overhanging rock on the ancient path of the elephants, deep in the bush, where they had often played together as children.

He needed to know what had happened down by the river, and there was only one person who knew the true story.

Eza.

Chapter Nineteen
The Doctor

True to his word Sir Christopher, with the help of Nicholas Gabeni, started the process of getting Sara moved to The Haven, the private hospital situated in the Winelands, an hour from Cape Town.

Every month he had visited her, tracking her progress with the medical staff in charge of her. He had sat with her on numerous occasions, coaxing her to speak to him. But Sara spoke not one word.

Although she still refused to speak to anyone and only nodded when necessary, she was a model prisoner. Her tiny barred room was locked at night and monitored, and she followed all the rules of the institution without question.

Her days followed a numbing routine. Breakfast was served at seven, followed by a brief walk around the courtyard outside. Then she would choose books from the well-stocked library, and like her father many thousands of miles away, she would lose herself in another world.

Various activities were available for the female prisoners, from craft classes, sewing, bridge, computer lessons and courses in writing, law, languages, psychology and many other subjects.

Sara's passion for research and writing, a throwback from when she was a news reporter, and the hours she spent in the library drew the attention of one of the warders. The previous prisoner who ran the library had served her sentence and been released. The warder offered Sara the vacant position, Sara nodded her acceptance. Books allowed her to escape into other people's lives, somewhere she could lose herself for a few precious hours.

Three times a week she would spend an hour with a psychiatrist, but said nothing.

Four long years after her incarceration Sir Christopher and Nicholas Gabene, with their diplomatic and legal skills managed to get Sara transferred to The Haven.

Here Sara was able to walk around the grounds of the old Cape Dutch Manor House and once more feel the warm sun on her arms and legs, to touch the flowers, feel the grass under her feet, and find a semblance of peace and contentment in the freedom she and the other inmates were given. The Manor house and the grounds were surrounded by walls with hidden cameras placed at strategic points, the tops of the walls studded with spikes to deter any thoughts of escape from their cloistered world.

As a child Sara had loved to paint and here she had discovered that passion again. In her silent world she found comfort in producing canvas after canvas as she sat on the same bench every day, unless the weather dictated otherwise.

The two-hundred-year-old heavy iron slave bell, pitted with age, housed in a simple sturdy white arch, summoned the inmates for dinner. When they had been accounted for, the heavy wooden doors at the entrance of the house were closed and bolted from the outside. The sash windows in all the bedrooms were discreetly barred with heavy Perspex strips, giving the illusion of no bars at all. But it was only an illusion.

The letters from her father were delivered by the Embassy car. They were left unread.

*****

It was a beautiful afternoon, Sara sat on the garden bench, her legs straight out in front of her, enjoying the sun. She put down her paintbrush and looked up at the old Manor house with its thick white walls, deep green shutters and main double doors.

In the distance, beyond the walls, Sara could see the grape vines, marching in straight lines as far as the eye could see, the blue grey metal coloured mountains creating a dramatic backdrop.

Sara imagined how it must have been long ago, the ladies of the manor strolling under the shade of the old oak trees, parasols held aloft, their muslin dresses fluttering in the breeze as they skirted the pathways, their soft shoes causing puffs of dust. Their hair in fashionable ringlets, delicate fans in their hands.

Farm vehicles would have rumbled past, loaded with grapes, on the roads surrounding the estate; the pickers calling cheerfully to one another, under the brutal sun as they sat on the crates of freshly picked fruit.

A much gentler world, Sara thought, than the one she had found herself plunged into.

For the past four years she had thought of nothing else but her children.

The hope had been bled from her, taking her far away from the world, the safe world she had always known and sometimes she lost all sense of time and being.

She was startled by a voice next to her. "Hello, one of the nurses pointed you out to me. You're Sara, aren't you?"

Sara frowned, annoyed by the intrusion into her silent world.

"I'm Karen," she held out her hand but Sara ignored it.

"Mind if I sit down?" She didn't wait for an answer. "So, how long have you been here?"

Sara leaned forward and dabbed at the canvas she was working on, wishing the woman would go away and leave her alone. Sara had noticed her at the long refectory table in the dining room. The tousled short hair, the colour of butterscotch, the dark brown intelligent and friendly eyes. Karen had moved around the table introducing herself as though she were at a holiday camp and not an institution for women with deeply disturbed minds.

Sara had ignored her then as she ignored her now.

Karen leaned forward and studied the painting Sara was working on. "Hey," she said with her slight Irish accent, "that's grand. I like the way the sun is burnishing the river, and the surrounding bush is spot on with the colours you've used. Who's the kid standing next to the water?"

Sara snatched up her brushes and paints, snapped closed her folder of paintings and stood up abruptly, then marched back to the house.

"Hey!" Karen called out to Sara's retreating back. "Sorry if I upset you, only making polite conversation is all!"

*****

Karen studied Sara across the large table. Watching her picking at her food, ignoring everyone, saying nothing. She was a nice-looking woman, in her mid to late forties she guessed, but painfully thin. Clearly disturbed though. Her blue eyes expressionless, her blonde hair tethered back with indifference, her high cheek bones gaunt. Her face a landscape of grief.

Karen's experienced eye took in Sara's body language, the way she held herself stiff and aloof, as though she had built a wall around herself, avoiding any contact with anyone, physical or otherwise.

As if sensing she was being studied, Sara looked up and for a brief few seconds looked at Karen, then quickly averted her eyes.

In that split-second Karen saw unimaginable grief in Sara's eyes, and for the first time she saw the woman behind the self-made mask. Whatever medication she was on, Karen knew, it would never heal the pain in those blue eyes, or fill the empty hole of grief in her thin body, where life seemed to be seeping away.

Karen watched Sara leave the room, ignoring everyone. She turned to the woman next to her. "So, what's up with the mystery woman who doesn't talk. What's she in for?"

The woman shrugged her shoulders, chasing the last of her dinner around the plate with her fork. "How the hell would I know, if she doesn't talk? Listen, everyone here has done something bad, something wrong, it's why we're locked up here. Not everyone wants to talk about it, you know. Why don't you mind your own business and let everyone else do the same, hey?"

"Only trying to be friendly," Karen muttered, pushing her chair back. "Bunch of nutters, to be sure." She made her way back to her own room, dreading the months of being incarcerated here, surrounded by a lot of tormented minds, including her own.

Karen lay back on the pillow on her bed. The woman called Sara was bothering her. In the Haven inmates were only known by their Christian names, and sometimes these were not real. But Karen was convinced she had seen Sara, whatever-her-surname-was, somewhere before.

She searched her impressive memory. The woman, she felt sure, had been quite well-known. Karen closed her eyes and concentrated, trying to imagine Sara in an ordinary situation outside the high walled gardens of the Haven. Sara with make-up, Sara with a hairstyle more becoming than the one she effected now. Yes, with a choppy hairstyle Sara would look like an older version of the whacky actress Meg Ryan.

Karen sat bolt upright, and swung her legs to the side of the bed. Got it! Her name was Sara Courtney-Saunders. A high-profile news reporter based in the UK. Sara's father had been a Diplomat somewhere in Africa. A child had gone missing somewhere, the body was never found and Sara had been charged with murder. She had murdered her own child, a boy if she remembered correctly.

Karen paced the confines of her small room, trying to recall as much detail as possible. The judge had found her guilty whilst of unsound mind. Karen clicked her fingers – Rohypnol. She had taken the drug Rohypnol.

Karen stopped her pacing, pulled open the curtains and stared out across the dark gardens. Rohypnol had been a fantastic drug used for treating a variety of different symptoms. She had prescribed it herself for many of her own patients, confident with its abilities. But then the drug had fallen into disrepute. Abused by rapists and murderers.

If Sara had taken Rohypnol then she would have had no recollection of her actions that day, if this were the truth.

Karen thought back to a few days ago when she had sat next to Sara on the bench in the gardens, admiring her painting. Yes, the river, the missing child, it had all been there in the painting.

Karen felt a wave of pity for the woman, instinctively wanting to help her, knowing Sara was a deeply disturbed woman, and who wouldn't be? Being incarcerated, hidden away from the outside world was one thing, but carrying the heavy weight of guilt of killing your own child was another.

She knew evil didn't always show in a person's face, a person's eyes. Even the most angelic face could conceal the heart of a monster. What Sara had done was unspeakable, but she didn't think she was a monster. The monster was the drug called Rohypnol.

Karen made up her mind. She wouldn't give up on Sara, somehow, she was going to try and reach her, wherever she had gone in her mind. It would give her a project, something to do with her time here, a challenge if ever there was one.

Chapter Twenty
The Shepherd

Eza sat under the branches of the old acacia tree, puffing on his home-made pipe, deeply troubled. Mirium, his wife, stitched quietly at the quilt she was making, the vibrant colours of blue, red, green and yellow in sharp contrast to the powdery grey dust under their feet.

Eza leaned down and took a handful of dust in his hand and let it trickle back. "*Eish*," he muttered, looking up at the darkening sky, "this rain must come soon or there will be trouble with the crops and the animals."

Mirium nodded, a worried frown spreading across her brow, but she said nothing. She paused and let the needle she was working with lie still, her eyes travelling around the almost deserted village. Some of the round houses with their conical roofs were already disintegrating. Birds nested in the collapsed thatch of the roofs, their hardened droppings making an ugly carpet on the dusty floor. Lizards scuttled in and out, looking for insects with their darting tongues.

"It is true, my husband. The young ones are leaving, some with their elders, seeking work and money in the towns and cities. If the rains do not come, there will be no food to eat." She clicked her tongue and picked up her sewing.

Eza could see his daughter Kia down at the dwindling river playing with her friends. His son, Jabu, now tall and strong, always close by watching over his little sister, protecting her.

Kia was bright and intelligent and she had learned how to collect water and balance the clay pot on her head without holding it steady with her hand, and acquiring the graceful female walk, head high, back straight with a slight swaying walk. She had learned how to gather firewood for her mother to cook the evening meal, and sweep the hard-baked floor of their house with twigs tied together with leather binding.

At the end of each day she would join the other young girls from the village down at the riverside, singing softly with them as they washed themselves in the shallow sweet soft water before adorning themselves with necklaces made of wooden beads, matching the colourful bracelets they wore on their ankles and wrists, then tying the short, soft, leather skirts around their slender waists. Jabu keeping his eyes on the boys who watched the young girls budding bodies with longing.

Still singing the girls plaited their hair threading more colourful beads through their braids, before filling their clay pots with water and returning in a single file back to the village.

Eza rose from his wooden three-legged chair and rubbed his aching back. He walked over to the pens where he had once kept many goats and sheep. Now the flock was much depleted. Only eight sheep and six goats, soon they would have to be slaughtered to feed his family and dwindling neighbours.

*****

Jabu stirred the dying embers of the fire with a stick, then looked up at his father. "Papa, we cannot sit here and wait for the last villager to leave, we must make some plans of our own, now the rains have not come.

"For us to survive we must also find another life," he glanced at his little sister Kia. "Kia is clever, she must have her chance to make a better life than carrying pots on her head. Perhaps the quilts Mama makes could be sold in the town? Myself and Kia should move into this new world, where there is much money and a future, more so than goats and sheep in a village which is slowly dying? Education, Papa, this is the way to go forward?"

Eza glanced at his wife and children, their shadowed faces glowing in the dying embers of the fire as darkness gathered around them.

Eza sighed. Perhaps the Gods were angry with him for what he had done, perhaps he should consider his son's advice. But his heart was heavy.

*****

Mirium saw her husband's troubled face and knew it was time. The future was their son and daughter. Not theirs.

"My husband? Let me take the children to the town and see what there is to be seen? Jabu is right, we are here in a dying village. I will take the children to this town and see if it will be a better place to be. Better than living here in this village with little water and no crops. Perhaps, as Jabu has said, I will be able to sell some of my quilts in the market."

"Mirium, it is true our children need a better future. But I will not leave my village. This village has given me more than a poor man could hope for. A wife, two children and my goats and sheep. I will wait here. Take the children," his voice broke, "lead them to this better life. I will not leave my village. I cannot take my sheep and goats to a town where they will not know where to graze and where I will not know how to live."

*****

Eza pulled his cloak around him and went to his sleeping quarters, so his family would not see the tears sliding down his cheeks. He had been given a gift from the Gods, a child, and a loving wife who had blessed him with another child. Was this now the price the Gods would ask him to pay?

He lay down on his bed and pulled the soft rabbit skin cover over his thin bones. Tomorrow he would find someone to write his letter, someone he could trust. He would have to go to town with his little family to do this. It was time.

Someone, surely, would be able to find the mother of the child. The mother he knew did not sleep well at night. The mother he knew grieved for her child with every breath she had in her body.

Yes, he would *have* to go to the town with his family in the morning and find someone who could write this letter for him. Then he would have to find a way to get it to the city in the south of the country. The place with the big flat mountain.

He would look for his old friend Sipo and seek his advice.

76

Chapter Twenty-One
The Shepherd

E za, Mirium and their two children, Kia and Jabu, trudged through the dry cracked bush, Kia and Mirium carrying the brightly coloured quilts, Eza and his son, two battered cardboard cases, until they came to the main road leading to town. They waited in the sun until the old bus arrived; it barrelled to a halt in front of them, covering them in dust, and belching black smoke from the exhaust pipe.

Mirium had insisted Kia wear a dress which she had made herself, and Jabu trousers and shirt like his father.

"*Eish*, my daughter, you cannot go to this town wearing only your beads and skirt, in this town they dress like the white people." Jabu had hastily agreed she was right. He didn't want young boys and men staring at his half-naked sister.

In silence they watched the flat brown parched lands stretching out in front of them, the sloping hills in the far distance and the occasional village looking as empty and forlorn as their own. Bony cattle being herded along, their ribs arching against their thin skin, their heads and necks sloped as they searched for water and something to graze on.

Two hours later the bus rumbled into the Willow Drift bus station and its weary passengers alighted. Eza looked around in dismay. *Eish*, how would he find his friend Sipo in this big noisy place with many cars, shops, houses and busy people?

Jabu picked up the small cases and turned to his father. "I will take Mama and Kia to the market with the quilts. Papa you will never find your friend here without help. Your friend Sipo was working with the police? It is so he might still be there, or they are knowing of his whereabouts? He will advise you on the future of our village and what should be done? I will ask someone where the police station is."

But is wasn't only Sipo, Eza needed to find. He needed someone who could write his letter for him. A letter he did not want Sipo to see in case it brought trouble with the police again. He would have to be careful and seek his advice on finding such a man who knew these English words.

The police sergeant, at the station, eventually looked up at Eza, who had been standing patiently waiting. "Yes?"

Eza realised the sergeant in front of him probably did not speak the language of his people. He would struggle with these English words, of which he knew only a few.

"It is Sipo I am looking for," he stammered. "It was with the police he was working?"

The sergeant shook his head impatiently. "Sipo? Sipo who? What is his family name?"

"Klassens. This is the family name of Sipo."

"Are you family?" the sergeant asked, his face softening.

"I am his friend from when we were children. My name is Eza, Sir."

"Then I am sorry for your loss Eza. Sipo died some years ago in a car accident."

Eza looked down at his bare feet and his carefully darned trousers, trying to make sense of this news of his friend. He nodded at the sergeant and made his way slowly back to the bus station and the market.

He passed small shops selling clothes, shoes, electrical goods, outside food stalls cooking pieces of chicken and yellow corn cobs, small stands piled high with bright fruits and green vegetables. He swallowed the saliva in his throat realising he was hungry, his nostrils immediately assailed with the smell of meat cooking, marked with the tines of the grill, but knew he did not have money for any of the things the traders were selling.

There was a dripping tap at the road side of one of the trader's stands, he filled his hands with water and drank greedily, the water staining the front of his thin shirt and splashing on his dusty feet. Feeling dizzy with hunger and with all the noise around him, he wished with all his heart he had stayed in his village, away from all of this.

Eza sat down on the pavement, his head in his hands. He jumped when he felt a hand on his shoulder.

"Here my friend, drink from this."

Eza looked up and took the tin can full of water, nodding his thanks.

"You are a stranger in town old man, but you are a Griqua, yes?"

Eza lapsed back into his familiar tongue. "Yes. I am Eza. I came to seek my friend of many years ago. I came to seek some help from him, but he has gone to be with our ancestors."

The stranger hunkered down next to him. "What is this help you are seeking, old man?"

"I am needing someone who is able to write in this language called English. It is a letter I need to send to the big city with the flat mountain."

The stranger laughed. "This place with the flat mountain is called Cape Town. But I know of such a person who will write this letter for you. He is one of us. He will help you."

Eza sighed. "I have no money for this letter to be written. But my wife Mirium is selling some things in the market. I will pay with this money."

The stranger stood up. "Come Eza. I will take you to this man. His place of work is only a short walk from here."

Eza and the stranger stood outside a small dark shop, the stranger indicated he should go in. Then waving cheerfully he went back to his stall.

Eza smoothed down his shirt and entered the shop, his eyes adjusting from the bright glare of the sun outside and the dark interior. A man sat at a simple wooden desk, a side light glowing over the papers on his table.

Seeing the poorly dressed, but proud man in front of him, he gestured for him to sit in the chair opposite.

"You are wishing for something to be written? A letter perhaps?"

Eza nodded gratefully and answered the man in his own language. "I have no money yet, but I will pay you, and for this I give you my word. My name is Eza."

The man smiled. "If I came to your village looking for food, water and shelter, would you not give it to me Eza?"

"We are of the same people. My home would be yours, yes."

The letter writer opened his large notepad, removed a pen from behind his ear, and looked at Eza. "I will write this letter for you."

Eza hesitated. "Have no fear, Eza, I will reveal to no-one the contents you will trust me with?"

An hour later the task was completed. The letter writer searched around for an envelope, sealed the letter, and waited, pen poised, for Eza to give him the address.

"Eza, who must this letter be going to?" he prompted.

Eza looked up, his face blank. *"Eish.* This part will be most hard for me. The man is a big white chief, who is working for the British Queen across the seas. His name is like a long way from one place to another in a bus. If you know this name for a long way from one place to another, I will know it."

The scribe looked up puzzled, he scratched his head with the end of the pen. "From one place to another by bus? You mean the time this journey takes?"

"No, I am meaning how long the road is?"

"Ah! You mean kilometres then?"

Eza shook his head. "Yes, this is what I am meaning but the British chief, his name is like these kilometres but in English."

"Ha! Then it is miles you are meaning; this is what the English use to measure their roads from place to place."

Eza's eyes lit up. "Yes, this is the name of the white chief – Miles!"

Laboriously the scribe wrote carefully on the envelope.

The White Chief Miles

Head of the British People

Cape Town

The Griqua man put the pen back behind his ear and stroked his thin wispy beard.

"I am thinking this letter will not get to the Chief Miles, more information is needed for this envelope?"

Seeing Eza's stricken face, he smiled at him warmly. "But this you must not worry about. There is a European doctor here in the town. He is often to Cape Town going. I will take this letter to him and he will surely know who the Chief Miles is and where he is living."

Eza thanked him profusely, promising to return with the money required for the writing of the letter.

"Eza, we are of the same tribe, we are of the same people, we help each other. I have no need of the money. One day you will be able to help someone who is also in need. This is payment enough for me."

Eza, made his way back to the market, his steps steadier, his heart lighter. But he would not be able to tell his wife or his children where he had been after the visit to the police station.

But what he had done was the right thing, in his heart he knew this, perhaps he should have said more, but this was impossible for him to do. His family and his life were already changing. He thought back to the letter.

Greetings,

It is I, Eza. Many rainy seasons ago you are coming to my village where you are meeting with our Chief. To this Chief you are giving your house in the bush and the land on which it is standing. The Chief was most pleased with this gift.

Before the rainy season is coming your daughter is coming to live in this your house which was to be given to the Chief, when you go to meet your white ancestors. Also, in this house was an African woman called Beauty. It was Beauty who looked after the two small ones, when Missus Sara was busy with making her things with beads and selling them to the place where many people come from across the seas, to see our animals in the bush.

The Chief's son, Joseph, went sometimes to check on this house but did not disturb your family there, they did not know he is being amongst the trees near the river watching. He saw many things which troubled him.

When the fires came, they were burning all around, and now, I am sorry to tell you that you and the Chief are only having one burnt house with the land.

This was being a very bad time for your daughter and the two little ones, for at this time the smaller child went missing and was not found. The Police searched for this child but it was gone. My boyhood friend Sipo, also looked for this lost child when it was with the police he was working. Sipo has also gone to be with his ancestors.

The Police they are taking your daughter away to this place with the flat mountain, they are saying she killed the child. They are taking her and putting her in a prison for people with bad things in their heads. They are saying she cannot see her other child because she might hurt this one as well.

I do not know where the other boy is staying now. Perhaps he is in this place for children, this place where kind people take small children and give them food, where there is only little love for them because there are many children in this place and not enough love for all.

It is I, Eza, who knows the truth of what happened to the little one. Joseph also know this truth, for he was the one who told me. From this place where he was hiding, he saw what he saw.

The mother did not kill her child.

It is with sadness I must tell you the old Chief has died. His son Joseph, who is my cousin, is now the Chief. But what use is this when the new Chief has no people left to be the Chief for?

When the rains did not come for many many months, the people are going to the town to look for work and food. The village is dying. I too must leave this village with my wife and children to find a place where there is money and food. The new Chief will also have to leave here and take his goats and sheep to another place where the rain is coming, but he will no longer be the chief of any place.

There is only your burnt house left there now. The bush will take this burnt house and cover it with the wild bushes and it will be forgotten.

I am sorry for your troubles.

Greetings from Eza.

Chapter Twenty-Two
The Teacher

Diana Templeton made her way through the bustling market, in Willow Drift, a straw hat covering her short grey hair, sunglasses shielding her brown eyes from the fierce glare of the Eastern Cape sun. She brushed a persistent fly away from her face with her free hand, in the other hand she held an empty shopping basket.

Diana had lived in Kenya and South Africa for over twenty-five years, but still she couldn't get used to the heat and glare of the merciless sun of Africa. Sometimes she yearned for the changing seasons of England where she had been born and brought up until she met her husband who was working in Africa. But not so much she would ever give up her life here, a place she had come to love, although it could be harsh and unpredictable, like a bad-tempered husband.

Norman Templeton, her husband, was far from being unpredictable or bad tempered, even though sometimes she wished he wasn't so predictable. Norman had been a consulting engineer on many projects in both East and Southern Africa, travelling often in the old days but not much recently.

Diana and Norman had always wanted a family but, in his predictable way, Norman had pointed out to his wife, living in Africa with all the travelling they would be doing was not conducive to having children, who, in his opinion, would have to end up in a boarding school where the fees would be horrendously high and they would hardly see them, except during the holidays.

Diana had to admit there was some truth in this, but still hid a secret desire for at least some grand-children but, of course, it was out of the question. So, to compensate she taught a small number of local children at her home, just out of town, three afternoons a week. Although she herself had a degree in the History of Art and had been good enough to go on and get a further degree at the prestigious art academy, the Courtauld, in London, she realised this would be of little benefit to local children in the Eastern Cape of South Africa; she stuck with reading, writing and basic arithmetic.

Her simple white cotton dress stuck to her ample body as she leaned over a vegetable stall, squeezing the tomatoes and avocados for ripeness, chatting to the smiling stall holder as he wrapped the fruit and vegetables in newspaper which she placed in her basket.

Diana always bought as much as she could from the local farmers, avoiding the noisy supermarket, and their plastic bags, on the main street of the town. She only bought her meat from there. She walked through the crowded stalls, trying to ignore the calls of the chicken traders, their birds trussed and bound, ready to be slaughtered. She shuddered; she would buy a few chickens later from the supermarket, at least there she wouldn't have to look into their eyes.

Sitting slightly to one side of a stall, under the shade of a tree her attention was drawn to a mother with two children, surrounded by colourful square quilts.

The mother of the children smiled shyly and a little anxiously, as Diana approached and bent over to admire the woman's handiwork. "Oh my," Diana exclaimed, "these are exquisite, did you make them?"

Mirium nodded. "Yes Mama," she said softly, using this word as a mark of respect for an older woman. "I am making them with the help of my daughter Kia," she nodded her head towards her daughter.

Although her mother tongue was Griqua, Mirium had learned a little English from her friend in the village who had worked for an English family in Cape Town, before returning to the familiar and comforting warmth of her family and village life. Mirium had encouraged her children to learn a little English as well. Eza had refused.

Diane looked through the small pile of quilts before she made up her mind. "I would like to take four of them. These four." Diana pulled them out, separating them from the others.

"How much are they?"

Mirium turned to her son, flustered. She had not thought about the worth of her hand-made quilts. Jabu, smiled at the woman. "They are four hundred Rand each, Mama."

"No discount if I buy four?"

"No, Mama, each quilt has taken my mother many hours to make, each one has its own worth, how could it be I would give this discount?

84

It would not be worthy of my mother's many hours to make them cheaper."

Diana grinned at him. "A business man in the making, hey! Alright but I will need some help to carry them back to my car and then my house. Would you be able to do this?"

Jabu and Kia both stood up. "My sister and I will help you. My mother will come too. She does not know this market, or this town, we will not leave her alone here."

Diana drove them all back to her house. Mirium watched as Diana placed her precious quilts on the beds, Kia helped to straighten them out.

Jabu felt the money in the pocket of his shorts, trying not to show his immense pleasure at such a large amount. Now they would be able to find somewhere cheap to stay and perhaps sell the rest of the quilts tomorrow. But now they must go back to the market and their father who would be waiting anxiously for them.

*****

Diana and Norman sat out on their patio, sipping a glass of wine, enjoying the stillness of the evening, hearing only the faint rumble of traffic from town.

Since meeting the quilt maker and her children Diana had been thinking. She had proudly shown Norman the quilts she had bought from the small family.

Norman glanced at his wife. "What are you thinking so deeply about, my dear? You've got that look on your face…?"

Diana put her glass down on the table next to her. "I was thinking about the quilt maker and her two children."

"Oh yes? What about them?"

"Jabu, the boy, is around twelve I would think, tall young man, and Kia, the girl, probably ten. They both seem like bright intelligent children. But clearly, they don't go to school out there in the bush in their village. Such a waste. South Africa needs more educated children for the future. Something really should be done about it Norman."

Norman refreshed his glass of wine and smiled at his innocent looking wife. "We can't turn our home into a boarding school, my dear, despite your aspirations for the future children of this country."

Diana shook her head. "Well it's not really what I'm suggesting, besides their parents would probably not want any change, they want to keep their children close. But…"

"But what, my dear?"

"Well I was thinking. Perhaps the children might like to do some light work around the house and garden, and in exchange I could teach them, educate them a little. They could sleep here, in the little cottage in the garden, then go home to visit their parents at the end of each month, if they so wish? What do you think?"

Norman knew when he was beaten, Diana had made her mind up. "I'm happy to go along with whatever you decide, my dear. Now, what's for dinner, I missed lunch so I'm famished!"

*****

The next morning Diana made her way back to the market and found the quilt maker and her two children sitting with their merchandise. A middle-aged man, his back against a cardboard suitcase, sat watching the crowds swirling around the stalls, a look of utter bewilderment on his face.

Jabu stood up when he saw Diana. Perhaps she would like to buy some more quilts he thought hopefully? Instead Diana wished them all good morning then turned to the man, who hurriedly scrambled to his feet.

"This is my father, Eza," Jabu said by way of introduction.

Diana shook his outstretched hand. "Good morning Eza. You must be proud of your family. Your wife's quilts are beautiful and your children quite charming!"

Diana took her sunglasses off. "I've been giving your children a great deal of thought. I'd like to help you and your family. I'm a teacher and I have a proposition for you?"

Jabu listened to the teacher lady's proposition, although he was not quite sure what the word meant, then he translated for his parents.

He watched and listened anxiously as his parents discussed, in their own language, what the woman in front of them was suggesting. Although he was fiercely protective of his sister, Jabu knew if they were to have any chance in life, outside the village they had known all their life, then this was a good opportunity, probably the only one they would ever get. An education.

"Papa, I have seen the house where this teacher lives, it is a good place and I think she is a good woman who wishes to help. What harm can there be in teaching us to read and write, these are valuable things to know?"

*****

Eza, though a simple man himself, knew the words his son had spoken were true. He would have to let his daughter go. The time would come when she would go anyway. What harm could come of her staying with this teacher woman and learning this reading and writing? But not his son. He wanted to keep Jabu close by.

He looked at the teacher. "My son, will stay with us." His son's face dropped with disappointment.

"But it must not be what we want. It is for Kia to decide if she would like to do this learning. Kia?"

Kia stood up, the beads in her braided hair clicking softly. "I would like to learn these things Mama," she glanced at her father eagerly. "Papa? With this knowledge I can help you and Mama when you are old. I will work hard for this knowledge."

She turned to Diana. "I thank you for wanting to teach me these things. I will work hard for you. I will be no trouble."

Diana clapped her hands. "Splendid! Now, Kia, when would you like to start to learn to read and write?"

Kia looked once more at her parents; her eyes bright with hope. "It is now I would like to start," she said bravely, her face anxious. "I will come with you now to your house for learning."

*****

Jabu had also tasted a little of life beyond his village, had felt the reassuring weight of money in his pocket. Although he was disappointed not to be given the same opportunities as his sister.

He also wanted to learn to read and write. Perhaps in time this teacher called Diana might teach him as well, maybe he could work in her garden? But first he would go back with his parents to the village for they would miss Kia, the loss of two children would be too much for them.

Chapter Twenty-Three

The letter writer, true to his word, entrusted Eza's letter addressed to Chief Miles, to the doctor he had mentioned he knew. The letter was delivered to the British Embassy in Cape Town as promised.

The receptionist at the Embassy looked briefly at the name and address on the envelope and raised an eyebrow at the childish writing.

That morning she had been fired for failing in her duties, spending too many days off sick and various other misdemeanours. She didn't have a clue who Chief bloody Miles was, nor did she care much.

Angrily she shoved the envelope in one of the files she was archiving, clearing the desk in readiness for whoever was going to take over from her.

Eza's carefully worded letter would lie in the dark of the filing cabinet, unseen by anyone for years to come.

Chapter Twenty-Four
The Doctor

Karen found Sara in her usual place on the bench. For the past month she had joined her there gazing out at the gardens. Oblivious to the obvious resentment of Sara, who completely ignored her, dabbing away at her paintings.

Initially Karen had not spoken to her at all, after the first attempt to get to know her, who she was. She sat there for half an hour or so, then stood up and left.

Then when she felt Sara was getting used to her presence, she would make a comment about the weather, or about the latest book she was reading. Lapsing back into silence, not expecting any response.

Feeling the time was now right she once more approached the bench and sat down. "Sure, it's a lovely day Sara." She looked around the gardens, the rays of sun sucking up the moist ground from the rains the night before.

No response.

"Sara, I want to help you. I don't know how long you've been locked up, or how long you'll be staying, but this I can tell you. If you don't make some effort to communicate, they won't let you out of here."

Sara ignored her and lifted her brush. The same river, the same child amongst the reeds.

"You know Sara, everyone in this place has secrets, to be sure. Everyone has done something wrong. Every single woman here is struggling with some kind of emotion, be it guilt at what they have done, or no remorse at all for whatever crime they have committed. But they all have one thing in common. They want to get better, serve their time, and then be released to start a new life. They're all working hard at it, as I am myself.

"You need to get better, learn to talk, to communicate, open up a little. Otherwise, as I said, you won't have the chance of being free again, of walking along the beach, going to the theatre, or shopping, or building a new life. They won't let you out. Believe me they won't.

"I know you can talk. You weren't born without a voice. Every human being needs some kind of contact with another otherwise they become withdrawn. Like you."

Karen stood up and was about to squeeze Sara's shoulder, then changed her mind when she saw the paint Sara was furiously mixing seemed to dilute. It was enough for one day.

Karen waited a few days before going back to the bench. She opened her book and started to read until she felt Sara relax slightly in her presence, as she worked on a new painting with the same subject. The river and the child. But never the child's face.

"You're probably not interested, ensconced in your own little world, but I had a grand life before this you know. I did something bad like everyone else here."

Sara's brush strokes stilled slightly, as though she might be listening.

Karen puffed out her cheeks and sighed. "The world I lived in, the job I had, was probably one of the most stressful in any profession. I came over from Ireland full of hopes and dreams, like any other young woman. I was good at what I did. Seven hard years of studying and I ended up with a dream come true, a doctor with my own practice."

Sara's brush lifted slightly and wavered. She was listening. Karen continued. "My practice grew, this was truly my calling, I'd never been happier. But, blimey, it was tough going. Health care professionals are fallible human beings who sometimes make mistakes. As I did.

"I did something I deeply regret, something I thought I would never forgive myself for. But here's the thing, Sara. The first step towards recovery is acknowledging what made you do the bad thing in the first place. The second thing is learning to forgive yourself for something which cannot be changed. Life offers chances each laden with hope and possibilities.

"At first, with me, it was recreational drugs, then amphetamines, then because my brain was screwed up, I couldn't sleep. That's when I started on the Rohypnol. I could take it, sleep well, and then still treat my patients the next day with no ill-effects, no thick head. I prescribed it often."

Karen stole a look at Sara, her brush was stilled, she was listening. One word had grabbed her attention as Karen knew it would.

90

"One day a female patient of mine told me she was going abroad for eight months and would I give her a supply of Rohypnol. Stupidly I did, two days later she committed suicide. She wasn't going anywhere. Just wanted to kill herself."

Karen stood up, tucking her book under her arm. "See you tomorrow Sara."

Sara looked up, as if seeing this woman for the first time. She nodded her head then ground her paintbrush into the palette of colours in front of her.

Karen looked back. Sara was finally still, her hands in her lap, looking into a distance at the past. A past Karen now knew a little about.

Her plan for Sara was working well so far.

Then Karen heard a sound, a sound she hoped she would never hear again. From the bench, a wail, a clean note of grief. A soul piercing eruption of pure loss. Sara, her arms wrapped around her knees her head buried in her lap, the sound raw and savage.

Karen's instinct was to run back to the shattered woman, but she didn't. Steeling herself she carried on walking back to the house.

Only a crack in the wall of silence, but Karen sensed that over the past few days Sara had lost the disinterested expression which had seemed to parallel her muteness.

Sara had made a sound, not a good one, but she had made it. A human sound.

Chapter Twenty-Five

After the death of her patient and the autopsy, Doctor Karen O'Hara had been hauled in front of the Disciplinary Board. She knew full well she was in a lot of trouble, no doctor should have prescribed eight months' supply of Rohypnol. The Board had insisted she underwent a full medical where the results of the blood tests put her squarely in the substance abuse category.

Despite many letters of support and satisfaction from her patients, the Board suspended her from practicing medicine for two years, with a proviso they would re-look at her case at the end of that period providing she could prove she was no longer a drug user.

Knowing the first steps to recovery would be to get out of the environment she was in, she would have to find somewhere different to start the treatment. Karen had heard of The Haven in Cape Town and decided it would be the ideal place, a grand place, to begin her recovery from addiction.

Six gruelling months later the medical facility pronounced her clean of any substance abuse.

With eighteen months still to go before she could apply to the Disciplinary Board in the UK for a review of her case and re-instatement of her licence to practice, Karen looked at her options. Staying in Cape Town was one, all she had to do was apply for another tourist visa. But then she would have to find somewhere to rent, find something to do. Going back to the UK with winter approaching was not an option. Perhaps she could find another solution.

That's when she approached the Senior Director of The Haven, Doctor Pretorius.

"I've done my time here, Doctor Pretorius, and I'm clean. I'm not asking you to let me practice. I know this wouldn't be allowed in South Africa without the correct legal licence. But I think I can contribute in other ways. I know what it's like to be a drug addict, how hard it is to beat.

"I could talk to the inmates; show them it can be done. Perhaps try and work with some of the other more traumatised patients? There's one in particular, her name is Sara. I think I can help her if I know a little more about her?"

Doctor Pretorius studied the woman in front of her and smiled sadly. "Sara doesn't speak, not ever. There's no physical reason why she shouldn't and we know she's intelligent. But she's locked the doors of her mind against the world, and no one's ever found a way to unlock them. We certainly haven't. If we knew why she never speaks we might make some sense out of what she did."

She rubbed the dark shadows under her eyes tiredly. "We've tried all different kinds of therapies, we know she likes to read and paint, but nothing's worked, but we won't give up. I'm not sure what you hope to achieve Doctor O'Hara?"

Karen leaned forward eagerly. "Let me at least try? You have nothing to lose?"

Doctor Pretorius picked up her glasses and rubbed them briskly with the hem of her white coat. "You're right we have nothing to lose. Let me put it to the Board and see how they feel about your proposal."

The Board of Directors deliberated her request over the next two days. It was true Karen was a well-qualified doctor and now clearly recovered. Her contribution to the other inmates could be invaluable. It had been noticed she mixed well with the other patients. It had also been noticed she spent time with Sara. The one woman the doctors, psychiatrists and psychologists had failed to make any headway with, despite their high rate of success with other inmates.

So, it was agreed Karen would mix with all the inmates on an informal basis, and, of course, she would not be paid a salary without a licence to practice in South Africa. Perhaps she would be able to help Sara, it was a risk worth taking, when all else had failed.

*****

Karen, after her visit with Sara an hour ago, knocked tentatively on the office door of the senior director.

Doctor Pretorius, surrounded by mounds of files indicated she should sit. "You're looking pleased with yourself Karen. What can I do for you?"

93

Karen crossed her legs and smiled. "It's Sara. I've been spending time with her in the gardens. She hasn't said a word, but today I'm hopeful. It wasn't pleasant hearing her cry like a wounded beast, but it was a sound, Doctor Pretorius, she finally made a sound! It was a grand thing to hear!"

"Well that is good, if unexpected news, Karen. Well done. What will you do from here?"

"I'm going to keep sitting with her, talking to her. I'm optimistic she'll eventually say something. But there's something which would help tremendously? Would it be possible to see her file? I know all records are confidential, but I am a doctor. It would help if I could get a better feeling for her and what she went through?

"I vaguely remember seeing her story on television in the UK, in fact I recognised her as an excellent reporter on one of the channels. Having a bit more background would help me considerably."

Doctor Pretorius removed her glasses and squeezed the top of her nose. "I'm not sure the other directors will agree to this. But given your background the least I can do is put it to them and see what they have to say. You'll have to sign a confidentiality agreement, of course. If they allow it that is."

"Sure, I'm happy to do that."

*****

Karen read carefully through Sara's case file, making notes as she went along.

Jesus, Mary, Mother of God, she crossed herself quickly. No wonder Sara was in such a state.

Karen stared out of the window watching the shadows lengthening on the lawn, she checked her watch. Out in the gardens the slave bell tolled. Time for dinner.

She watched Sara sitting across from her in her usual seat, she would do everything in her power to help her recover. It wouldn't be easy, she knew she was no miracle worker, but she had to do something. She had to gain her trust.

Sara looked up briefly without smiling, but Karen had seen something in those dark blue empty eyes – hope.

Chapter Twenty Six

The following morning Karen walked around the gardens looking for Sara. Puzzled at not finding her in her usual place on the bench, she ventured back into the house, checked the communal sitting room and the library, but Sara was no-where to be found.

Once more she scanned the grounds, more than a little concerned. She had pushed Sara hard yesterday. Then she spotted her, sitting under the shade of one of the ancient oak trees, partially hidden beneath their heavy boughs, squeezing her empty hands. No paints, no brushes no half-finished painting on her lap.

Karen sat down next to her. "I thought you might have escaped Sara; you gave me quite a scare. How are you feeling today?"

Sara turned and looked at Karen, properly now, without her eyes sliding away as they normally did. Her face betrayed her. Her decision almost written on the air above her. To talk, or not to talk? But the need seemed too great for the moment. Karen fell silent, and waited for a few moments.

"The child in the painting, the little one standing in the reeds? That's Ben isn't it?"

Sara shook her head, her eyes brimming with the tears she had held back for too long.

Karen tried again. "Then it must be Charlie, right?"

"Yes," she whispered, her voice rasping in her throat.

Karen tentatively put her hand over Sara's and she didn't pull away. "Listen to me Sara. I think I can help you, in fact I know I can help you. As you know I'm a medical doctor, and, yes, I also made a terrible mistake. But I have paid for it. Now I want to help you. The doctors here have agreed to let me try. Anything you tell me will stay between the two of us, I need you to understand this. I need you to trust me."

Sara nodded. "Tell me about Rohypnol, Karen," her voice was hoarse. "I need to know about it, what it can do?" She whispered, squeezing her hands. Soft cracked words breaking through the barrier of disbelief and silence.

*****

For two hours they sat under the oak tree, the words finally emerging from Sara, her voice breaking as though she had a scratchy raw throat. Then she would stop as though gathering herself, not speaking for periods of time. Karen waited, listening carefully, interrupting with a question only when absolutely necessary, and handing her a bottle of water to sip from, to lubricate her throat.

Finally, Sara leaned back spent, looking up through the thick branches of the trees, emotionally drained.

"So, you haven't spoken to your father for seven years? Jaysus, and you haven't seen Ben in all this time?"

"My father wrote to me several times but I never opened any of the letters. Everything was too raw. I was ashamed of what I'd done, ashamed I never told him about the birth of Charlie. We've always had a tempestuous relationship. I didn't think he would understand and knew he wouldn't approve. He's a bit old fashioned about things like that and a staunch Catholic.

She cleared her throat again, and winced with the effort. "Ben didn't want to see me."

Karen glanced quickly around and withdrew a cigarette and lighter from her pocket. "Yeah, I know, bad for you, but you'd be surprised at how many doctors and nurses smoke. Pressure of the job and the misery and sadness in patient's lives. I should have stuck to smoking and avoided the drugs.

"So, where's Ben now, do you know?"

Sara nodded her head. "The Embassy wrote and told me he'd been fostered out for four years. Then, when he turned fifteen, his grandfather, my father, arranged for him to fly back to the UK. Ben was accepted into a top private school; he was a boarder there and spent the holidays with my father in the West Country."

Sara wiped her eyes with her sleeve. Karen passed her the bottle of water and a tissue.

"My father would have been thrilled I'm sure, it's what he always wanted you see. He said Ben was running wild out there in the bush

96

with me, he needed some discipline. It was the last time I spoke to my father and we had a blistering row about it. He didn't approve of my career, didn't approve of my husband, rightly so as it turned out, and he most certainly would not have approved of a child born out of wedlock."

Sara's shoulders slumped and she took a deep breath, her voice easier and clearer now. "Being a Diplomat, he was always rigid in the way he behaved and he expected me to behave accordingly. Scandal was abhorrent to him. Something he would never tolerate. I let him down badly."

Karen blew a perfect circle of smoke from her cigarette. "But you love him, right?"

"Yes, of course, I love him, even though he wasn't like any of the other fathers I met. There was no lightness about him. But he did have one lovely disarming feature – a laugh, a deep laugh, which seemed to rumble up from his well-polished shoes and make his shoulders shake. I used to wait for those moments."

Sara smiled softly at the memory. She reached for the bottle of water and cleared her throat again. "He loved Christmas, like a small boy emerging from a grown man's body. He fussed over the tree and decorations, tramping the countryside looking for holly, berries and fir tree branches. He became like a real living breathing father and, of course, his wonderful laugh."

Nervously biting slivers of skin from her lips, she continued, her voice fading to a whisper. "Then when the festive season was over, he would revert to his normal aloof and private self."

Karen turned to Sara and put her hands on her shoulders. "See here my girl, there's a promise I'm going to make to you, but I'll need your help.

"In nine months', I'll be out of here. I could have left before now, but I wanted to help other patients here – you especially. You'll be due for release then, and as you're now talking, there's no reason on earth for them to hold you any longer. You will have served your time.

"I'll work with you every day, if you'll let me?"

Sara looking apprehensive. She chewed the inside of her cheek using her finger to gain traction.

"In time your strength and courage will come back to you. You were a top war correspondent, Sara, covering all the hot spots, the Gulf, Bosnia, Afghanistan, Iraq and God knows where else. You're tougher than you think."

She lit another cigarette. "You need to see Ben and work on your relationship with him. You're his mother, and he needs his mother even though he's eighteen now. You also need to mend some bridges with your father. He won't be around forever and you don't need any more guilt."

Karen ground out her cigarette and flicked the butt into a nearby bush. "Tell me something, Sara. Why didn't your father send for Ben before? Why did he wait four years before he did anything?"

Sara shrugged. "Perhaps he thought Ben would be too difficult to handle under the circumstances. Asking a man in his seventies to look after an eleven-year-old child, is a lot to ask. I don't have the answer to that."

Karen stood up. "Now let's go back to the house. I want you to read those letters from your father, then I want you to respond to them okay?"

"Okay," Sara whispered, her voice breaking. She rocked back and forth her head in her hands, a ritualistic calming motion. Karen sat down again and put her arms around her thin shoulders, stroking her back with a circular motion, holding her once more as she wept for the life she had lost.

She lifted her face briefly. "I need to know what happened to Charlie, Karen. It's the one thing I can't get out of my mind," she rocked back and forth again, consumed by tears.

"Shhhh, Sara, one step at a time. One step at a time, okay?"

*****

Karen had made some headway, letting Sara talk about her childhood, her career, her marriage and its fall-out. But she had said precious little about Charlie.

They talked about the drug they said she had taken – Rohypnol. Was it possible, she asked, that she could have killed Charlie?

Karen had chosen her words carefully. "Yes. It's why it became such a terrible drug in the wrong hands. A potential predator could drop a pill or two in a drink in a pub somewhere, once he had identified who he was after. The woman, or man, would return from, say, going to the toilets, and continue with the conversation, enjoying his, or her drink. Next thing, let's stick with a woman here, she'd be seen walking out of the pub with the predator, chatting away, smiling, with no fear, looking consensual.

"The next day she would wake up and have no recollection of being violated, being raped, which clearly she knew she had been. The Police were helpless, after all she had been seen leaving the pub quite happily with whoever had popped her the pills. As far as they were concerned, she had taken the guy home, had consensual sex with him and that was that."

She lit a cigarette. "In the wrong hands Rohypnol was a devastating drug. Eventually it was taken off the market.

"So, in answer to your question, yes, you could have been responsible for the death of Charlie, and you would have no recollection whatsoever of what had happened. Sorry, but it's the hard truth. It's a tough one though, because there was no intent there. This you'll have to learn to accept."

Sara sat up straight, flicking her hair behind her ear. Karen noticed the small white scar reaching from her hairline to her eyebrow, but said nothing.

Sara stared at the faultless blue sky, the clouds like distorted spines. Doves cooed in the shady trees, their leaves rustling as the breeze caressed them. Her hands stilled and she turned to Karen.

"Is it in the genes do you think? What is it that makes a person kill someone else? Did I have relatives who maybe had a bad streak in them. Did it skip a couple of generations and I inherited the gene?"

Karen shrugged. "I suppose it's possible, but unlikely."

Sara picked up a leaf and began to shred it. "After it happened, I could hardly move. I would wake up in that terrible place they locked me up in and for a brief second there my mind saw and heard nothing. Then the memories would come tumbling back crowding my mind with questions and no answers, until I thought my head would burst into flames.

"The warders sedated me three times a day, but I didn't swallow any of the pills. I needed to keep my mind clear, needed to go over every single second of what happened. But Charlie always remained a blank. The only time I was content was when I was asleep, because when you're asleep you're neither happy nor unhappy."

Karen raised her eyebrows. "That's an odd thing to say, but quite true when you think about it. But go on."

"I could speak, but I chose not to. I thought if I did it would make it all too real and I knew it would break me. There was no-one to hold my grief, lift it from me for a few precious seconds, so I could breathe properly. The grief was all mine. The emptiness was all mine."

Karen brushed a persistent fly away from her face and let Sara talk as she lifted the all concealing black veil of torment and utter grief.

"Then one day, a few weeks ago, I was sitting here and I noticed how blue the sky was, I watched a bird swoop down to feed from a flower. I noticed the shimmering iridescent colours of its wings, and for a brief few moment I didn't think about me, or Charlie. That was the moment I knew I was starting to heal, starting to accept the fact I couldn't change anything at all. I would have to go on. I would be alone, but I would go on."

She turned and looked at Karen. "That's when you came into my life."

Karen lit another cigarette, masking her own emotions at Sara's words.

But there was something Sara was holding back. Something she was not telling her about the day Charlie disappeared.

Chapter Twenty-Seven

For the following month's Karen worked hard to gain Sara's confidence, encouraging her to talk about her childhood, her years as a war correspondent and any fragile plans she had for when she was released.

Although Sara remained aloof from the other inmates, barely acknowledging them, Karen could see she was working hard to gain back the confidence she once had.

Karen talked to her about her life in London, her home there, the friends she once had, and her patients. Her favourite bars, restaurants and shops. She knew it would be a difficult transition for Sara, to go from eight years of isolation and discipline, to a world where she would finally be free to begin her new life.

She would, as she had promised, be there for Sara, guiding and helping her as she made her way back into the world she had been hidden from.

*****

Sara watched the airport buildings speeding past her window. She felt the powerful surge of the mighty engines as they pulled the aircraft up into the black velvet sky. She took a last long look at Cape Town, glittering below her, like a glorious box of fabulous jewels, Table Mountain a grand silhouette watching over the City.

The aircraft banked slowly and she whispered goodbye to Charlie and the country that had given her the greatest happiness and joy she had ever known, and the greatest tragedy a mother should ever have to bear.

Sara pressed her forehead against the cold window, the tears coming before she could stop them. She didn't try.

"Goodbye, Charlie." she whispered. "Sleep well in this beautiful country, your home. Goodbye, my darling. One day I'll come back to our house in the bush, back to the place where I lost you. I'm sorry I hurt you, I loved you very much. I'll always love you and although you'll be far away, in my mind you'll always be asleep in my arms, right here with me. Once there were two hearts beating inside of me. Now there's only one. But if I hold still, I feel the beat of your heart. It will stay with me for as long as I live. I'm not alone, Charlie, I still have the memory of you, I can still feel the weight of you in my arms."

Karen squeezed her arm, letting Sara whisper her last poignant farewell to her child.

In her handbag she had a letter from the Chief Medical Officer at The Haven, praising her enormous success with their patient Sara. The patient no-one had been able to reach. Doctor O'Hara's determination and understanding had produced results, excellent results, where they had failed. They strongly recommended Karen be allowed to continue to practice as a doctor on her return to England, and made it quite clear she had not been practicing medicine with her patient, nor had she been paid for her impressive results.

Karen knew the letter, when she produced it to the Disciplinary Board, would be in her favour. She had put Sara back on the road to, what she hoped, was a full recovery. Now she wanted to get back to practicing medicine again.

Over the last nine months Sara and Karen had become close friends, the friendship built on complete honesty and trust.

Karen flicked through the in-flight magazine and sipped a glass of wine. "Come on Sara, have a glass of wine or something. You're at the start of a new life now, it'll be a challenge but you've made grand progress. I'm not going to let you slide back, I'll be right by your side."

Sara, as promised to Karen, had finally read the letters from her father and felt even more guilty. His words were full of compassion and advice, and gradually they had been in touch every month.

But there was one subject he was adamant about. He wanted no mention of Charlie or what happened. It was the only way, he told her, he would be able to come to terms with it all.

Sir Miles had brought her up to date on Ben, how he had settled well into his new school and was thriving. They always spent school holidays together at the family home in Dorset.

Ben, he told her proudly, was a fine young man, despite his troubled time in Africa, although he refused to talk about her, and

Charlie's tragic death. It was a subject not to be mentioned until such time as Ben wanted to talk about it. He told her Ben had thrown himself into his new life and wanted to forget all about his previous one, so much so he was in the process of changing his name legally to Courtney.

Her father suggested when she returned to England, they should plan a week-end where she could finally meet up with her son again, at the family home in Dorset.

He told her how much he looked forward to meeting her doctor friend, who had given her all the help and support she needed to get back to a normal life, as normal a life as possible given the circumstances. But he didn't say if Ben was looking forward to seeing her again…

Sara visibly relaxed as soon as the flight reached its cruising height. She ordered a glass of wine from the stewardess and put her seat back. "We seem to have spent so much time taking about me Karen, and I know quite a bit about you but nothing about your personal life? Have you ever been married?"

Karen looked up from the in-flight magazine she was flicking through. "No, fell in and out of love numerous times, but nothing came of it. Running a busy practice in London doesn't leave much time for romance. There was someone…but he was married, a fellow doctor. I knew there was no future in the relationship.

"My parents and my sister live in Dublin, on high days and holidays I go over to see them. I had a lot of friends in London, but when I got into drugs they fell by the wayside," she shrugged, "and I don't blame them."

She grinned at Sara. "Now I have my hands full with you, and I consider you a good friend who trusted me. I'll be busy trying to get a new practice going again. I'm sure a few of my old patients will come back. But, of course, I need to get my licence back before I can do anything.

"I'm going to try and sleep now. I have to say I'm not looking forward to the weather in the UK. Cape Town will be a hard act to follow!"

Sara was already asleep. Karen covered her with a blanket and removed the glass from her hand. Her first drink in eight years, no wonder it had knocked her out! She put her seat back and fell into an uneasy sleep.

Chapter Twenty-Eight
The Teacher

Kia had been with Diana for nearly two years. Although she missed her family her hunger to learn overcame her longing for her family and the life she had once known. Jabu came from the village for her once a month, and returned her three days later. Bringing her school books with her Kia spent those three days teaching her brother what she had learned.

In the morning, at Diana's house, she would help with the housework and accompany Diana to the market. Three afternoons a week the other four pupils would arrive. Although they were more advanced in their lessons than she was, Kia soon caught up, surprising Diana with her quick grasp of the English language and the written word.

After the other pupils had left Kia would help Diana prepare the evening meal. Both Diana and Norman insisted she ate her meals with them. In this way Kia learned her table manners, learned about food, how it was cooked and served, and Norman taught her about wines and where they came from, showing her on the large map in his study. Diana pulled her into conversations as they ate, gently correcting her sometimes halting English as she searched for the right words.

Diana taught her about money, making sure she had a small allowance for helping around the house, so that when they went to town the child could select and buy her own simple clothes and anything else, she needed.

Kia, once she had finished helping Diana clear the table and wash up, went to her own bedroom, where she would prop herself up on her mother's quilt and do the homework Diana had prepared for her.

Diana hung the dishcloth over the sink and went to join her husband out on the patio. Sipping her coffee, she stared out into the night, listening to the croak of the frogs around the pond at the bottom of the garden.

Norman shook his paper, then folded it and placed it on the table between them. "So, my dear, what's up? Something is. When you go quiet it makes me nervous!"

Diana twisted in her chair, carefully placing her coffee cup on the table. "Well, yes, there is something on my mind Norman. It's Kia. We've both become quite fond of her?"

Norman nodded as he prepared his pipe.

Diana continued enthusiastically. "Kia is one of the brightest pupils I've ever taught! Her English is near perfect now, she soaks up everything I teach her. I think she has real potential to be something. That's what I wanted to talk to you about."

Norman stood up and smiled. "I think I might need a drink then. May I get you one?"

Diana shook her head, drumming her fingers on the side of her chair impatiently, anxious to continue the conversation. Norman poured himself a gin and tonic and sat back down.

"Okay, fire away, my dear. The gin will steady my nerves for whatever is coming next."

"I don't want Kia to grow up thinking she will only be able to work in a shop, or someone else's house. She's worth much more, I promise you."

She pulled her cardigan around her against the sudden cool breeze. "There's a private girls school in Port Elizabeth. I've made some enquiries, only tentative ones Norman, I promise," she said hastily. "Kia could either be a boarder there, or a day girl. They have a school bus which goes from here.

"On my recommendations the Head Mistress is prepared to enrol her, with her parent's permission of course, for next term. She'll need to do some tests to see if she's up to the school's standards of education – but I have absolutely no worries there. She's more than qualified to meet their exacting requirements.

"It's an excellent school with a lovely mix of children from all over South Africa and beyond its borders.

"In order for these young adults to learn how to conduct themselves with confidence it's essential they learn to mingle with confidence at social and business functions, learn the importance of good grooming and style, that sort of thing," she finished lamely.

Norman raised his eyebrows, as he puffed at his pipe. "Bit ambitious for a young girl from an African village isn't it? I mean I know you went to a finishing school in Europe, but surely it's not necessary here?"

"Oh, but it is Norman," Diana said fiercely, "even more so here. In today's world, if you want to succeed, these skills are paramount. First impressions are important.

"I want to give Kia every advantage I can. I want her to have an international education and this school can give it to her. Yes, I could teach her a lot of these things but she needs to be in an environment where she can interact and use the skills the school will teach her."

Norman nodded and took a large mouthful of his drink.

"You know, Norman, Kia is like a daughter to me. I love her as if she were my own. I know I'll never be her real mother, Mirium is. But this is such a wonderful opportunity to round her off, as they say, she'll learn more than I can ever teach her. She needs the stimulation of other pupils, to mix with children from all walks of life. It's what I want to do for her. The only thing is," she crossed her legs nervously, "it's terribly expensive, especially if she becomes a boarder."

Norman seemed to be mulling over his wife's dreams for Kia. He stood up and leaned against the patio balustrade, puffing at his pipe. Then sat back down again.

"You've worked hard with her and achieved what I thought would be impossible. I see no reason why she shouldn't get "rounded off" as you put it. Yes, why not. Let's look at the boarding fees and day girl fees. Personally, I think boarding will be too much of a challenge for her. Maybe the first term as a day girl and take it from there?"

He held up his hand. "However, you will need to get her parents' permission, but more so, you need to make sure Kia is happy with the idea. She's led a sheltered life so far. Plunging her into a private school environment, far away from her village, her family and our home could be traumatic for her?"

Diana jumped up and threw her arms around her husband's neck. "Thank you, Norman, thank you! She's ready for it, I promise you!"

She ran back into the house, calling over her shoulder. "I'll go and talk to her now. See what she thinks!"

Norman smiled to himself and picked up his newspaper. He loved the child himself, loved to hear the soft clicking of the beads plaited through her hair as she moved around the house, her chatter in the

106

kitchen as she helped Diana prepare dinner. Diana was right, Kia was bright, and now had an accent nearly as English as his own.

Diana knocked softly on the bedroom door. "Kia? I need to speak to you, may I come in?"

There was no response. Diana knocked again, then quietly opened the door, thinking maybe Kia had fallen asleep over her homework.

Diana heard the soft fall of water from the shower. She smiled. Her good news could wait a moment or two, she would come back.

A few moments later Diana was back. Once more she knocked and let herself into Kia's bedroom.

Kia stepped from the shower, reaching for a towel, not seeing Diana standing there with her hand to her throat, a stricken look on her face.

Quietly Diana backed out of the bedroom and fled to her own.

She had only thought about it fleetingly, thinking it was all in her imagination.

But now she knew.

Kia would not be able to attend the boarding school, she would have to be a day girl, boarding was out of the question.

Chapter Twenty-Nine

A t the end of the month Jabu arrived, as usual, to collect Kia and take her back to his village to see her family. Diana was waiting for him.

"Jabu, I should like to come back to your village with you and Kia. There's something I would like to discuss with your parents," she laughed. "It's alright, don't look so worried. It's a good thing I want to talk to them about! We can all go in my car. Come along now."

Diana drove along the main highway until Jabu indicated she should turn to the left onto a dirt road. Although the rains had been reasonable the year before, the drought had once again taken hold, the road was rutted and baked dry, pot holes hard to avoid. They arrived at the village and Diana parked gratefully under the shade of a small tree. Brushing the dust off her dress, she picked up her bag and followed Jabu and Kia.

Her heart sank when she saw how dilapidated the village was, with only a few dwellings occupied. Like many other villages in the Eastern Cape the people had migrated to the nearest town, looking for money and food to feed their families. A few chickens pecked disconcertingly at the dusty ground, next to one humble round house two light brown tethered goats bleated plaintively.

*****

Eza and Mirium were sitting outside their home, waiting with anticipation to see their daughter again. Eza stood up when he saw the teacher woman, an anxious look on his face. Was Kia in trouble, had this woman brought her back because of this?

Kia hugged her parents and spoke to them in her own tongue. Then she rushed inside and brought out an old cane chair, with a sagging seat, for Diana to sit on, brushing the dust off with her sleeve.

108

Once they had exchanged pleasantries Diana nodded towards Kia.

For the next hour Kia told her parents about Diana's plans for her to attend one of the best private girls' schools in the country. Mirium and Eza's face showed no emotion, only anxiety, as they stared at their daughter in her European clothes.

When Kia had finished talking, she took her mother's hand. "I want to do this Mama. I love learning all the things Mrs Templeton has taught me, but I want to know more. I would like to go to a proper school?"

Eza said nothing as he filled his home-made pipe and waited for it to smoulder. Once satisfied, he leaned back on his three-legged stool and puffed quietly before he spoke.

"This school? It is costing much money I am thinking? Where is this money to be coming from? It is not a good thing if there are boys there. This we would not be happy with."

Diana fumbled in her bag and pulled out the school brochure, blowing off the thin film of dust it had acquired during the drive.

Eza looked at the photographs of smiling girls, the grand school building sitting amidst lush gardens, the tennis courts, the stables and the pictures of the girl's dormitories. Mirium peered over his shoulder.

"*Eish,* this is a fine place for a child to learn in Eza," she pointed at the photograph of the building and the green lawns. "There is much water there for the grass to grow. A fine place for goats and sheep to eat."

Mirium looked at her daughter's animated face. "Is this what you are wanting my little one? It will be much different from the village you know well."

"Yes Mama, this is what I want. What good will this village be for me now? I have taught Jabu to read and write but he needs more than looking after four goats here. I want more, Mama, much more. Mrs Templeton will be paying for me to go to this fine school. Papa?"

Eza looked down at his splayed toes before speaking to Diana. "The Gods have been good to us, they sent you to find Kia and give to her this fine learning." Kia translated for Diana.

"For Kia to be in this big house with other girls would also be a good thing, for we have no money to do this. I see Kia is grown up now and knows the way of the Europeans. She will never return to the village, this I know.

"But my heart is heavy for my son Jabu, who has learned this writing from Kia, but he needs more learning now. Perhaps the Gods will be good again and take my son for this learning with you?"

When Kia finished translating, Diana nodded her head with enthusiasm.

"Yes, of course! My husband and I have discussed this. We would like Jabu to come and live with us, just like Kia did. He will have the same opportunities to learn as his sister.

"In return for his lessons he'll be able to help me with my garden. I will bring them back to the village to see you during the holidays?"

Eza nodded. He turned to his wife.

"This is a good thing for the children Mirium, more than we can give them. We must let them go and find their own footsteps to the future."

Mirium nodded in agreement, her eyes filling with tears. "It will be hard, my husband, for then we will have no children left. But they are growing fast now and there is nothing for them here. If they are looked after and have much learning, it is a good thing."

Mirium stood up, carefully laying down the quilt she was working on. "Come, my son, we must collect your things for this new life you will be having."

Kia hugged her father. The joy in her face hard to ignore. She sat down at his feet and rested her head against his bony legs.

Diana cleared her throat. "Eza, there are some things I will need for the school; papers and documents will be required. I will need Kia and Jabu's identity book and their birth certificates? Also, their immunisation cards?"

Eza looked anxious. "*Eish,* I am not having these papers. These papers are only needed for people living in the big towns. We have no such papers as this. When this village was full of our people, we had no need for such things as we are all knowing who each of us is."

Diana frowned; this was going to be a problem. In her experience all births had to be registered with the authorities but perhaps being far away from anywhere, the village people saw no need for documentation.

"I must have some documentation Eza, otherwise the school will not accept Kia or Jabu?"

Kia looked up at her father. "Papa, you must come to town again! We will come with you to get the papers. There is a place I have heard of; there they will issue the birth certificates. Once we have these, we

110

can get our identity books. This is necessary, everyone in the country must carry their identity books, it is the law."

*****

Eza looked worried, as well he might. But he would trust his daughter to help him with these papers. He hoped the office for birth certificates would not ask for his or Mirium's, because neither of them had one.

Perhaps if he told them Jabu was fourteen rainy seasons and Kia was twelve rainy seasons this would be enough for these papers which everyone is needing now Mr Mandela was the big Chief of the country.

But what of the years when there was no rainy season? Would he count those as none years of age? He had no idea of his own age, or Mirium's, and more worrying, he did not know if he had the second name they would be requiring.

Eish, he thought to himself. It was easier to look after goats and sheep than children. But perhaps one small story which would not be the true one, would not hurt anyone and then they would have these things called documents.

*****

At the end of the month Eza and Mirium travelled back to the town with their children after their week-end together.

Now they were gathered around the dining room table in Diana's house, surrounded by forms she had collected from the Home Affairs office in town.

"Now, Kia, Jabu, you can fill out your own forms. I will help Eza and Mirium with theirs okay?"

Kia and Jabu picked up their pens and carefully looked at all the questions which had to be answered.

Kia frowned. Falling at the first hurdle. "Papa what is the family name? Also, how old am I?"

Diana looked up startled. "You don't know how old you are? What about you Jabu?" He shook his head.

Eza cleared his throat. "In the village we only know age by the seasons. This family name you are needing? It is Klassens."

He looked down to hide the guilt in his eyes, taking the name of his friend Sipo was surely not a crime? "I am thinking Jabu is maybe fourteen seasons, for he is tall. Little Kia was born after, she is maybe twelve rainy seasons."

Kia and Jabu stared at each other, looking as confused as Diana.

Diana sighed with frustration. "Alright let's start there then. Your family name is Klassens. Kia is twelve and Jabu is fourteen, well, it's a start. I don't suppose for one second you know the day and month of the births?"

Mirium and Eza shook their heads miserably.

Diana tapped her pen on the table. "Look, perhaps this part is not important if neither child was registered at birth. So, let's make Jabu's birthday the same as mine 5th January. Kia you shall have Norman's birthday 9th June. Let's fill those bits out and worry about the rest when we hand them in."

Relieved they now had proper birthdays and a surname, Kia and Jabu set to work, whilst Diana tried her best with Mirium and Eza. Their forms, when completed, looked somewhat blank, except for their names.

*****

They arrived at the office of Home Affairs early the next morning, and joined the long queue. Two hours later they were standing in front of the officer in charge of issuing birth, death and marriage certificates. He didn't show any emotion as he carefully checked all four sets of forms. A Griqua himself he knew the ways of his people. He knew births, marriages and deaths were rarely recorded by these nomadic people in their faraway villages. He also knew most of the information on the forms was a little shy of the truth, but they were his people and he would help them. Without the correct identification papers these young children would have no chance in the new South Africa.

An hour later, after taking their fingerprints he handed them the forms stamped by his office. "You must take these forms to the Police Station in town and they will sign them for you, declaring the information true."

He smiled at their anxious faces. "All will be well."

Once outside Kia hugged her parents. "I love my name Kia Klassens! All *will* be well Papa. Soon we will all have what the authorities require. Come let's go to the Police Station and get this Affidavit signed, then we can go home. Mrs Templeton wants you to stay in the little cottage in her garden. You must be tired after the journey and all the questions you had to answer.

"Only Jabu and I need to return to the office for the temporary certificate that nice man promised us. He will let us know when we can collect our birth certificates and identity books."

Grinning happily Jabu and Kia led their bewildered parents to the Police Station.

Chapter Thirty
The Mother

Sara wiped the window of the taxi with the sleeve of her coat and watched people hurrying past the brightly lit shops like shoals of fish. The only sound was the thud of the windscreen wipers which she found oddly soothing. Then the traffic started moving, the driver increased the speed of the wipers and put his side lights on against the gathering gloom of the closing day.

Africa seemed a million miles away. She had been back in London for two weeks, staying with Karen at her flat in Notting Hill, it was taking some time to get used to life generally, especially back in the city where she had worked as a journalist.

She had phoned her father the day after she and Karen had arrived back. He'd sounded cautiously pleased to hear from her, but also slightly aloof. Informing her he would have to make arrangements with Ben to see when it would be convenient for him to come to the house in Dorset and be re-united with his mother.

"Don't expect too much Sara," he'd said. "As you know the subject of Charlie and what happened afterwards has never been discussed. I thought it might help Ben to talk about it with me. But he absolutely refuses to.

"I know this is going to be hard for you, but he doesn't talk about you either. It's like he's blocked out his life in Africa. As if he was never there. I thought about seeking medical help, but he's doing well at university mixing with his fellow students, mentally he seems absolutely fine. Rather than dredge the whole thing up, I've chosen to let sleeping dogs lie.

"I've no idea how he is going to react when he sees you again. I'm sorry I can't be more positive."

"Well, Daddy," she had replied, "I hardly expect a hero's welcome. I know it's going to be difficult. But I'm looking forward to seeing you both as soon as you can arrange things."

She'd sat with the phone in her lap absolutely crushed. She'd hoped Ben might be looking forward to seeing her. But it was a foolish hope.

The taxi pulled up outside Karen's flat, Sara collected her shopping bags, paid the taxi and let herself in.

"Hey, Sara, how did the shopping trip go? What was it like to be amongst the frenzy of London shoppers?"

Sara dropped her bags on a chair, shrugged off her coat and eased her feet out of her shoes, before sinking onto the sofa, rubbing her feet together.

"Too ghastly for words! What a contrast to the silence I became so used to. I didn't get much. A few clothes for the trip to the country, a pair of boots, two pairs of shoes. It all felt strange. No-one recognised me from my glittering old world of television, thank goodness."

Karen smiled at her friend. "I remember you on television with all that blonde hair, absolutely gorgeous, half the nation fell in love with you. Even when you were getting shot at in one of those hell holes you used to cover, you still managed to look fabulous with a tin helmet rammed on your head! How did you do that, by the way, when you took it off on camera, your hair still looked great? If it had been me, my hair would have been stuck to my head, I'd look like a seal emerging from the depths of the sea!"

Sara laughed. "Much easier now, not having to bother with hairdressers or make-up artists. I might get something done with my hair though, don't want to frighten my father or my son, or the horses, if they still have any. We always had horses. I think I need a glass of wine. May I get you one?"

"Sure, why not. I've been sitting here twiddling my thumbs all day waiting for the phone to ring with some good news about being allowed to practice again. But bugger all so far."

"Nothing from my father then?"

Karen took the proffered glass of wine. "No, I expect he's trying to sort something out with Ben. After all Ben has a full life from what you told me, might even have a girlfriend, for all we know, after all he's nearly twenty, it's when they normally become extremely interested in girls!"

They both jumped as the phone rang. Karen reached over for it. "Dr O'Hara speaking." She grinned at Sara, it sounded good to her ears, getting her identity back again.

"Sure, Sir Miles, she's right here." Karen listened for a few moments. "I did what any other doctor would have done. But thank you, I look forward to meeting you as well. Here's Sara, here's your daughter."

"Hello Daddy." Sara nodded her head as she listened. "Right. I'll travel down on Friday. I'll see you then. I'll take a taxi from the station."

Karen twirled the glass in her hand watching Sara's hand shaking slightly as she took a sip from her own glass.

"Would you like me to come with you Sara?"

Sara shook her hand. "Thanks, but this is something I really have to do on my own. If the whole thing is a disaster at least no-one will be there to witness it. I'm nervous though."

Sara reached for one of the shiny shopping bags. "I bought Ben a present. It sounds ridiculous, but I couldn't remember what colours he liked, or if he liked patterns. I mean, I don't even know how tall he is! Anyway, I went for navy blue, what do you think?"

"Looks expensive, but nice, I'm sure he'll love it. Pick your time to give it to him though. Be cautious Sara, don't overwhelm him. Don't expect too much?"

Chapter Thirty-One
The Ambassador

The taxi made its way up the sweeping driveway, pulling up in front of the impressive front door. Sara collected her weekend bag, handbag and heavy coat, paid off the taxi and stood still, staring up at the house she had spent so much time in, between their overseas postings. Unlike her own life, nothing had changed here. The greyness of a November afternoon made the place look cold and forbidding.

She hesitated. Should she just walk in or perhaps knock? Where was her place now in the order of things? Her father and her son were waiting for her, she had every right to open the door and walk right in. Her father must have heard the taxi arrive? The barking of a dog?

Sara went in, leaving her bag, her coat, and Ben's present in its own glossy bag on a chair in the sitting room; she looked around. Same comfortable though faded chairs, facing the large fireplace, same pictures on the walls, the cluster of silver framed photographs on a side table, as they had always been.

The house felt cold and unwelcoming as she made her way down the long corridor to the kitchen where her father had always had his favourite chair in front of the fireplace built into the wall. The fire was lit, but the chair was empty.

Maggie came bounding into the room, pushing herself at her legs, her tail wagging furiously. "Well hello! You must be Maggie! I've heard all about you!" She bent down and ruffled her head.

"Where is everyone Maggie? They can't be out walking, not without you?"

Maggie dashed back to the kitchen door, looking over her shoulder. Sara followed her. "Daddy, it's me, I'm home. Where are you?"

Then she heard the familiar voice she had longed for. "In my study Sara."

Sara frowned. He might at least have come out to welcome her. Sitting in his study waiting for her was not a good sign.

She hesitated briefly then pushed the study door open. Her father stood up; she was surprised at how he had aged since she last saw him. She waited for him to come around the desk and hug her.

He didn't.

"Sit down Sara. I'd like a few words with you before you see Ben. He's upstairs in his bedroom. He would have heard the taxi arrive, heard Maggie barking, as I did. He knows you're here."

With a sense of foreboding she did as she was told. "I didn't expect balloons and banners, Daddy, but it would have been nice if you had at least hugged me." Her voice hardened. "But then it was never quite your style was it. What on earth was I expecting?"

Sir Miles cleared his throat and sat down. He polished his glasses carefully as he looked at her. "I know we have had our differences in the past, Sara, and nothing will change that. I've thought long and hard about this meeting today. Searching my soul to find some way of forgiving you. But I'm afraid I find it impossible. The damage you have caused to the family name is unforgivable. What you *did* was unforgivable."

Sara blinked back her tears. "Then why did you try to help me Daddy? Sir Christopher told me you tried everything. You wrote to me saying you were thinking of me. You were sorry about everything that happened. What made you change your mind?"

"Seeing you standing in front of me. Yes, I tried to support you with my letters. It was my duty as your father. Seeing you now brings the whole ghastly mess back. Makes it all too real. Makes what you did real. Standing there I don't see my daughter anymore. Only a stranger, fresh out of prison, who committed an unspeakable act against her own child. A child I knew nothing about."

Shocked by the bitterness, the harshness and anger, in her father's voice, Sara didn't see the tall figure standing in the doorway.

"Well, hello Mother."

Sara turned and stared at her son, a smile spreading across her face. "Oh Ben, look at you! So tall!"

She stood up and took a step towards him, then stopped abruptly, her arms falling to her sides. Taking a step back she sank into her chair.

She had seen hatred in the eyes of the enemy in the course of her career, but she had never seen the cold hard look of pure hatred her son was giving her now.

118

Ben strolled over to the window and leaned against the bookcase, not taking his eyes off her. "So, my mother has returned. My mother who went to prison. My mother the killer of her own child."

"Now Ben," murmured her father, "that's quite enough."

He scowled. "Oh no, Grandfather, it's not enough. This woman ruined my life, ruined the family name. Made me famous on television screens across the globe as the son of a killer! I even had to resort to changing my name, for God's sake."

Suddenly Ben lunged forward, putting his hands on either side of her chair. Sara flinched and drew back.

"Get out! Get out of this house," he hissed. "Get out of my life, like you did before."

"Ben!" her father shouted. "I said enough!"

Ben backed off and glanced out of the window. "Ah, here comes the taxi I ordered for you. Now get out!"

Sara heard the sound of Ben's boots running back up the stairs. She turned and stared at her father, her face the colour of ash, shock leaching the brightness from her too hopeful eyes.

"One more thing Sara. I've changed my Will. I thought I should tell you. Ben will now get half of your inheritance, half of this house and the contents, plus the right to live here should he choose. The house in Mayfair will be yours, you may do whatever you wish with it. Your mother left it to me, as you know, but it is now in your name. Despite this upsetting reunion, I would suggest you leave the Mayfair house to Ben and, of course, your half of this one. Too much water under the bridge Sara, but he is still your son."

Sara stood up slowly. "Is this it then Daddy? You don't want to see me again do you?"

Sir Miles stood up and came to his daughter. He patted her awkwardly on the shoulder. "I'm sorry Sara. But some things can't be put right. Ben and I are close. He's all I have now. I think it's best don't you? Let me help you with your bag. The taxi's waiting."

Picking up his cane he steered his daughter back to the front door, he caught her arm as she stumbled down the steps. The driver took her overnight bag and opened the back door for her.

Sara stopped and looked at her father, then threw her arms around him.

"Don't let it end like this daddy, please give me a chance to put things right?"

Sir Miles eased her arms from his neck. "Come on, my girl, or you'll miss the next train. Let's give things a little more time, eh?"

"Please daddy, don't push me away like this..." her voice caught in her throat as she climbed in the back of the car.

Sir Miles watched as the taxi pulled away from the house. Closing the front door, he went back to his study, brushing the sleeve of his jacket across his eyes. Seeing Sara's tearstained face watching him from the back window as the car took her away from him and her family home.

Sara's gift to Ben stood unwanted in its glossy bag next to the chair.

Upstairs Ben also watched the taxi make its way down the drive. His eyes as cold and dead as the child his mother had killed.

Chapter Thirty-Two
The Doctor

The hammering on the front door, the next morning, woke both Maggie and Sir Miles, who was asleep in his chair, with a start. Maggie staggered to her feet barking and raced to where the noise was emanating from. Sir Miles fumbled for his cane and followed her out of the kitchen.

Ben came running down the stairs to see what all the noise was about. If it was his mother wanting to cause more trouble, he would call the police.

He threw the door open and stopped short. "Who the hell are you, and what's all the noise about? Has something happened?"

The tall woman with the tousled blonde hair stared at him. Her large brown eyes glittering with fury. "Has something happened? Yes, something damn well has happened, and you and your grandfather are fully responsible for it."

Sir Miles opened the door a little wider. "Perhaps you should come in out of the rain. I'm presuming you're Doctor O'Hara. Am I correct?"

"Yes. Sara's doctor. Her closest friend."

Sir Miles led her into the kitchen and helped her off with her coat. "Perhaps I can get you a coffee, or something Doctor O'Hara?"

"No, thank you, I haven't come here to exchange pleasantries, or be social."

Karen sat down her body rigid with unadulterated fury. "I find it inconceivable anyone, least of all her family, could treat Sara the way you two did yesterday!"

Ben stared at her coldly. She looked as though she were about to implode with rage. "I don't think our family business has anything to do with you, Doctor O'Hara."

"Is that so Ben? Well, I disagree. It has everything to do with me. Let me tell you something. What you did yesterday nearly destroyed all my work with your mother. I worked bloody hard putting her back together again, giving her back her confidence, her self-respect, helping her forgive herself, to understand what happened."

"She is not my mother." Ben interrupted.

"Oh yes, she damn well is, whatever you say! I understand what you went through Sir Miles, and you Ben, but you kicked her out like an unwanted dog yesterday. It was unforgiveable!"

Karen turned to Sir Miles. "I think I know Sara better than both of you put together."

She stood up and paced around the kitchen. "Did you know Ben that Sara was on suicide watch for three months after Charlie died? She was catatonic with grief, for years afterwards. I don't know how much you remember of that day Ben, but she has no recollection of what happened, and, believe me, that is even harder to live with. How can you forgive yourself for something you have no recollection of doing?

"Your mother was a top war correspondent. Ruthless in uncovering the truth in some of the most God forsaken places on the planet. She believed in the truth whatever it might be."

Ben stared out of the window saying nothing. Sir Miles sat in his chair with his eyes shut, a shooting pain in his leg. Maggie had her head between her paws, her eyebrows twitching, nervously watching the woman who was doing a lot of shouting.

"Sara saw things in those war zones no human being should ever see, children with their limbs blown off, pregnant women bayoneted, beheadings and hangings in the local village. But she didn't flinch, sending back her reports to the television station, sometimes under fire herself.

"Amidst all the death, decay and chaos, Sara fell in love with a fellow journalist. Did you know that? No, of course you didn't! A man with the same guts and courage for uncovering the truth and making the world sit up and do something about it."

Sir Miles opened his eyes, looking surprised at this side of his daughter he knew nothing about.

"The man she fell in love with was called Greg. They were filming the remains of what was once a small town in Bosnia when they came under fire themselves. The helicopter was shot down. Greg was killed instantly, Sara badly injured. She crawled away from the wreckage but kept on filming until she passed out. Now that's what I call guts and courage. What do you call it Sir Miles?"

Sir Miles hand shook as he gripped his cane and rubbed his leg. "I didn't approve of Sara's choice of a career; she was always reckless. I knew she covered stories in some difficult countries, although she never talked about her job to me. She most certainly didn't mention any accident..."

Karen stood in front of him. "Do you know why Sir Miles?" she said softly. "Do you know why she never talked to you about it? I'll tell you why! Because you were never interested in her as a person, as your daughter. You were too busy with that stiff upper lip you British so admire. Too busy with being the perfect diplomat, sorting out your country's little problems, whilst your daughter was out there saving dozens of lives and risking her own. Probably whilst you were swanning around some Embassy party in Cape Town, with your gin and tonic, making polite small talk about nothing of importance, or relevance."

Ben stood up. "I think you've said enough Doctor O'Hara. I think you should leave now; you're upsetting my grandfather?"

"Well, I'm sorry about that, to be sure, but I haven't finished. I'll go when I'm ready."

Karen fumbled for a cigarette and lit it, ignoring the protestations. "After losing Greg, and nearly her own life, Sara decided to throw in the towel. To leave the world of war and death. She didn't have the stomach for it anymore.

"That, Sir Miles, was when she decided she wanted to be with her family in Cape Town, wanted a more normal life. But still you were never there for her, not as a real father should have been. Sara's mother liked to party, from what I can gather. If she wasn't out shopping for her next party dress, she was asleep trying to recover from yet another hangover. She wasn't there for Sara either." Karen flicked her cigarette into the fire grate.

"Sara wasn't in love with her husband, Simon. She was in love with the idea of being in love again. Hoping to fill the gaping hole Greg had left in her life. As we all know, the marriage to Simon ended in disaster, so much so she had to hide out in the bush in the Eastern Cape, far away from the prying eyes of the media, the world she had once loved, respected, and lived in. Her world.

"You, Ben were everything to her. Someone who was truly hers, someone she loved like only a mother can."

Karen shrugged on her coat. "Sara is the bravest, most courageous and compassionate woman I've ever met. I wouldn't have been able to do any of the things she did in those wars and I'm a medical doctor.

"Sara came here yesterday to see you both, especially you Ben. She was desperate to see you. She knew it would be difficult, she didn't expect to be greeted like the prodigal daughter, but she had paid the price for Charlie's death and thought you would forgive her. Clearly this was not what happened. You threw her out without even listening to her side of things."

She snatched up her bag from the table. "You should be ashamed of yourselves! Sure, if you don't want to see her again, then so be it. But there could have been a kinder, more compassionate way of handling the situation.

"I'll see myself out."

Then she turned around, a smile hovering on her lips. "I hope Sara leaves the half of this house and the one in Mayfair to Battersea dog's home. Where would that leave you Ben? Half a house is not better than one."

There was silence in the kitchen after she left. The only sound, the ticking of the kitchen clock. Maggie closed her eyes with relief.

Chapter Thirty-Three
The Mother

After the disastrous reunion with her son and father she had moved into the flat in Mayfair, bitterly accepting she had lost her entire family.

Over the ensuing months Karen's practice was slowly picking up. When she asked Sara to work with her there, Sara didn't hesitate. Karen was the only constant in her life now and they were as close as sisters.

"I know you don't need the money Sara, but it will give you something to do, you'll meet people. It will help with the healing process."

Sara dropped the Courtney from her name and became Sara Saunders. Moving seamlessly into the melting pot of humanity which was London, she painstakingly began to rebuild her life. After a day at the surgery, she would return to her flat.

Sara reached for one of the several remotes on the table next to her chair. The curtains closed silently blocking out the relentless sweeping rain sounding like handfuls of sand being thrown against the windows, the naked branches of the swaying trees scratching on the glass. A siren screamed past the windows, a chorus of barking dogs followed, and then there was silence.

Soft lights now lit up the sumptuous flat. Expensively framed pictures of African wildlife dotted the walls, at odds with the style of the rest of the room. She looked around the familiar room with its heavy upholstered cream cushioned armchairs, and tasselled skirts; the low square table, polished to a high sheen, crowded with books and magazines, a bowl of white tulips at its centre. At the tall windows, long cream velvet curtains brushed the surface of the floor, a tall carved wooden giraffe stood sentinel next to the front door.

The soft lights revealed her in the mirror opposite. Every time she looked at herself, she felt a wave of depression and anger. Prison had not been kind to her, now in her early fifties she looked ten years older.

The obscene cruelty of age, she thought, as she saw her beauty descending. The distortion of smooth velvet skin into the beginning of a spider's web of fine lines, criss-crossing a face she had always presumed would stay the same – a foolish thought which came with thinking she would never get old – this happened to other people. As she had thought being locked up only happened to other people.

She pushed up the sides of her face, seeing, briefly, how she used to look, lowering her hands she watched the lines fall into place, gathering around her mouth, jaw and neck. There was no going back, there was no place to return to. The imperfections impossible to camouflage with the magic of a soft brush and a palette of make-up. Clothes, shoes and jewellery enhancing nothing, only highlighting the inevitable. Sara didn't have the energy, or the interest, to try and improve how she looked.

Oh, what she wouldn't give to turn back the enemy called time. She had had a rich and varied life, but growing older when one was alone was not for the fainthearted. Somehow, she hadn't seen it coming. The darkness, the silence of an empty flat. It wasn't what she had expected; in her head she had painted a different scenario.

The soft chime of the front door startled her. It wouldn't be Karen; she knew she had a date this evening. Sara peered through the circle of glass and stepped back, pulling her hair back and hastily fashioned it into a bun at the nape of her neck.

She slid back the safely chain and opened the door.

Ben was standing there.

"Hello Mother. Sorry I didn't call in advance but I don't have your number. May I come in?"

Flustered she opened the door wider. "Yes, of course."

Ben shrugged off his coat and threw it carelessly over a chair before sitting down.

Sara stood, smoothing down her skirt nervously. "You look well Ben. I'm surprised to see you though, after our last meeting. It's been quite some time."

Ben took the chair opposite her. He leaned forward his elbows on his knees. "Yes, a year, in fact. But I've had a lot of time to think, Mother. Perhaps Grandfather and I were a little hard on you, but seeing you was a shock. I'd forgotten what you looked like.

126

"Grandfather, I'm afraid, still wants to live in his quiet world in the country. He's stubborn as you know and he won't change his mind about seeing you. I'm sorry. It's his way of dealing with things."

Sara stared at her son, saying nothing, not sure what was coming next, but deep inside a flicker of hope teetered. Carefully she lowered herself into the seat opposite him, fleetingly seeing, and remembering, the small boy now an adult.

His eyes traversed the flat before returning to hers. "I'd like to get to know you again. See if we can put the past behind us, but there is one proviso. I don't want to talk about Africa. Can we be clear on this Mother?"

Sara looked at him warily. "Alright, if that's what you want. Tell me, how are you getting on at university, have you thought about what you'll do afterwards?" Stay on safe ground she told herself.

"Grandfather has a lot of contacts in the city, as you know," he smiled at her, and her heart skipped a beat. "I've always had a flair for figures. Top of the class every time!"

Sara smiled. "Yes, I remember, go on."

"I want to become a trader; I think I'll be good at it. Grandfather has found me a position with one of his old pals. So, when I leave, I'm going to come up to London and start my internship with them. Grandfather will support me financially until they put me on the payroll."

Sara bit her tongue. Too early to tell him he could live with her until he started earning money and found a place of his own. "That sounds wonderful Ben."

Ben stood up. "Well, must go. I'm meeting a friend for dinner, then tomorrow I go for the interview."

Sara stood up. "Maybe we could have dinner tomorrow night, if you're still in town, and you can tell me all about it?" she said hopefully.

"Sorry, Mother. It won't be possible; I must get back. But next time I'm in London we'll have dinner."

Sara nodded her head, speculating how many months it might be from now. Wondering if he would contact her again.

"Let me give you my number Ben." She reached for her bag and pulled out a card. "Please keep in touch, won't you?"

Ben took the card and slipped it inside his jacket pocket. He bent his head and briefly kissed her cheek. "Goodbye Mother."

Then he was gone.

Sara poured herself a glass of wine, her mind swirling with questions she had no answers to.

Having Ben back in her life was totally unexpected, but she wondered what had changed his mind. Perhaps Karen's whiplashing had given him something to think about? Maybe her father had persuaded Ben to make contact. Well, whatever it was, it felt positive.

She ignored the little voice niggling in her brain, the little voice saying *"but why now, after all this time, after the terrible scene at your father's house, what made him change his mind?"*

It didn't matter. Ben was back. Tomorrow she would make an appointment with a hairdresser, buy some skin care products, some new clothes. Go to a make-up specialist and return to the woman she was before.

Ben had grown even taller, his thick dark hair flopped over his dark eyes; he was a good-looking man, but, she frowned, was she expecting too much? His dark eyes had shown no emotion at all, they were as hard and as cold as the last time he had shouted at her to get out of the house.

Chapter Thirty-Four

O ver the next few years Sara saw her son on his brief trips to London. Normally with a new girlfriend in tow, although she never met any of them. Ben would eat at her apartment.

"Why don't you ever bring your girlfriend around for lunch, Ben. I'd love to meet the people in your life?"

"You know the answer to that, Mother," he had snapped at her. "I don't want any awkward questions asked."

"Well, you do have a mother, Ben, you can't keep me hidden like a specimen in a jar forever you know."

"I'll decide when and where I want to introduce you to my friends, Mother. Not you."

Sara backed off at the coldness in his voice and the hardness of his eyes. The door slammed behind him, making the plates clatter in protest in the kitchen.

*****

Karen and Sara strolled through Green Park. The leaves on the trees were changing colour and a spiteful cold wind was blowing them around in circles at their feet. Sara wrapped her scarf more tightly around her neck before plunging her gloved hands back into her pockets.

"So, Sara, what's up? You've been quiet for the past few days and you know how I hate that; it reminds me of when I first met you. Is it Ben? Come on, let's go sit on the bench over there and you can tell me what's going on?"

Sara sat huddled in her coat, trying to get some warmth into her bones. The stinging wind bringing unwanted tears to her eyes.

"Yes. It's Ben. I was pleased when he came back into my life, Karen. Before he came up to London, I didn't see much of him, but I did think when he found his flat and started his job, he would include me in his life a little more.

"I know he's living life in the fast lane, fast cars, fast girls, great social life. He's been hugely successful in his job and clearly his company are impressed with him. Well, as I said, I thought he might include me in his new life. But it hasn't happened. I haven't even seen his flat or met any of his friends. He's still ashamed of me. I know he is."

Karen reached into her pocket for a cigarette, then spent a few minutes trying to light it as she battled with the wind.

"Look, it wasn't any kind of moral obligation that made him contact you again Sara. You know damn well why he did!"

"Of course, I worked it out for myself. I think he hates me Karen, I really do and it hurts. My father stopped supporting him financially as soon as he started working. I've been helping him out a bit. Like many others he felt the bite of the financial meltdown."

Karen ground her cigarette out under her boot, picked up what was left and leaned over, depositing it in the bin next to the bench. She turned to her friend.

"Ben wants to make quite sure he gets the other half of your father's country heap. It's as simple as that. You're trying to buy his love with your cash hand-outs Sara. I know your mother left you a considerable trust fund, but you need to think of yourself and your own future. Your relationship with your son is built on sand. Sorry, but that's the truth of it. If he was genuine about building up a relationship with you, he would include you in his life. When did he last take you out for dinner?"

Sara averted her eyes. "He's never taken me out for dinner, or lunch, or even a drink. He comes to my flat, when he has a moment – which isn't often. Only when he needs money."

"So, what are you going to do?"

"I'm not sure." She looked up at the bruised sky as she felt the fine mist of rain on her face. "God, I miss Africa."

Karen stood up and shook out her umbrella. "Yeah, I can understand that, this weather really sucks. Come on let's go grab a cup of coffee, or a glass of wine or something."

Sara linked her arm through her friend's, as they trod through the wet leaves.

130

"Sometimes Ben scares me, Karen. I don't know him anymore. That temper of his is going to land him in trouble one day. He doesn't love me. I can see it in his eyes."

*****

Sara knew Ben was over compensating with his relationships with women. Making mistakes, catapulting in and out of disastrous relationships on a regular basis. It seemed when he came to visit there was a different woman's name on his lips. It wasn't difficult to work out, his obvious indifference and disrespect for women, the way he talked about and dismissed them as shallow. His complete lack of empathy for anyone's feelings other than his own. She wondered how much of this she should blame herself for.

Sara reached down the side of her chair for the ever-present rabbit, holding it close to her heart and stroking its threadbare back. The rabbits had been an Easter present for the children. One each, both identical. Ben had preferred his catapult and collection of beetles, frogs and lizards and had generously given his rabbit to Charlie.

The police, of course, had taken one, the one the sniffer dogs had used to search for the child, and bagged it with the other evidence. But this second little one Sara had retrieved from Charlie's empty bed before she and Ben had moved to the game lodge.

All her possessions had been listed and sealed when she went into the psychiatric institution to serve her sentence. On her release from the Haven her things were returned to her, including Charlie's forlorn little rabbit.

Sara clung to it like a talisman, her last contact with her child.

She held the rabbit up in front of her then kissed his faded pink nose. Her time in London had been enough.

She wanted to go back. Go back to the place where Charlie had died. There should be some sort of memorial plaque put there.

She wanted to sit by the river, in the silence of the bush and remember her child.

She had seen too much horror in her career. Too many tears, too many broken bodies and dreams, too many with no hope for anything better, the utter hopelessness in their eyes.

Sara yearned for the high blue skies, the dark velvet nights, studded with silent non-judgemental stars.

London was perceived to be glamourous, and, yes it was, if you had money. Sara had money, but to her the seething mass of shoppers, the frenzied spending, the women clutching handfuls of shiny designer bags, full of things they might never wear, but they shopped because they could; and on the other side – run down high streets full of cheap fast food outlets and shabby charity shops, full of things of people long gone. The crowded commuter trains where eye contact was avoided, the red buses full of people who had left their dreams behind. The windows steamed up by their once breathless hopes, and now the breath of despair and the brutal recognition that this was their life now – the grinding reality of routine.

Sara took out her palette of paints and started a new canvas. An older child, on the edge of the river. She tried to imagine what her child might look like now.

As she worked a plan began to form in her mind. A plan which would put her in more danger than she had confronted when covering stories in war zones.

Chapter Thirty-Five
The Shepherd

Eza returned to his village alone. It had been decided Mirium would stay in Diana's cottage and make her quilts which she could sell on a regular basis in the market.

When Eza entered his village, he was struck by the silence of the place. It was deserted. The carcass of one of his goats lying in the dust outside his hut, buzzing with the drone of busy flies. The other one gone.

He looked around his home seeing the shabby furniture steadily being eaten away by termites, the few plates and mugs chipped and broken on an upturned wooden crate. Birds had pecked away at the mattresses, pulling the foam out to make their nests.

He pulled his three-legged stool out and sat under the shade of a tree wondering what he should do next. Through his children he had learned to speak a little English, but now with no goats and no home, what should he do?

With no money to support his family he would have to return to the town and look for some work. Perhaps there would be a farm he could work on. In this town they must have goats and sheep for looking after?

As his pride fell into despair he tried to imagine not living in his village. In town he would have his wife next to him, as it had always been. He would see his children when they came home from school. Missus Diana had said he could live in the cottage with Mirium, so he would have a home, though not his own. If he found work, he would have money, although he knew it would be hard for an old man like him. Even if he did not know how old he was, his body certainly did with its aches and pains.

He stood up and walked around his hut again. *Eish,* there was nothing left here to be taking to the town. He eyed his three-legged chair. This he would take with him on the bus, he would be able to sit outside Missus Diana's cottage and look up at the stars at night.

Eza trudged back through the bush to the bus stop. Placing his stool under a tree he sat down and waited.

Chapter Thirty-Six
The Teacher

Diana had explained to the children that much as she would have liked them both to go to university, for which they had more than qualified, it simply wasn't possible. They didn't have the money to pay the fees.

Kia, now seventeen, was keen to study photography, Jabu wanted to be a tracker. He had missed the bush more than he had thought. He wanted to be back in the wild, far away from the town, where he had spent his past few years. When he left school at the age of seventeen, Jabu found a job as a waiter in one of the restaurants in town. He worked there for two years waiting for Kia to finish school. The money he earned helped his parents, but he worried for their future. His father had worked in some of the neighbour's garden, but did not have a permanent job. Jabu could tell he was unhappy, how much he yearned for his old life.

Kia would spend a year at the Cape Town Academy of Photography. Diana, with all her contacts, had found a friend of a friend who had a room Kia would be able to rent, until she could afford a place of her own.

Jabu had been accepted by one of the top lodges in the country, who offered game ranging and tracker courses.

The day the children left was tough. Diana hugged them both fiercely. Norman cleared his throat and tried to stay dry-eyed; he would miss them.

Kia took her brother's hand and they stood in front of the Templetons. "We thank you for your gift of education, for all the love and kindness you have shown us and our parents. This we'll never forget." Tears filled her eyes. "Of course, you are not our blood parents, but we love you as much as we love them."

Jabu put his arm around his sister. "Kia speaks for both of us. We won't forget you, and the opportunities you gave to us. We will both miss you very much. Thank you, thank you for everything you have given us."

Then they turned and left the room. Now they would say goodbye to their parents.

Norman and Diana drove the children to the station where Kia would catch the train to Cape Town, and Jabu a coach to Johannesburg where the game lodge manager would be waiting for him, to take him up to the lodge, to begin his training.

*****

Norman sipped at his gin and tonic then reached across for Diana's hand. "I'm proud of you, my dear. What you achieved with Kia and Jabu was magnificent. Both are well equipped now to make their way in the world, thanks to you."

"And you, Norman. You paid for everything. That's something to be proud of too. But it's so quiet without them though…"

Norman cleared his throat as he folded his paper and dropped it down the side of his chair. "My dear, we need to talk about our own future now? In six months, my contract will be up. I'm afraid South Africa doesn't offer the kind of safety net we need in our so-called golden years. Most of our savings have gone on educating the children, although we're not poor by any stretch of the imagination," he added quickly, seeing the concern on her face.

"I've loved my time here but I think we should think about returning to England. I know you love this country, as I do, but the government has enough on its plate meeting the demands of its own people. There's not much concern for older Europeans here now."

Diana sighed, and reached over for his hand. "I've been thinking the same thing. If anything happened to you, I would be quite alone here. I can't bear to think about it but I have. Both of us have relatives in the old country and we have our pensions there and free medical aid. It will be a huge adjustment though…"

She sat up straight in her chair. "The one thing I have missed living here, are the changing seasons. In Africa it's either, wet, dry, hot or cold!"

Norman smiled. Diana always looked on the positive side of things. "No rush to do anything, my dear, we still have plenty of time."

He looked at the little cottage nestled amongst the trees at the bottom of the garden. "I'm a little concerned about Eza, now the children have gone. He doesn't seem to be happy, and I think Mirium needs glasses."

"Yes, I've noticed. But she won't go near a doctor, they prefer their own ways. Using the old traditional medicines. We'll have to make some sort of plan for both of them when we eventually have to leave. But let's not think about it now."

*****

Eza sat out on their little veranda at the cottage, on his three-legged stool. Mirium working hard on her latest quilt. Eza noticed she held the cloth much closer to her eyes than before.

Mirium rubbed her eyes and put her quilt aside. "What troubles you my husband?"

Eza tapped his pipe out carefully collecting the dying embers in a pile next to his foot. "I am not liking this town Mirium. There is no work for me. Every day I try to find some work for money. But there is nothing for an old man."

He looked up at the dark skies. "Here in this town a man cannot see the stars for all the lights in the houses. Cannot hear the wind breathing through the grasses. My soul is heavy for my home and the bush."

Mirium rubbed her tired eyes again. This she could not help him with, but her own heart was full of sadness, for she knew he was unhappy in this town with many lights.

Chapter Thirty-Seven

Some weeks after his children had left, Eza slipped away from the cottage before the sun rose. He took only his pouch, with its hidden secret, his rabbit skin cloak, his bows and arrows and the clothes he was dressed in.

The bus dropped him off. He set off in the direction of his old village, his loping strides eating up the distance with ease. He felt the life of the town's people slip away behind him, the crowds the shops and the houses already forgotten.

Without stopping in his deserted village, he followed the path he had taken so many years ago.

There was something he had to do.

Two days later he was at the wide river. The water meandering towards the steep drop after the rapids. The river where he had found the child.

He crossed over on the same slippery rocks as before and with uncanny instincts found the exact spot. He stood looking down at the thick reeds and smiled. Hunkering down he remembered the joy of this child and the one born shortly after. Jabu and Kia. He missed them.

He stood up and scanned the banks of the river, his eyes noticing where the river twisted and turned. Walking slowly, he looked for where the child might have come from. Three hours later, with the sun burning high above, he retraced his footsteps. Noticing things only a man at one with the bush would see.

At some time, there had been a village here, or maybe a small house. There had been a fire. He bent down and picked up a square stone.

"*Eish,* this stone is what the white people build their houses with." He muttered. He scratched his head, carefully moving through the thick bush.

The burnt-out skeleton of a house stood in front of him. Cautiously he moved towards it, noticing a smaller dwelling slightly to the back of it.

A startled monkey leapt from the bush. With the swiftness of a striking snake he drew an arrow from his pouch and with deadly accuracy brought the young animal to the ground where it lay still.

Eza smiled. This was a good omen. He had not eaten for two days and the monkey would be a good meal. He would give thanks to the Gods before skinning it.

The inside of the house was empty, thick vines and branches clinging grimly to its sides. The wooden door had collapsed and was seething with termites and white ants.

Eza made his way to the small round house at the back. This too was empty. The thatch now home to birds, lizards and other creatures. He hunkered down again and studied the floor and the walls. In the corner debris from storms and strong winds had formed a pile of detritus. This then was the house of the woman called Beauty, who looked after the small ones.

Then using his arrow, he laboriously carved his name on the wall in the corner.

Eza.

Collecting the dead monkey, he loped along an old bush track to the river, the animal bouncing against his back. At this spot tall trees swayed and clattered in the wind. Eza looked down the river. Yes, this was the spot where the child had tumbled into the river. Of this he was quite sure.

The child belonged to the woman who must have lived in the house before the fires. The woman who was the daughter of Chief Miles. Therefore, this burnt house must belong to his dead Chief, but because he was with his ancestors, his son Joseph it would belong to now.

He bent his head and stared at the river. The daughter of the Chief Miles had gone to prison many seasons ago. This Sipo had told him when they had met in secret many years ago. Perhaps the letter writer had not found someone to deliver his letter to the Chief Miles, in the place with the flat mountain?

He stood up; his heart leaden with guilt. He had saved the life of the child from certain death, this he knew, but in doing so he had caused much grief to the mother of the chid. The mother who had been locked away for something she did not do.

He reached into his pouch and withdrew the one thing he had never shown to anyone.

The child he had rescued had lost one shoe, but he had the other.

Holding the shoe and an arrow, he looked for a place between the strong roots of the big tree near the banks of the river. Wedging the shoe in the thick tangle of roots, he plunged his arrow into it to hold it fast.

Perhaps one day the mother, when she came out of this prison, would come to this spot to remember her child. As he had done.

He crossed back over the river and headed south. South to where he and his people had come from.

His life had come full circle, he needed to be out in the desert again, in the wilderness where his ancestors had been born. Where they had lived for hundreds of years, somewhere perhaps where the Gods would forgive him for saving the life of a child, but bringing much grief to the mother.

He turned towards the land of his ancestors. The tears coursing down the creased furrows of his cheeks as he loped through the dry bush. Each dusty step taking him further away from his family, the wetness cooling on his chest as he ran.

Chapter Thirty-Eight
The Son

Sara finished grating the cheese over the pasta dish. It had always been one of Ben's favourite dishes when he was small. She called it nursery tea and the name had stuck. Sara hoped it would bring a smile to his face if he remembered the dish, or how to smile for that matter. The last few visits hadn't been what she would call successful. She wasn't particularly looking forward to this one. He wouldn't be happy with what she was going to tell him.

The doorbell chimed followed by a rapid knocking. Her heart sank as she opened the door. Ben's face was red and blotchy, as he pushed passed her, she smelt the alcohol on his breath.

"Well hello Ben, and a good evening to you too. Would you like a drink? Or do you think you might have had enough?"

Ben scowled at her. "I've had a rough day at the office, Mother, I don't need you to start nagging me. I'll help myself to a drink. Is dinner ready? I haven't long to hang around."

Sara smiled at him brightly. "Yes, dinner is ready. I made your favourite – nursery tea!"

He turned from the drinks table. "What the hell is nursery tea? Is this some kind of a joke? I'm not a child, in case you forgot, well, yes, you did, didn't you? You weren't there."

"You and Charlie loved it as children…" her words trailed off as she saw the fury in his face.

"Don't ever, ever, mention Charlie to me again, Mother. We had an agreement remember?"

She stood up abruptly. "I'll go and get dinner."

Setting it on the table she motioned for him to sit. He didn't.

"It looks like something I wouldn't even give to a dog... You honestly can't expect me to eat it can you?"

"Don't be ridiculous Ben, sit down and eat. It might help soak up some of the alcohol you've clearly consumed. You're drunk and it doesn't suit you. You need to take a close look at yourself and get that temper of yours under control. It's not attractive."

Ben angrily reached for the coat he had thrown over the back of the chair. "Forget it, Mother. I'll eat later with someone who appreciates me and doesn't mind me having a little fun at the end of a rough day.

"I was a bit short of fun when I was growing up, I'm sure you understand that. By the way I need more money, I'm in a bit of a squeeze at the moment. I'll need more than usual, say five thousand pounds? You have plenty to spare and not much to spend it on judging by your lack of a social life."

His face twisted with malice. "But I understand the social life part, it would be difficult to talk about your life to strangers wouldn't it, especially Linda who I plan on marrying. Mind you, some people might find it fascinating to hear about life in prison. What do you think, Mother?"

Sara stood up; her food untouched. "I'll tell you what I think Ben," she said her voice shaking with anger.

"I think this relationship is never going to work. I will not be subsidising your lifestyle any longer. You're not the son I remember. You've grown into a complete stranger, a cruel one, someone I no longer know, or care to know. I'm happy you've found someone who loves you. Linda you said?

"Obviously you won't be introducing me to her anytime soon. I hope she'll make you happy, which I clearly don't. Unless I'm giving you money, of course!

"You threw me out of my father's house and now I'm asking you to leave mine."

With a swiftness that surprised her he lunged towards her putting his hands on her shoulders, towering above her.

"Who was Charlie's father?" he hissed at her. "Or is that something you'll take to your grave with you?"

Sara stumbled trying to back away from him. He pushed her roughly into a chair, then shrugged on his coat.

"Charlie's father?" she said bitterly. "What does it matter who the father was? It won't change anything will it?"

Sara stood and walked towards the door. "Goodbye Ben."

Ben wrenched the door open. "Get out of my way, Mother." He pushed her roughly aside, Sara staggered and fell back.

142

The force of the slammed door, dislodged Sara's most loved wood carving. The tall giraffe tottered briefly then fell on top of her, gouging a deep cut in her cheek.

The crockery in the kitchen clattered against each other, then the flat was still; as still as Sara lying on the floor, her tears mingling with the blood she had once shared with her son.

Chapter Thirty-Nine
The Doctor

Karen looked at the clock on the wall. Where the hell was Sara this morning? In between patients she'd tried her phone, but there was no response. She left messages but none were returned.

Her appointments were back to back today, she wouldn't have the time to go around to Sara's flat.

Then finally as she was preparing to leave the surgery, Sara called.

"Karen? I'm sorry I didn't come in today. Something happened last night. Would you come over when you've finished up there?"

Karen sighed. "Something to do with Ben, no doubt? I'll be over there in half an hour. Shall I bring a bottle of wine. Some food?"

"No. I have a pasta dish already made," she laughed hysterically. "But no-one seemed to have an appetite for it. Bring your medical bag. I think I might need a few stitches?"

"Dear God," Karen murmured, "Ben came calling, didn't he? Did he hurt you?"

Sara laughed uncontrollably. "No. It wasn't Ben. He was here of course. It was a giraffe who did the damage."

"Well clearly you're delirious Sara. I'm on my way."

*****

Karen tended to the wound on Sara's cheek before she asked any questions. "There we go then Sara, all fixed, my best needlework. Much better than whoever stitched you up before. The scar near your hairline could have done with a woman's touch."

She handed Sara two pills and a glass of water. "Take these, it will help with the pain.

"Now what exactly happened here?"

"It was the giraffe." Sara pointed to the heavy wooden carving of the giraffe lying on its side. "It toppled over when Ben rampaged out of the flat, it's not the giraffe's fault." She snorted with laughter, then winced with pain.

"Look, Sara, I've had enough of Ben and the effect he's had on you since you came back. I know we're close. I know you've told me a great deal about your life in Africa. What happened to you there. But I know there are things you haven't told me. I think it's time you did?"

Sara, feeling the effect of the painkillers Karen had given her, decided to tell Karen the things she had held back. But not everything.

"You might want a glass of wine Karen, maybe I'll have one as well."

"Not for you, my girl. Doctor's orders, but I sure will have one. I'm not going to like what I hear right?" She poured herself a generous glass of red wine.

"Right. But I need you to help me Karen, I need you to put your career, as a doctor, at risk again. I'm not sure I can ask you to do this."

Karen took a long gulp of her wine. Unsure of what was coming next.

"Let me be the judge of that, Sara. I know you've seen suffering in your career, as I have. If something must be put right, then so be it, I'll help if I can."

*****

Karen drove slowly back through the traffic, the relentless rain slew across the windscreen, the wipers as steady as a heartbeat, as they washed away the grimy tears of a London night.

Of all the patients she had dealt with over the years, Sara had been the most complex.

She would help her and to hell with the consequences. She would go along with Sara's plan and it would take some planning. Complex and, yes, dangerous. If the truth of what they planned ever came out she faced the possibility of being struck off.

But Sara's story needed the truth to come out.

Chapter Forty

Four months after the incident with Ben at the flat, Doctor Karen O'Hara strode across the driveway of the stately building, now converted to a private care home, knowing the cameras would be observing her every move. She knew the authorities would come after her later.

"Good afternoon, Doctor O'Hara," the cleaning lady said cheerfully, taking a final look around the luxury suite. "I'm all done here. I'll leave you two together then."

Karen moved through to the bedroom admiring the snowy white sheets taut across the bed, and the bowl of apricot roses on the table. Her patient, her best friend, sat in her chair staring at her hands and ignoring the sumptuous grounds outside her window.

A soft knock at the door announced the arrival of Sara's lunch. The nurse deposited the silver tray and retreated.

Karen spread a linen napkin over her Sara's knees, their eyes met briefly and a ghost of a smile crossed her patient's lips.

*****

The nurse looked out of the window and watched the two women sitting under the oak tree, their heads close together as though deep in conversation. How lucky Sara was to have such a loving and caring friend who was also a doctor. The only doctor Sara would let near her.

Doctor O'Hara had checked Sara into the home herself, providing all the necessary paperwork. Apart from Karen she only had one other visitor, her son, Ben.

*****

Ben had visited her rarely, spending as little time as possible with her, watching in frustration as she stared blankly out of the window, saying nothing, unaware of his presence.

He clearly remembered the telephone call from Karen.

"She's deteriorating quickly, Ben. We need to look at all possibilities. Her father can hardly take care of himself, as you know, and your mother needs a lot of looking after. She could come and live with you perhaps? She can't be on her own anymore. I have a busy practice to run so I won't be able to help out I'm afraid. The only other alternative would be a private care home…"

Ben was now struggling to pay the mortgage on his expensively furnished apartment and the lease on his Range Rover. His girlfriend, Linda, was high maintenance. If he wanted to keep her, which he did, he would have to make a plan. Maybe this situation could be to his advantage.

Much better to put her in a home and be done with it. Safely hidden away. His mother would be able to afford the substantial fees charged by the home. There would still be plenty over for him when the time came. He wasn't prepared to give up one moment of his life to accommodate what was left of his mother's.

With indecent haste, he had co-signed the required papers for her admittance to the private care home.

Chapter Forty-One
The Son

Ben Courtney parked his Range Rover under the shade of a tree and switched the engine off. He turned to the woman next to him.

"It's not going to be pleasant for you, darling, but it's something I have to do, though hopefully for not much longer. Now we're getting married, you have to meet her. Then you'll understand the hell I have to go through. Not that she'll have a clue who you are, or even speak to you. She's a mess to look at, with all that grey straggly hair. Ignore her like I do."

Linda followed Ben, dreading what was to come. His mother wasn't her problem and she didn't care whether she met her or not - by all accounts she would never come out of the home. But she was in love. Not with Ben, but rather the money he would inherit, the impressive home in Dorset, and the town house in London, which she was eager to get her hands on. His mother was wealthy and would leave him her fortune now that Charlie was no longer around. He wasn't the most attractive man she had dated: his hair was beginning to recede; bags had appeared under his eyes and he was carrying too much weight. She glanced down at her hands. She would have to make an appointment for a manicure when she returned home.

One reason she had agreed to this visit was to check out exactly how frail his mother was and how long they would have to wait for the inheritance. Then when his grandfather died, which couldn't be far off, Ben would inherit everything including the contents of the country estate.

They were an odd family though. Grandfather having nothing to do with his daughter, Mother and son not speaking to each other. She knew a little of what had happened in the past but she wasn't interested anyway, only the future beckoned. Ben had changed his name, no-one needed to know his mother had gone to prison.

Ben had told her about the last argument he had had with his mother, how she had thrown him out. She knew he was nervous of his mother's best friend and doctor, Karen. They would have to make sure the damn doctor didn't persuade Sara to leave her money and assets to her, or some worthy medical cause. By all accounts the final parting of the ways between Sara and Ben had brought on her illness. Suddenly she had stopped talking, seemed unable to take care of herself. Some kind of mental condition eating away at her.

Now they sat awkwardly in the guest chairs as Sara stared at her hands or looked out of the window. Ben looked across at Linda and shrugged his shoulders dismissively.

"This is a waste of time. I've never been that close to my mother, she nearly suffocated me with love when I was a child."

Linda glanced briefly at his mother. "Before Charlie came along do you mean?"

"I don't remember Charlie! But because of Charlie I was fostered out to a couple, who I couldn't stand, any more than they could stand me. Then I was sent back to live with my grandfather, as you well know."

He gestured to the woman staring out of the window. "You have no idea what it was like after what she did to Charlie!"

He patted his jacket pocket and pulled out his cigarettes. "You can't smoke in here Ben. You'll have to go outside and I don't want to be left here with her. You'll have to wait."

He thrust the pack back in his pocket and paced around the room. "See, that's all she does for hours on end – stares out of the bloody window at nothing. Doesn't say a word to anyone."

Linda looked at him through narrowed eyes. He grinned at her wolfishly and she shuddered. She dearly hoped when he had his hands on the money, he would spend some time smartening himself up a bit. She looked away and snatched up her handbag.

"Come on Ben, I really can't stay another minute in this room. Let's go and have lunch."

Sara's eyes followed them as they left.

*****

Sara knew who would come to her suite of rooms during the day, and when: the cleaner, the nurse with her meals, the laundry staff, and for them she played her part. The staff were cheerful and the service excellent. Most week-ends Karen would collect Sara and take her to her flat in Notting Hill; they would dine out, go to the movies, or the theatre.

On Friday night she would be leaving the home and a large bill, for Ben's account. The price she had already paid was more than enough.

*****

Karen had collected her from the care home, then drove her to the flat in Mayfair where Sara had packed two small suitcases and collected the documents she would need. Then they had returned to Karen's Notting Hill flat.

Sara took a sip of her champagne watching Karen throw together a salad for their dinner.

"I wish you were coming with me Karen. I'm going to miss you terribly. I won't forget this. The risk you're taking for me."

Karen gave the salad a final toss. "I wish I was coming with you as well, but I have to stay here to make sure everything goes to plan.

"The police will be searching everywhere for you and all roads will lead to me. I've covered every possibility and my story is watertight. When I tell them about your time in South Africa, it will add a lot of weight to the whole situation.

"They won't be able to find you. I'll play the grieving best friend and deal with the media. Because of what happened to Charlie, and the fact that a lot of people might remember your days as a hot shot war correspondent, there will be plenty of interest in your suicide, especially when your body doesn't pitch up.

"The media will only have one recent picture of you. The one I took of you last week – not looking your most glamorous best I have to say, but it should do the trick."

Karen reached over and ruffled Sara's hair. "Looking gorgeous now though, absolutely no comparison at all! Marvellous what a top hairdresser can do these days, and a bit of make-up helps."

Sara took a sip of her champagne and checked her travel documents. "I'm feeling a bit nervous now it's all going to happen. Let's run through my travel plans again?"

150

Karen sat down next to her. "Tomorrow morning, before it gets light, I'll take you to the station. My good buddy Luc will be waiting for you in Paris."

The two women smiled at each other. "He'll take you to his place. No-one ever comes to visit him; you'll be safe from prying eyes. In two months' time, when the fuss over your death has died down, and the media have lost interest, he'll take you to Marseilles for the boat to Cape Town. Then it's over to you.

"Come on let's eat our last supper, so to speak."

Chapter Forty-Two
The French Detective

On a busy square in the centre of town, surrounded by old plane trees, tables were set with white tablecloths anchored at the corners with metal clips, the menu scrawled in white chalk on blackboards, tables already filling up for lunch. Tourists and locals were meandering along the sidewalk, stopping to study menus before deciding where to have lunch in this old town of Menton, with its maze of narrow steep cobbled streets leading to tall houses painted pink, apricot, yellow and ochre. The medieval steps snaking through dark narrow alleyways, steeped in history.

Cluttered on the Promenade and in the old town were cafes and bars, shops selling postcards crammed onto spinning display stands, kitchenware, clothes, antiques and food. Down in the busy daily market, fresh fish, oysters, homemade tapenade, meat, fruit, vegetables, fat glistening salamis, oils and flowers were sold by noisy vendors to busy, basket wielding, housewives. Small supermarkets displayed their fruit and vegetables outside in sloping crates nestled in fake grass, under brightly coloured awnings.

People promenaded through the streets, the women exquisitely dressed, poised and elegant, walking with purpose, poodles and French bull dogs trotting alongside their owner's slim ankles and well shod feet.

The tall man made his way through the old town, a bottle of wine in his shabby coat pocket, another held by the neck from which he took regular sips, frequently stopping and sitting on a step, or a bollard, muttering to himself.

He was a regular sighting in the old town, tourists would stare at him wondering how a good-looking man such as this, albeit badly in need of a shave, a haircut and a shower, could be drunk so early in the morning.

The locals were used to him and greeted him although he never acknowledged them. If he was hungry, he would help himself to a piece of fruit from one of the small wooden crates outside a grocery shop, or a baguette on display close to the door of a Boulangerie. No-one berated him for his theft, only shrugged and shook their heads. He was harmless.

Rumours abounded about his past. No-one in and around town had seen him sober from the day he had appeared on their cobbled streets, no-one knew where he came from, or where he lived. Mothers pulled their children close when he passed, his penetrating blue eyes raking over their bodies as he sometimes paused, gulping from his wine bottle, before mumbling and laughing, and patting his pockets.

Some of the local mothers had reported him to the police, complaining he was dangerous, they feared for their children. Who was this man? Where did he come from?

The police had hauled him to the station on more than one occasion and questioned him. Where did he live. What was the purpose of his stay in Menton? He had stared at them with incomprehension, his eyes wavering and unfocussed as he reached for his bottle. Making no sense of their questions, giving only slurred responses to what he thought they had asked.

He was harmless the police assured the locals. He had committed no crime, there was no law against being drunk and harmless in France, or staring at pretty girls. Was it not a national past time, *non*? The man was a little simple in the head. No threat to anyone. His papers were in order.

*****

They were unaware that he was observing them all.

The tall man with the bottles of wine walked the streets from morning 'til night, talking to no-one, sometimes he moved to another town for the day, and when darkness began to fall, he would make his way to the foothills of the mountains. To the simple cottage where he lived his secret life.

Once he was inside, Luc triple-locked his door, filled his two empty wine bottles with water, ready for the morning, then went through to the only other room in the small cottage. Lining one wall were photographs he had taken with his highly sophisticated camera which he kept in the pocket of his jacket. Hand written notes with dates and

153

places were pinned to a cork board. He sighed and ran his hands over his face, then looked at the time.

It was time to call Sara and bring her up to date on what little progress made so far, then he would take a shower, and make ready for his trip to Paris to meet her off the train from London.

His six months of searching had brought no results – another dead end. The French connection had come to nothing. No father and no child.

Having little to work with, Luc had found it nearly impossible to find Charlie's father, despite the accurate description Sara had given him and his possible locations.

But Sara had insisted he try and find Charlie's father, so she could be sure he hadn't kidnapped the child and smuggled Charlie out of the country. Every possibility had to be covered, then eliminated.

Luc had accepted the challenge but knew too much time had passed, he didn't have the heart to tell her she was clutching at straws.

Chapter Forty-Three

"You'll have to start at the beginning Sara."

Luc leaned forward and tapped a cigarette out of his packet.

"If the press gets wind of the fact, you're back in South Africa they'll track your every move. Waiting for you to return to the scene of the crime, they'll be baying for your blood again.

"The police will be watching too. It may be a cold case but as soon as they know you're back in the country, they'll be watching you."

Sara frowned. "But you have all the paperwork sorted out, Luc?"

"Yes, as I promised I would. As far as the world is concerned you committed suicide. Karen will verify with the British police you were of unsound mind and threated to kill yourself on several occasions. You had hinted it wouldn't be done in the UK, but somewhere in Europe – that should muddy the waters even more."

Luc ran his fingers through his long dark hair and leaned back in his chair. "Karen will arrange a memorial service for you. Attended by your not so distraught son, Ben, and your father. That will be the end of it."

Sara looked down at her hands, her lips trembling. "I desperately wanted to phone my father and say goodbye. But Karen said it would be too dangerous. It's something I regret. He might have been a difficult man, but he is my father. I hate to think what he will have to go through."

Luc shrugged and held out her passport. Sara flicked through it

"You must know a lot of, um, unusual people to have pulled this off?"

Luc grinned. "Yes, I know a lot of people, most detectives do. An old friend owed me a favour or two. So, you are now Annabel Courtney.

"Have you still got your old South African identity document?"

She nodded. "I always kept it with me, in my handbag, you have to in South Africa it's the law. That's why it escaped the fire which destroyed everything else."

"Okay, try not to use it. It's in the name of Sara Saunders I presume?"

"Yes."

He stubbed out his cigarette and immediately lit another one. "If you're asked for identification use your new passport, as far as the South African authorities are concerned, you're a tourist. You'll have to judge each situation as it arises. If you're stopped and asked for your driving licence, you'll have to make up some story about it being lost or stolen.

"You have money?"

Sara nodded. "Don't worry about that. I opened a South African bank account on line, in a small town called Greyton. A tiny little place, out in the country. I thought it would be safe enough. They, of course wanted my ID number which I felt confident enough to give them. So, I have a bank account and a credit card, in my old name, which they sent to me by courier. I've transferred more than enough money. It should see me through."

Luc ground out his cigarette. "After that Sara, you really will have to accept Charlie is dead."

Chapter Forty-Four
The Mother

Two months later Sara boarded the ship bound for Cape Town. In the evenings she would sit in the elegant Champagne Club - an intimate and more expensive venue compared to the huge lounges scattered throughout the vessel. The passengers who frequented the club were from the first-class decks, as she was, and happy to pay the money for an expensive glass, or bottle, of champagne before dinner.

Emile Beaumont studied the woman sitting in the bar alone, as she watched the churning, heaving, waves through the large glass picture windows. During the day he had looked for her but, as yet, had not spotted her anywhere on deck.

The following evening, she appeared at her usual time and looked around the crowded room, every table seemed to be full.

Emile stood up and gestured for her to join him. Reluctantly she made her way to the only empty seat in the intimate bar. "Madame, Emile Beaumont." He lifted her hand to his lips. "Please join me for a glass of champagne?"

She waited for him to pull out a chair for her before sitting down. He poured her a glass of champagne. She introduced herself as Annabel Courtney.

"You're enjoying your cruise, Emile?" she said politely. "You have been to Africa before perhaps?"

"Indeed, I am, and I have been to South Africa before – I sometimes have some business there.

"Have you been to South Africa before Annabel? Perhaps you are going on holiday there, on safari? Or do you have family there?"

He was surprised and interested in her reaction to his question. The slight flicker of wariness he saw in her eyes.

"No Monsieur, Emile, this will be my first visit."

Although in his seventies, Emile was still an attractive man with a fine mane of silver hair and a body which could have been the envy of a man ten years his junior.

"I do not like to discuss my private life, Emile. It would not be of interest to anyone, believe me."

"You are French, Madame, if I am not mistaken?"

"My mother was French," she said abruptly. Then she softened her voice. "Tell me about you and your life, Emile," she smiled at him. "I'm sure it has been far more interesting than mine?"

He told her that before he retired, he had owned an art gallery in Paris. What he didn't tell her was he had made his money by buying and selling on the black market, the dark underbelly of the art world. His income had been sporadic to say the least. Cruise ships were a good hunting ground for wealthy widows willing to pay for his company, or, as had happened often, pay for him to keep his mouth shut.

Whilst they talked, he studied her. A beautiful woman, although not so young now. Her blue eyes gave nothing away. He was intrigued with her.

She stood up quickly, obviously uncomfortable with the way he was watching her. "Good night, Emile, thank you for the champagne and your company." His eyes followed her as she made way through the tables. A woman with a past, he surmised, she had deftly avoided saying much about herself. He smiled. What better way to run from your past than on a cruise ship which didn't stay anywhere for long?

*****

Emile Beaumont stood at the rail of the ship looking out over the swelling waves of the sea. He was thinking about Annabel Courtney.

He was going to find out as much as he could about her. She was definitely cagey about her private life, which to him in his experience, meant she had something to hide. There was a story here, and he was going to find out what it was. Perhaps there would be some money in it for him. Thoughtfully he made his way to the purser's office and placed a ship to shore phone call to Paris.

"Felix, I want you to find out as much as you can about someone for me." he said to the private investigator he had used many times before. "But I have only the smallest information at the moment. Her name is Annabel Courtney but I don't believe it's her real name."

158

He gave Felix as much information as he had. "I'll call you in a few days' time – see what you can find out."

*****

Emile tapped his foot impatiently as he waited for his second call to connect.

"What have you managed to find out for me, Felix?"

Felix took a generous mouthful of his cognac then wiped his mouth with the back of his hand and lit a cigarette. "I did a lot of research and came up with bugger all. No Annabel Courtney anywhere. I threw the net wider and checked the English papers."

"Come on Felix! I haven't all day. This call is costing me a fortune."

Felix continued, ignoring his interjection. "Then I stumbled on an article in an English newspaper, on the internet, about a woman who disappeared from a care home in England some months ago. Her name was Sara Saunders. There was a photograph of her.

"She was suffering from one of those diseases where your brain doesn't function any more. Saunders had a close friend, a doctor, who was questioned about the disappearance from the care home of her patient. The doctor had found a note addressed to her from this Sara Saunders, telling her of her plan to travel to Europe and end her life there.

Emile waited tapping his foot impatiently again, watching the churning seas from the Purser's office, wondering where the story was going and what possible connection could there be to Annabel Courtney. But he knew Felix was good at his job, slow but thorough, but someone who depended a great deal on his instincts. He heard Felix light another cigarette.

"I did some more digging on this woman Sara Saunders and came up with something most interesting. Some years ago, she lived in South Africa. She had two children. One child disappeared without trace. The police searched for weeks but came up with nothing. The body was never found.

"They were deeply suspicious that Sara Saunders knew exactly what had happened to the child and she was arrested.

"There was a witness, whose name was never made public to the Press. She was sentenced to eight years in a psychiatric prison in Cape Town. After she had served her time, she left the country and was never heard of again. As I said there was a photo of her on the internet along with the story.

"I compared the photo of Sara Saunders with the one you emailed me taken by the ship's photographer at the welcoming party on your first night at sea."

Emile raised his eyebrows. Now the story was becoming interesting. Felix continued. "When a child goes missing and is never found, the public are always intrigued. I think Annabel Courtney is the supposedly dead Sara Saunders. I'll send my report through to you."

Emile smiled into the phone. If this was indeed the case then Annabel was becoming more than interesting to him. Travelling first class she was likely to be wealthy. A wealthy woman with a guilty past. A murderess and a woman who was supposed to be dead.

The perfect target for blackmail.

Chapter Forty-Five
Cape Town

Sara stood at the rail at the back of the ship, unsheltered from the elements, and looked out into the black night. The sea, churned up by the mighty engines of the ship, turned silver white as the propellers gouged through it. She didn't hear Emile's stealthy approach.

"Ah, Annabel, there you are I was looking for you."

She spun around at the sound of his voice and felt a prickle of unexpected fear.

He joined her at the rail. "I'm looking forward to another glimpse of the great continent of Africa, Annabel, as I expect you are. After all, did you not live here once?"

He was watching her carefully, waiting for her reaction. She looked back at him steadily. "I have never been to Africa, as I told you.

"Monsieur Beaumont, are you following me? If you are, I don't care for it," she said uneasily.

"Indeed, I am following you and why not, you are a beautiful woman, Annabel, or should I call you Sara?"

Fear seeped through her and she steadied herself with the handrail, feeling the colour leaching from her face. "Please leave me alone or I will report you to the Captain."

"Perhaps it should be me talking to the Captain. I'm sure he will be most interested in knowing he has an ex-convict on his ship, and even more so to learn Sara Saunders is this person using a different name. Killing a child turns the stomach of the strongest of us. What do you think, Sara?"

"I think you are letting your imagination run away with you, Monsieur. Now please go away."

"No. If you wish for me to keep your little secret, the fact you disappeared from a nursing home and apparently committed suicide…well, you will need to pay me to keep the information I have to myself. I also find it extraordinary for one suffering from a disease of the mind you are remarkably well versed in the art of conversation. Another lie I think?"

She thought quickly, calculating how to handle the situation. Her honed instincts for survival moved smoothly into position. "I'm afraid you have your facts wrong. I have never heard of Sara Saunders. I think perhaps a little too much cognac has muddled your brain." She turned and started to walk away.

She felt his fingers bite into her arm. "I had a private detective looking into your past. I have his report. You lived in South Africa – *non*? Did you know the South African police never closed the case of the missing child called Charlie – your child?

"Why would you want the world to know you had committed suicide? If the Police have any knowledge of this supposed suicide, I think they would be intrigued and probably like to question you again. Heading back to Africa could become a dangerous thing for you. Perhaps you would like to reconsider my request?"

She was thinking on her feet now. He knew too much. Far too much. "Perhaps you will give me some time to think about this?"

He looked at her dispassionately. "We reach Cape Town the day after tomorrow. I need your answer before then."

"I will meet you here this time tomorrow. I will need some guarantees from you, Monsieur, and what it will take to ensure your, how can I put this, discretion? I will also need the report from your so called detective?"

"Let us both think about how this can be agreed amicably shall we? I will see you here tomorrow." He turned on his heel and left.

*****

He was waiting at the stern of the ship the following night. He licked his lips with anticipation when he saw her shadowy figure walking along the deck towards him, dodging the fine film of sweeping rain.

"Changing the colour of your hair will not save you, Sara Saunders. Only I can do this."

"I have not changed the colour of my hair, Monsieur, this is my own hair. And the dark wig was worn in case anyone should recognise me.

162

"You have the envelope with the report from your private investigator?"

He handed it to her and she opened it. After glancing at the contents, she put it back in the envelope and dropped it into her handbag.

He leaned easily against the wet rail of the ship. "So now we must agree a figure and discuss the terms of payment when we arrive in Cape Town?"

She leaned towards him; her voice raw with fury. "There will be no money Monsieur," she hissed at him. "I despise people like you who prey on others, a common thief who feeds off of others misfortune.

"It is I who will inform the Captain of your attempts to blackmail me. I have paid the price for what happened to my child. I have no intention of paying any more. You have no proof of anything. My papers are in order…"

He lunged at her, his face suffused with anger. But she was too quick for him, she lifted her knee and brought it up hard between his legs. He bent over with a howl of pain.

Sara pushed him roughly back against the rail. "Maybe you will learn a lesson from this Monsieur." She watched with horror as he seemed to lose his balance, scrabbling for the slippery hand rail of the back of the ship. Within seconds he had gone overboard, his arms wind milling through the air, his screams of terror drowned out by the mighty throbbing of the engines.

Sara looked down and saw the coil of rope his feet had become entangled with, his empty shoe turned on its side. She clamped her hand to her mouth, searching wildly for a lifebelt.

Breathing heavily, she pushed the hair out of her eyes and scanned the back of the ship. The white of his shirt was lost in the churning mass of the sea. She tried to imagine what it must feel like to be alone in the black sea watching the brightly lit ship, festooned with twinkling lights, disappearing into the distance. Then the black lonely silence, the surging waves of water. Then nothing.

Panic streaked through her body like acid. She threw the shoe over the side, picked up her handbag and ran back quickly into the shadows of the deserted deck.

Back in her cabin she sat on her bed, clasping and unclasping her hands, unable to believe what had happened.

A terrible accident that's all it had been. An accident with devastating results.

She sat up straight rubbing her arms to get the circulation going again, thinking quickly.

Emile Beaumont would not be missed for perhaps two days. In the early hours of the next morning the ship would dock in Cape Town; the steward who looked after his cabin would assume, he had gone ashore. When the ship sailed again, and his steward had not seen him change for dinner, he would raise the alarm.

A search of the ship would reveal nothing. The police in Cape Town would be alerted to the fact one of the passengers was missing. A search for him would be called off when his passport was found with his personal effects. An accident at sea would be assumed.

She anticipated his body would not be found; the shores around the Cape was famous for their plethora of sharks. She pulled out her week-end bag, she would fill it with as much as she could, the rest of her things she would have to leave behind. She had intended to disembark in Port Elizabeth, but now it would have to be Cape Town where she would leave the ship and disappear into the labyrinth of the city.

The ship would sail without her. It would probably be a day or two, when the ship was at sea, before she too would be discovered missing, her luggage still in her cabin. A *do not disturb* sign on her door would not deter the steward for long. It would be reported to the South African police. They would be looking for her. A chance she could not afford to take.

She crossed herself, then clasped her hands together. "May God forgive me," she whispered to herself, "it was just a terrible accident."

Pulling the report from her bag she screwed it up into a ball and tossed it over the balcony of her suite.

*****

Private detective Felix Arnaud read the article in the newspaper of the disappearance of Emile Beaumont whilst on a cruise to South Africa. He smiled to himself as he sipped his drink at an outside bar. So, the wily old fox had been no match for Sara Saunders.

He shrugged his shoulders dismissively; losing one client was not a disaster but obviously his client's cruise had been. Perhaps one day he would be able to use the information to his advantage, perhaps the police in South Africa would be interested. Then he quickly changed his mind; he was not, and never had been, comfortable around the police, there was no money to be made there. Meanwhile he had plenty of work to keep him going in the city of lovers, spying on errant husbands and unfaithful wives.

Chapter Forty-Six
The Game Ranger

"What time will we see the elephants?"

The game ranger, Andrew, rolled his eyes with disbelief – true the young model was beautiful in a vague sort of way, but the question was ridiculous beyond belief.

With what he hoped was an engaging smile he looked at his watch and told her they would be here at three. Some people on safari really did ask the most stupid questions. How the hell was he supposed to know what time a herd of elephants might pitch up on any given day? Elephants are elephants and do what they want to do when they want to do it.

He turned the opened top vehicle towards the waterhole where he knew the elephants would be – if nothing else he would impress the young model. It had been a lean season and the American magazine crew had taken the entire camp for a week, earning some much-needed revenue.

The week had been a challenge and tested all his people pleasing skills. The camera crew had focussed on their work and been little trouble, but the four young models had squealed and squeaked at everything unfamiliar. Throwing tantrums when it was either too hot, or it rained, or they found something small and furry in their tented suites. Okay, the snake slithering around outside had been a big bugger, even he had to admit that, but, hey, they were out in the bush with Mother Nature, not in a cocktail bar on Madison Avenue.

As for the meals – a complete nightmare! Two of the models were Vegan, wouldn't eat anything with a face, then it had to be wheat free, lactose intolerance was an issue, gluten free… Everything had to be organic and on it all went.

Later, sitting round the camp fire, before dinner (well what was left of it when all the dietary requirements had been met) was normally a highlight with guests as they waited to eat. The fire crackling away and shooting sparks up into the night, the Milky Way like the gossamer of a bridal veil floating across the heavens above was something truly special.

Screwing her eyes up one of the girls piped up. "Do you think you can get the smoke to blow the other way? It's making my eyes sting?"

Resisting the urge to put his hands around her slender neck and squeeze, he suggested perhaps they should go into the dining area and have an early dinner. He was relishing sinking his teeth into the impala steak and watching their horrified faces.

Only Kia, one of Marianne's moody photographers, seemed unperturbed by snakes, furry creatures or bugs. He had asked her if she was nervous of the close proximity of the elephants to the camp when they came to drink at the waterhole. Their grey wrinkled bodies bathed in the soft pink of the approaching sunset, making them, in his opinion, far more beautiful, and gracious, then their two-legged visitors.

Kia had shrugged. "Nope, I'm not scared. I don't have any fear of elephants or any wild animals only mad humans like bloody Marianne. God the woman is a nightmare to work with!"

When Marianne had asked him if he could organise for one of the elephants to have his tusks straightened out with plaster of Paris and whitened for a black and white shot with one of the models, he thought he might scream.

"Marianne, these are wild elephants, not tame horses. There is no way in hell, me, or any of my staff will be able to accommodate your request without being trampled to death. Sorry, we're doing the best to accommodate you and your crew and models, but that particular request is out of the question."

He had shaken his head and held his temper, barely managing a fixed smile.

Marianne had raised an eyebrow and folded her arms in front of her. "Now, look here Mr Game Ranger, I'm paying big bucks for this shoot and I want the shot with an elephant. I know it's been done before. Don't give me the bullshit about it not being possible! Damn well get it organised."

"The particular shot you are referring to was taken in Botswana. There is a safari camp there who do elephant back safaris. All the elephants are rescue elephants brought back to Africa from America, where they performed in a circus. They are trained and relatively tame, used to humans, hence the film crew were able to get the shot.

"If you want this so badly then may I suggest you get in touch with them and see if they will accommodate you, because, believe you me, I'm not going to be able to."

Andrew walked away, jamming his hat on his head, never, never, ever would he have a camera crew and models at his camp again.

"*What time will we see the elephants*" he mimicked to himself. For Christ's sake…

The Creative Director, Marianne, was as tough as they come in the fashion world and worked the crew and models pitilessly, allowing only a few hours break in the heat of the afternoon, otherwise they were all up to catch the light at sunrise and allowed to relax only after the sun had plunged into the bush and the chilly dark night was descending.

Kia looked bored and fed up. For the entire week she had taken the photographs then took off on her own to read a book. No internet deep in the bush of Africa.

When the party had arrived and were informed their cell phones and whatever other devices they were planning to use would not function, there was a collective look of absolute horror and disbelief on their faces – Andrew always enjoyed that part. No point in coming thousands of miles to see spectacular wild life and then spend hours staring at a flickering screen.

At dinner, Andrew made a point of sitting next to Kia.

"So, Kia, where do you come from, you're obviously not American?"

"Cape Town," she said shortly, stabbing unseeingly at whatever was on her plate. "This is my first assignment as a professional photographer, after two years of hard work, I'm thinking I might have chosen the wrong career if clients are going to be anything like Marianne. She's almost impossible to please, I can tell you."

Kia, Andrew noticed, didn't have the staggering good looks of the models around the table, but she was striking in her own way. Tall and slim she was wearing dark brown leggings and a bright yellow top that rode high at the front and dipped low at the back. Her shoes like slivers of gold on her feet, a seam of shimmer through her toes and around her ankles, her toenails tipped with gold polish.

Her plaited hair, threaded with small beads of ochre, yellow and green hung down to her waist. Her golden hooped earrings, as big as small saucers, caught the sun when she moved her head, throwing prisms of light across her lovely face. Her skin bare of any make-up, her large expressive green eyes listless and disinterested in what was going

168

on around her. It appeared to him being a photographer on a fashion shoot had defeated her already.

He tried again. "Do you know anything about the galaxy? The stars?"

She looked up at him and scowled. "No, although I'm a Gemini, does that count?"

"Not really. I'll take that as a no, then shall I?"

Kia sighed dramatically and put her fork down. "I grew up here in South Africa. Stars don't hold any great fascination for me."

He watched her wondering why she was so tense. He tried again. "Where do your family live?"

"My mother lives in the Eastern Cape. My father left her. Didn't even say goodbye." She slapped, harder than necessary, at her arm as a mosquito alighted on her. She picked it off and wiped her hand on her napkin, leaving faint red welts on her upper arm.

Her face softened. "I have a brother, Jabu, he's a game ranger too, up near the Kruger Park. I don't see him often. It's too expensive to fly from Cape Town to the lodge and he works, like you, seven days a week. He seems to have found exactly what he was looking for in life, he's happy – he's content with his lot in life."

Andrew felt a stab of pity for her, she was clearly not happy. "Tell you what Kia. There's a Sangoma in the village not far from here, I could take you to meet him? The guests always love the experience."

"Sangoma? What's that? Some kind of cocktail?"

He threw back his head and laughed. "No! A Sangoma is a sort of witch doctor, medicine man, someone who can see your spiritual path. He's much respected by everyone around here. Maybe he'll suggest a new career path for you, you never know."

He saw a glint of humour in her eyes. "Sure, why not, it beats sitting around here with a bunch of giggling girls who don't have a brain between them. What on earth are they going to do when their looks begin to fade?

She gave him a small smile. "Of course, I know what a Sangoma is! But I've never met one. So, yes, why not?"

*****

The Sangoma was an old man, the skin on his face like parchment. The interior of his round hut, dark and smoky. Adorning the walls were animal skulls, skins of animals, necklaces of teeth and shells. Around his skinny shoulders he wore a skin cloak made of long dark fur, around his neck, weighing it down, were necklaces of baboon and hippo teeth. His ankles and wrists were covered in heavy bracelets made of brightly coloured beads, leather and heavy metal.

The old man clapped his hands softly and murmured, "I see you; you are welcome here."

Not knowing how to respond Kia nodded, her eyes beginning to water from the smoke spiralling up from the smouldering fire as she adjusted her eyes to the dark interior of the Sangoma's hut.

He gestured for her to sit. She looked around for a chair, not finding one she sank onto the thin straw mat in front of him.

The Sangoma crouched on his haunches, staring at the ground for a long minute, his head down. Kia waited her heartbeat speeding up as she became aware of the aura around this medicine man, this Sangoma, feeling the energy emanating from him.

Suddenly he gave a shriek and Kia's hand flew to her mouth with fright. The old man threw a handful of bones onto the dusty ground in front of him and stared at them, his lips moving but saying nothing. Then he scooped them up and threw them down again, pointing at one then another.

He rocked back on his heels; eyes closed. For a moment he was still: then he looked straight at her.

"There was much evil in your past. I see your brother. That which is lost must be found. Beware of this evil - it is around you still. Stay in the land where you now live or you will weep forever for what has been lost. This the spirits have told me."

Kia shivered, not understanding what he was telling her although he spoke in stilted English. All she wanted to do was stand up and run away from this old man who seemed to be able to look into her soul.

"You are much loved by your mother...this mother hides secrets from you."

The Sangoma stood up, seemingly weakened by his revelations. He shrugged his cloak around him and disappeared into the dark depths of another room.

Kia waited for a few moments, then, realising her audience with the Sangoma was over she stood up and left the smoky hut. Andrew was waiting for her.

"Well?"

She scowled at him.

"Well what? He spooked me out, is what. All those smelly animal heads and that stinking fire, God know what it's done to my lungs! I think I'll stick to horoscopes…"

Disappointed, Andrew led her back to the vehicle and they made their way back to the lodge. "Are you always this angry with life, Kia?"

"Yes," she said abruptly.

"Look, why don't I take you on a game drive? You haven't left the camp since you arrived, well, apart from the visit to the Sangoma, which perhaps wasn't such a good idea after all."

She bit her lip. "Look, Andrew, I appreciate you trying to cheer me up, but some things can't be fixed. I don't want to go out into the bush. I was brought up in the bush. I don't belong there anymore. Okay? But thanks anyway."

Andrew parked the vehicle and turned off the engine. The setting sun threw a golden glow across her face, the beads in her plaits clicked softly in the wind.

Kia clambered out of the vehicle and made her way down the dirt pathway to her tented suite. Andrew watched her rigid back, her gold sandals and hooped earrings glinting from the lit hurricane lamps lining the path.

*****

Kia lay down on her bed, her arm across her eyes. She thought back to her days at the private school, where she had mixed with girls from all over the country. Some of the students came from other parts of the continent, professionals on contract there sent their daughters to South Africa for their education.

As her confidence grew, she had thrown herself into this new life. Eza and Mirium never came to the school. It was not a world they knew, or wanted to know.

Secretly she was pleased they didn't visit. She didn't want her new friends to know of her lowly beginnings. She wanted to be like them. Have parents who came to the school in their shiny big cars. It was only a small lie, she had told herself. Everyone assumed Diana and Norman were her parents, that perhaps she was adopted.

But she was, nevertheless, ashamed of herself for denying her birth right.

When her father had finally disappeared from their lives, she felt anger, although her anger didn't diminish her love for him. She had grown too far away from him. He clung stubbornly to the old ways of his people, whereas she wanted so much more. Their worlds were too different now, on a different trajectory.

The smelly old witch doctor had disturbed her a great deal. What had he meant when he said her mother held secrets back from her? Was it about Jabu?

Kia punched her pillow in frustration. Stupid old man, mumbling about spirits and ancestors and chucking his smelly bones around.

She'd be glad to get back to Cape Town, away from it all, taking photographs was not enough. A lifestyle magazine had offered her a good job, and she had decided to accept it. She would get her life together and start making some serious money. After all what was there to inherit from her parents?

Nothing

Chapter Forty-Seven
The Mother

The tentacles of her past had found her. She would have to lie low for a while Sara Courtney Saunders would have to disappear again. Using the toilet at the waterfront, she removed her wig and threw it into the garbage bag. Pulling her hair back she tied it in a severe bun, washed all the make-up off her face and donned the black rimmed eye glasses she had bought at the shop on the ship. Satisfied she no longer resembled Annabel Courtney, Sara walked towards the taxi rank.

She found a cheap hotel in an area of Cape Town called Green Point. It was run down but would service her needs until she found a flat for a few months.

She picked up a newspaper from reception and took it to her room. The story of the missing passenger from the cruise ship didn't take up much space on the front page. It wasn't unheard of for a passenger to topple over the side of a ship, after a few drinks too many. When her steward realised she wasn't on board, the Captain would report it to the Cape Town Police. She had been seen with Emile on a couple of occasions, joining him at his table. It was then the two pieces of the puzzle would come together. The Police would be looking for her. A passenger falling off the back of a ship was one thing, but two? Not likely. There would be an investigation.

She turned to the classified section and spotted an advertisement for a one bedroomed furnished flat, with a sea view. Sara rang the number.

Following the directions she had been given she found the shop situated on the main road through Sea Point. Taking a deep breath, she entered. Shelves lined all four walls of the room packed with old long-playing records; long tables ran down the length of it with more records, CD's and music books precariously balanced on top.

A man in his late sixties was writing laboriously in a large ledger, his glasses perched on the end of his nose, tufts of white hair clung defiantly to his balding head. He looked up. "May I help you?"

"Hello, are you Mr Kruger? My name's Jenny Marshall, I phoned about the flat?"

He smiled at her as he cleared some books from a chair and beckoned for her to sit. "Hello, Jenny, yes, I'm Edward Kruger. The flat is small, but it does have a balcony, a small one, with a nice view of the sea. I would prefer a long-term rental, but I'm happy to rent it out for a few months. I'm afraid no pets are allowed though."

She could see him looking her over as they sat opposite. He was sizing her up. Her simple blue striped dress was clean and well pressed, her overall appearance plain and ordinary.

"Tell me a little about yourself, Jenny?"

"I've come from London," well that was true enough, "and before I lived in various places in Europe. I was an au pair before I married. I've just arrived in Cape Town. I wanted a complete change in my life, a new start, and I'm hoping to find it here, now I'm divorced. I'm doing some research; I need somewhere quiet to work. Oh, and I don't have any pets!"

"Research? Are you writing a paper of some sort?"

"I'm looking at the long-term effects certain drugs have," she shook her head, "It's not easy to explain in a sentence or two."

Edward stood up smoothing down his tufts of hair which immediately sprang back up.

He glanced at his watch. "Let me show you the flat, it's in the same block as the one I live in. It's not far from here."

She hesitated before answering. Living on the same premises might cause problems, she had to keep her distance from everyone. She looked at his honest face, his kindly brown eyes, deciding to take a chance.

He slipped his jacket on and patted his pockets searching for his keys. "Things are quiet at the moment, everyone's probably at the beach enjoying the weather. I don't particularly like the city at this time of the year, too many tourists filling up the place."

Sara picked up her handbag. "I'll take it, Mr Kruger, and move in right away if it's alright with you?"

"Are you sure you don't want to see it first?" he asked, surprised.

"I'm sure it will be fine and I don't have the time or the energy to look at dozens of places."

174

"Well, if you're quite sure? Don't won't worry about a lease as you only need it for a couple of months, but I will need a deposit? If you like, I'll help you move your things."

Grateful for his kindness and concern she accepted his offer. "I only have a small case, but in this heat, I would appreciate a hand with it. The rest of my luggage will follow later. I'm in a small hotel in Green Point called The Point."

*****

Edward waited in the dingy reception area of the hotel whilst she went to her room to pack. He asked the surly receptionist to order a taxi for them.

Sara returned to the reception desk to settle her account and he glanced idly at the luggage tag on the small case the porter had carried down. Obviously, she had come by ship and not air as he had presumed, and by the look of things on the same ship where a passenger had gone missing. There had been a small article in the Cape Times which he remembered reading.

He hauled her luggage up the two flights of stairs into the flat, and paused to wipe his brow, before unlocking the door. She looked around wordlessly, it was basic to say the least, but the light was good and there was a tiny balcony, only big enough for two chairs and a small table, but the view over the ocean was spectacular, it would compensate for the lack of any luxury. The fact Edward was not requiring her to sign a lease was in her favour. A lease meant identification. Sara straightened her shoulders and turned to him. "Thank you, Mr Kruger. I appreciate your help with everything. This is exactly what I'm looking for."

Thoughtfully Edward climbed two more flights of stairs to his own flat. Ms Jenny Marshall was pleasant enough, well educated. She was evasive though, carefully avoiding any more personal questions about herself. Well, who didn't have secrets? He had more than enough of his own.

*****

Sara unpacked her bag and put both her passports into her handbag and left the flat, locking the door carefully behind her. Mr Kruger seemed like a nice enough man, but she had fallen into that trap before. She had learned the hard way. Mr Kruger might have a spare

175

key to her place and be curious enough about her to snoop around when she was out. She doubted it, but it wasn't worth taking any chances.

She walked along the sea front breathing in the familiar salty air. Even though it was getting dark the early December evening was still warm, with plenty of people around: cyclists, joggers, couples, children playing on the swings, dogs and their owners and a group of boys running around with a rugby ball.

She retraced her footsteps and walked back to her new flat. Despite all the memories it was wonderful to be back in Cape Town again. As beautiful as she remembered it.

Tomorrow she would find a hairdresser to cut her hair shorter and get herself a new look, she would buy the biggest pair of sunglasses she could find and a wide brimmed hat to hide the rest of her face.

Then she would find an art shop. She needed to keep steady. She needed to paint.

Chapter Forty-Eight

E dward was more than happy with his new tenant. Respecting, as he perceived, her need to keep her private life exactly that, the conversations they had, if they bumped into each other, were non-intrusive.

It was the time of the year he disliked the most. Christmas was a fairly good time for the business but when the shop closed over the festive holidays, he normally went back to his empty flat and waited for the long days to be over with.

He stared out at the Christmas lights, then, making up his mind, he went and knocked on her door. "There's a Christmas carol concert this evening, Jenny. I don't normally go to these sorts of things but perhaps you might like to? It will be your first Christmas in South Africa and you shouldn't spend it on your own with no family around. They're having it down on the promenade. What do you think?"

*****

Sara hesitated. Was this an innocent invitation or was he going to make some sort of move on her and ruin the comfortable relationship they had enjoyed so far? But like him, the thought of the empty flat and spending Christmas alone had little or no appeal. She accepted.

After the concert they walked back in the warm balmy air. She had enjoyed it and been amused. Edward, his back ram-rod straight and wearing a tie and jacket, had sung along robustly with the rest of the crowd. Their hand-held candles hardly flickering in the still night air. She had attempted to join in but found her throat constricting with tears as she remembered past Christmases as a child, remembered her father and his love for this time of the year, remembering his laugh. Remembering her children and the excitement of it all.

Slowly they made their way back. At the entrance to the block of flats, Edward hesitated. "It's a beautiful evening and it's Christmas. Please join me for a glass of wine, my dear?"

She saw nothing but care and kindness in his soft brown eyes and relented, despite the promises she had made to herself not to get close to anyone ever again. Edward had kept his distance from her and behaved impeccably. "Thank you, that sounds lovely, Mr Kruger."

"Please call me Edward, my dear. I think we know each other well enough now?"

Whilst Edward busied himself with finding glasses and selecting a bottle of wine from his fridge, Sara looked around his flat. Although the furnishings were sparse the place was immaculate. As in the shop, there were lots of books everywhere but not a single photograph. There were a few paintings of ships and military battles gracing the walls, then a small painting propped against a pile of books caught her eye. She leaned forward and picked it up, feeling the beat of her heart ratchet up.

A young child was standing near an expanse of water which glittered in the sunlight, arms held aloft as if in worship, deep in the background was the silhouette of an elephant. She turned the frame over and clutched at the table to steady herself, the painting was called "*The Lost Child.*"

Sara, her legs unsteady, walked carefully out onto the wide balcony and sat in one of the two chairs, carefully avoiding the cushioned bench seat. The painting in her hand.

Edward brought the drinks out and placed them on the table, glancing at her with concern. "Are you alright, my dear? Are you feeling unwell?"

Sara shook her head, her smile unsteady. "I was admiring this little painting, Edward. It's exquisite, quite perfect."

"Yes, it's one of my favourites painted by an artist in Kenya called Jake Henderson."

He leaned forward and took it from her, staring at it fondly. "I've often wondered why that particular country, Kenya, attracted so many aristocratic Europeans. Lots of books been written about their antics over the years. They were called The Happy Valley crowd. Murders, affairs, drugs and general bad behaviour, but that was way back.

"Jake Henderson was born there, he was a brilliant artist, known internationally. Then one day he went out riding and never came back. All sorts of speculation about what happened to him. Anyway, I was

178

wandering around a gallery in London, some years ago, and I saw this and fell in love with the colours and the landscape.

"I thought the child looked vulnerable out there in the bush, close to the water's edge. So, I bought it. Jake Henderson's work became extremely collectable. I'm hoping it was a good investment. Not that I would ever sell it. I love my little lost child.

"Are you sure you're feeling alright, my dear, you look a little shaken. Is there anything I can get you?"

She shook her head and took a sip of her wine, listening to the faint sound of Christmas music coming from a neighbouring flat.

"I expect you find it odd spending Christmas in a hot country," he smiled at her contentedly, enjoying the unexpected company. "It always amuses me how families continue the European tradition of cooking a full festive feast in thirty degrees or more. That part of Christmas I don't miss."

"Have you no family, Edward?"

He shook his head. "Only my brother Johann, he lives in the Karoo."

"You never married then? No children?"

Again, he shook his head as he topped up her glass. "No, I was brought up in the Karoo, where there are more sheep than people. My family farmed sheep but when I grew up, I decided I didn't want to be a farmer. South Africa was going through a traumatic stage in its history. I joined the Defence Force and became a soldier, to fight for my country."

He looked up at the black sky, the stars tiny pin points of light. "I love this country Jenny. It's the most beautiful place on earth."

He shrugged his shoulders and took a sip of his wine. "It has its problems, like every country, but I wouldn't want to be anywhere else."

"I spent time in Angola and what was South West Africa, now Namibia. I liked being a soldier. I liked the discipline of the life."

He leaned back resting his head on the back of the chair for a few moments. "There were things about my life I'd never told anyone. Then one day I made a mistake. I met someone and thought the feeling was mutual, but I was wrong. From that moment on I was a target. Eventually I lost control and badly beat up a fellow officer - he died."

He looked at her impassive face and continued. "There was a Court Martial and I was found guilty, with mitigating circumstances, and sentenced to ten years in prison."

He laughed. "They say time flies but I can assure you when you're serving time the days crawl past!"

She nodded but remained silent. A curious coincidence.

"When I came out of prison I applied for many jobs. A further career in the military was out of the question. In desperation I came to Cape Town and having exhausted every other opportunity I decided to try and start my own music shop. My parents had died by this time and because they never forgave me for what I did, they left the farm to my brother."

A look of genuine regret passed over his face. "Johann and I had always been close and he felt I should have inherited half of the farm, so, being the decent man he is, he financed the buying and setting up of the shop. Have I shocked you?"

She shook her head. "Not really. I suppose one can reach a point when something snaps and consequently the price has to be paid. But why did you beat up a fellow officer, Edward?"

He twirled the liquid around in his glass and looked into its depths as though he might find the answer there. "Why did I kill him you mean? Well when I was a teenager, I discovered I wasn't attracted to women in any way. By joining the army, I had hoped I could be shaped into a real man but the opposite happened. As I said, I became a target and the bullying and abuse became intolerable. The officer pushed me too far and I lost my temper."

"Do you think God forgives someone who kills, Edward?" she asked him softly.

He raised a bushy eyebrow, looking surprised at her question. "I think he is a forgiving God. In a war situation, a soldier obeys orders and men kill each other. Out of a war situation, things are different. But, yes, I think he is a forgiving God. We Afrikaners are fiercely religious. My brother and I were brought up on the bible – my belief in God was the only thing that pulled me through my time in prison. Why do you ask?"

She looked down avoiding his eyes. "No reason. I was just curious. Do you regret what you did?"

"No. Sadistic bullies have no place in society. They contribute nothing. Some people deserve to die. I'm not proud of what I did because I'm not violent by nature. It happened and I paid my debt to society."

He looked at her over the rims of his glasses. "I'm going to put some music on, my dear, let's lighten the mood a little, shall we?"

180

She smiled absently, going over what he had told her. The first bars of a Mozart clarinet concerto filtered out into the night and she closed her eyes to listen.

*****

He sat down and watched her. Yes, he thought, we all have our secrets, our cross to carry in life and if he wasn't mistaken, this woman was carrying more than her fair share of sadness. She never talked about her family or her childhood, where she had lived. Either way he felt her real name was not Jenny Marshall.

Feeling his eyes on her she opened hers and looked steadily at him. "You have trusted me with your truth, Edward, and I know you're curious about mine. Perhaps one day I'll tell you. But not now. Thank you for the wine, I really must go now."

He walked her back to her flat and made sure she was safely in before he returned to his chair out on the balcony. The moon, like silver beaten to airy thinness, threw a shimmering light across the sea.

He had yet to ask her about the ship she had arrived on but he often thought about the newspaper article he had read. It was possible she knew something about the passenger who had disappeared. Another article had appeared in the local paper a few days later. The police were anxious to find another passenger called Annabel Courtney who had not returned to the same ship as the missing passenger. It was thought the couple were known to each other having been seen together on numerous occasions.

He re-filled his glass and put the empty bottle down next to his chair. He picked up the painting again, puzzled by Jenny's reaction to it.

Chapter Forty-Nine

Sara and Edward had become close over the past four months and his companionship filled the empty places in her life. Sometimes she would go to his flat and cook dinner for him, or they would go to the theatre, or walk through the busy waterfront and enjoy a cup of coffee together. Once she had discovered Edward would only ever ask of her to be his friend and companion, her fear of being approached sexually by him faded like the fiery sun now sinking into the blood red sea.

Edward took a sip of his coffee and sighed heavily. "I hope sales improve, Jenny, business this year has been slow. I've cut back expenses as much as possible. I don't know what else to do to improve the cash flow."

"As long as you don't get rid of my flat," she said with a nervous laugh, "I'll try not to worry too much."

She covered his hand with her own and gave it an encouraging squeeze. His familiar ram-rod straight back was now slightly stooped and his slim frame had become thinner as he worried over his future, or perhaps it was something else.

"Your friendship means a lot to me, Jenny. I thank God for the day you walked into my shop looking for somewhere to rent. Now let's cheer up a bit. It's your birthday tomorrow, you told me. I'm sure we can rustle up some funds to go out for dinner. There's a new Italian restaurant around the corner from the shop. It's not expensive. I'd like to take you there?"

"Let me cook something for you, Edward. No need for expensive restaurants, especially when things are a bit tight?"

Edward longingly watched a young tanned man saunter past their table. He sighed and turned to her. "I don't think any of us thinks one day we'll be old, it's a hard fact to face. But you're still a beautiful woman Jenny, if you don't mind me saying so, and yes, I would love you to cook dinner for me!"

She watched the crowds and envied the young teenagers, their glossy hair and arms laden with expensive designer bags, chatting and laughing without a care in the world. It was hard to think Charlie would have been a young adult by now. No, she couldn't think about it; if she did her well-structured emotional world would tumble down around her ears.

Chapter Fifty

The South Easter screamed its way up and down the streets of Cape Town, tossing plastic bags and newspapers high into the air. White clouds tumbled down over Table Mountain, then came a deluge of rain.

Edward shook his newspaper then folded it. He wasn't feeling well and the howling wind was rattling his nerves.

His phone growled on the table next to him.

"Edward Kruger."

"Mr Kruger? My name's Christopher. I think you might have an issue in your other flat. The ceiling of mine is starting to leak, I think your tenant might have a water problem somewhere, but there was no reply when I knocked at the door. Maybe you should check it out?"

Edward collected the key to Jenny's flat and made his way down the stairs. He had never been inside since she moved in. If there was a problem then it was his responsibility to sort it out, but he didn't feel comfortable about the situation.

He knocked on her door but only silence emanated from inside. He hesitated, knocked again more loudly, then let himself in. Jenny had left the balcony doors open, obviously not expecting the sudden change in the weather. The rain had saturated the floor and caused the problem with the tenant downstairs.

He struggled with the doors, battling with the strength of the wind. Then he turned to survey the damage. Nothing that couldn't be fixed with a bit of mopping up. He looked around the sparse room. No photographs, nothing personal at all. In the corner was a small easel, a canvas propped up with a work in progress. He had no idea Jenny was keen on painting, she'd never mentioned it to him.

He smiled as he remembered her reaction to his favourite piece "*The Lost Child.*" He walked over to take a closer look then stopped dead in his tracks. A small child next to a river. Nothing like his

184

painting, but the similarity was obvious. A small thread bear rabbit was leaning against the leg of the easel. A child's toy. He peered at the painting again, in the child's hand was the rabbit.

He mopped up the water then returned to his flat. Jenny would know he had been here; she would notice the now closed balcony doors, the damp floor. She would know he had seen the painting.

The mopping up had tired him. More so than usual. He picked up his painting and stared at it then sat down, thinking back over the past few months. Jenny's reluctance to talk about her life. Jenny's asking him if God was a forgiving God, her complete non-reaction when he mentioned he had spent time in prison. But her strong reaction to his painting.

He tapped the frame of the painting. Jenny had never asked him any questions about South Africa and now everything seemed to slot into place.

Of course, she hadn't. Jenny obviously already knew South Africa. She hadn't flinched, like most tourists did, when the noon day gun boomed over the city, sending pigeons scattering into the sky. Hadn't asked him what it was – because she already knew. Edward searched back in his excellent memory.

Now he knew exactly who she was.

Chapter Fifty-One
The Doctor

Karen O'Hara tapped her cigarette on the ashtray as she waited for her call to connect.

"Luc? It's Karen. Have you heard from Sara at all?"

She could hear the smile in his voice. "No, I haven't, but then I didn't expect to. You know the plan. It would be too dangerous."

"I know. But Sara promised to call in from an internet café' where an email wouldn't be traced. To let me know she was alright. I'm worried about her Luc."

"You always worry about her, but she's quite capable of taking care of herself. She'll be in touch when she's ready."

"Luc, this whole plan was to take no longer than six months. She's been gone nearly eight months' now and I am seriously worried. She wouldn't do this to me. Not after all we've been through together?"

"Let's give her a little more time Karen. She's off on her own private pilgrimage. Try not to worry okay? She'll be in touch when she's ready."

Luc put his phone down and looked out over the yachts bobbing in the harbour of Marseilles, where he now lived.

Unlike Karen, he knew what the problem was. Through his network he had heard about the missing Frenchman on the cruise ship en-route to Cape Town. Sara had not run off with him, of that he was quite certain. But she had been seen with this particular passenger on a couple of occasions his contact at the shipping office had told him. Whoever he was he must have recognised her.

He reached for his cigarettes. She might have no recollection of causing the death of her child Charlie. But must know something about the missing passenger.

Sara must have fled the ship in Cape Town and gone to ground. She wouldn't get away with another unexplained disappearance. The police would be all over her like mosquitoes.

Whatever Sara's plan was there was nothing he could do about it. He didn't know where she was either.

Chapter Fifty-Two

Edward was woken from his afternoon nap, by the loud rapid knocking on his door. He stood up and straightened his jumper, holding onto the back of the chair until the wave of pain had passed, then he took a deep breath and opened his door.

"Hello Jenny," he said tentatively, "here give me your jacket you're soaked." He hung it over the back of a chair and turned back to her. "Have a good day in this ghastly weather?

"Sit down and I'll make us some coffee; it'll warm you up a bit."

He watched her from the kitchen. She looked nervous, upset, and more than a little angry.

"Here we go." He handed her mug over then sat back down in his favourite chair with the view over the ocean.

He linked his hands around his mug. "Looks pretty wild out there doesn't it. Not a soul in sight. So, what have you been up to?"

Sara put her mug carefully down on the table. "Edward, someone's been into my flat. I left the balcony doors open, now they're shut. Did you go in?"

He blew on his coffee and took a tentative sip. "Yes, my dear. I'm sorry but I had no choice." He explained the situation.

"I had no idea you had such talent as an artist. No wonder you were taken with my painting."

She stared at him, saying nothing and he saw the emptiness in her eyes.

Then to his horror, she doubled over, hugging her shoulders as they shuddered. "Oh, God…"

He leaned across and squeezed her shoulder. "Please don't cry, my dear. I'm sorry I invaded your privacy, but I had no choice."

He stood and walked to the window, the steam from his coffee blurring the view. "Everyone has a secret, or two, Jenny. I'd like to help you if I can."

She stood up, ready to take flight, but he turned back to her and eased her gently back into the chair.

"Your name isn't Jenny is it?"

Her body seemed to shrink before his eyes. "Whatever you tell me, if you wish to tell me anything, will go no further. You have my word."

Sara dabbed at her eyes with his proffered handkerchief. "My name is Sara. It's a long story… and like you, I've paid for what I did, Edward. I need to go back to where it all happened."

He handed her the mug of coffee, she took a sip and continued. "I can't tell you why there is all this secrecy. Not yet. But it's terribly important no-one knows where I am, who I am. There are too many people involved, you see?"

Edward nodded. "It's alright Sara. You'll tell me when you're ready, if you want to."

He looked at his watch. "Tell you what, how about a glass of wine? I think you promised me dinner, happy birthday, by the way, although it doesn't seem to have been one so far does it?"

He smiled at her. "Come on, choose a nice bottle of wine, I'll close the curtains and put on some lights, the weather seems to be closing in again."

He came back into the kitchen rubbing his hands. "Now, what are we having for dinner? I'll help you if you like, I'm good at peeling potatoes?"

He lifted his wine glass to her. "Here's to you, my dear, and here's to our friendship. Happy Birthday!"

"Thank you, Edward," she gave him a shaky smile, and touched his glass with her own. "Here's to our friendship."

Chapter Fifty-Three

The next morning, Monday, Sara woke feeling lighter. Perhaps one day she would tell Edward her story, he was one person she knew would understand – but not yet. They were meeting at eleven and going down to the waterfront for brunch. The skies were once again clear and the wind had stopped its endless rampage through the streets of the city.

When he had not arrived at her door by midday, she became concerned. Edward was always punctual.

She knocked loudly on his door. "Edward, it's me. Is everything alright with you?"

Silence greeted her, she knocked again. Looking around to ensure she wasn't being watched she reached inside the pot of a lush potted fern and retrieved the spare front door key.

"Edward? It's me. Where are you?"

The two empty glasses sat unwashed next to the sink, the only sound in the room was the repetitious tick of his old-fashioned clock. Sara called out his name again. Silence.

He surely would not have gone out for brunch on his own? They had a date. "Edward?"

Sara pushed the half-opened door to his bedroom. He was lying on his back with his eyes closed, a half smile on his face. A raw sound escaped from her lips.

"Oh, Edward....!"

She touched his cold hand and looked at him. Knowing it was futile she shook his arm gently. "Oh, Edward," she whispered again.

She sat on the bed holding his hand knowing yet another chapter in her life was over. She closed the bedroom door behind her. Sara washed the glasses, putting them carefully away in the kitchen cupboard along with the empty bottle of wine. She looked around; there was nothing to indicate Edward had had company the night before. Letting herself out of his flat she placed the key inside the fern and walked back to her own.

The last thing she wanted to do was call the police. They would want statements and probably ask a lot of questions. She knew they would ask her for some kind of identification, of which she had none she was prepared to produce. She wanted as little to do with the police as possible.

That evening she sat in her flat fully aware Edward was lying dead in his bedroom. She would miss him. Her only friend in South Africa had gone and her world without him was already shrinking. Numbly, she sat sipping a glass of water. It was all over. Perhaps it was safe enough now to head towards the Eastern Cape. It was time.

"Forgive me, Edward," she whispered to the silence.

*****

The following evening there was a rapid knocking on her door, an unsmiling policeman was standing there.

"Yes, officer, how may I help you? Has something happened in the building?"

"Good Evening, Madam. This is the flat belonging to Mr Edward Kruger?" He removed his hat and tucked it under his arm.

She nodded.

"We had a call from his brother who was concerned he couldn't get him on the phone at home. We checked with the other tenants and no-one seems to have seen him around today. Unfortunately, we had to break down the door to his flat to check if he was alright."

She raised her eyebrows. "Is he alright?"

The young policeman cleared his throat. "I'm afraid Mr Kruger has passed away. There are no reasons for us to be suspicious about the circumstances of his death. His brother told us he was ill, and had been for some months."

He took a notepad out of his top pocket. "It looks as though he died in his sleep. But an autopsy will confirm it. His brother asked us to let you know, as his tenant, about his death?"

"Thank you, Officer. I'm sorry to hear this. I didn't know him well, but he was a pleasant enough landlord. I've only been here a few months."

The policeman made a note on his pad and replaced it in his top pocket. "I'm sure Mr Kruger's brother will be in touch with you. Thank you." He turned to go, then frowning he turned back, and scrutinised her face.

"May I see your ID book please, Madam?"

She spread her hands out in front of her. "I'm sorry officer, my handbag was snatched in town a few days ago. My ID book, passport and wallet…everything gone. Sorry." She gave an apologetic shrug of her shoulders.

He scribbled something in his notebook.

"You have a case number for your stolen handbag?"

"Um, no, not yet. I'll do it tomorrow."

"Please let me have it. May I have your full name?"

"Yes, of course. Jennifer Marshall."

She took his proffered card hoping he couldn't hear the rapid beating of her heart in the quietness of the hallway.

He turned smartly on his heel and left.

Sara leaned against the closed door. If the young policeman put her name into the system, he would soon realise Jenny Marshall didn't exist. She wandered out onto the balcony and sat down. No. There would be other Jenny Marshall's living in South Africa.

He had given her a long hard look though. She would have to leave Cape Town as soon as possible after Edward's funeral.

Four days after the death of his brother, Johann, arrived at the flat. A taller, rounder version of his older brother. "You must be Jenny? I'm Johann, Edward's brother."

She held out her hand. "I'm sorry to hear about your brother's death. It was such a shock. We'd become good friends."

"*Ja*, it was a big shock, but he had been ill for some months, so not unexpected. Perhaps I could come in?"

Flustered she opened the door wider. "Of course, please come in, let's sit out on the balcony. I'm sure you'll enjoy the view after the dry Karoo and all those sheep!"

He looked briefly at the ocean then turned to her. "The flat Edward lived in belongs to me, but I won't be selling it. Perhaps one day I will sell the family farm and come and live here." He looked out over the traffic snarled up on the main road and the seething pedestrians crowding the pavements and the promenade.

"But perhaps not. I prefer the silence of the Karoo. Anyway, the flat will remain empty until such time as I make a decision for its future. This one, however, I will be selling."

"I see," she murmured.

Johann looked at the woman across the table. I'm sorry," he said gently "I'd like you to stay until it's sold, if this is acceptable to you?"

She nodded. "I was thinking of leaving Cape Town in the next month or so anyway. So, yes that's fine with me. I'll let you know when I'll be leaving."

"Edward wanted you to have this." He handed her a carefully wrapped small square package. "I found it with his papers."

Sara took it wordlessly, deciding to open it when Johann left.

*****

Now she stared at the small painting of the young child standing on a jetty at the edge of a lake, holding its arms up to the sun as if in supplication. A letter was enclosed with the painting.

Dearest Sara

I want you to have this. I'm not sure what it would be worth today. But perhaps one day it may help you.

Your friendship meant a great deal to me and I thank you for it. What I didn't disclose to you, because I wanted you to do this in your own time, when you felt ready, was that I have known for some time of your history. Cape Town is a sophisticated city and it's not difficult to research someone's past – if they have one. It took me a long time to go through old newspapers, and the internet, looking for clues to what happened to you.

You see, when I first met you and we became friends I realised you had lived in South Africa before, and spent time in Cape Town. Nothing obvious, but you didn't ask the usual questions someone new to the country would ask, and, of course, I knew your real name long before you told me last night. But, as I said, I wanted you to tell me your story in your own words, but only when you felt comfortable enough to do this.

I would imagine to lose a child, whatever the circumstances, is the cruellest cut of all for a mother. I remember your case well.

Prison was hard enough for me, but I did kill someone and deserved to pay the full price. For you to lose your child and be charged with murder is beyond my imagination. My thoughts are you have come back to this country to search for the memory of the baby you lost, something you will have to live with for the rest of your life.

Tonight, after you left, I decided the painting should be yours after my death which I fear is not far off. I have been ill for some time now. I'm looking forward to the day when you tell me all about yourself, however you will only inherit this when I have gone. I'm putting it with my private papers which my brother will find, but even so I wanted to write this letter to you tonight.

Now I have gone and you are looking at this charming painting which the artist called "The Lost Child," it is my gift to you to do with as you will. Goodbye my dearest Sara. You deserve to be happy after everything you have been through and this is my only wish for you.

Enclosed in this package are the keys to my car. You will find it impossible to hire one under your assumed names. Using your real name, Sara Saunders, may set a few bells off. After all you're supposed to be dead as well!

The car is parked in the underground parking bay. It's a small white Toyota, the registration number is with the keys.

Johann is unaware that I own a car, so you will be safe.

Edward

Sara held the little portrait close to her chest as the tears slid down her face.

*****

She stood with Johann at the graveside and watched the gravediggers cover the coffin with wet soil. Gale force winds once again ripped over the Cape peninsula bringing the lashing rain with it. She pulled her jacket around her and stared unseeingly at the coffin until it was covered, then she turned and walked slowly away.

Like Edward, it was time for her to make her final journey.

Chapter Fifty-Four

M iss Harrington hung up her jacket and placed her handbag in the office cupboard. It was good to be back. She was always available to fill in when secretaries went on leave, or had their babies, or resigned.

The secretary at the British Embassy had called her in to archive documents and generally put some order back into the bulging filing cabinets and the tall piles of even more documents.

She pulled up her sleeves and rubbed her hands together, working out where she should begin. Large boxes lined one of the walls and into these would go old files which would be shipped back to the United Kingdom where, no doubt, she thought, they would end up on the dusty shelves of some ancient building.

Each file would have to be gone through then referenced, the relevant information loaded into the computer, then placed alphabetically in the boxes.

It was in her second week at the Embassy when she opened one of the old files and found Eza's letter. She frowned at the childish writing on the envelope then smiled at the address: ***The White Chief Miles, Head of the British People, Cape Town.***

Probably a school child doing some kind of project maybe. Miss Harrington turned to her computer and did some research.

The letter was clearly intended for Sir Miles Courtney who had retired and left the country some years ago. She wondered how long the letter had been lying in a totally unrelated file, the subject of which was the up and coming State visit of the Prime Minister of the United Kingdom at the time.

Miss Harrington was tempted to open the letter and see if a follow up would be necessary, but she hesitated. Opening someone's private mail, whether from a child or an adult, went strictly against her belief of a person's right to privacy.

She would send it on to London in the diplomatic pouch which went out every night and ask for it to be forwarded to Sir Miles Courtney. He would be quite elderly by now she thought, checking his personal details on the computer. But he might find it amusing to receive a child's letter from when he served Her Majesty's Government in the Republic of South Africa.

In the top right-hand corner of the envelope she addressed it correctly: *Sir Miles Courtney – please forward.* Then she put the official Embassy stamp on it and put it on top of the paperwork leaving on this evening's flight for London.

Sir Miles would find the letter anything but amusing.

Chapter Fifty-Five
The Ambassador

Sir Miles leaned heavily on his cane as he lowered himself into the chair close to the fire. Maggie sat down next to him and put her slightly greying muzzle on his knee.

Sir Miles stroked her head, more out of habit than anything else, and reached for his newspaper. He was lonely down here in Dorset, finding the journey to London becoming more difficult with each visit. The crowds pushing their way through the train barriers, the long wait in the queue for a taxi to take him to his club and the endless traffic, the intolerable noise.

Perhaps he should think about renting a flat near his club, at least he would have some company there amidst retired Diplomats and Civil Servants.

Ben wouldn't want to move out of London to come and live in the house. He and Linda enjoyed their odd week-ends there with him, but he knew Linda wouldn't want to live here, once they were married, whilst Ben commuted back and forth to London and his job. She enjoyed her life in London and Ben wouldn't have the time or the patience to do the two-hour commute there and back.

Miles had a cleaning lady, Emma, who came in once a week. It was the one day of the week he ate properly. Emma would prepare his dinner leaving it for him to warm up when he was ready to eat. Apart from that he had ready-made meals, shopped for by Emma.

He would lock the place up and Emma could come in each week and keep her eye on things.

He looked down at Maggie. "You wouldn't mind would you, old girl. Lots of parks in London, new things to sniff at and lots of dogs to play with along the way. I think that's what we'll do Maggie – go and live in London. I can eat at the Club with the other members. We can pop back here for the odd week-end when we feel like it."

Maggie's deep bark startled the peace of the house. Sir Miles waited as he heard the letterbox clang shut. "Go fetch the post Maggie. Only be a pile of bills, maybe The Spectator. Off you go."

Maggie came back, the post clamped between her soft jaws and stood in front of Sir Miles, her tail wagging.

He leaned forward and took the letters. "Thank you, Maggie. Now let's see what we have here."

He flicked through the mail, half of it went into the waste paper basket next to his chair. The bills he put to one side. One envelope remained, from the Foreign Office in London. He lifted the flap and pulled out another envelope.

His eyebrows lifted in surprise. A letter from a child in Cape Town?

He smiled. Probably someone asking for money whilst he was stationed there. The letter had obviously lost its way over the years. He slid his thumb under the thin cheap flap and pulled out the letter from Eza.

Greetings,

It is I, Eza. Many rainy seasons ago you are coming to my village where you are meeting with our Chief. To this Chief you are giving your house in the bush and the land on which it is standing. The Chief was most pleased with this gift.

Before the rainy season is coming your daughter is coming to live in this your house which was to be given to the Chief, when you go to meet your white ancestors. Also, in this house was an African woman called Beauty. It was Beauty who looked after the two small ones, when Missus Sara was busy with making her things with beads and selling them to the place where many people come, from across the seas to see our animals in the bush.

The Chief's son, Joseph, went sometimes to check on this house but did not disturb your family there, they did not know he is being amongst the trees near the river watching. He saw many things which troubled him.

When the fires came, they were burning all around, and now, I am sorry to tell you that you and the Chief are only having one burnt house with the land.

This was being a very bad time for your daughter and the two small ones, for at this time the smallest child went missing and was not found. The Police searched for this child but it was gone. My own

198

boyhood friend Sipo, also looked for this lost child when it was with the police he was working. Sipo has also gone to be with his ancestors.

The Police they are taking your daughter away to this place with the flat mountain, they are saying she killed the small child. They are taking her and putting her in a prison for people with bad things in their heads. They are saying she cannot see her other child because she might hurt this one as well.

I do not know where the other boy is staying now. Perhaps he is in this place for children, this place where kind people take small children and give them food, where there is only a little love for them because there are many children in this place and not enough love for all.

It is I, Eza, who knows the truth of what happened to the little one. Joseph also know this truth, for he was the one who told me. From this place where he was hiding, he saw what he saw.

The mother did not kill her child.

It is with sadness I must tell you the old Chief has died. His son Joseph, who is my cousin, is now the Chief. But what use is this when the new Chief has no people left to be the Chief for?

When the rains did not come for many many months, the people are going to the town to look for work and food. My village is dying. I too must leave this village with my wife and children to find a place where there is money and food. The new Chief will also have to leave here and take his goats and sheep to another place where the rain is coming, but he will no longer be the chief of any place.

There is only your burnt house left there now. The bush will take this burnt house and cover it with the wild bushes and it will be forgotten.

I am sorry for your troubles.

Greetings from Eza.

Sir Miles read the letter over and over again. Then held it to his aching chest and closed his eyes. Was this person Eza telling the truth? Did he make the whole thing up about Sara not killing Charlie? Maybe to extract some money from him?

He read the letter again. No, there was someone out there who knew the truth. Sara had not killed her child. His Sara who had gone to prison for something she had not done and he, her own father, had turned his back on her. Found her as guilty as the Judge who had sentenced her.

He felt the unusual sensation of his eyes prickling with tears. He let them fall. Maggie whimpered with concern, nudging Sir Miles' hands with her muzzle, licking the wetness from the back of them.

"Oh, God, Maggie. If this letter is to be believed then a terrible wrong must be put right."

He reached an unsteady hand out for his phone and stabbed in the private number of his lawyer, James Storm. He didn't waste his words.

"James? Miles here. I need to see you urgently? Tomorrow if possible?"

With the promise of his lawyer arriving the next day, he poured himself a large whisky and sat down again. He picked up his address book until he found the number he was looking for.

The receptionist put him through. "This is Doctor O'Hara?"

"Doctor O'Hara, its Sara's father here. Miles Courtney."

"Good afternoon Sir Miles, I trust you are well?" He ignored the coldness in her voice. She had every reason to dislike him.

He cleared his throat, holding Eza's letter in his trembling hands. "Where is Sara?"

He heard the sharp intake of her breath. "Sir Miles are you sure you're alright? I know you didn't come to the memorial service, but I'm afraid this doesn't make it any more unreal. Sara has gone from us. You must accept this. Look, is there someone I can call? Someone who could pop around and see you?"

"Please don't patronise me Doctor O'Hara!" He tried to rein in his anger.

"I know Sara isn't dead! I didn't come to the memorial service because I knew the whole suicide thing was a farce. Sara wanted to disappear. She wanted to go back to South Africa. I now have reason to believe she didn't kill Charlie. I think I'm holding proof of this in my hand right now."

There was silence at the end of the phone. "Are you still there?"

"Yes, I'm still here, Sir Miles. I don't know what to say to you."

"Then listen. Sara called me before she disappeared. She told me what was going to happen. She didn't want me to live with her lie. I gave her my word I would go along with it, even though it would make me complicit in the eyes of the law. I didn't agree with it, but with Sara I knew there was no use fighting any of her decisions."

Sir Miles took a deep shaking breath. "I was interviewed by the police, after Sara disappeared from the care home. I told the truth then, before she called me."

200

Karen gave an audible sigh. "Sara loves you Sir Miles, despite your tempestuous relationship. She didn't want you to suffer in any way. I suppose we have to trust you to keep your word?"

He exploded. "Of course, you can damn well trust me!" he tried to calm down, ease his blood pressure. "I need to know something and it's important. More than important. Did Sara ever admit to you she had killed Charlie. You two were close. If you had asked her, she would have told you the truth. Did you ask her?"

"Yes, I did ask her, of course I did."

"So, when you asked her, what did she say?"

"She said it was impossible for her to believe she had killed her child, drugged or not. That's all she would say, nothing more. She wouldn't talk about it."

Sir Miles took a large gulp of his drink, thinking rapidly. "Doctor O'Hara I must find Sara, it's urgent. I have a letter here from someone called Eza. I knew the Chief from his village. In fact, I left him my house there, the house Sara fled to after the unsavoury business with her ex-husband Simon. Did Sara ever mention the name Eza?"

"No. I would have remembered a name like that."

"Eza tells me the Chief's son Joseph was in the area on the day Charlie disappeared. He tells me Sara didn't kill the child."

He heard her breathing heavily. "But how can you trust this letter and what's written there? I would like to believe it Sir Miles, of course I would, but this is no proof at all? When was this letter written, what date?"

"There is no date on the letter but I think Eza is telling the truth. I *must* find my daughter," his voice broke. "Please help me?"

He heard the sound of a siren screaming past her window, then there was silence again. "Sara did go back to South Africa it's true. She promised to keep in touch to let me know she was alright. The problem is she hasn't. She seems to have disappeared."

There was silence at the end of the phone. "Are you still there, Sir Miles?"

"Yes. I think Sara is out there somewhere. Despite what you think, I do know my daughter. She's gone undercover for some reason."

"So, what are you going to do?"

Sir Miles rubbed his aching knee. "I'm going to use one of my contacts. Someone I trust implicitly. I'll protect Sara's wish to lie low. But I shall find her. I think Sara will, at some stage, go back to the Eastern Cape."

"But why Sir Miles, what's there to go back for?"

"Sara was an excellent war correspondent, fearless, you told me."

He tapped his glass on the arm of his chair. "She'll go back to the Eastern Cape.

"Sara's going back to find the truth about what really happened. That's what she does, right? Her whole career was built on that premise.

"I know her relationship with Ben became impossible. They were almost strangers to each other. I know she severed all her ties with him, and he with her. Even so it's extremely difficult to accept. I must carry the burden of knowing the truth and not be able to tell him.

"But I made a promise to Sara, rightly or wrongly. One way or another she is dead to him. I think she thought it would be better that way, maybe to give him a chance to put everything behind him and get on with his life, without her hovering over him and reminding him of what happened. Perhaps a loving gesture on her part? Her final gift to him?

"If she can heal herself, find some peace in her life, it will be more than any father could wish for. But we must find her."

*****

Karen paced the room, puffing nervously on a cigarette. How on earth was Sir Miles going to track Sara down, and more to the point, how would he protect her, Karen? It was a serious offence to lie to the police. Just how much had Sara told her father? How much of the truth?

She knew she would have to go back to Sir Miles' house, sooner rather than later, and try to find out exactly what he did and didn't know. More than anything she wanted to read the mysterious letter from this person called Eza.

She sat down abruptly, fumbling with the gold cross around her neck. No, she had only told the police Sara was suicidal, had talked about it, then disappeared and presumably killed herself. Yes, she had lied to them. But they would have to prove it.

Her hand shook as she lit another cigarette. Despite all her best efforts to help Sara she knew her friend was far from accepting what had happened and was capable of doing anything. She was a long way off leading a normal life.

Karen squashed down her next thought as fiercely as she ground out her cigarette.

202

Sir Miles' lawyer, James Storm, sat back in his first-class compartment on the train and watched the rolling countryside slide past his window, his clients changed Will tucked safely in his leather briefcase.

He looked down at his expensive black coat and frowned. A fastidious man by nature, but like most English men, fond of dogs. But his client's dog Maggie seemed to love to share her fur coat with all and sundry. Sir Miles' beautiful home with its faded furniture had not escaped Maggie's largesse. Nothing escaped unscathed.

As he picked off each piece of golden fur, his thoughts went back to the meeting with Sir Miles. At first, he thought his old friend might be losing his marbles when he told him the changes he wished to make to his Will.

Families, he thought to himself, thank God he had never gone down that road. Sir Miles had given him another envelope which was not to be opened until his death. Of course, he would respect his wishes, but he was intrigued.

He picked another clump of fur off his coat, closed his eyes and fell asleep to the soothing clack of wheels on the rails and the swaying of the carriages.

Chapter Fifty-Six
The Daughter

The small aircraft lined up for landing on the dirt airstrip out in the middle of the bush. The trees and thick bushes sped past Kia's small window as it began its descent then rapidly lifted into the air again. The passengers looked at each other smiling nervously, then looked down to see what the problem might be.

The plane banked then turned around swooping low over a group of impala. Startled they scattered in all directions, leaping and springing into the air like seasoned ballet dancers.

The pilot brought the plane around again and landed. The plane bumped and jumped, rattling over the corrugations of the baked earth, then came to a halt, a cloud of red dust in its wake.

The pilot turned and smiled at her five passengers. "Sorry about that, the animals sometimes like to lie around on the airstrip, we have to clear them off before we can land. She undid her safety belt, her fingers busy with the post flight checks, flicking switches and pressing buttons. "Here we are. Welcome to the bush!"

She slid her window open and opened the door, the propellers slowed to a stop. Jumping down she opened the passenger door and lowered a short flight of steps for her passengers to disembark.

The waiting lodge vehicle made its way from the shade of a tree and pulled up next to the assembled, somewhat relieved, passengers and their luggage.

Kia dropped her cameras onto an empty seat and climbed into the vehicle. With the luggage now stowed the ranger hopped into the driver's seat and turned to introduce himself to his guests.

"Hi, I'm George. We're going to wait a few moments so your pilot can take off again. Once she's safely on her way we'll head for the lodge."

The two American couples smiled happily now they were safely back on the ground, on terra firma.

"Slightly smoother landing on the big jet." One of men said laughing. "Nearly had a heart attack with that landing!"

George smiled at him. "Yes, it can come as a bit of surprise. No time to warn passengers when a bunch of animals decide to take a snooze on our airstrip. We have to turn the flight, then swoop back over them to get them to shove off."

George smiled at Kia. "You must be Kia, Jabu's sister. He wanted to come and meet the flight but got caught up with other things at the lodge. He's been bouncing around with excitement since he heard you were coming to visit! I believe you are our VIP?"

Kia grinned at him. "Yes, I can imagine he's a bit excited. Its three years since we've seen each other, so quite an occasion. VIP hey? Nice thought, but I'm here to work for the magazine. We're doing a feature on the lodge, as you know."

George waited until the aircraft had lifted off into a cloudless sky, then turned on the ignition and headed slowly back to the lodge.

Kia breathed in the dry smell of wood, wild sage, trees and dusty dirt roads. It was too hot for many of the animals to be out. George pointed out giraffe, impala, kudu and warthogs. The Americans clicked away with their cameras, pointing to things in the distance, as excited as children on Christmas Day.

Kia smiled. The magic of the bush. It worked every time. Even the most hardened international businessman seemed to soften at the first sighting of the elegant haughty giraffe, or the gentle pantomime look of the zebra, with their soft brown eyes and long eyelashes. Kia always had the desire to throw a saddle over the back of one of them and gallop off into the bush.

Slowly George brought the vehicle to a halt and turned off the engine. A troop of baboons sat in a dry river bed, busy with their grooming. A big female leaned over her mate, meticulously parting his fur searching for ticks and other parasites. The younger ones cavorted around their parents, chasing each other around the rocks and through the trees. A lone male sat high on a rock watching for danger. Suddenly he raised himself up on his haunches and gave a sharp bark. His troop scattered into the trees and rocks, rapidly hiding themselves from danger.

"There's a leopard around," whispered George, his experienced eyes searching the surrounding bush.

The bush was silent except for the ticking of the hot engine as it cooled down. Finding no leopard, not the easiest animal to spot, George started the engine again.

Kia prayed there wouldn't be any enthusiastic bird watchers on board, they were the worst of all, making the ranger stop every time a bird was sighted. It would be a mind- numbing drive if this were the case. She glanced at the Americans, no-one seemed to be clutching a bird book or any binoculars, no twitchers on board. The Americans were probably more of the big five type. Elephant, rhino, lion, leopard and buffalo, and for the amount of money they would have paid for this safari they fully expected to see them.

Kia smiled to herself. If anyone could find them it would be her brother Jabu. He could find anything in the bush, big or small, even the tiny dung beetle, battling its way along pushing and rolling dung, fifty times its size, would not escape his trained eyes, or the busy activity of ants, who marched with such purpose, although what the purpose was, no human was capable of fully understanding.

Tonight, around the camp fire, sipping cocktails before dinner, the Americans would sit chatting as smoke from the fire billowed over them. There would be a bit of coughing and spluttering, their eyes would be streaming, but still they would sit, having the great adventure under an African sky. The vast stretches of bush turning gold in the evening sun. The smoke would pervade their lungs probably causing more damage than a life time of smoking unfiltered cigarettes. These same Americans who would be outraged if someone lit up a cigarette anywhere near them in America.

Something happened to people in the bush. Years of civilisation seemed to peel away from them, making them more human somehow, bringing out their more basic instincts.

All the guests wanted to see a kill. Hearing the thunder of hooves across the bush, a female lion crouching in the bush with only her ears visible, then the chase as the lioness gained on a panic-stricken buck as it zig-zagged across the plains, separated from its herd. Its hooves thudding in terror as it tried to outrun the big hungry cat. The other females flanking each side to ensure there is no escape.

The lioness leaping onto its back, bringing it down kicking and bucking until it collapsed, then sinking her jaws into its throat until it lay still. The cameras would click and whirr as the guests watched the male saunter up and take his fill of meat first, before allowing his

206

females and cubs to share the kill, tearing into the still warm body, their jaws and beards bloodied and dripping.

Most people in the civilised world, Kia thought, would avert their eyes rather than confront the bloodied bodies of fellow human beings involved in a car crash, choosing not to look at death strewn on a highway somewhere. But not out here in the bush.

Afterwards the hyenas would circle for what was left of the kill, skulking and giggling in the shadows waiting for the pride to leave. High up in the trees the vultures would rhythmically goose-step, waiting impatiently for their turn.

Kia picked up one of her cameras, tapping George on the shoulder and pointing up into a tree. He stopped the vehicle, lifting his binoculars.

The leopard was draped along the branch, one leg hanging languidly, his face resting on his paws, the size of small side plates. The dappled sunshine through the leaves giving him all the natural camouflage he needed.

"Oh my," whispered one of the Americans, awestruck, "he's magnificent."

The leopard lifted his head, sensing them. Then he yawned widely and resumed his nap.

Not bad Kia, my girl, she thought to herself. You might not be as good as your brother but you're not bad. She had spotted the leopard before the ranger.

Smugly she took a few more shots. Jabu would be proud of his little sister.

Chapter Fifty-Seven

Jabu carried his sister's small safari bag to her suite, Kia following along behind, her keen photographer's eye missing nothing. The path through the discreetly hidden suites with their decks overlooking the water hole, was well swept, hurricane lamps lined the sides ready for nightfall. A slight breeze blew discarded leaves in their wake, crisp and curled from the dry summer heat.

Jabu had not stopped grinning since he met her at the impressive entrance to the lodge. He seemed taller to her and as handsome in his ranger uniform as he had always been. He had picked her up and swung her around, so pleased was he to see his little sister.

"We've put you in our honeymoon suite, Kia, so you can get a feel for the place. The owners of the lodge are expecting great things from you for their exclusive in your magazine. So, no sitting around and admiring the view! I'm to be your personal guide whilst you work, so we can spend plenty of time together."

He lifted his hand and flicked her braids. "Still the same hairstyle I see. I thought Cape Town might have changed that. Made you more modern."

"I happen to like my braids, brother dear, I don't have to bother tying it up or back, easier to work with."

Jabu stopped at the last tented suite, put her suitcase down and unzipped the entrance. "Here we go!"

She looked around the white canvas suite. "Wow! This is what I call camping. How fabulous is this? It will make a great feature!"

Sumptuous furnishing and fabrics, with natural coir matting covering the floor and a private sundeck overlooking the water hole, the perfect spot to watch the animals as they came down to drink.

Heavy wooden chests featured brass corner pieces, two old leather suitcases and a hat box stood in the corner, a round ochre clay pot full of guinea fowl feathers next to them. The centre piece of the suite was the carved wooden double bed with its embroidered white cotton covers, turquoise silk cushions and bolsters and swathes of soft white gauzy mosquito netting suspended from a wood frame hung from the rafters, like a bridal gown.

Kia wandered into the bathroom. A claw footed bath looked out onto the endless savannah through sheer glass from top to bottom. A Butler's tray held soaps, creams and lotions, and a colourful beaded container for shampoos and conditioners. A plush chaise longue, artfully draped with a soft blanket and a dressing gown enhanced the exquisite room.

Out on the private deck a beaten copper topped round table held binoculars, a brass hurricane lamp, and two comfortable looking chintz armchairs either side.

On the edge of the deck another low round table, a constellation of candles of all sizes nestled in a silver tray. When night fell, they would cast a halo of light around the deck whilst not detracting from the deep navy skies with their promise of a staggering display of heavenly lights.

"A bit different from camping out under the stars in our village." Jabu murmured behind her, making her jump.

"Seems like a hundred years ago, Jabu. Show me the rest of the lodge, if it's anything like this suite, it'll be a joy to work with."

As he walked her through the rest of the lodge, Kia made notes, quiet corners with cushions embedded in the base of a tree, a small library looking more like an English private club with deep green leather chairs studded with brass.

An elegant dining room, tables laid with silver candelabra and crystal glassware, napkin holders and condiments again featuring the bright Ndebele beads. The tablecloths impossibly white, bowls of pale roses nestling in ceramic bowls. The inside and outside lounges with invitingly comfortable chairs, low carved tables with binoculars and telescopes mounted on tripods trained on the water hole where thirsty animals would assemble to quench their thirst after another hot day in the bush.

Returning to Kia's suite they settled in the armchairs on the deck. A cold bottle of wine nestled in a silver ice bucket, condensation sliding down the sides, had been delivered whilst they were on the inspection tour.

Jabu lifted the bottle and wrapped a snowy white napkin around the neck before pouring the wine into crystal glasses. "So, my little sister is now working for one of the most prestigious magazines in the country. I'm proud of you Kia."

Kia grinned at him. "And you're one of the best game rangers in the country. Quite a jump from being a tracker hey! Other lodges trying to head hunt you, I hear?"

"Yeah, it does happen. It's a tough job though. Might look glamorous, but the hours are long and hard. No social life to speak of, we have to stay until the last guest has gone to bed which is mostly fairly early, but there are always some who stay up 'til the early hours. Then we rangers have to be up at five to prepare for the early game drives. But I love it. Life in the bush is all I ever wanted. So, yes from tracker to game ranger. I have my sights set on managing this lodge one day. It might take a couple of years but it's my goal."

"No girlfriends then Jabu?" she asked innocently.

He laughed. "I get hit on by guests sometimes. The bush seems to bring out the animal in some women. There was one wealthy American woman, older than me, she wanted me to go back to New York with her! Can you imagine?"

"Did you think about it at all?"

"Not for a second! Can you picture me wandering around a city in a suit? I've never even travelled out of South Africa, nor do I wish to. Anyway, I have a girlfriend. I'm not sure if it will evolve into anything. I don't see her often enough. I'm definitely not giving up my job to live in town, and although we're allowed to have girlfriends to stay now and again in the staff quarters, having someone permanently living here is against the rules."

Kia smacked her leg then peeled the mosquito off her leg, leaving a faint smear of blood. "Bloody mosquitoes, I hate them. I mean what was God thinking when he made them? They're rubbish. They're not good for anything, they don't contribute anything!"

She took a sip of her ice-cold wine. "I mean did God sit there one day and create them? What did he say, do you think?

"Hmm, I think I'll make a little black thing with striped legs, and it will carry a disease of some sort. I'll make them super intelligent so they can squeeze through miniscule holes in a mosquito net, find one tiny pore not covered in two inches of insect repellent, and give them a high-pitched zinging noise which will wake the dead. I think I'll do spiders next. Now, where's my goblet of wine. I need another drink!"

Tears of laughter streamed down Jabu's cheeks. "I didn't know you had developed a sense of humour Kia. You didn't have much of one before. Always so serious."

Kia smiled at him. "Yes, I suppose I was. We had an odd sort of life when I look back, but I'm grateful to the Templetons for everything they did for us. I still keep in touch with them, not as often as I should, but I hope they understand. It took a bit of an effort for them to settle back in England from what I can gather.

"Have you seen Mama at all Jabu?"

He shook his head. "I feel guilty about it, but I don't have the time. Have you seen her?"

"Months ago. I also feel guilty. Mama can hardly see at all now. I think she misses being able to sew. I knew there was something wrong. She said so little and seemed a little confused as to who I was. It was good of the Templetons to make all the arrangements for her and pay for everything. But I blame Papa for some of it, up and leaving her like that. I don't think I can forgive him for not coming back."

Jabu leaned back and looked up at the darkening sky, lapsing back into the Griqua language of his childhood, the soft and lilting words peppered with clicks and strange sounds only they could understand.

"I think Papa's heart was broken when the village people left, he couldn't adapt to living in a town. He couldn't find a job. I think he felt it would be a noble thing to leave and not be a burden on his family. I think he went back to the desert of the San people. He won't return. But he'll remember us and give thanks to the ancestors."

"Bugger the ancestors Jabu, and stop speaking in that language. Speak English for goodness sake! The old world our parents belonged to has long gone. I don't want to be part of it anymore. For God's sake they didn't even know how old we were! The Templetons had to hazard a guess!"

Jabu held up his hands in surrender. "Okay, don't get mad at me. You did ask?"

His eyes traversed her face and he sighed. "You and I are so different in many ways, Kia..."

He shook his head and stood up. "Come on drink up. Let's go and eat. I expect you'll want to be up at the crack of dawn to start your work. I've booked one of the vehicles so we can get going on a game drive as soon as you're ready. I know you want some animal shots. I've organised with the Chef to have a cold box for us to take with us. I'll personally cook you breakfast in the bush – how's that?"

Kia jumped up. "Sounds fabulous. I think I'll have an early night in that case. I'm feeling a bit bushed after the trip from Cape Town."

Arm in arm they walked down the now hurricane lit pathway to the dining room. "What about you Kia, have you anyone in your life?"

"Nope. I've had a couple of flings but nothing came of them. Anyway, I'm planning a trip to England in the next month or two, who knows who I might meet!

"I want to see the Templetons whilst I'm over there and maybe see a bit of the country. It'll be my first trip out of South Africa.

"I'll take some shots of you out in the bush wearing your smart uniform. They'll be keen to see how you turned out. What you look like now. Maybe someone could take some photographs of us together, they'd love that!"

*****

Three days later Kia had wrapped up her shoot. Now she and Jabu were heading back to the air strip. Jabu stowed her bag in the back of the plane, along with the other five passengers.

Kia reached for her camera. "Hang on Jabu! I forgot to get some shots of us together!" She looked at the other passengers who were milling around waiting to board. One in particular stood out.

She approached him with her wide smile. "Excuse me? Would you mind taking a few shots of me and my brother? Next to the plane would be good?"

The young man reached for the camera. "Sure." He looked around then back at Kia. "Which one is your brother?"

Kia laughed. "The good-looking ranger – he's my brother, Jabu."

The young man looked momentarily flustered, but took the required photos and handed the camera back. "There you go. How did the shoot go, I was watching you work?"

"It went well, thanks. I'm Kia." she held out her hand. "I'm based in Cape Town."

"Josh Headley. Pleased to meet you." He held out a small card. "I'm a photographer too, mostly interiors of flashy houses in Cape Town, I live there as well. I came here for a couple of days break. Come on I think the pilot's waiting to get under way."

Kia hugged her brother goodbye. "He's cute," she whispered in his ear, "definitely going to look him up when I get home!" She clambered up the short steps and disappeared inside.

212

The small plane roared down the dirt runway, Jabu raised his hand in farewell and watched until it was only a tiny dot in the sky.

He smiled to himself. Kia needed to find someone to hang out with. The young photographer seemed to have caught her attention.

Maybe something would come of it.

Chapter Fifty-Eight

Sara made her way out of Cape Town fighting her way through the heavy traffic, getting used to the feel of Edward's old car. The traffic thinned out as she reached the bottom of Sir Lowry's Pass, she hoped the little car would make it up the steep mountain road.

Once over the pass, she glanced to her left admiring the long fields of grapes, the farm stalls and the cattle grazing in the fields.

The road opened up; she was making good time. Five hours later sticking to the main highway she saw the shimmering sea in front of her as the road dipped slightly. Mossel Bay was on her right, the highway passed George on her left, then she slowed down as she came to Sedgefield, a quaint village town full of antique shops, fast food outlets, garden centres and a Classic car sales lot.

Sara glanced at her watch, still another five hours before she reached her destination. Crossing the bridge into Knysna she slowed down again. The town hugged the lagoon, its surface choppy with the strong wind blowing. She decided to stop in the next town for the night, then set off early the next morning.

A short time later she turned right off the highway and made her way through Plettenberg Bay. She would look for a small bed and breakfast place where they would be unlikely to ask for any identification.

June was a quiet month for most seaside towns. There was little traffic on the roads and the weather, cold and blustery, didn't lend itself to residents venturing out to sit at the many open-air bars and restaurants the town had to offer.

Sara made her way down towards the sea and, despite the weather, admired the beauty of the place. In the high holiday season of December, she remembered the town would be heaving with local and international tourists enjoying the glorious sweeping beaches, the background of mountains and the hot summer weather.

She turned left when she saw the sign for a bed and breakfast guest house. Pulling into the driveway she turned off the engine.

There was no-one at the little reception desk, but there was a bell which she shook vigorously.

A young African girl materialised, smiling a welcome. Yes, they did have availability would she care to sign in?

Sara filled in the form using the name Jenny Marshall, still careful not to use her real name.

"May I have some ID please, Ms Marshall? I'm afraid it's a requirement these days."

"Yes, I know. Unfortunately, my handbag was stolen in Cape Town. Everything was in it. Passport, credit cards, wallet. Sorry."

The young African rolled her eyes. "Crime is a problem in our country, that's for sure. Let's hope you won't get stopped by the traffic cops; you'll be in trouble without a driving licence to show."

"Oh, no problem there," Sara said airily, "I have a case number for my bag being snatched. It should see me through."

"How will you be settling your account, Ms Marshall?"

"I'll pay cash." She took the key to her room. "Thank you."

Sara went back to the car and collected her luggage. She would take a quick shower and find somewhere to eat. Then an early night before setting off for her final destination.

It would not be an easy day.

*****

Sara made her way down the familiar dirt track. The small villages she remembered were gone. She waved at a solitary goat-herd as she passed. The area had an abandoned look about it, as if all life had seeped away by the years of drought.

In the distance she could see the wide river glinting in the sunshine. She turned right onto another dirt track and headed towards her old home.

Sara stopped the car and looked around. The old palm tree still stood in front of what had been her father's cottage. Beauty's round house was still visible, although the thatched roof had caved in on itself. Her father's cottage still blackened by the terrible fire of that night and the following days. Only three walls remained and over one cascaded a yellow shower of determined flowers she remembered.

The roof was rusted and bent held up precariously by a rotting pole, slimy with dead leaves and clinging ivy. The base of the house splashed with mud like an old torn skirt. Creepers had grown up through the open roof only to hang down the outside like a rotting fishing net. The shutters bent and lopsided on one side of the window.

She stepped out of the car, the silence cloying. Her memories crowding back. She didn't want to go inside the house but sat on what was left of the crumbling veranda. A dove called breaking the silence, followed by an answering call from its mate.

Sara closed her eyes. In her imagination she could hear the laughter of her children whispering through the garden.

Charlie's laughter. The joy on the children's faces as they unwrapped Christmas presents on a hot sultry morning.

Sara opened her wet eyes and stared at the dust beneath her feet. She picked up a small piece of china, blowing the dust off of it, then wiping it with her sleeve.

She recognised it immediately, a broken piece of Charlie's favourite Peter Rabbit bowl. She rubbed it with her fingers then carefully put it in the pocket of her skirt. "I'm coming darling, I'm coming," she whispered.

She wrapped her arms around her, remembering the weight of her baby. To outlive a child went against the natural order of things, and it had happened because she had caused it.

At last Sara gave into the anguish and the pain which had never diminished. Her raw crying carrying across the still bush.

Emotionally drained she stood up unsteadily. This then would be the most difficult part.

The river.

The river was slow and gentle today, meandering its way through the deep bush, a faint swirl of mist crept over the water disappearing into the restless reeds, bending and nodding in the faint breeze.

She stood on the banks of the river, staring at the water. What was the point of putting up any kind of memorial for Charlie? No-one would come looking for it. It would be lost like thousands of others buried in the wild bush of Africa, overtaken by the ruthless tread of time and nature.

Charlie would be another name added to all the others. A child's face, laugh, touch, voice, already forgotten. Maybe someone would stumble across the plaque and fleetingly wonder about a dead child; then move on. Forgetting a life ending so abruptly on a stormy day in Africa.

216

No. She would not let the ruthlessness of Africa take her child forever.

But she wanted to be here for a while and remember, before she said her final goodbye. She looked for somewhere to sit and found the ancient tree trunk, its old twisted roots deeply embedded in the soil, stretching towards the river.

She reached for her bag, then clasped her hands together and prayed for forgiveness.

As she fumbled to open the buckle on her bag, she saw something wedged in the roots of the tree. She leaned forward, reaching out her hand.

A shoe – a baby's shoe.

Sara frowned as she wrested it from the arrow pinning it to the root. She dusted it off with the hem of her skirt, then held it to her lips. Her heart beating rapidly.

Charlie's blue shoe.

*****

Everything had been destroyed in the fire after Charlie disappeared. The dogs, the police and the trackers, would have found the shoe.

No, it had been placed here long after the event. Someone had placed it there for a reason. Perhaps knew the mother of the child might one day return.

Why would someone do this? Why would someone leave a message like this?

Sara looked wildly around, then sank to her knees. What she had planned to do would not now happen. The plan that would take her back to Charlie.

Working with Karen she had had access to all the drugs any doctor would have. The hypodermic in her bag and its deadly accomplice would have to wait another day.

*****

Sara ran back to her car. She knew exactly where she was going next. The game lodge and Paul, the lodge manager. The game lodge where she had been arrested and Paul who had looked after her, shielding her from the press before they gathered around her like hyenas, and she had no place left to go.

She knew the chances of him being there were slim. Too much time had passed.

Two hours later she arrived at the lodge. There was an air of abandonment about it. The entrance gate heavily padlocked. No bustling guests, no vehicles lined up.

*****

The guard brushed down his faded uniform and watched the vehicle approach, seeing the long line of dust dissipating into the atmosphere. The car stopped at the gates. He recognised her.

The ghost woman from long ago had returned.

Chapter Fifty-Nine
The Editor

Sir Miles wandered around his old house, deep in thought. Maggie followed him around then went back to the kitchen and the crackling warmth of the fire.

Sir Miles followed her then reached for his address book. "I need to be careful with this situation Maggie. If I get it wrong, the results could be disastrous."

Maggie closed her eyes and dozed off, her whiskers and legs twitching with dreams of chasing rabbits when she was young.

Where had he gone wrong with his daughter? Her upbringing was unusual, yes. But no different from thousands of other children who, either military or otherwise, followed their fathers around the world. She had been born in Singapore, but as a roving Ambassador he never stayed anywhere longer than two years. The tight knit world of diplomats was a transient one. Life was all about moving on at random and unpredictable intervals. Friends would disappear, shipped out somewhere around the world never to be seen again. Nobody ever said hello or goodbye. You were either there today, or gone tomorrow.

Sara's life had been a blur of new places. Not owning anything in the many fully furnished houses they had lived in. A different culture, different languages to contend with. Had this made her unpredictable? Was this why she had chosen a career as a journalist so she could still travel, not putting roots down anywhere?

She had attended excellent international schools in every country they had lived in, learning the skills which would carry her through her life. Sara had excelled in languages, the arts, music and sport.

Did she blame him for not providing a more stable life?

He shook his head and found the name and number he was looking for. Harry Bentley, the editor of *The Telegraph*. He knew what he was going to say without giving much away. He had to find his daughter.

"Ah, Harry. Miles here."

"Good to hear from you Miles. I'm sorry to hear about Sara. We ran a small piece for her in the paper here."

"Yes. I saw it. I know it's been a long time since we spoke, but I wanted to thank you for the way you covered the story. You showed more compassion than most of the other newspapers. They tore into her and ripped her apart once again dredging up her past."

"Least I could do, Miles. We go back a long way. It must have been painful for you. We did our best."

There was silence at the end of the phone. "Are you still there, Miles?"

Harry heard the scrape of a chair, the tapping of a cane on a stone floor.

"Harry. I need your help. There's no-one else I can trust this with. You'll need to think carefully about who you choose to do this. You see, I received a letter two days ago. It doesn't have a date. I don't know when it was written."

Harry held his breath. He could smell a story. "No post mark then?"

"No, it was found at the Embassy in Cape Town and came in the diplomatic pouch then posted on to me here. It looks as though it's some years old."

"Is there a story here for me Miles?"

"Yes. I need someone to go to South Africa. You see, Harry. If this letter is to be believed there was another witness to the child's murder.

"The writer of the letter said it wasn't Sara who killed Charlie. It was someone else. I need to find that person. I need to find the author of the letter?"

Harry felt the familiar fizz of excitement. If there was one thing he loved more than anything else it was a big story out of Africa. The last one was a cracker. An abandoned house in the bush in Kenya, two sisters, a murder or two and a long search for the truth. The newspaper *The Telegraph*, of which he was editor, had made a packet out of it.

"Leave it with me Miles, I'll give you my best journalist. Jack Taylor. He specialises in cold cases. We'll be discreet until we find the truth. Hold on a moment. He cupped his hand over the phone.

"Jack!" he bellowed into the press room. Then continued.

"I'm going to ask Jack to follow this one Miles. I'm going to ask him to come and see you. He'll have questions and obviously will want to see the letter. Okay with that?"

Sir Miles sighed into the phone. "I appreciate this Harry. It was a great shock to get the letter. My Sara, she went through all that and she was innocent, if this letter can be believed."

"Leave it with Jack, he'll uncover the truth. Now, how soon can he come and visit you. Are you still living in the great draughty heap in Dorset?"

Despite everything Miles smiled. "Yes, Harry, still in the big heap as you call it. I'm thinking of renting something in London. Too bloody quiet in the country for me, with only Maggie to talk to."

"Maggie?"

"Yes, my Labrador. I would have gone mad without her company. I'll expect this Jack tomorrow then? I don't drive anymore but there are plenty of taxis at the station in Dorchester. They all know where North End house is."

Harry put down the phone and punched the air. Then strode into the office where a bevy of journalists were talking into phones or thumping stories out on their computers.

"Jack!" he bellowed again, get your butt over here."

Jack skidded into the office and sat opposite his boss. "So, what's the story, you look excited, which is unlike you…"

Harry leaned back, his navy-blue braces, his signature trademark, straining against his shirt. He ran his fingers through his thick white hair and grinned. "Ah, well. A missing child in Africa always does it for me. The public may forget the journalist who covered the story, but never the name of the child.

"Yes, a child who disappears leaves a huge question mark…"

Chapter Sixty
The Journalist

Jack Taylor lived and worked in London. He had started out as a cub reporter on a national newspaper when he was eighteen. He had a keen eye and a good nose for unusual stories.

Over the years he had worked his way up to the position of Crime Reporter with *The Telegraph*, his success rate with digging out the truth in cold cases had been the envy of his colleagues. Now, at thirty-two he was at the top of his game

He knew an event couldn't change, but the understanding of how it happened could. Looking through statements taken after a murder, sifting through the case files often contained the secret to cracking a cold case. It was all there if you could find it. A discrepancy, a hidden clue a contradictory statement, an investigator's hand written notes in a margin. Re-visiting a witness, speaking to detectives who had worked the cases. He loved his job.

*****

Now he waited in Harry's chaotic office for him to brief him on this missing child.

"This one's for you Jack, right up your street, except it must be handled with the utmost discretion."

Jack ran his hand through his untidy blonde hair, and leaned forward in his chair already feeling the usual excitement spinning up his spine, his dark brown eyes alert with anticipation.

"Ever heard of Sir Miles Courtney?"

Jack shook his head. "Should I have?"

"Perhaps not. He spent a great deal of his life out of the country. Singapore, Middle East, South and East Africa, at the bidding of Her Majesty the Queen."

222

Jack raised an eyebrow. "Diplomat?"

"Yes. He has an impeccable reputation. Not an easy man, doesn't suffer fools gladly."

"Ah, it's why you want to send me eh!" Jack grinned at his boss.

"He asked for my best journalist. That's you. I need you to get down to Dorset and see what it is he wants. You might want to run a brush through your hair before you meet him. Smarten up a bit, maybe find a tie somewhere?"

Jack grinned at him again, and raked his fingers through his hair. "Any background stuff on Sir Miles, Harry. Anything I need to know that I won't find with Mr Google?"

"There's a lot on Sir Miles, his career etc. and even more on his daughter Sara Saunders. She did a stint in prison for killing her child in South Africa. The body was never found. Sir Miles seems to think he has proof she didn't do it…"

Jack was already out of the door. Grabbing his jacket and laptop he raced out of the office and back to his flat to pack an overnight bag.

*****

Jack was on the morning train to the south of England. The grey sprawl of London with its endless view of back yards of dark sooty houses, back to back gardens, identical fences and washing lines. Some strewn with discarded tricycles, prams, broken furniture, others equally neglected, as though they had given up competing with the endless procession of sleek trains leaving Waterloo.

Through the rain streaked windows London had given way to earth tones of cultivated land, and drab farm buildings, with the occasional glimpse of grand houses, and all their secrets, hidden and shrouded by hundred-year-old trees, arrogant with age they stood amidst vast lawns and ancient forests.

Small villages filled the windows for a few seconds, a post office, a pub, a station with parking lots, and the obligatory dark stoned church with its steeple, the crumbling tomb stones, green with age, nestling in its grounds. A village shop and used cars for sale, the forecourts festooned with bunting.

Jack turned back to his laptop and was soon lost in the numerous articles about Sara Saunders.

*****

Jack paid off the taxi and crunched up the path to the front door of the house. He rapped on the door and looked up at the old building.

He knocked again, more loudly, and was rewarded with the deep bark of a dog.

He stepped back to see if there was any other sign of life apart from the dog barking. A light was on in one of the rooms upstairs. Maybe the old man was having a lie in, or perhaps getting dressed. He glanced at his watch. He cupped his hands to his mouth and called up to the lighted window.

"Sir Miles? It's Jack Taylor from *The Telegraph.* We have an appointment?"

Only silence greeted him then more barking from the dog. He turned as he heard a car pulling up. A middle-aged woman with short brown hair, streaked with grey, stepped out carrying a basket full of what looked like cleaning products. She stopped and frowned at him.

"Morning! My name's Jack. I have an appointment with Sir Miles. I've come down from London?"

The woman gave him a tentative smile. "He should be up and about by now. He normally lets Maggie out first thing. I'm Emma by the way, his housekeeper."

She dug into her coat pocket and extracted some keys then unlocked the big wooden door, with an equally big ornate key. "Come on in." She put down her basket and pulled off her gloves with her teeth.

Maggie came bouncing into the kitchen barking and whimpering. "Hey, Maggie, where's the boss?" She bent and scratched her behind the ears. "Sir Miles?" she called out, "Are you up yet?"

Maggie whimpered and ran back to the kitchen door, looking over her shoulder, then barked again.

Emma frowned. "I'd better go and check upstairs. I saw his bedroom light was on, maybe he's not feeling well. Alright, Maggie, I'm coming. Stop all that barking, will you?"

Jack waited in the kitchen, noticing the Aga, the ancient pots and pans, a big walk in larder, the heavy square table pitted with age and the worn faded chair next to the fire, stuffing beginning to seep from one corner, a silver topped cane leaning against it.

Propped up next to the coffee machine was an envelope with his name on it. He picked it up, then hastily put it back again. Sir Miles was a bit of a stickler, by all accounts, he would wait until he gave it to him

224

personally, wouldn't do to get off on the wrong footing. He smoothed his hair down then pulled at the unfamiliar tie around his neck.

He heard Emma's hurried footsteps coming down the stairs. "Oh my God. Oh my God." She put her hands to her face and stared at Jack, panic written all over her kindly face. "He's not breathing, his eyes are open. I think, I think…Oh God I think he's gone."

Alarmed, Jack stepped forward and helped her into a chair. "Sit down Emma. Would you like me to go and double check?

She shook her head. "No. He's gone. There's nothing to be done now."

*****

The ambulance crawled up the driveway, a police car following. Inside Jack had started a fire and put the kettle on, as he tried to calm and comfort the distraught housekeeper.

The policemen entered through the front door, removed their hats and identified themselves. "We don't normally accompany the ambulance when a death is reported. But Sir Miles is well known in the area. His personal physician is on his way." They nodded at Emma.

"Mrs Gates? You're the housekeeper? This must be very hard for you. We know you've been with Sir Miles for years. I'm sorry."

Emma tried to hold her tears back and failed. "Yes, she whispered, "I'm his housekeeper."

The police in Dorchester, Jack surmised, were familiar with Sir Miles. Who came and went in his house, and who worked for him?

"Your name, sir?"

"Jack Taylor. I had an appointment with Sir Miles this morning."

The taller of the two took out his notebook. "May I ask you what business you had with him?"

"I'm a journalist, with *The Telegraph,* my boss, Harry Bentley, is the editor of the newspaper. Sir Miles was an old friend of his." He handed the policeman his business card.

The two policemen looked at each other. The tall one glanced at Jack's card and spoke again. "Any idea why Sir Miles wanted to meet up with a journalist? I understand he had a strong dislike for them, no offence, sir."

Jack hesitated. "No, I've no idea what he wanted to see me about."

Sir Miles' doctor bustled into the kitchen, nodding at Emma and the policemen. "I know my way. Morning Emma. I'll find him in his bedroom?"

Emma nodded and distractedly made some more tea.

Within minutes he was back. "Looks like a heart attack. I'm afraid Sir Miles is dead."

He put a comforting hand on Emma's shoulder, as the young constable went out to the ambulance to summons the medics. The doctor accompanied them upstairs.

Jack stepped aside as the stretcher passed him. Judging by the sweat on the ambulance crews faces, Sir Miles was a heavy man. They crunched over the stones with the body, then slammed the doors to the vehicle closed.

The doctor followed the ambulance as it made its way down the drive, accompanying Sir Miles on his final journey.

The sound of the ambulance's engine faded and there was silence in the kitchen. The two policemen finished their mugs of tea.

"Right, sir, we'll be on our way then." The tall policeman seemed to be the spokesperson of the two. "I suggest you lock up the house, Mrs Gates, and don't forget to set the alarms. We'll contact his next of kin. A grandson if I recall?" They put their hats back on.

"Yes. His name's Ben." She recited his number and he wrote it down.

Maggie nuzzled Jack's hand, he looked down surprised, then stroked her golden head. "What about Maggie?" he asked Emma.

She put her hand over her mouth. "Oh, my goodness, what will happen to Maggie. We can't leave her here! I can't take her unfortunately. My cats are terrified of dogs and I live in a small flat in town."

The tall one scratched his head. "Well, we can take her down to the dog pound. Maybe keep her there until the grandson comes down?"

Emma shook her head, her mouth turning down. "Maggie and Ben don't get on I'm afraid. Ben won't want her. I can't bear to think of her in the dog pound, it'll break her heart. She'll know Sir Miles has gone, they somehow know don't they?" She dabbed at her eyes.

Jack put a comforting hand on Emma's shoulder, seeing the tears again. "Look, if it's alright with everyone I'll take Maggie. Harry, my boss, talked about her, said how fond Sir Miles was of her. Harry lives out in the country I'm sure he'll take Maggie in for his old friend, until her futures decided?"

The tall one nodded his head. "Seems like a good solution to the problem, for the moment. Thank you, Mr Taylor. Perhaps we could give you a lift to the station, no point in hanging around here now. We'll wait in the car."

"I'll get Maggie's bowls, her toys and her leash, Mr Taylor. I'll give you my number in case your boss has any questions about her. Oh, and he'll need to give Maggie her heart pill every evening."

Now alone in the kitchen, Jack deftly pocketed the letter addressed to him.

*****

Maggie lay at his feet on the train looking miserable. Jack bent down and patted her head. "You'll like Harry, Maggie, I think he has a couple of labs, you'll make some new friends. Harry loves labs, you'll be happy with him."

He picked off clumps of golden fur from his coat. "What are you thinking here, Maggie, that everyone should wear a fur coat?"

Maggie thumped her tail weakly, putting her face between her paws.

Jack went back to a thought which had crossed his mind many times before. Does someone know when they are about to die, outside of the usual situations, war, execution etc. What are their last thoughts as the darkness descends? It's like the other question. Is there life after death? Only the same people can answer that one, and, of course, they can't. It was a world he knew well, a world he moved in.

Jack pulled the envelope from his inside pocket and lifted the flap.

Chapter Sixty-One
The Editor

Jack made his way back to the office, Maggie on her leash next to his side. He tapped on Harry's door and went inside.

Harry looked up surprised. "That didn't take long. How was Sir Miles, and where did the dog come from?"

Jack slumped into a chair. "Sorry Harry. Sir Miles died last night. I was too late. This is Maggie his dog. Or rather your dog now, until someone finds her a new home."

Harry raised his eyebrow, resting his thumbs against his braces. "I'm sorry to hear this. He was a nice old boy. I guess one more dog won't make much of a difference. My wife is going to kill me. Come here Maggie, don't look so worried. We'll give you a good home."

Maggie answered to her name and lay down next to Harry's desk.

Harry steepled his fingers and looked at Jack. "Well there goes the story then. He took whatever he wanted to tell you to his grave with him. Damn."

Jack waved the envelope in front of him, and grinned. "Not quite. He left this for me, as though he knew something was going to happen. It's the letter he told you about on the phone."

Harry reached over and snatched it out of Jack's hand, scanning the handwriting on the inner envelope. "Looks like a kid wrote it."

He finished reading the letter then read it again. "So, how are you going to handle this Jack. Have you ever been to Africa?"

"No. I've always wanted to go, but never quite managed it. I'm going to start by sniffing around here first. I've done quite a bit of research. Sir Miles mentioned in his note, a Doctor O'Hara here in London who knew Sara, she was her patient at some point. I want to speak to her. Then I'm going to find Sara's son Ben and see what he remembers."

Harry nodded, only half listening, as he re-read the letter again. "See here, Jack. Africa isn't easy if you don't know your way around. There was another story we handled some years ago, in Kenya. We had a journalist working for us, Alex Patterson, he used to be full time, but he was too expensive. The bean counters didn't approve of him flying back and forth to various places in Africa and here.

"Alex decided to go freelance and based himself in Cape Town where he filed stories back to us. Our readers like all the white mischief stuff, deadly deeds and doings in deepest darkest Africa."

He tapped the letter rhythmically on his desk. "An elderly woman collapsed near a restaurant where he was eating lunch, he went to help her and that was the beginning of a brilliant piece of journalistic investigation. The story was fantastic. All the ingredients were there. Two sisters going missing, an abandoned house deep in the Kenyan bush, a magnificent Steinway Grand boarded up on the top floor. Husbands and lovers, it had it all - even a nun.

"Alex ended up in Kenya. He's still there. When you've done the groundwork here, I think you should meet up with him. Go to Cape Town via Kenya. Alex will be able to give you plenty of advice and guidance on how to navigate things in South Africa. He probably still has contacts there. I'll let him know you're coming."

He leaned back and pulled a book out of a sagging shelf. "Read this. *The House Called Mbabati.* Alex wrote it. It'll give you an idea of how Africa works, or doesn't, depending on your point of view!"

Jack looking out at the ash coloured sky, the rain slashing across the window. He rubbed his hands together at the thought of blue skies and that elusive thing called sun. "Sounds like a good contact. Thanks Harry. I'll get onto it straight away, starting with the doctor."

He lifted the bag containing Maggie's fur covered blanket, her bowls, toys, her pills, and a well chewed ball and put it on Harry's desk.

"Bye Maggie."

Jack whistled through his teeth as he cleared his desk.

Africa.

He was an avid watcher of National Geographic on television. Thundering great elephants, golden lions, gorgeous tanned women, long white beaches, and, from the books he had read, an alluring place for interesting people with interesting lives. Forget the South of France with its reputation of being a shady place for shady characters. Africa wasn't shady, it was full of sunshine – and shady people with nowhere to hide.

But first he had to visit Sara's doctor as Sir Miles had suggested.

Chapter Sixty-Two

Jack waited patiently in the waiting room of the surgery. He looked up when he heard a door opening. Doctor Karen O'Hara, wearing a white coat and a stethoscope looped around her neck, ushered her patient out of the door, then turned and looked at him, her brown eyes cool and appraising behind expensive looking glasses. She checked her watch then walked behind the empty receptionist's desk and checked the appointment book.

Turning, she raised a perfectly shaped eyebrow at him as she carefully pushed her glasses on top of her head. "You don't seem to have an appointment?"

Jack gave her what he hoped was a beguiling smile, it normally worked. He stood up and extended his hand. "Jack Taylor. I wondered if I might have a chat with you?"

"In connection with what. I'm about to close the surgery?"

"I won't take up much of your time but I would like to talk to you about Sara Saunders? You were her doctor according to the newspaper reports?"

Her head jerked up. "Who are you exactly?"

"I'm a journalist with *The Telegraph*. My editor is an old friend of Sir Miles Courtney, Sara's father. I'm afraid Sir Miles died at his home in Dorset a couple of days ago." He handed her his card.

"I'm sorry to hear that. I'm not particularly fond of journalists, Mr Taylor. I won't be able to help you with any details of Sara Saunders. It would be a breach of patient confidentiality. I'm sure you understand?"

Jack ran his fingers through his hair and gave her a lopsided grin. "Absolutely. Sir Miles left a letter," he patted his pocket and pulled it out. "He suggested I meet with you."

He pulled out the letter from Eza. "Perhaps you should read this? Then, if you agree, we can discuss the contents?"

Karen took the letter and sat down in the chair opposite him and crossed her legs. He watched her closely for any reaction.

Karen read the letter twice then folded it and handed it back to him. "How did you obtain the letter Mr Taylor?"

"Please call me Jack. I had an appointment with Sir Miles, he wanted to discuss his daughter and this letter. But I was too late, when I arrived at his house he had already passed away. But I think you will agree he wanted me to check out the contents of the letter, because if Sara didn't kill her child, then who did?"

"Perhaps you would give me a bit of background on Sara, I know a fair bit but I need to talk to someone who knew her. This would be you Doctor O'Hara. You first met her in South Africa, at a place called The Haven? I understand you looked after her there, but I know for a fact you wouldn't have been able to treat her in a professional capacity, you wouldn't have been licenced to practice in another country. So, I assume you had personal reasons for being there?"

Her face hardened. "What I was doing there is of no concern of yours Mr Taylor."

He could see the contents of the letter had shaken her, but her reaction to it was not quite what he had expected.

Karen checked her watch and stood up. "If there's any truth in the letter, this will make Sara innocent?"

He leaned forward, his hands on his knees. "Look, this might sound a bit crazy, but supposing when Sara disappeared from the nursing home she didn't travel to Europe and kill herself. Supposing she went back to South Africa? It's possible?"

"I told the police Sara was unpredictable. She had threatened suicide often. Sara was unbalanced, and if there is any truth in the letter, well, one can understand."

"But," Jack persisted, "her body was never found. Supposing Sara isn't dead? Don't you think she has the right to know about this letter and, more to the point, about her father's death?"

"Another thing that bothers me; no-one walks out of a care home, they're normally secure. I'm thinking perhaps she had help?"

Karen sat down again. "I'm sorry Mr Taylor, I can't discuss Sara's medical condition with you."

She removed her stethoscope and put it in her coat pocket. "The police have closed the case; missing presumed dead. I'm afraid you'll have to accept their findings, as I have. Sara was a friend as well as my patient. She often stayed with me at the week-ends. The care home was quite happy with the arrangement. One Sunday morning, when I went downstairs, I found she'd gone. That's all I'm prepared to say. Now I really must go. Please see yourself out."

"I'll let you know if I come up with anything Doctor O'Hara," he said to her retreating back "When I return from South Africa."

Jack made his way to the underground. Doctor O'Hara was not telling the truth. She'd tripped herself up by using the present tense.

This will make Sara innocent.

Also, she had said *the letter,* not, *this letter.*

Therefore, he concluded, she knew about the letter, before he showed it to her.

No, for whatever reason, he fully believed the doctor had been involved with the disappearance of Sara Saunders, and if he was not mistaken, she knew where Sara was. But why all the secrecy?

Jack stood at the back of the filled church. Sir Miles, by all accounts, had been a difficult bugger, but the pews were packed with people he must have known over the years, including some obvious looking Foreign Office types.

After the service he followed the queue of cars back to the old house where drinks and snacks were being served, the caterer's watched over by the housekeeper Emma. Her eyes lit up when she spotted him.

"Mr Taylor, how kind of you to come! How's Maggie? The house feels so empty without her."

Jack kissed her on both cheeks. "Maggie's fine. She's settled down in her new home, with Harry, and is happily sharing her fur with everyone and everything."

Emma's eyes filled with tears. "Oh, that is good news, I do miss her. Ben, Sir Miles' grandson, wants me to stay on and clean the house once a week until he decides its future. There he is over there. Would you like me to introduce you?"

Jack looked across to where she was pointing. A young, rather overweight, man was standing alone, pouring himself a large glass of gin with a top up of tonic.

Emma continued. "He probably doesn't know anyone here, most of the guests are from Sir Miles old life. He looks a bit over whelmed doesn't he?"

"I'll go over and introduce myself Emma. Let you get on with the caterers."

232

So, this is Sara Saunders son, he thought to himself. Maybe he could get him to talk about his mother. No time like the present after her father's funeral when he would more than likely be feeling vulnerable.

Ben was standing next to a large window overlooking the wintry grounds. "My condolences Ben. I'm Jack Taylor."

Ben turned and Jack dismissed the bloodshot eyes as signs of grief, more like booze he thought.

Ben shook his hand. "Thanks for coming," he mumbled. "You're younger than most of his friends here. Where did you meet him?" The ice in his glass clinked.

"I didn't actually meet him. My editor, Harry, was an old friend. He asked me to represent him at the funeral."

Jack looked around the room noticing the large framed black and white photograph of a rather beautiful woman. He knew who it was. Sara Saunders. He turned to Ben. "Must be difficult being the only one left of the family…"

Ben narrowed his eyes, the red spider veins on his cheeks deepening. "Which newspaper are you with?"

"*The Telegraph.* Harry wants me to do a piece on your grandfather."

Jack pretended to study the grounds outside. "Sir Miles must have found it difficult to accept what happened to his daughter and his grandchild, as you must have," he said casually.

"Difficult to lose a sibling. But, a long time ago now. You probably don't remember much about it. A terrible time for your mother though." He turned and pointed to the portrait with his glass. "That's her isn't it?"

With a shaking hand Ben poured himself another drink. "If you've come here to dig up information on the past then you're wasting your time. My mother's dead." He took a large mouthful of his drink and wiped his mouth with the back of his hand, then turned back to Jack.

"I'm going to ask you nicely to leave my house now Mr Taylor. I have nothing to say to the Press, they destroyed my life. Write your piece, finish your drink and leave."

Jack put his glass down. "Nice to meet you Ben. Oh, by the way, I'm off to South Africa at the week-end. Really looking forward to it."

Jack threaded his way through the crowded room and put the small framed photograph of Sara in his jacket pocket. Emma might miss it when she dusted the small table in the drawing room, crowded with framed photographs, but Ben certainly wouldn't.

*****

The last guest had left the house. Emma and the caterers had cleaned up and gone home.

Ben wandered around the silent house a glass of red wine in his hand.

He stood in front of the portrait of his mother and felt the rage rise inside of him. She had wrecked the family, besmirched its name, and brought shame on them all.

Lifting his glass, he hurled it at her. The wine glass shattered; the contents slithered down his mother's face like endless bloody tears.

Chapter Sixty-Three
The Lawyer

James Storm looked at the faces seated around his highly polished table. It was time for the reading of Sir Miles Courtney's Will.

Sir Miles had been specific about who he wished to attend the reading. His housekeeper, Emma. His old friend Harry. Doctor O'Hara, his dog Maggie and his grandson Ben.

James picked a piece of dog fur off his jacket. Sir Miles revenge, he thought to himself. The old boy did have a sense of humour after all.

James looked at his watch with irritation. Where was Ben?

Maggie growled softly, then the door opened and Ben strode in.

"Sorry I'm late. Overslept." He took the last remaining seat and leaned forward on the table. "Come on, let's get on with it shall we?"

He heard the soft growl and looked around the table, spotting Maggie looking at him. "What the hell is a dog doing here?"

He peered more closely. "It's bloody Maggie isn't it?"

Harry smiled. "Well, it would appear you didn't have much time for Maggie, never bonded I believe. Otherwise you might have noticed she wasn't around your house. One of my journalists, Jack Taylor, was at the house the morning after your grandfather died, he brought me the dog."

Ben scowled at him. "I met Jack Taylor at the funeral, representing you he told me. What was he doing at my house the morning after my grandfather died?"

Harry stroked Maggie's head. "Sir Miles wanted me to send Jack to him. There was something he wanted to discuss with him. Something private maybe? Anyway, if you feel strongly about Maggie, then you should take her with you after we finish here?"

Emma cut in, panic in her voice. "Oh no, Mr Bentley! Maggie could never live with Ben. She was always nervous around him. No, definitely not. Sir Miles would be happy knowing Maggie has gone to a good home. It would have meant everything to him, absolutely everything."

Ben glowered around the table, his face reddening with anger when he saw Karen sitting there. He ignored her. "Look Mr Storm, can we get on with this. It shouldn't take long. Cut and dried I would presume as I am the only family member left?"

James gave him a wintery smile. He cleared his throat. "Sir Miles' Will was drawn up some years ago, most of his requests have stayed the same. However recently he made some changes. Here are his last wishes.

"To Emma, my housekeeper, who looked after me, Maggie, and my house with great love and kindness. I leave to her ten thousand pounds, with gratitude."

Emma's eyes opened wide, then filled with tears. She reached for the handkerchief in the sleeve of her cardigan, overwhelmed with his generous gift.

"To Doctor Karen O'Hara who helped my daughter through a difficult time in her life, I leave fifty thousand pounds. I am grateful she didn't desert her as many others did."

Karen jerked back in her chair with surprise. This was most unexpected. Perhaps she had judged him too harshly. Perhaps she should have spent more time with him, tried to understand him and his relationship with his daughter. After all she had only ever heard Sara's side of the story. Fleetingly she thought back to the awful confrontation in his kitchen when she had been beside herself with fury at the way he, and Ben, had treated Sara. How she had wanted to meet him again to discuss his daughter, and the mysterious letter. But it was too late now.

"To my old friend Harry, I leave the gift of a story. He will understand this bequest."

Harry grinned and twanged his navy-blue braces.

James once again cleared his throat. He looked across at Ben, who was already rubbing his hands in anticipation.

"Recently, as I mentioned Ben, Sir Miles changed this particular part of the Will. Initially you were to inherit half the house in Dorset and all its contents. However, he changed this.

"The entire estate is left to Sara. It will be up to her to decide how she distributes the estate."

Ben looked wildly around the table, then back to James. "There must be some mistake. My mother is dead!"

236

James put the cap on his fountain pen. "I can't explain this Ben, but these were his instructions. I have to respect his wishes. Without your mother's body being found it will take seven years before she is officially declared dead.

"When it is proven beyond reasonable doubt that Sara Saunders is dead, half of the house will revert to Doctor O'Hara. The other half will be yours, along with the contents and any other assets."

Ben stood up, his face suffused with blood, the veins in his neck protruding. "Doctor O'Hara is not even family! You can trust me, Mr Storm, I will engage the services of a top lawyer to contest this ridiculous Will. My grandfather could not have been of sound mind when he made these changes."

James looked at the fury in the young man's face. "I can assure you he was, Ben."

He glanced back at the document in his hand. "There is one final request. Your grandfather has bequeathed the small Monet painting to Maggie and whoever gives his beloved companion a loving home. That's you Harry. When Maggie passes on, he gives his full permission for you to sell this piece and do what you will with the proceeds, or perhaps you might like to keep it?"

James thought Ben was going to implode. "Look," he blustered, "maybe I was too hasty. I'll take Maggie back. I'm sure she'll settle with me. So, no problem there. The Monet stays in the family." He looked over at Maggie.

"Come on Maggie, let's not break the family up over a painting!"

Maggie bared her teeth and growled deep in her throat.

Harry laughed. He hooked his thumbs behind his braces again. "No way, Ben, the dog doesn't like you. Maggie belongs to me now. Suck it up. Your grandfather was passionate about wildlife in Africa. It seems animals gave him more love than his family ever did.

"So, I'll tell you what I'm going to do. I'm going to give Maggie the loving home she deserves. When she passes on, I will sell the painting and donate the money to an elephant shelter, and the foundation who look after them, in Kenya. It will make a massive difference to the good people who try and help those who cannot help themselves."

James closed the file.

Ben stood up, knocking over the chair. Maggie's growl followed him out of the office before he slammed the door. The cups on the tray rattled in protest.

The meeting was over, everyone stood up and reached for their coats and umbrellas.

Harry touched Karen's arm. "I know you met with Jack?"

She nodded.

"Given the media exposure you were subject to, and in view of Sir Miles's Will, perhaps now is the time to work together? You want the truth as much as we do. Would you consider helping us Karen? We'll protect you. I give you my word."

Karen nodded. She liked Harry; an instinctive thing.

"I need to know as much as you do, Harry. I need to know what happened to Sara. Sir Miles would have expected this of us."

Harry followed Karen to the lift. "Tell you what, why don't we have lunch together. I need as much information as you can give me so when Jack leaves this week-end he has everything he needs to chase this story?"

The doors to the lift opened and they stepped inside. Karen stared at the light as it illuminated each floor. "You realise Harry, whatever I tell you has to remain confidential. To give you the full story I'll have to divulge a bit of Sara's medical history which legally remains confidential between a doctor and her patient? I'm not sure I feel comfortable about this."

Harry nodded. "Your name won't appear anywhere in Jack's report, you can tell me about Sara as a close friend, not her doctor. That should sidestep any moral and legal obligations you may have?"

They stepped out into the cold and Karen pulled her coat around her. Harry put the leash on Maggie and buttoned up his own coat.

"I didn't really lie to the police, Harry. I might have been a little economic with the truth though. The only reason I'm going to help you is because once Jack discovers what really happened, Sara needs to come back to England and clear her name. This will go a long way to finally curing her.

"Ben will be a problem. She left him once, now she's done it again. But maybe I'm getting ahead of myself. Perhaps something's happened to Sara – she might never come back. I don't know."

Harry pressed the button for the pedestrian light. "Let's see what happens Karen. We can confront those problems if and when they arise.

He took her by the elbow and steered her through the throng of pedestrians. "If Sara is out there, dead or alive, Jack will find her. I've known many journalists in my time and Jack is one of the best. He has an uncanny nose for digging deep and finding the truth. Cold cases are his speciality.

"Now let's find a dog friendly restaurant and have lunch, shall we?"

*****

Ben pushed through the crowds of people in Knightsbridge. Seeing nothing and hearing nothing only the pounding of blood in his ears, incandescent with rage at the contents of his grandfather's revised Will.

He needed a drink. He pushed his way through the bar, ignoring everyone, found a seat at the end of the counter and ordered a double gin and tonic.

So far, the New Year had been a disaster. His girlfriend, Linda had dumped him.

*****

The Press, on learning of the death of Sir Miles, had dug the whole story up again.

Linda had been hounded by journalists who knew of her relationship with Ben Courtney.

She had been keen to find out how much Ben was going to inherit from his Grandfather. They had met for lunch and Ben told her the outcome of the meeting.

She had made her decision immediately. Ben had more problems than most men she had met. He drank too much and she knew for a fact he had other girlfriends on the side. London might be a mighty big city but it had a tight social circle.

The story of Sara Courtney Saunders had once again made it to the front pages of the tabloids. There was no way she could now be associated with a man with such a distasteful, publicly exposed background. It would be social suicide. The Press had been a nightmare, chasing her all over the place, yelling and shouting questions at her.

"Look Ben," she had said after lunch, "I'm afraid this isn't going to work for me. I have my reputation to think of here in London. My parents have insisted I disassociate myself from you.

"Now your own inheritance is in such a mess, I'm afraid marriage is not an option. My father would never give his consent. Not after all the scandal in the newspapers."

She had slid her engagement ring off and dropped it on the table, picked up her handbag and walked out of the restaurant, leaving him with a bill which made his eyes water.

*****

Ben trudged back to his flat and lay on his bed. In the corner of the room were three cardboard boxes containing the things he had packed from his office when they fired him two days ago. A few of their top clients had complained about his erratic moods and the lingering smell of alcohol after too many late lunches. After two warnings the Chairman had called him in and given him his marching orders.

With no income he now had to think of how he was going to pay his bills and there was only one option. He would get hold of Sotheby's Real Estate and put his country house in Dorset on the market.

He wouldn't be able to use Sotheby's in London, the bloody lawyer James Storm would soon hear about it, and it wasn't his legally to sell. Not yet anyway. But, no harm in getting it valued, that wasn't against the law?

He thought for a moment, then smiled. He would use Sotheby's in South Africa, give them an exclusive for that particular market, and no other.

Once he knew the value of it, he would work out the next step of his plan. Clearly his grandfather thought his bloody mother was still alive somewhere. Based on what he had no idea. The visit from the journalist had something to do with it, but he had been too late. However, the fact the editor from *The Telegraph* had attended the reading of the Will must mean something. What had his grandfather said, something like "*To Harry, I give a story.*" What the hell did that mean?

Hadn't the journalist Jack whatever his name was, when he had asked him to leave the house after the funeral, said something about going to South Africa?

Harry had been an old friend of his grandfathers, someone he obviously trusted. Something had happened to make his grandfather change his Will again.

240

Well, whatever the mystery was, let them work it all out. All he wanted to know was whether his mother was dead or alive. It would make all the difference to his future and his inheritance. He would fight Doctor Karen O'Hara tooth and nail through the highest court in the land if he had to.

And to hell with Linda as well.

He reached for his phone. Time to start the ball rolling. He needed to know exactly how much his grandfather's house and land was worth. Maybe the bank would let him borrow against it.

Chapter Sixty-Four
The Journalist

Kenya Airways started its decent into Nairobi. Jack rubbed the window with his shirt sleeve to get his first look at Africa. Below he could see the beginnings of a pink dawn sky and the city sprawling beneath him.

The wheels of the aircraft bumped twice before thundering down the runway, then slowing down sedately made its way towards the terminal buildings. It came to a hissing halt and there was silence inside the cabin.

The seatbelt light went out and there was the usual clicking of seatbelts, the hurried scrum for the overhead bins, then the inevitable wait for the doors to open.

Jack walked towards the terminal building, the warm breath and scent of Africa snatching at his senses.

The arrivals hall was seething with excited people, some straining their necks to get a first glimpse of a loved one, others holding up name boards. He shouldered his way through the crowds and made his way to Avis, to collect his hired car. Harry had advised him to get a four by four, as according to Alex Patterson, the road out of the city towards Nanyuki, where Alex now lived, left much to be desired.

Adjusting his seat and mirrors he familiarised himself with the car. Satisfied he made his way out of the airport. Approaching the city of Nairobi, he found himself caught up with the commuter traffic. He whistled through his teeth. London could be a nightmare during rush hour but this was something else altogether.

There was traffic coming from everywhere, springing from all directions without any semblance of order. Motor bikes, brightly hand painted trucks and buses, cars and even a donkey cart, piled high with watermelons, all pushed and jostled for a position. Pedestrians dashed in between the traffic, some with briefcases, mothers with babies tied to their backs, mopeds whizzing through any opening in the traffic. He would have to keep his wits about him. A red moped crawled past his window and he grinned at the passengers being carried in the paniers. Four indignant chickens their beaks and combs jerking, squawking with indignation.

Booming music blared from the slogan painted, ten-seater taxis, the honking horns and squealing brakes adding to all the confusion. Black smoke belched from the exhaust pipes of old trucks with wooden frames, a sharp contrast to the polished shiny Mercedes with their tinted windows, which seemed to glide along oblivious to everything around them.

With some reluctance Jack closed his window, already feeling the heat of the sun burning his arm. He put the air-conditioning on and there was a buffer between him and the chaos outside.

The traffic started to clear as he picked up the road to Nanyuki. He looked around with interest. Open savannah and swaying golden grasslands stretched for miles around him. He passed forests and fruit sellers, villages with their cultivated fields of cabbages, maize and potatoes, sprawling markets and donkey carts weighed down with produce on the way to market.

Four tall Maasai warriors watched his vehicle imperiously as he passed, their red-gold ochre smeared bodies, elaborately plaited hair and brightly beaded thick necklaces and ankle bracelets, a startling splash of colour on the dusty landscape. He lifted his hand in greeting and in return they raised their spears courteously, in an almost regal gesture.

Three hours later he reached the busy market town of Nanyuki. He slowed down to a crawl as he passed rows and rows of shops selling fruit, vegetables, colourful material, drinks and food, electrical appliances, bicycles and shoes. Dotted in between were internet cafés, their signage roughly hand painted in bright colours. In the middle of town there were more sophisticated, but small supermarkets, garages, hotels and restaurants.

Soon he was back out on the road heading for Alex Patterson and the country house called Mbabati. He was making steady progress, not bothering to stop for food. There were two bottles of water provided by Avis, and he sipped from these as he absorbed the sights and smells of Africa.

Occasionally he passed a village with its round houses and thatched roofs, goats, chickens and plots of vegetables. Near to one village he slowed as a donkey with a mountain of cut wood, piled high and swaying perilously from side to side on its cart, stubbornly refused to pull over and let him pass. He went off road and shouted an apology to the owner of the stumbling beast as he covered him in red dust.

He raised his hand with thanks, and apologies, then joined the rough bush road again. He glanced at the directions Harry had given him, then looked for the fork in the road which would lead him to Mbabati. He passed a flat roofed building with a bright red iconic swinging sign which proclaimed it sold, amongst other things, Coca Cola. He laughed out loud. Coca Cola must have their signs up in every corner of the globe. Whether deep in the African bush, or out in the paddy fields of China.

He found the fork in the road and turned right. The vehicle bucked and rattled over the deeply rutted and pot-holed road making his teeth chatter. He clung grimly to the steering wheel, keeping his eyes on the road, waiting for his first glimpse of the now famous house called Mbabati.

An elegant sign proclaimed he had reached his destination. He stopped and looked around. In the distance he could see a flattened area with a wind sock. Alex, when he had phoned him to give his arrival dates, had suggested he fly straight to Mbabati as they had their own private landing strip. But Jack had insisted he wanted to drive, he wanted to get a feel for the country.

He took his sunglasses off and wiped the dust off the lenses with his shirt sleeve. Pouring some of the water into his cupped hand he also wiped the half-moons of dust from under his eyes. He eased himself out of the vehicle and stretched, then walked around taking in the dry smell of the bush, feeling the intense heat of the sun on his arms and the back of his neck.

Getting back in the vehicle he ran his hands through his hair, put his sunglasses back on and made his way to the entrance of Mbabati.

The grand iron gates to the house, swung open silently. A smooth, well maintained dirt road led to the grand entrance of the house with its elegant portico. The walls of the house were painted a rich apricot tone reflecting in the late afternoon sun. Fine sprays of water clicked and arched over the immaculate green lawns. Birdsong echoed through the gardens as brightly coloured birds swooped to bathe in the cool spray.

A formal rose garden exuded a heavy scent from the nodding pink, white and yellow roses, the bushes bending slightly from the weight of the flowers.

Jack was impressed. An oasis of luxury in the middle of nowhere. He pulled into the parking area at the side of the magnificent building and slid out of the driver's seat.

A tall man, wearing a ranger's uniform, was waiting for him at the top of the sweeping steps leading into the house. "You must be Jack. We've been expecting you. My name's Bruce, I'm the lodge manager. Welcome to Mbabati."

Jack shook his hand. "You must have one of the best jobs in the world Bruce. What a place. It's fantastic!"

Bruce smiled. "Yes, it's pretty spectacular. Wasn't always like this, of course, well maybe forty years ago. Come on in out of the sun. Amos will bring your luggage and take it to your room. I expect you'll want to freshen up after the drive."

Jack propped his sunglasses on top of his head, adjusting his eyes after the bright sunlight outside. "A shower sounds good, thanks Bruce."

Bruce pointed to the top of the grand staircase. You're in room six, ah Amos, thank you." Amos went nimbly up the staircase to room six carrying Jack's soft leather safari bag.

"Sorry Alex wasn't here to meet you. He'll be along in about an hour. So, take a shower and have a look around, Amos will fix you a drink or perhaps something to eat?"

Jack let the warm water of the power shower cascade down his body, then when he was sure all dust had been removed, he dried himself and changed into long khaki trousers and a loose white shirt. He thrust his bare feet into his loafers and wriggled his toes with delight.

He made his way down the staircase, admiring the impressive chandelier hanging in the centre of the lofty ceiling. Then he stopped short. Filling almost one wall was a magnificent portrait of an equally magnificent looking woman. The blue of her long dress shimmered with life, her golden arms looked so real he wanted to stretch out his hands and touch them. Around her elegant neck she wore a triple strand choker of pearls. Jack knew without any doubt this was Nicola, the world-famous pianist who had featured strongly in Alex Patterson's now legendary book. *The House Called Mbabati.*

He wandered through to the dining room with its dark wood panelled walls, small tables with snowy white cloths, set with silver and crystal glasses awaited guests for dinner.

The sitting room walls were decorated with prints of English hunting scenes, comfortable chairs plump with cushions were arranged with small tables. There was a large fireplace with bulging wicker baskets stacked with wood positioned either side, shelves of books took up two corners of the room.

He nodded at a small group of guests who were chatting in the corner enjoying their first, he presumed, drink of the day.

He went back to the entrance to take another look at the portrait then made his way up to the top floor. Pushing open the double doors he sucked in his breath. A beautifully crafted Steinway Concert Grand stood centre stage in the room. The Rolls-Royce of all pianos.

Above the fireplace at the end of the long room was a large black and white photograph of another beautiful woman with short dark hair, a cigarette held between her fingers, the smoke drifting upwards as she gazed unseeingly out of the window at the African bush.

Jack shook his head. Alex had indeed discovered a magical place, full of mystery, in the middle of no-where.

Jack checked his watch. Alex should be here any minute. He was looking forward to meeting him.

Amos was waiting for him at the bottom of the stairs. "Mr Alex is waiting for you in his study. I will show you the way. Perhaps I may get you a drink?"

"Thanks Amos. I could murder an ice-cold beer please."

He ushered Jack into the study. Alex stood up a broad grin on his attractive face. He was a man in his early fifties, his short hair peppered with grey, deep lines fanning out from his steady eyes. "Welcome to Mbabati Jack. Good to meet you. How's my old boss Harry? Still wearing those old blue braces and twanging them when he smells a story?"

Jack laughed. "Yup. As cantankerous as ever! He sends his best and promised to fire me if I don't come back with a story as good as the one you wrote about this place!"

They waited for Amos to place their beers in front of them. "Harry told me he'd given you the book I wrote on the sisters, Jack?"

"Yes. A real cracker it was too. I can imagine what this place looked like when you first found it. The renovations are remarkable.

"Is the old retainer Luke still around? It would be great to meet him, although he would be pretty old by now?"

Alex glanced out of the window, a shadow crossing his face. "No, Luke died a year ago. But his last few years were happy here. The house full of life again."

246

Jack took a sip of his beer. "Africa sure attracts some remarkable characters!"

Alex smiled. "It certainly does. I guess some people like the ordinary, secure, routine of life. Then, as history has shown, there are the ones who are curious about a different sort of life – adventurers, if you like. They're the ones with an insatiable thirst for something different."

He looked out of the window at the lengthening shadows of the trees. "Africa has always attracted people who want more, India is another example. Imagine where the world would be now if these people with adventure in their heart hadn't followed their dreams? Instead of a semi-detached house in Croydon, living a mind-numbing existence, they now had sun filled houses, servants and a glorious social life. But, of course, that's all gone now, although there are still thousands of so-called expatriates, still living their dream, but with no guarantee that the country they loved and lived in will care for them when they're old. We call them scatterlings."

He reached over and turned on the small lamp on his desk. "Some went back to the land of their birth, others stayed on. Anyway, I'm rambling

"So, Jack, tell me your story?"

Jack took another long sip of his beer. "As Harry told you I'm chasing a story in South Africa, your old stamping ground, when you were Harry's man in Africa for the newspaper.

"The daughter of the British Ambassador who was once stationed in South Africa, allegedly murdered her child. A boy called Charlie. Her name was Sara, she went to prison for eight years, then returned to the UK.

"Eight months ago, she disappeared…"

He stopped and lifted his head. The house was suddenly filled with the most exquisite music he had ever heard in his life.

Alex smiled at him. "It's Nicola, playing her beloved piano. She plays for the guests every night, recordings of course. Guests come from all over the world to stay here and listen to her play." He glanced at his watch. "Tell you what, let's go into dinner and you can tell me the rest of your story. Then I'll see if I can point you in the right direction with any contacts I have in South Africa."

They finished their meal in the elegant dining room. Alex sat back in his chair. "Chasing a case in Africa is a whole lot different to chasing one in England or Europe. But first I need to know what you have on this Sara."

When Jack had filled Alex in on all he knew so far, they took their coffee back to the study. Alex stirred some sugar in his and took a tentative sip.

"So, let's take a look at what you have here." He pointed to the small silver framed photograph Jack had brought with him. "The Ambassador's daughter Sara, who was sent to prison for the murder of her child, the body of which was never found. A child's bloodied tee shirt hidden under the mattress of the bed where she was staying at the lodge. A burnt-out house where any other potential evidence was destroyed. Drugs found in Sara's washbag suggesting she was in a hypnotic state when she killed the child. An English doctor herself a drug addict, befriends Sara in a rehabilitation centre in the Cape. Sara and the doctor return to the UK together and become friends. Good friends."

He took another sip of his coffee. "We also have a mysterious letter from someone called Eza who claims there was another witness at the river that day, who saw what happened, and tells Sara's father, in the letter, she didn't kill the child."

Jack nodded. "Right."

"Then Sir Miles inexplicably changes his Will after he gets the letter from this Eza. Sir Miles believes his daughter is still alive and has returned to South Africa, where once again she disappears."

He picked up the photo of Sara again. "Tell me about the boy Ben?"

Jack tried to stifle a yawn. "Angry young man is how I would describe him. Looks like a bit of a drinker with temper to go with it. Obviously has, or had, a difficult if not impossible relationship with his mother. After she went to prison, he was in a foster home until his grandfather agreed to take him in. He was a bright kid by all accounts. I would say he's a deeply unhappy person. But who wouldn't be given his turbulent history?"

Alex tapped his spoon on the side of the table. "My question is this. Sara had paid for her so-called crime and there was no reason why she shouldn't return to South Africa. Why all the secrecy and fake suicide?

"Finally, from everything you have told me, not one person will talk about Charlie, not the mother, not the son, not the grandfather. Why is that? Was there something wrong with the boy?"

Jack shrugged and leaned back in his chair. "A lot of questions and not many answers, I agree. Normally with cold cases I've cracked, I know where to start. I know the country, how it all works. But this one is going to be a challenge." He grinned at Alex. "One I'm up for, by the way!

"But I don't know how the country works, I have no contacts there. God knows why Harry picked me for this one. He should have used you?"

Alex laughed. "I'm out of the game now. I have my hands full here. But maybe there's an advantage to not knowing the country, or how it works, you'll have fresh eyes. You'll see things from a different perspective."

Alex stood up and gazed out over the immaculate grounds of the estate. "In my experience in Africa, it's best to start at the end and work back. Obviously, you need to go to the scene of the crime. Talk to people who were around. The local clubs are a good source of information, the white folk who drink there love a good bit of gossip.

"That's how I chased the story of the two sisters who disappeared for twenty years and how I ended up here…"

"Find out where retired police officers hang out in their spare time, find their favourite watering hole. Someone in the area might have worked on the case, or knows someone who did.

"Eza, this African who wrote the letter, is first prize of course. He could be anywhere, to me it's going to be your biggest challenge. He's key to the whole thing, as is his mate Joseph. Then there's the nanny, Beauty. Good luck with tracking her down, it's a common name there and they're a transient people, difficult to find.

"Another thing to keep in mind, these people will often refer to each other as brothers, or cousins, or sisters. But it doesn't mean they are blood relatives."

He sat back down again. "South Africa is known as the Rainbow Nation, and for good reason. They have Whites, Blacks, Indians, Chinese, Malays, and Coloureds, plus eleven official languages! I know everyone else in the world think Coloureds is an offensive word, not politically correct as they say. But the Coloureds are a race of their own and proud of it. As much a part of the landscape as all the other races."

He tilted his chair back. "This Eza chap, judging by his name, could well be a Coloured and not an African. The Eastern Cape is a place close to the heart of the Griqua people, they consider the area sacred, they're part of the Coloured population.

"Then you have to track down Sara…if she is indeed alive."

Jack stifled another yawn his eyelids feeling suddenly heavy. "Sorry, the flight and the drive are catching up with me, and the heat."

Alex smiled at him and pushed his empty cup away. "South Africans are a friendly lot, unlike the Brits who are mostly suspicious of strangers. You'll find them happy to give their opinions on things. I'll give you a couple of contacts who might be able to help you. Ted Ford is a journo friend of mine based in Cape Town. He's Australian. Tough as they come and loud, but he'll remember the story. You'll find him at the Press Club if he's not chasing stories all over the continent. There's an old hotel, the Mount Nelson, a lot of journos hang out there. Ted spends time there as well."

Jack stood up. "Thanks Alex. I think I'll turn in. Early start back tomorrow for the airport. I'll let you know how things progress."

Alex shook his hand. "One other question? Where is the father of this Charlie? Who was he?"

Jack shrugged. "No-one knows and no-one is telling. Another unanswered question. Goodnight Alex."

Darkness had come quickly. Jack lay back on his bed, still fully clothed. He hated sleeping with an air-conditioner mumbling away in the background.

Fresh air, that's what he needed. He padded over to the window and drew back the curtains, throwing open the shutters and then the windows. The silence of the bush was balm to his soul. Only heavy silence with the odd belly laugh of the hippo down in the lake, the cicadas chirping rhythmically to each other interspersed with the hearty burp of frogs, big ones by the sound of it. Soft lights glowed through the gardens.

Unexpectedly there was a slash of jagged lightening which lit up the black night, followed by the deep rumbling of thunder, then another slash of lightening and a great boom of thunder overhead. Jack jumped and ducked his head instinctively.

Within minutes the rain arrived, pounding on the roof of the old house, the wind came from no-where roaring through the grounds bending bushes and trees with its mighty strength. Like rods of steel the rain plunged to the ground, dancing off the dry parched earth. Jack

250

watched the fury of nature, strangely exhilarated, as he felt the spray on his face and arms. The scene outside was biblical, then as quickly as it started it slowed down, as if nature was taking a break, exhausted after its own personal display of fury.

Now there was only the sound of the patter of rain. But it was the smell that overwhelmed him, heat, dust and wetness all mixed together, cleansing the air, the bush, and the gardens below. Then the rain stopped and all he could hear was the hollow steady drips on the wide leaved plant below his window.

Jack smiled to himself. It would be easy to fall in love with Africa with its stark contrast to London. No foxes making their stealthy way through gardens of private homes looking for dustbins to overturn and rummage through.

No screaming sirens, boom boxes, banging doors, crying babies, arguing couples or the forlorn barking of a dog. No screeching of brakes, or the grinding of garbage trucks or the endless sound of jack hammers digging up the roads. No rumble of the underground trains as they made their way through the belly of London, jam packed with commuters.

Jack smiled. Yup, he could become very attached to Africa.

Chapter Sixty-Five
The Daughter

Kia watched the throngs of locals and tourists wandering around the Waterfront in Cape Town. The restaurants and bars were packed, the waiters bustling between the tables, their shirts sticking to their backs in the blistering January heat of summer. Tourists' boats chugged around the harbour, sleek shiny seals surfacing briefly to entertain the passengers with their round liquid eyes and long whiskers.

Large ferries crowded with people ploughed back and forth to Robbin Island, returning passengers looking more sombre then when they set out for the famous island where Nelson Mandela was incarcerated for many long years.

Kia glanced at her watch. Josh was late again. She had looked him up on her return to Cape Town after the shoot at the lodge where her brother Jabu worked. Josh, had been more than happy to hear her voice again.

Through their mutual love of photography, they had become the best of friends. Meeting up three or four times a week for coffee, lunch or dinner. Kia had been attracted to him the moment she saw him on the air strip when she had asked him to take a photograph of her and Jabu together.

To say she was disappointed when he told her he was gay was an understatement. Cape Town was known as one of the biggest gay capitals in the world, she knew that better than anyone. Even so she enjoyed his company, his sense of humour and, of course, he was gorgeous to look at with his dark floppy fringe and big brown eyes and a smile that could stop you in your tracks.

"Sorry Kia, there was a massive queue for parking. I hate this time of the year, everywhere clogged up with tourists."

He kissed her on the cheek and dropped his cameras on the table before flopping into a chair and waving his arm around listlessly trying to attract the attention of a waiter.

Kia grinned at him. "Yeah, I'm not too keen on this time of the year myself. That's why I'm looking forward to the trip to the UK. I've worked out my itinerary. A few days up in Yorkshire, Bronte territory, then a couple of days with the Templetons before I meet you down in Dorset."

Josh, who was famous for his talent with interiors of houses had been asked by Sotheby's in Cape Town to travel to the UK and take some atmospheric shots of an old country house which had come onto the market.

Kia had looked puzzled when he told her. "But Sotheby's have offices in the UK, why do they want you to do it?"

"Because, my lovely, I'm the best! No, seriously, they want to market the house exclusively here in South Africa. I know what South African buyers look for when they see shots of houses overseas. It'll be great, I need a break from the heat and the bloody tourists with their bulging wallets!"

*****

Two weeks later Kia looked out over the rolling hills and watched the rain sweep across the Yorkshire countryside. Idly she wondered where all the gentleman farmers had gone. She had imagined them all tall and broody looking roaring through the country lanes in Range Rovers splattered with mud, wet Labradors hanging out of the windows, pink tongues flapping in the wind, or clopping past on shiny horses. She decided they must have emigrated to Kenya or Europe where the weather was better, much better.

This rural idyll, in reality, gave only the opportunity to meet little old ladies with funny accents and ancient dogs staggering around on their last legs. But it was the greenness of the land that struck her, having been brought up in the drought stricken and dusty land of her childhood.

To Kia, country life in rural England had conjured up images out of Wuthering Heights. She had imagined Heathcliff silhouetted against dark brooding hills battered by gale force winds, his cloak billowing as his horse galloped along at breath-taking speed to meet his Cathy. All she had seen so far were creaky old men tottering through the village on their way to the pub.

Still, she had enjoyed her three days up North. She had spent her time with her camera visiting derelict churches, old graveyards and ancient pubs. The gloomy weather had added an atmospheric touch to her work.

Now she was heading south again on the train to spend the week-end with the Templetons. This she was really looking forward to having not seen them for nearly five years.

Kia boarded another train at Waterloo which would take her to the pretty town of Christchurch where the Templetons had retired to when they left South Africa.

They were waiting for her at the station both smiling broadly as she stepped off the train.

Diana and Norman Templeton hugged Kia with delight. All talking over each other in their excitement.

"Darling Kia, look at you! As beautiful as ever! I'm happy to see you still wear your hair in braids. I expect you turned a few heads in England!"

Kia tossed her braids and laughed. "Possibly, well definitely in some of the pubs I went into up in the North. Forget about the elephant in the room, I felt like a giraffe."

Norman picked up her small suitcase and Kia linked her arm through his and her other through Diana's. "It seems odd to see you in another country all bundled up with coats, scarves and boots!"

Diana grimaced. "Yes, I expect it is. We still haven't settled down I have to say. To be honest we would go back to Africa in a flash if we could, but we can't, so there it is."

Now they were sitting in front of the fire sipping glasses of wine. The cottage was small but cosy, the curtains drawn against the blackness of the night, blocking out the sound of the wind and the rain pattering on the windows.

Diana tucked her legs under her. "Now, I want to hear all the news. How is Mirium? How is Jabu?"

Kia brought them up to date. Her mother's health had not improved but this had been expected. She told them about her few days with Jabu at the game lodge, her life in Cape Town and the work she was doing with the lifestyle magazine.

Nothing was said about Eza.

The Templetons told her about their life in England, how difficult it had been to settle down, if they ever had.

254

"It's not only the weather Kia," Diana said, "It's just the sky seems so low here and the weather does get us both down. But having said that in the summer, brief though it often is, it can be quite beautiful. No nasty snakes creeping around the garden. We go for long walks through the woods and fields and it is rather nice not to have to look over your shoulder all the time. Yes, it's safe here but, my dear, so predictable. Give me Africa any day, at least living on the edge adds a bit of zest to life. We even miss the power cuts!"

Kia shook her head in sympathy, the beads in her hair clicking softly, seeing how unsettled they both were.

Norman re-filled their glasses before giving the fire a desultory poke and settling back down into his chair. "I remember sitting around various fires in Africa, watching the sparks soaring up into the sky." He shook his head.

"It's not the same here, of course it's not, and we certainly didn't expect it to be. I mean the people are nice enough but they don't understand about the life we used to have. Some even look downright disapproving as though we abused the Africans by using them as servants. They simply don't understand that anyone we employed was paid a good salary and were well looked after."

Kia looked surprised. "Surely they watch television here and can see what Africa is like now?"

Diana shook her head. "I'm afraid not. You know what the media are like, they only want to show misery and unhappiness. All they see are starving children with flies stuck all over their faces, people dying of terrible diseases, tribal wars and riots and corruption, terrible corruption, that eats away at anything good going on there. They imagine all white people live a privileged life there and spend their days drinking gin and tonics whilst the Africans clean and sweep their impressive houses and swimming pools!"

Norman interjected. "It's not that the people here are ignorant, it's because they have no perception of life in Africa and, quite frankly, they don't seem to be in the least bit interested. Unless, of course, they've been there on holiday and had a jolly good time. But even then, they don't understand how it all works. We don't even talk about our life there anymore…"

Kia put her glass down in front of her, standing up she went and hugged both of them. "Perhaps people here don't understand your life there. But Jabu and I both know the good things you achieved. If it hadn't been for you where would Jabu and I be now?"

Diana fumbled for her tissue. Norman cleared his throat finding some imaginary fluff on his trousers which seemed to demand his immediate attention.

Kia continued. "You've looked after my mother now for years. Without your financial assistance she would have died long ago, quite alone and with no-one around her."

Kia stood up. "There's something I want to give you."

Diana and Norman looked at her retreating back, and smiled. "Lovely to have her back, but it's going to be hard when she leaves." Diana dabbed at her eyes as Kia came back into the room.

In her hands she held a large photograph in a silver frame. It was the shot Josh had taken at the airstrip. Jabu standing proudly in his ranger's uniform, one arm protectively around his sister. Kia was looking up to him a loving happy smile on her lovely face.

This was too much for Diana as she picked up the frame and stared at it, the tears making their steady way down her lined cheeks.

"Darling Kia, how sweet of you. What a glorious pair you make. You make me so proud of you. We both miss you; you seem so far away now."

Kia took the frame from her hands and handed it to Norman. Crouching down she took Diana's hands in both of hers.

"Why stay in a place where you're both unhappy? Why stay somewhere because it's safe? Why stay somewhere which is eroding your soul with longing for another place?"

She passed Diana another tissue. "Over the years I've thought about my father. I was angry with him for deserting us. But then I stopped thinking about us as a family. I began to think about him as a man and not only a father. Once I took the name of Papa away from him and called him by his given name Eza. Then I understood him. He was a very loving and caring man, that's why he did what he did."

"You see Eza tried hard. He gave the best he possibly could to his wife and children but it wasn't enough. His roots were deep with his people. I think he tried to be part of this new world he found himself in – and he couldn't. Not much different to you, I think.

"Eza knew his unhappiness would make us, his family, unhappy. He did a noble thing by leaving us. He was true to himself. Both Jabu and I have forgiven him. I think Mama, though she may be muddled at the moment, has also forgiven him."

Diana and Norman were mesmerised by the wisdom of this young girl's thinking.

256

Kia returned to her chair. "Jabu wants no part of the modern world. He is exactly where he should be. Out in the bush with nature. This is what he understands. I, on the other hand, have embraced a different world."

Norman gave another desultory poke at the fire and slumped back into his chair.

Kia paced around the room. "May I open the window? I must have air on my face?"

Norman and Diana rose together. "Of course, but let's go outside for a moment, it seems to have stopped raining."

It was bitter out there. Kia sucked in the cool fresh air and turned to the shivering Diana and Norman.

"Come home. Why exist when you can be happy and live in the place you came to love?

"There's still a need for teachers. You can be something again." She turned to Norman. "You have years of experience in Africa, you're an engineer, you can help and advise? Mentor the young people, give them vision as to how the country might be?"

Kia looked up at the thick dark night. "Yes, you must come home. You are existing here. You need to come back and live."

Diana squeezed Norman's hand.

*****

They took Kia back to the train station the next day. She was off to Dorset to meet her photographer friend, Josh.

Diana and Norman held Kia close. Promising they would think about her proposal to return to Africa.

Diana and Norman returned to the silence and darkness of the cottage they had rented. Norman drew the curtains as he had done for the past years, knowing that tomorrow would be exactly the same as today and he felt his soul shrivel in anticipation. The view would be the same, the sheep in the fields, the sweeping relentless rains, the dampness and the dullness of it all.

He heard the pop of a cork in the kitchen. Diana came bustling through with two crystal glasses on a silver tray, the bottle of champagne nestling in the ice bucket.

They sat in front of the fire, the photograph of Kia and Juba spearing the room with a vivid splash of the colours of Africa. The sun bright on their faces.

257

Norman's bushy eyebrows met. "So, my dear, what are we celebrating?"

"Life, my darling. Life. Kia was right. Life is an adventure. We're merely existing. You get to a certain age and then you take the back seat. Well, it's not what we do Norman. We never have."

Norman kicked off his tartan slippers and removed his socks. The air felt good on his feet, bringing back memories of soft rain on his skin during a tropical storm.

Diana filled their glasses. "We're going home, my darling, back where we were truly happy."

Norman smiled. "Let's give it a bit more thought, my dear. We have our lease on the cottage to fulfil first. But we can use the time to decide our next move."

He rubbed his feet together. "I feel ten years younger just thinking about going back. Come on let's put layers and layers of clothes on and go down to the pub for dinner. We've a lot of things to discuss.

Chapter Sixty-Six
The Photographer

Josh drove carefully down the curving narrow country roads, watching out for oncoming tractors and other traffic. Twice he stopped to let a herd of cattle cross the road. There was a definite art to driving in the country. Twice Kia had squealed with fright as they rounded bends and come face to face with tractors loaded with hay, or trucks filled with cattle and sheep on the way to the abattoir.

Finally, they came to the village of Larks Town which consisted of one road. Dotted each side were chocolate box classic thatched cottages, that belonged on a souvenir box of chocolates or a puzzle. A village shop, a church and a pub. Josh pulled into the car park and turned off the engine.

"There's only one pub in the village. This must be it." He peered through the wet windscreen. "Come on let's check in. The estate agent is meeting us at the house in half an hour. Maybe put a warmer jumper on, my lovely, the house has been closed up for months now, it'll be freezing inside.

"Apparently, there's a cleaning lady who comes once a week, but I doubt she puts the heating on. I wanted to have a good look around outside but it's bloody gloomy, I probably won't be able to see a thing. Maybe tomorrow the sun will shine!"

"Don't put your money on it Josh," Kia muttered, pulling her warm coat tightly around her and winding her scarf around her neck. "It is January after all."

The pub was warm inside with a cheerful fire blazing in the corner. A couple with their dog sat in the corner, close to the fire, otherwise it was empty.

They looked around for some kind of reception area. "Well, hello there!" A plump woman appeared behind the bar wiping her hands on a dishcloth. "You must be the photographers. Welcome to Larks Town. I'm Polly." She reached under the counter and pulled out the register.

"If you'll sign in, I'll show you to your rooms. You haven't picked the best of days to see our village, but, who knows, tomorrow the sun may blaze forth." She grinned. "Or maybe not."

*****

Josh and Kia drove to the end of the road and turned left up a sweeping driveway. The outline of the house had been clearly visible from the road although it was shrouded in mist.

The estate agent, a middle-aged, stern looking woman wrapped in an unflattering puffy coat and thick boots, was waiting for them as they climbed out of the car. "Hello there. I'm Monica. Welcome to North End House. You must be Josh?" She glanced at Kia, and frowned. "I didn't realise there were two of you?"

Josh gave her his beguiling smile. "This is Kia. We've worked together on a couple of projects back home. She'll give you a copy of her passport if that makes you feel more comfortable? Kia is going to help me, if that's alright with you?"

Monica frowned. "Well, I suppose it will be alright. But I will need some identification, the owner is a bit of a stickler…"

She removed a large bunch of keys from her handbag and bustled up to the front door. "This is the main entrance, although the owner normally used the kitchen door. She put her shoulder to the door and tried to push it open.

Josh stepped forward. "Here, let me help you with that, it looks as though it's jammed."

Monica stood aside laughing, her cheeks red from the cold. "That's why they probably used the kitchen door. This one is tough to open as you can see!"

The door opened with a loud screech. Monica put her umbrella down next to a row of wellington boots, and unbuttoned her coat, then opened another door and reached swiftly for the alarm flashing on the wall. A few more flicks and the entrance flooded with light.

"I've written down the security code for you so you can get in and out without bringing the local security company screaming up the drive. Please remember to put it on when you leave the house. There are a lot of extremely valuable things here and the insurance company are strict."

"Got it." said Josh.

Monica checked the list of notes on her clipboard. "A few more things to point out. If you'll follow me to the kitchen."

They followed her down the long corridor as she turned on more lights. Kia noticed a large study on her left, the sitting room on her right. The long staircase leading to the bedrooms upstairs, and an elegant drawing room on her left. Monica stopped next to a small room with a large sink, bags of dog biscuits and dog bowls. An assortment of coats, hats and dog leashes, hung from heavy ornate hooks.

"Here are all the thermostats for hot water, underfloor heating and the heating generally." She flipped switches up and turned three dials. "There, the heating is now on. I'll come and turn everything off when you've finished. I understand you'll be here for two days?"

Josh shivered. "Yes, at least two days. There's a lot of work to be done here to get the lighting and atmosphere right. You wanted to show us something in the kitchen?"

"Yes. This way please."

The agent flicked on the kitchen light. Along one wall behind glass fronted doors were shelves and shelves of glasses of varying sizes. "Under no circumstances must these glasses be touched," she said sternly. "They're over four hundred years old and quite priceless."

Kia giggled. "Won't be putting those in the dishwasher then Josh!"

Monica gave her a withering look. "Sorry, Monica, only making a joke. Of course, we won't touch them."

"Would you like me to show you the rest of the house?"

Josh shook his head. "Thanks Monica, I'd prefer to wander around with my sketch pad and camera, and make some notes. Plus, we need to get our equipment in before dark. But thank you. Rest assured we'll take great care of everything. I'll send Kia's passport details through in the morning."

Monica looked at her watch. "Right. I'll be off then. I'll see you on Monday. If you need anything here's my card. Oh, there's no internet here. Sir Miles didn't care for it. The phone signal is also rather weak. But they do have facilities at the pub. You'll have to use theirs."

She pulled on her gloves. "Oh, one more thing. The owner of the property, Ben Courtney, may well pop in at some point to meet you. He can be, um, a little gruff shall we say. But I suppose it's always hard to part with something that's been in your family for generations.

"There's a lot of complicated history here. Ben is Sir Miles' grandson. Lots of rumours, gossip and scandal about the place, but I suppose that's inevitable. People who live like this are not like the rest of us are they?"

Kia and Josh watched the estate agent's car until her taillights disappeared. Then turned to unload their car.

Whilst Josh studied each room, switching lights on and off, Kia explored the house. There were eight bedrooms upstairs and four bathrooms. Large oil paintings graced the walls, rows of cupboards at the top of the stairs held linen bedding, feather duvets and pillows. Stacked at the bottom were several suitcases. She glanced at one of the luggage tags – Cape Town.

The gloomy drawing room, with its tarnished silver candelabra, looked as though it was never used. It felt cold and uninviting. She turned the lights on.

Here there were hundreds of books in glass bookcases, beautifully bound, and probably hadn't been read for decades. Dotted around on small tables were carved elephants from India, silent wooden African butlers holding empty trays, West Africa she thought. A portrait of a military man, in full uniform dress, stiff and unsmiling. Probably Sir Miles.

Over the fireplace was a framed black and white photograph of a beautiful woman in her prime. Her blonde hair fell to her bare shoulders, her large eyes and exquisite cheekbones caught at an angle by a remarkable photographer. She peered at the signature in the bottom right hand corner. *Snowdon.* Husband of the Queen's sister. A society photographer of some note. Even Josh would be impressed.

Kia lifted her camera and took some shots. An original Snowdon! She prowled around the house again looking at all the photographs, twice she lost her way in the sprawl of the place, bumping into Josh when she least expected to, as he too searched for angles and inspiration. She knew better than to interrupt his creative juices from flowing.

Next to the kitchen there was a small cloakroom with a toilet and hand basin, and there she found another Snowdon. This was a much smaller one. A woman wearing a back-pack, cameras slung around her neck pointing at the remains of a small house its walls pock marked with bullet holes. Snowdon had managed to capture the full horror of war in the expression on her face, beneath a protective helmet. Kia lifted her camera again. The photograph was a sharp contrast to the dreamy woman in the drawing room who looked as though she had never experienced anything horrible in her entire life.

She heard Josh calling her and tried to work out which direction his voice was coming from. Giving up she called back.

"Hey, Josh, if you can find the drawing room come and have a look at this photograph – it's a Snowdon!"

Josh followed the sound of her voice. They both studied the photograph. Josh was more than impressed. "Come on, my lovely, time to lock up and get back to the pub. I don't know about you but I could murder a couple of beers and something to eat. We can leave all our kit here. Judging by all the security in and around the place it should be quite safe."

The pub was now busy, but Polly had reserved them a small table close enough to the fire to feel a bit of warmth. They studied the menu. Kia decided on the scampi and chips, Josh went for the chicken pie with chips.

Josh took a large mouthful of beer and wiped the foam from his top lip with pleasure. "Bloody good at making beer here, I have to say. Not ice-cold like at home, but its good stuff, lots of body. How's the wine?"

Kia wrinkled her nose. "Not a patch on ours, then I would say that wouldn't I? But I like this little pub, it's probably hundreds of years old. I have to say there's a great sense of history here in the UK. It's like everything has stood still and in a hundred years' time, it will still look the same. Something nice about that. Are you all set to get to work tomorrow?"

Josh stabbed at his chicken pie watching the thick creamy gravy seep over the pastry. "Yup. Good to go. I can see how it should all look, have to use loads of lights though to make it look less gloomy. I had a bit of a poke around to see what I could use as props. There's a drawer full of candles, I'm going to use them in the original sconces. Probably been there since before electricity was invented. So, interiors tomorrow and, if the weather perks up, I need to get exteriors and some atmospheric landscapes. You can help me with those if you like?"

He picked up a crust of pastry with his fingers. "All the fields around the house are part of the property, even though the owner isn't selling them, unless of course the buyer of the house wants them, then he'll negotiate.

"When I was looking for the candles, I opened a lot of drawers. Every single one was packed with old stuff. Cutlery with yellowing ivory handles, kitchen utensils I've never seen in my life. I mean who would want all those old things? If the house sells what's this Ben

Courtney going to do with all the priceless heirlooms. You'd need an aircraft hangar to store it all in.

"There's a wine cellar in the basement, packed to the rafters with fine wines covered in cobwebs. Been there for a hundred years no doubt."

He used a piece of bread to mop up the last of his chicken pie. "The way I see it possessions possess you in the end. To inherit all that stuff must be like a rock around your neck. I mean, it's a beautiful old house but I wouldn't want to live in it. It would spook me out. I bet there are loads of ghosts creeping around at night, going through the drawers looking for their things."

Kia threw back her head and laughed, attracting a few admiring glances from the patrons at the bar. "I agree. Not my kind of place at all, but then, as you know, I come from a long line of people who owned pretty much nothing. This North End place really fascinates me."

"Excuse me?" They both turned and looked at the middle-aged woman who had approached them. "Forgive me for interrupting but I wanted to say how much I love your hair my dear! Do you plait it every morning with the beads?"

Kia laughed. "No. It's like this all the time. Easy to wash too. I stand under the shower, rub in the shampoo, rinse, and I'm good to go."

The woman patted her tight perm wistfully and smiled. "I think next time I go and have my hair done I'm going to ask Doris to thread a few beads through mine! You're the two South Africans taking photographs of the big house I understand?"

Josh and Kia looked at each other. "There are no secrets here, my dears. We all know Ben Courtney wants to sell the place. Sir Miles was such a gentleman, he spent some time in Africa, Kenya, I think? We all miss him. He's buried in the local churchyard here, in amongst all his ancestors, and their dogs. Ben is the only surviving member of the family. Nothing like his grandfather of course..." she left the question floating in the air.

"Anyway, let me not take up more of your time. Good luck with the house. Sometimes buyers love a whiff of scandal, whilst others don't want to know, it puts them off. Nice meeting you both."

Josh and Kia looked at each other again. Scandal? What scandal in a tiny village like this?

Josh paid the bill. Said goodnight to everyone in general, then escorted Kia upstairs to their rooms.

"Goodnight, my lovely. See you tomorrow at breakfast. Eight o' clock sharp. It might still be dark but we have a full day ahead."

Kia hugged him. "I'm going to try the internet and do a bit of research on this Courtney family. See you tomorrow."

Kia snuggled under the duvet and flicked through the photos she had taken of the house. Again, and again she went back to the Snowdon shot of the woman in the portrait and the one of the woman in what was clearly a war zone.

It was the same woman. Of this she was now sure, having studied them both.

She propped up her laptop and tried to log on. There was no signal. For a moment she was frustrated then put her head back. Having no access to the internet was in a way liberating. There was nothing she could do about it. The sound of a lone car swished through the puddles outside. A light mist surrounded a solitary street lamp. There was an ancient stillness about the place.

An owl hooted outside, then all was silent. Kia fell asleep with the image of the woman in the portrait prowling after her through her dreams.

Chapter Sixty-seven

The smell of breakfast cooking lured both Josh and Kia downstairs. They were obviously the only two guests staying in the pub. The friendly owner, Polly, served them large plates of eggs, bacon, beans and sausages, with crisp toast and strong coffee.

She bustled around refilling their cups. "I'm quite sure there's no food up there in the big house. I've made up a lunch hamper for you. All local produce, like your breakfast. Can't work on an empty stomach now, can we? There's cold ham, cheeses and chicken. I popped some of my home-made bread in and relish as well, oh, and a flask of coffee. Not sure if they've turned the heating on up there."

Kia was quite overwhelmed at the kindness. "How lovely, thank you so much, we do have a long day ahead. I didn't even think about lunch."

Josh stood up and kissed her soundly on the cheek. "You're a marvel, Polly. I think I'll take you home with me."

Polly blushed. "To Africa? No, I don't think so. Not one for the heat and as for all those snakes and creepy crawlies…it always looks like such a troublesome place to me. I know it always looks beautiful on those travel shows on telly. But it's what lies beneath that bothers me."

She cocked her head. "Not unlike here sometimes. But I'm not one for gossip. I'll reserve your table for dinner tonight."

*****

Kia left Josh with his cables, lights and cameras to get on with the job. By midday a watery sun had appeared. Finding a pair of wellington boots which more or less fit, she set out for the fields surrounding the house. Blobs of white were dotted over the fields as fat sheep went about their business. Briefly she thought of her father and his small herd with their thin grey matted coats.

Cattle, with their swishing tails grazed in the pastures. She pushed her way through the wooden gates dividing the fields and keeping the animals where they should be. High up on a hill she looked around at all the greenness, the calmness of an unaltered landscape.

Finding a sturdy rock, she sat down. Now she understood why the British had fought hard for their country during the great wars. It was a small island, but the backbone of the people who fought for peace reminded her of the Afrikaners who had shaped the future of South Africa and lost in the end. Kia had the greatest respect for them. The Afrikaners had lost their country, their flag, and their national anthem. But still they were a proud and mighty people. Determined to embrace the new order of things.

Although many white people had fled the country in fear of the new order, most Afrikaners, had stubbornly refused to leave the land they loved. The country where they had their roots. The country they now had such high hopes for under the guiding hand of the new President.

Kia made her way back to the house. It was nearly mid-afternoon and she was looking forward to sampling the delights of the contents of the hamper provided by Polly.

Parked in the driveway was a mud splattered Range Rover. Not the estate agent she surmised, but probably the so-called gruff owner of the estate Ben Courtney.

Easing off her boots before entering the main house, Kia padded softly towards the kitchen anxious for a mug of the promised coffee in the hamper, glad she was wearing her thick creamy polo necked jumper. The house still felt cold to her.

"Who the hell are you and what are you doing in my house?"

Kia turned, startled at the harshness in the man's voice. She smiled nervously and held out her hand, which was ignored. "I'm Kia. A friend of Josh from Cape Town. I'm helping him with the exterior shots of the house."

"I only gave police clearance for someone called Headley. No-one told me about you. There'll be hell to pay for this with Sotheby's. How dare they include another photographer in this without telling me. You could be anyone!"

Kia stood her ground staring at the man in front of her. His hair was greasy and lank across his forehead. His thick padded jacket stained down the front. His cheeks flaming with anger.

"So, you're a South African, are you?"

Kia smoothed down her jumper. "Yes, I am."

"Never had much time for South Africans myself. Screwed up bunch of people as far as I'm concerned."

Kia smiled tightly unable to move even if she had wanted to.

"Well don't just stand there, where's Headley?"

He pushed her aside, Kia backed herself against the wall and closed her eyes. Feeling light-headed she ran to the downstairs cloakroom and splashed cold water on her face, trying to calm herself after the disagreeable encounter.

Ben entered the drawing room.

Without turning, Josh held up his hand, twisted one of the lights and went back to his cameras. Satisfied with what he saw he turned around. "Hi, you must be Mr Courtney. I'm Josh Headley. Nice to meet you. May I say what an honour it is to work in such an amazing house," he gave his boyish smile. "Alongside the great Lord Snowdon."

He looked at Ben Courtney's face and his smile slackened.

Courtney looked as though he was about to explode. "Your brief, Mr Headley, was to take interior and exterior shots of my house. It did *not* include taking images of personal photographs!

"How dare you come in here and invade my privacy! You will delete all the shots you have taken of that woman," he hissed, pointing at the portrait. "And I'm going to stand here and watch you do it. Understood?"

Josh shook his head bewildered. "Sorry Mr Courtney. My understanding was I would have free range of the house and take shots of anything which would enhance the sale of the place. The portrait is exquisite, the centrepiece of the entire room…"

"I said delete all the shots you have taken of her. Now!"

Josh picked up his camera and carefully deleted any of the shots depicting the woman in the portrait. A waste of two hours hard work.

*****

Ben Courtney looked carefully around the drawing room with its pale yellow and beige colours, then headed towards the drinks tray by the window. Next to the bottles was a small table crowded with silver

268

framed photographs. He lifted the bottle of gin and started to pour himself a drink. Then his arm froze in mid-air. Carefully he put the bottle down and scanned the photographs. One of them was missing. Only a trace of dust indicated where it had stood.

He turned to Josh. "I want you to pack up all your equipment and assemble it in the kitchen. I will see you both there in ten minutes." He left the room.

In the kitchen Josh and Kia looked at each other. "Now what?" Kia whispered.

Josh shrugged and began to gather his cameras, lights and cables, his face taut with anger. "I think I've just been fired."

Ben came in and closed the door behind him, leaning against it. He folded his arms and stared at them.

"I want you to open all your equipment bags Mr Headley, then turn out your pockets. Including your jacket and your coat. The same goes for you girl. I'll need your identity number as well."

Kia felt her temper rise. "My name is Kia. Please don't insult me by calling me *girl*."

Ben laughed at her. "Ikea? Like after the Swedish company who make cheap furniture – yes, it suits you."

Kia glared at him. "I will not empty my pockets, or allow you to go through my handbag, unless you tell me what you are looking for? Or, more to the point, what you think we might have stolen from you. Because that's what you're assuming isn't it Mr Courtney?"

Ben ignored her. "There was a small silver framed photograph of my mother on the small table next to the drinks tray. It's no longer there. I want it back! No-one has been to the house for weeks. I was with the estate agent when she came to view the house, she was never alone. Our housekeeper, Emma, comes in once a week. She would have noticed if the photograph was missing. So that leaves you two. Empty your bags."

Kia lost her temper. "How dare you imply we're thieves. How dare you! I know you have a low opinion of South Africans, or is it because I am a person of colour, Mr Courtney? You seem to have spent a lot of time looking at me, more than Josh, but then again he's white, isn't he?"

"Kia," Josh murmured, "let it go. We have nothing to hide. Let him search our bags, what the hell. I'm out of here."

Ben, with a triumphant look on his face rummaged through their belonging and found nothing.

Kia was furious. "Satisfied Mr Courtney? Or would you like to do a body search now? I've seen the way you look at me?"

Ben ignored her and thrust out his hand to Josh. "I want the keys back. You may leave now. I want all the photographs you've taken. I've paid for them and they belong to me."

Josh finally lost his temper. "The photographs belong to me Mr Courtney! I will not be using them. Find someone else, or let the agency find someone else to complete the project. I find your remarks about South Africans, and Kia in particular, deeply offensive.

"The money paid to me to do this job will be fully refunded. I want you to apologise to Kia for your racist remarks."

Ben snatched the keys from Josh hand. "Get out. I have nothing to apologise for."

Kia and Josh collected all their equipment and bags and stowed them away in the car. Josh started the engine.

Kia hesitated as she opened the passenger door and looked back.

The mist was swirling around the great house, upstairs a single light lit up one of the bedrooms. The silhouette of Ben Courtney was outlined against the light. Kia lifted her head and watched him. Then she climbed into the car.

Pulling her coat around and wrapping her scarf around her neck, she turned once more to look at the house. The light had gone out and plunged the house into darkness. She shivered.

Josh took hold of her hand. "Well that wasn't a huge success was it Kia. I have to say I've met plenty of rich and famous people but Ben Courtney is something else."

Kia squeezed his hand. "He has some connection with South Africa. How else would he know about identity numbers? Why would he ask for mine? Also, there was a South African Airways luggage tag on a suitcase in one of the cupboards, and whoever the woman was in the portrait he clearly hates her. My guess is she's his mother, or maybe his sister?"

She shivered. "I need a large glass of wine and the friendly face of Polly. What a ghastly day all round."

Josh drove back to the pub. "Yup, it sure was. I'll call the estate agent tomorrow and tell her we're unable to complete the project for personal reasons. Then I'll get in touch with the guys in Cape Town and tell them to find another photographer, South African or otherwise. Then we'll head home, I think. You okay with that?"

270

Kia nodded and reached for her camera. "By the way Josh, bloody Ben Courtney forgot to check my camera. I've plenty of shots of the Snowdon portrait in the drawing room and some of the smaller one in the downstairs cloakroom, at least we didn't leave empty handed. To spite him I'm going to have them blown up and put them in my office, I quite fancy having a couple of Snowdon's hanging on the wall."

Josh locked the car and rubbed his hands together. "Let's hope there's some kind of signal for the internet. I need to catch up on a few things. Did you get on line last night?"

"No. I gave up waiting. Anyway, I was only interested in doing some research on the Courtney family. I thought it might give a bit of an edge to our work. But having met that dreadful man I have to admit I'm not remotely interested now. Come on let's go inside. No need to tell Polly what a disastrous day it was. We'll check out tomorrow and leave it all behind. To hell with the Courtney's."

Josh stopped walking. "But what about all the lovely food Polly packed for our lunch? She'll be really hurt to see we haven't touched it. Hang on, I need to get the hamper."

Kia shrugged. "I'll tell her we were too busy to eat. We can take the food with us when we leave tomorrow. Come on I'm freezing."

Chapter Sixty-Eight
The Journalist

The Kenya Airways flight dropped as lightly as a feather at Cape town international airport. Jack Taylor waited with the queue of passengers for his luggage to come through the flapping skirts of the carousel. Scooping up his soft safari bag he strode through customs and out into the arrival's hall, then made his way to Avis and the car he had booked.

He navigated his way out of the airport and headed for the city. Jack wound down the window, feeling the hot air on his face. It wasn't quite what he had expected.

Miles and miles of poverty confronted him. Endless rows of shacks lined both sides of the impressive highway. Washing was draped over sagging fences to dry, plastic bags and rubbish were strewn everywhere, some hanging in stubby trees and others clinging tenaciously to bushes. Skinny dogs foraged for food, their bones standing out through their dull patchy fur. Rusting cars, missing their wheels, stood forlornly abandoned.

Bridges for foot passengers were dispersed across the motorway, covered with iron mesh to stop anyone from chucking bricks at the steady flow of well pursed international tourists who came in their millions to this stunningly beautiful city.

Taking heed of Alex's advice, he had booked a room in a small guest house in an area known as De Waterkant. A tiny enclave huddled between the City and the Waterfront.

He checked in. His room was simple but elegant, far away from the opulent five-star hotels that littered the City. He unpacked and walked out onto the tiny balcony.

Below was a patchwork of cobbled streets, restaurants and tiny shops, bakeries, delicatessens and nightclubs. In the distance the vastness of the Atlantic Ocean. The clouds were gathering with the promise of rain, a strong South-Easter, known as the Cape Doctor for its ability to clean up the streets and dispense of any lingering pestilence with the might of its wind, was already whipping up the sea into a frenzy. The umbrellas outside of the restaurants were buckling with the force of the wind.

Jack withdrew to his room, closing the doors against the impending storm. He spread the map of the Eastern Cape out in front of him. The car he had hired at Cape Town airport came with maps, in book form, but Jack wanted one which would show him the fine network of secondary gravel roads. He had gone back into the airport and found a bookshop. The map he bought, was perfect although he never quite managed to fold it back to its original shape.

With his finger he traced what he thought might be the route of Sara Saunders from Cape Town to the Eastern Cape. It was a large area, a couple of fairly big towns but many small ones and then there was the vastness of the bush.

He reached for his notes when suddenly his room was plunged into darkness.

Within minutes there was a tap on his door. A waver of light beneath it.

"Come in!" he shouted.

The smiling African, his face lit up by a lamp padded into the room. "Sorry Mr Taylor. We have a power cut. One of many. Eskom, is like a difficult child. Unpredictable! Our power company leaves much to be desired, but nothing to be done about it."

He placed the light on the table, next to the map. "Most of the restaurants around and about here have generators, you'll be able to have a meal. Perhaps the power will come on again, but who can say?" He shrugged his shoulders helplessly and left the room.

*****

Jack lay in his bed resigned to the elements. The wind roared around the city, whipping the rain every which way. He had run through the pelting rain to the nearest restaurant, had a quick meal, unsettled by the screaming wind, then returned to the guest house.

Tomorrow he would find the local watering hole for local and international journalists and look for Alex's old buddy, Ted Ford.

The next morning, tempted though he was to take his first good look at Cape Town and spend the day exploring, he made his way to the world-famous Mount Nelson hotel. The grand old lady of Cape Town had hosted international politicians, celebrities, Prime Ministers, authors, film stars and royalty. Steeped in two hundred years of history she still retained her young pink blush of colour as she nestled amidst her sumptuous grounds.

Jack parked his car and made his way through the hotel's impressive entrance. Although time had marched on the grand old lady still retained an aura of gracious days gone by, her elegant public rooms still whispering their stories.

The hotel had preserved one of the oldest bars in the City -The Lord Nelson. Here the old stalwarts of the town still came to drink. With its long bar, high leather padded seats, and old sepia photographs of famous people, it had retained the original atmosphere of an English club. This, Jack knew from Alex, was where not only the locals came to quench their thirst but also the local and international hacks. What better spot to exchange gossip and news with the possible sighting of a celeb or two staying in the hotel?

Jack ordered a club sandwich. The lunch time crowd was beginning to arrive. The tall elegant Indian barman, complete with turban and red sash around his white uniform, reverently placed Jack's order on the bar in front of him.

It was huge. Jack smiled at him. "That should keep me going for a day or two, thank you." He looked at the badge on the elderly barman's jacket. "So, Imran, how long have you been working here?"

Imran wiped his cloth over an already immaculate bar counter. "Fifty years, sir. I am one of the oldest employees here."

Jack looked impressed. "Wow! That's a long time. You must know everything there is to know about hotel guests. Bet you've seen a lot of famous people? Probably a few in the photographs here." He pointed to the walls of the bar.

Imran smiled broadly. "Yes, of course, sir, but not something I would divulge. You are a visitor to our beautiful city. A guest perhaps?"

Jack nibbled on a perfectly cooked chip. "A visitor, from the UK. I'm a journalist."

Imran polished a glass and returned it to the shelf behind him. Jack continued.

"I'm looking for a journalist called Ted Ford. Do you know him at all?"

Imran smiled broadly at him. "Mr Ted! Yes, of course, he is a regular here, when he's in town. He has a loud voice! Perhaps, sir, if

274

you'd like to leave me your card, I will give it to him when next I see him here?"

*****

Jack returned to his guest house and once more spread the map of the Eastern Cape out in front of him. He drummed his fingers on the table.

"Where are you Sara? Where are you?"

His phone vibrated on the table next to him. He lifted the phone then hastily held it away from his ear. "G'day, Jack! Ted Ford here! Think you're looking for me?" Jack smiled, yes, he did indeed have a loud voice with a strong Australian accent.

"Hey Ted. Thanks for calling, that was quick. Any chance we could meet up somewhere? Alex Patterson thought you might be able to give me some information on a case some twenty years ago?"

He held the phone even further away from his ear in anticipation of Ted's response. "I'll do me best mate," he boomed. "How about meeting up at Larry's lobster shack down at the waterfront. Not the posh end. It's down in the old docks area. Lots of atmosphere, great food and not as mind buggery expensive as the restaurants in the modern waterfront. Say seven?"

*****

Jack followed the directions given to him by the receptionist at the guest house. He made his way into the restaurant. Bubbling tanks of lobster sat in the middle of the room. The lobsters waving their arms languidly at the diners who were probably going to eat them. Lobster pots and old fishing nets decorated the walls, displaying trapped dusty plastic fish. Simple wooden chairs and tables filled the rest of the room, hurricane lamps glowed on each table. Knives and forks were heaped in a tin bucket next to a pile of paper napkins.

A large tanned man sat at the bar, wearing a battered hat with a leopard skin band. Jack approached him, his hand extended. "Some corks on your hat would have helped Ted. Jack Taylor. Glad to meet you."

Ted threw back his head and laughed uproariously. "We Aussies don't all look like Crocodile Dundee mate." He shook Jack's hand and he winced.

275

Ted stood up. "Let's grab a table, order some beer and food and you can fire away with your questions. Twenty years ago is a long time, but if it's a juicy story, I'll remember it."

The waiter delivered their lobster dinner the size of two small loaves of bread. Ted ripped off one of the legs and crunched it between his teeth. "So, shoot Jack, let's see what you're after."

"Does Sara Courtney-Saunders ring any distant bells Ted?"

Ted ripped off another leg. "Sara Courtney-Saunders? Too right it does. Daughter of a British Ambassador who served in Cape Town. Bit of a scandal with her husband, so she divorced him, then took off for some hidey hole in the Eastern Cape with her son. Had another kid. Can't quite recall the name at the moment. Anyway, when the child was just a nipper it disappeared. Sara was arrested and stood trial for his murder."

Ted took a long drink of beer and went back to attacking his lobster. "Four or five us journos went scooting up to follow the story. At the time the kid had only disappeared, no body had been found. But then there was a huge bush fire and Sara's house was burnt to the ground. She was hiding out in some safari lodge but they wouldn't let us in.

"We followed the story obviously, her arrest and the trial, but we couldn't get anywhere near her. The Embassy closed ranks. She went to prison; her son was hidden away somewhere either here or back in the UK and that was it."

Ted tipped his hat back with his fork, took a handful of water from the finger bowl and wiped his face and neck. "There was plenty happening in South Africa at the time, so we moved on chasing the next story. Always plenty of interesting stories to follow here. White farmers murdering their entire families then topping themselves, husbands murdering their wives, passengers falling off the back of cruise liners, murders in fancy game lodges and hotels. Township violence, drug gangs, yup, South Africa can always keep a journalist busy!"

He scratched the side of his neck. "You married Jack?"

"Nope. Women don't look on me as a long-term investment for some reason," he grinned at Ted. "Anyway, I don't spend much time at home, I have a small rabbit hutch of a flat in Kensington, and if I did have someone in my life, I doubt whether they would want to hear about my day at work, probably put them off their dinner, like dinner out with an undertaker and asking him how his day went! But I have girlfriends here and there, up and down the country. Works for me at the moment."

276

Ted nodded his head in agreement. "Same here. So how was Alex, the lord of the manor in Kenya? Bloody good journalist, and what a story he unearthed about those two sisters who lived at Mbabati…

"But let's go back to the Saunders case. One thing I do remember. There wasn't a single photograph of her or either of her sons, not when it all happened or afterwards. Just some half assed black and white sketch of a child with curly hair.

"So, what's your interest in the story Jack?"

Jack, defeated by the size of his lobster pushed his plate to one side. "Sara Courtney Saunders father, Sir Miles Courtney, died recently. Before he died, he called my editor, an old pal of his, and said he had some recent information that perhaps his daughter wasn't guilty after all. Unfortunately, he died before I could talk to him. Apparently, Sara Saunders committed suicide a few years after she was released. But here's the question. The body of the child was never found right?"

Ted nodded, seemingly dismissing the theory that Sara Saunders wasn't guilty, and now dead. He eyed the leftovers on Jack's plate. "Right."

"Supposing the child didn't die, maybe he's out there somewhere?"

"Nah. You can't hide a white kid out in the bush in Africa. Not possible. The area is remote, or was then. Nah, like I said the crocs probably got him; they don't care what colour dinner is, or how many legs it has. You're wasting your time Jack, too much time has passed. The story is dead in the water, if you'll pardon the pun. Anyway because of the circumstances, the storm, the fires and a wide search revealing nothing, the Judge at the trial recorded the child's death, and a death certificate was issued. End of story."

"Maybe. But I specialise in cold cases. This one has my juices going. I'm going to nose around and see if I can come up with anything someone may have missed. But I need your help?"

He looked around the now crowded and noisy restaurant. "Can you remember the name of the lodge where Sara hid herself away before she was arrested? Can you remember where her house was before it burned to the ground? Any names you can recall like the safari lodge manager's, or any of the police involved in the investigation?"

Ted tipped his hat back again and narrowed his eyes. "Let me have a think…yes, Bushman's Way was the name of the lodge. The manager's name I wouldn't have a clue, mate. He wasn't exactly welcoming when we descended on his lodge. The detective in charge of

277

the investigation was someone called Joubert. He must have been around thirty-five then, probably been nudged aside by now. The ANC wanted their own police officers in the old Afrikaner's positions. The white officers were pretty much put out to grass. But he might still be around. Try the clubs and pubs for disgruntled ex-policeman."

The waiter came and removed the debris from the table. Ted's eyes followed the half-finished lobster on Jack's plate with regret.

Jack reached into his pocket and withdrew his map, spreading it on the table.

Ted raised his bushy eyebrows, and roared with laughter, causing a few heads to turn at nearby tables. "A paper map! You have to be kidding right? We're up with the best in technology here in South Africa, Jack. No-one uses a map anymore."

Jack shrugged, unperturbed. "I've always loved maps. It's the way my brain works best. Indulge me Ted. Now, maybe you would show me where you think the lodge might be, and also the house where she lived? The nearest town would help as well?"

Ted reached into his pocket for his glasses, and bent forward, moving the lamp closer to the map. "Okay. This is the Eastern Cape." His finger moved over the surface of the map. Jack handed him his pen.

"This is the nearest town to the lodge. It's called Willow Drift, yes, here it is." He circled it. The house would have been around here and the lodge was two hours away, so hereabouts. However, over the years loads of safari lodges have sprouted up all over the area. It won't be easy. The lodge could have changed its name. New owners may have re-branded it."

He peered at the map. "Sara's house was close to a river – ah yes, here's the river. Can't pinpoint the house exactly. You'll have to work it out for yourself. Probably impossible to find now. Twenty years of encroaching bush will probably have covered what was left of it."

Jack folded up the map messily, and put it back in his pocket. "I owe you Ted. Not really used to plodding around the African bush, I'm more into the deep dark belly of the bad streets of the UK."

Ted rummaged hopefully around his teeth with a tooth pick. "Personally, I don't think there is a story here. I'm not sure what you're hoping for after all this time. However, not only are you going to pay for dinner, mate, I want a promise from you. If you do dig anything up and come out with a story, you'll share it with me?"

"Harry has the exclusive on this. But I can promise, you will get some credit if we find out what really happened to this child called Charlie."

Ted drained his glass of beer. "Charlie is dead Jack. There's no way a toddler could survive a river in full flood or the raging fire surrounding the family home. The crocs got him or some other marauding predator, this is Africa, mate, not bloody London!"

Jack handed over his credit card to the hovering waiter. "Maybe Ted, maybe. But I'm going to find out one way or the other. I'll look you up when I get back. Thanks for all your help."

*****

Jack drove back to his guest house, feeling no guilt at all that he hadn't shared all his information with Ted, not the letter from Eza, or the fact it looked as though he was the only journalist with a photograph of Sara Courtney-Saunders, and he had met her son Ben. Ted, he had no doubts, would more than likely have tagged along with him if he knew about any of this. If he had told him he thought Sara might be back in South Africa, well, he would have found him camped outside his bedroom door, cameras at the ready, the next morning.

No, this was his story. His exclusive. All he had to do was follow his instincts and get to the truth.

Chapter Sixty-Nine

Jack took a flight to Port Elizabeth, hired a car and headed for the small town of Willow Drift. On the flight he had worked out his strategy.

First stop was to find the hotel, he had booked on line, and dump his luggage. Then he would set out for the Bushman's Way game lodge. He hadn't found it anywhere on the internet. Depending on what information he could gather there he would then try to locate Sara's old house and the river. The scene of the crime.

On the drive from the airport he passed small towns. Some with only the main road running through them, small houses dozing in the heat, few people around and a couple of even smaller shops, a service station with the obligatory wash rooms, ATM machines, fast food outlets and fuel pumps. Most of the towns looked run down, as if they had been left behind, in the dusts of time. Sometimes he caught a glimpse of couples sitting on their shade dappled verandas, watching what little of the world was going by.

He found the small hotel on the outskirts of the town. The Drop Inn was anything but modern, and Jack's heart sank as he pulled into the car park. He hoped the inside was more impressive than the outside.

The old hotel might have seen better days but his room was clean and bright, more than enough for his needs. He unpacked and took a quick shower.

The directions to the game lodge, according to his map, and Ted's directions, seemed easy enough, a one-hour drive at the most. He had taken an early flight from Cape Town which left him the whole day to explore.

He drove along the well-maintained road, a sharp contrast to the ones in Kenya, until he came to a worn sign pointing to the left, he could just make out the wording. *Bushman's Way.* He could only hope the lodge was in a better shape than the signpost.

The dirt road leading to the lodge was in dire need of some maintenance. He danced the vehicle around the numerous potholes, throwing up thick clouds of dust behind him, hoping he wouldn't wreck the vehicle in the process. It was obvious the road had not seen any traffic for some time. There were no tyre tracks anywhere, only dusty bushes and spindly trees, dotted with crumbling termite mounds. Occasionally he saw some goats and sheep, but no wildlife so far.

He stopped to stretch his legs and took a long drink from his water bottle. Apart from the ticking of the engine as it cooled there was no sound at all. Not even any birdsong. He hadn't passed a single person on his journey.

He looked around. In the distance he could see some hills but otherwise it was miles and miles of bush, the heat shimmering across the land distorting the flow of the landscape. He climbed back into the car and continued on his journey.

He finally reached the gates of the lodge and climbed out. The place was deserted. Heavy chains and padlocks secured the gates denying entrance. Propped up next to a pole was a hand written sign in three languages. *"Keep Out – Government Property."*

Puzzled Jack looked for another entrance but high wire fencing stretched either side of the gate as far as the eye could see. To the left of the gate was a small thatched office, the paint peeling from the door, the windows covered in dust. He wiped one of them with his shirt sleeve, shielding his eyes he peered inside. An old African was dozing in a chair, at least that's what he hoped and not a dead body.

He tapped lightly on the glass. The old man woke groggily, and struggled to his feet reaching for his bush hat before opening the door.

Jack prayed the old fellow could speak English. "Morning! I'd like to visit the lodge please. Might be a nice place to stay for a day or two?"

The old African shook his head and pointed to the sign. "This is not possible, sir. The lodge is closed now. It will not be opening again."

Jack took of his dusty sunglasses and wiped them on his sleeve. "How long has it been closed?"

"Many years, sir. There is no-one here now. It is only myself who is living here."

"Was it sold then?"

"No, sir, not sold. This land where the lodge is belongs to the local people. Many years ago, the white people came and built this place not knowing the land belonged to us. The new Government has returned the land to our people. Now no-one is allowed to come inside."

Jack thought quickly. Somehow, he had to get inside and take a look around, after all this was key to his investigation. This is where the story had unfolded.

The old man was staring at him. Jack reached into his back pocket and removed his wallet. He counted out five hundred Rand notes and held it out.

"Maybe you would let me have a quick look around? I've come a long way to see this place. It used to belong to some friends of mine?"

The African eyed the notes. He reached out, took the money and folded it into the ragged pocket of what once had been his smart guard's uniform.

"You will wait here, sir. When I return, I will unlock the gates and let you in."

Jack smiled. "Don't be gone too long, it's bloody hot out here in the sun!"

Twenty minutes later the old man returned his bike rattling over the corrugations of the lodge path. Carefully leaning his bike against the side of the office he pulled some keys out of his pocket and unlocked the gates so Jack could drive his car in.

"You will not be long, sir. There is nothing to see here anymore."

Jack nodded and started his car. He drove up the short path and parked outside the old entrance of the lodge and stepped out. The lodge consisted of about twenty thatched rooms. The windows bare and the doors shut. He looked through one of the windows. The room had been stripped of any furnishings. He wandered through the main building; a solid wooden reception desk was the only piece of furniture. What once had been the lounge for guests had also been stripped of furniture, as was the dining room. The outside viewing deck was deserted, what should have been a sparkling blue swimming pool had been drained, now it was full of leaves and dead branches.

The owners of the lodge had obviously cleared out all the furniture when they had been told to move off the land. Jack reached for his camera.

He wandered down one of the pathways leading to more rooms, all but one bereft of curtains. Parked under a thick canopy of trees was an old car covered in dust. He hunkered down and studied the fresh tyre tracks. Perhaps the only room with curtains and the car belonged to the

282

old guard. After all he had to live somewhere and Jack didn't think he slept in the office. He would also have to get his food from somewhere.

Feeling oddly spooked Jack made his way back to his car, with a final backward glance at the curtained room and the dusty car.

The guard was waiting for him. "Thanks, for letting me have a look around. As you say, nothing to be seen here anymore. It's sad to see the place deserted. It must be lonely out here on your own?"

The guard nodded and put the padlock and chain around the gates.

With a final wave Jack reversed into the bush and turned his car around. In the rear-view mirror, he could see the old African watching him. Then he rounded a bend and the guard was gone.

Jack glanced down at his map. Ted had told him that from the lodge the river would be to the east of him. He looked for any sign of a road. There were small paths here and there but nothing that would qualify as a road, dust or otherwise.

He slowed down and spotted a dirt road which had recently been used. Perhaps this was the road the old African used to go and buy his food. He turned left and followed the faint tyre tracks.

Now the river was on his right and the tyre tracks he had been following had ended. He stopped the car and got out. A small track led down to the banks of the fast-flowing river, shaded by numerous leafy trees. Jack stared at the water as it rushed past trying to imagine a small body being helplessly pulled along.

He wiped the sweat from his neck and sat down on a large stump of a long-gone tree. Overhead a canopy of leaves afforded him some relief from the hot sun, a faint breeze cooled his hot face and body. He was tempted to strip off and plunge into the river, but hesitated. God knows what was lurking under the surface or hiding on the banks, maybe crocs.

He eased his swollen feet out of his shoes and once again watched the river. It was a strangely peaceful spot. He glanced at his watch, time to get moving. He reached for his shoes and noticed the disturbance of the earth around the stump he was sitting on. Not animal prints. Maybe the old guard liked to sit here as well.

Jack clicked away with his camera then climbed back into his car. The steering wheel was red hot, he poured some of his bottled water over it to cool it down, fully expecting it to bubble and fizz. He looked at his map again. There was a secondary road which would take him back to the main highway, if he kept the river to his right, he should be able to find it and hopefully maybe a signpost to go with it.

With some trepidation he set off again.

*****

The watcher's eyes downstream, hidden in the foliage of a tall tree, had followed his every move, before fading back into the thick bush.

*****

The bush started to clear and Jack was making good progress, he passed a small village and knew he was on the right track. Over an hour later he was back at the hotel. After another shower he changed his clothes and made his way down to the bar already anticipating an ice-cold beer or two.

Chapter Seventy

The ice-cold beer slid down Jack's throat like nectar. Closing his eyes with pleasure, he wiped his hand across his upper lip, then smiled at the barman who was looking impressed.

"Another one Mr Taylor?"

Jack nodded. "Thanks. I needed that. I'm not used to this kind of heat I can tell you."

The barman slid another bottle across the counter. "*Ag*, you get used to it if you live here long enough. Are you on holiday?"

Jack took another pull from his glass. "Yes, getting away from an English winter. I've read a lot about the history of the Eastern Cape and thought I'd spend some time here and not in the usual tourist spots. So, tell me what goes on in this town. Where do all the locals hang out?"

The barman looked around his empty bar. "Well not here at The Drop Inn, as you can see. Mostly the locals hang out at the Settler's Way. It's in the middle of town. Oldest pub in the area with a long history. It's not what you might call sophisticated, most tourists have never heard of it and you won't find it listed in the must-see places whilst you're in the Eastern Cape. But everyone knows everyone there. It has a nice vibe. Beer and wine are cheap, food's basic but good, and that's about it."

*****

Jack drove slowly through the town. There were small farm shops advertising homemade jams and fresh produce, one complete with an ancient wagon wheel leaning against the front entrance. A bakery, a butchery, art galleries, some pharmacies, restaurants, coffee shops, wine shops, pavement café's with scrubbed wooden tables, steak houses, a post office, a police station, a couple of fast food outlets and one fairly large supermarket.

In the centre of the town was a magnificent Dutch Reformed Church, its elegant white spires stretching towards heaven and all it promised. The doors to the church were wide open which surprised Jack. Where he came from most of the churches were locked and barred against unsavoury people intent on stripping the place of everything that could be moved and sold on.

Neat cottages with thatched roofs and pretty patios decorated with what looked like, to his English eyes, lacy Victorian underwear made of iron. He would learn this was a typical adornment of many old houses in South Africa and was called *Broekie lace*. Roughly translated meant knicker lace. Brilliant colours of bougainvillea, scarlet, white, orange, magenta and purple tumbled over walls and he glimpsed small glittering blue pools in some of the gardens.

A defunct railway line, rusting and sprouting dried brown grass ran along the side of the town. The peeling letters announcing the name of the town were barely legible.

A few thin dogs dodged in and out of the pedestrians and cars, looking for scraps of food.

He spotted the pub immediately. Cars parked in a haphazard way along the pavements and on them. The faded name of the pub, painted on the outside of the brick building.

It was already crowded with people having a quick, or perhaps not so quick, drink before heading home. He made his way to the bar unaware of the curious glances of some of the locals, and the admiring looks of some of the women seated at small tables.

The place reminded him of old traditional pubs in England. Instead of horse brasses, fireplaces and football scarves decorating the place, the walls were covered with photographs of big burly rugby players, behind the bar the old flag of South Africa and the new one stood side by side. Rugby shirts were pinned to the walls. A large flat screened television, on mute, was showing a rugby match. Jack smiled. The South Africans were passionate about their rugby and bloody good at it.

All the stools at the bar were taken. He stood and waited for the barmen to notice him, which didn't take long.

"Hello meneer! Hoegan dit met jou? Wat kan ek vir jou kry om te drink?

Jack understood the drink part of the question. "Castle please?"

A few heads turned in his direction. An Englishman.

Next to him, staring gloomily into his glass of beer was a craggy man of about fifty-five. His short hair peppered with grey. He turned and looked long and hard at Jack, his eyes surprisingly blue and alert, fanned by thick dark lashes.

"*Ag*, take no notice of these people, my friend, they're not used to Englishmen here. They're curious. Tourists never come here. These are good people they mean you no harm, as I said only curious as to why you should pick this place when you have the rest of the country to choose from? I'm Piet Joubert."

Jack extended his hand. "Jack Taylor. Pleased to meet you. Only passing through. Wanted to meet the locals, not into tourists myself."

"Don't give me the *fokkin* bullshit Jack Taylor. I knew the moment you booked into your hotel. I can smell a journalist a mile off. I know the story you're after. I know because it was my case. We're not all wild woolly Afrikaners living in the bush you know, oblivious to what's going on in the outside world, we notice things in town – like you for instance."

Jack tried to hide his surprise at being rumbled so quickly. He sipped his beer. The ex-detective was smart; he'd sussed him out the moment he entered the town. He said nothing.

Joubert signalled to the barman for another beer. "We were the best in South Africa. But politics pushed us out, the new order of things. Felt like a dinosaur, tip-toing around trying to avoid political and racial potholes. Man can't do his job properly in those situations."

"Must have been difficult..." Jack murmured, trying to sound sympathetic.

Piet narrowed his eyes and studied Jack, he reached for his drink. "Knowledge is the gift of a good detective, knowing the people of this land and how they think.

"Our trackers are some of the best in the world. Each one of them could get a degree in botany without even setting foot in a university. So, I'm asking you why you are here?

"What are you looking for Jack Taylor, that hasn't been looked at before? You think you might find something we missed? *Ag,* man we missed nothing I'm telling you."

Piet Joubert slapped down some money on the bar, rammed his battered hat on his head and stomped off.

Jack sat down in the vacated chair. The man next to him was sporting an impressive beard with bushy eyebrows to match. He grinned at Jack, deep lines branching out from his dark brown friendly eyes.

"No flies on old Piet, my friend. He can be grumpy after a beer or two but he's a good man. I'm Tinus, pleased to meet you." They shook hands.

"You're a journalist hey? There's only one big story this *dorp* is famous for and that's the one about the kid who disappeared a long time ago. People here still talk about it. Is this what you're interested in?"

Jack signalled to the barman for another beer. "Yup. That's the one. The child's grandfather died recently. My editor wants a follow up on the story. The public are always interested in stories about missing children."

Tinus shook the ice cubes in his brandy and coke. "Nothing to follow up. The kid is dead. I was involved in one of the search parties looking for him. It was like looking for a blond hair on the beach. Impossible with the conditions at the time."

Jack's heart skipped a beat or two. "Here Tinus, let me buy you another drink. See, the thing is I'm here now and I'd like to see where it all happened. I don't want to upset anyone, especially Piet Joubert who was in charge of the case. Do you think he'll discuss it with me?"

Tinus shifted in his chair and reached a large hairy hand towards his fresh drink. "Nah, I doubt it. He doesn't like journalists," he grinned at Jack. "Especially English ones. But I'll show you around if you like?" He slurped his drink and grinned at Jack. "For a small fee, of course, nothing comes for free in this town."

Jack nodded. "I'm sure we can come to some sort of mutual agreement about a fee. Would tomorrow morning suit you?"

The big Afrikaner nodded. "*Ja,* I'll pick you up at your hotel, we'll go in my truck. I'll be there at eight. The Drop Inn, right? I even know your room number!"

Jack shook his head and finished his drink.

Chapter Seventy-One
The Farmer

Tinus arrived at the hotel as promised, his battered old truck splattered with dried mud. Jack was waiting for him. The inside of the truck was as bad as the outside. An empty beer bottle rolled around under his feet, the ashtray was overflowing with butts and the interior looked as though it hadn't been cleaned in decades. A KFC take out box, bereft of its contents, but not its smell, was wedged under the seat.

Tinus looked twice the size than he had appeared in the bar the night before. In his early sixties, his face was deeply lined with character, built by a life in the hot sun and merciless wind of harsh summers, his arms and legs deeply tanned, his bare feet encased by soft bush boots and an impressive belly straining against his khaki shorts and shirt.

Tinus caught the edge of the curb as he took off, oblivious to his frayed seat belt clanking on the handbrake. Jack who valued his life and obeyed the law, feverishly felt around for his and strapped himself in – tight.

Jack looked out at the flat landscape and took a sip of water from his bottle. "So, Tinus, have you always lived in Willow Drift?"

Tinus squinted through the dusty windscreen. "In the old days I had a farm, sheep mostly, but this is harsh farming land, not much rain, we always seem to be in the middle of a drought. So, five years ago I sold the farm and moved into Willow Drift.

"The Africans are hungry for land. They reckon if their great great grandfather had two goats that grazed on a piece of land two hundred years ago, then it belongs to them now. I wasn't going to get caught up in another situation like Zimbabwe and get kicked off my land. So, I sold it."

Jack opened his window to let out a persistent fly and the lingering odour of KFC. "Willow Drift seems to be the only decent sized town around here, according to my map. Did you ever see Sara Saunders and her children? She must have come into town to do her shopping?"

"*Ja*, I saw her once or twice. A stranger is easily noticed in a place like ours," he grinned at Jack, "as you know. But she never spoke to anyone, didn't go to any local bars or restaurants. Did her shopping in the supermarket and buggered off back to the bush. She never came with her children. They would have been left with the nanny."

"Did you know the nanny's name by any chance?"

Tinus shook his head. "I would have no idea. But listen, man, you're talking twenty years ago. You'll never find her. She could have come from anywhere. Malawi, Zimbabwe, Lesotho, Zambia, or anywhere in South Africa."

"Apparently her name was Beauty according to Sara's father."

Tinus thumped the steering wheel with his big fist and laughed. "*Ag*, Beauty is a common name, my friend. Unless you have a surname, you will never find her. Maybe Piet Joubert can remember it from the case file. But if I recall there was no nanny, Beauty or otherwise, when we were searching for the kid. Joubert is a good detective he would have spoken to everyone who knew Sara Saunders. If this Beauty person had an identity book, he would have put it through the system and tracked her down. But if she came across the border illegally from another country, he wouldn't have been able to. If she returned to her own country she probably would have stayed there."

Tinus turned off the tarmac road and rumbled onto a dirt track, but not the same one as Jack had taken the day before. They passed a monotony of dusty villages with poor shacks and poor people. Listless lines of washing catching more dust than sun. Children squatted in the dust with only their imagination to play with.

Women bent double carrying firewood on their heads and babies strapped to their backs. Other women worked over their patches of garden, or pounded and thrashed their washing on the rocks near a muddy brown stream. Their men sitting on stools under the shade of trees smoking and idling away the hours.

Dilapidated phone lines followed the road, the poles leaning like drunks crowned with large scruffy twigs for nesting birds, big ones Jack thought.

They came to a fork in the road, amateurish hand painted signs indicated guest farms and lodges. Tinus slowed down. "Used to be

290

nothing here but the odd village or two, now look at it. It seems anyone who has a bit of land and a house with a spare room, has turned it into a bloody game lodge or guest house."

A group of startled impala stood and stared at them, their tails twitching. Tinus snorted. "*Ag*, should have brought my rifle with me," he muttered, "and shot one of them for the pot. They make good biltong too.

"Now, the game lodge where this Sara woman was hiding from the Press has been closed down. So, no point in going there. The land has been given back to the people by the Government. The owners thought they might buy everything in the lodge but when the promised money didn't come through, they called the auctioneers in and sold the lot. Not sure the locals would know how to run a five-star game lodge, but there you have it. It'll fall down in time and be no use to anyone."

Jack wound up his window against the dust. "What happened to the manager who ran the place?"

Tinus snorted again. "Went to bloody Australia with all the others who left the country. Me, I would never leave. This is my land, my country. I was born here and I will die here. There is no-where else I could be happy."

Tinus dragged a grubby looking handkerchief out of his shirt pocket and wiped the back of his neck. "My two boys also left for Australia, some years ago now, they saw no future here. When I sold the farm, my wife went to live in Cape Town with her sister, she never came back. We're divorced now."

He looked at Jack, and for an instant he saw sadness in the man's brown eyes. Then it was gone. Tinus continued. "The trick is to ignore the politics and all the corruption in the government and keep plenty of candles around when the power goes off, which is often. That way you can survive and enjoy life here."

He gestured at the land around them. "*Man*, this is a beautiful country and no-one can screw that up. The beer is cheap and they have a generator in the pub, what more can a fellow ask for, hey?"

Tinus turned off down a narrow bush path, haphazardly crushing bushes and grasses on either side. Stones pinged on the chassis. He stopped the truck. "So, this is where it all happened Jack. I'll show you."

Jack hid a smile, feeling proud of the fact it was the exact spot he had found yesterday. He followed Tinus down to the river.

"According to Piet this is where the English woman got rid of the kid. Today the river is moving slowly, but underneath are strong currents and within minutes it can turn into a raging torrent. Further up are the rapids and the long drop to the fast-flowing water below. The kid didn't stand a chance. I'll show you where the house used to be. Watch out for snakes."

Jack followed him. He hadn't even glimpsed a derelict building of any kind, now he understood why.

Using a heavy stick Tinus pushed his way through the tangled undergrowth. Branches, tree roots, spiders' webs and vicious choking vines snared everything in its path as the relentless bush reclaimed its territory.

There was little left of Sara's house. The broken remains of walls left were blackened with damp and fire damage. One wall remained standing over which a determined cascade of golden flowers still flourished.

Tinus looked around. "There was another building here, a *rondavel*, as we call them. It means a round house with thatch. Apparently, it's where the nanny used to live. This Beauty you mentioned. Ah, there it is. Almost disappeared."

Again, he swiped at the undergrowth with his stick until he came to the remains of the nanny's house. The door had gone and the birds and insects had made short work of the thatched roof.

He stood back and let Jack take a look at what was left. Jack paused waiting to accustom his eyes to the gloom caused by the heavy trees overhead. Dry leaves crunched under his feet as he looked around the small circular skeleton of the house. Something was scratched on the wall, he bent down, swiping away a cobweb that settled on him, like the caress of a healing mask on a burn victim's face.

ZA

"Hey, Tinus come and have a look at this. Someone's scratched a word or something?"

Wheezing with the effort, Tinus crouched his great bulk down beside Jack then laughed.

"ZA stands for South Africa, Zuid Afrika. If you've seen enough, we should head back."

Jack nodded. "I'm going to take a few pics of the place, give me five minutes?"

*****

Tinus leaned against his vehicle enjoying his cigarette whilst Jack wandered around taking his shots. Why anyone would want to take pictures of nothing baffled him. But Jack was an Englishman so who knew what he was thinking?

On their way back Tinus pointed up through the dusty windscreen. "Vultures. Ugly bastards with their beady eyes, scrawny necks and ugly beaks. But they're the office cleaners of the bush. They'll float around there on the thermals then, when they spot the remains of a kill, they'll gather in squawking bunches and wait their turn for what's left. Everything has a purpose in the bush Englishman."

Jack let that one go. He thought of the vultures and remembered the photograph he had seen in a magazine of vultures surrounding a starving skeletal child, still alive, somewhere in Africa, their great heavy wings like black cloaks, waiting. He tried not to think of little Charlie. Africa for all its great beauty had a cruel, savage dark side to it as well.

Tinus pulled up outside Jack's hotel smothering the scarlet bougainvillea bushes in yet another layer of dust.

Jack pulled out his wallet and peeled off a wad of notes. "Thanks, Tinus. Appreciate it."

Tinus quickly counted out the notes and nodded, satisfied. "Maybe see you down the pub later, hey?"

Jack hesitated. "I don't think your detective mate would be pleased to see me again."

"*Ag*, man, he knows where you've been today and he knows who took you. I'm sure the ladies will be pleased to see you again." He bellowed with laughter as he took off down the road to the pub. Dust and gravel shot out in all directions as Tinus ground the gears and catapulted out onto the road, black smoke belching out of the exhaust pipe.

Jack returned to his room and took a shower then sat propped up on his bed flicking through all the photographs he'd taken. Then he went back over all the notes he had made about the case.

For the first time in his successful career he felt out of his depth here in Africa. He had no infrastructure to lean on, no back up.

But one thing he did have that no-one else had was the letter from Eza. He ran his hands through his hair. Was it a Christian name or a surname? It was the same with the nanny called Beauty. What was her surname. Where did she live? How was he going to find her?

He had no other alternative. He would have to befriend the grumpy ex-detective and show him the letter. He would either laugh in his face or maybe, just maybe, take him seriously.

He drove back to the pub. Maybe Tinus could help him after all.

*****

Tinus was at his usual perch at the bar and lifted his glass in greeting.

Jack slid on to the vacant stool next to him and looked around. It was only four in the afternoon but the locals had obviously decided it was the beginning of the week-end. Sitting at a corner table were two Africans in business suits, a table of six women who had paused in mid-sentence and eyed him with interest, as he walked to the bar. An elderly couple sat alone saying nothing to each other, watching everyone else. Briefly he wondered where the Coloured people of the town, and he had seen many, gathered for a drink or two. Tinus would know.

Jack ordered a beer and turned to Tinus and asked him.

"The Coloured people stick close together, you won't find them in any of the local bars. Of course, everyone can drink where they want to now. The Coloured folk like their *shebeens* where they can drink their own traditional beers and eat their own kinds of hot and spicy foods, and listen to their loud music. Friday is a big night for them, the end of a working week, they like to get stuck into their drinking!"

Jack nodded. "Detective Joubert not around today?"

Tinus wiped the wet ring his glass had made on the bar with his sleeve. "Nah, he's out of town for the week-end, visiting his sister. Should be back on Monday - if he feels like it."

Jack drummed his fingers on the bar. "I want to try and persuade him to discuss the Saunders case with me. There's a slim chance he could agree. I might have something he can help me with."

He saw a flash of interest in the big man's eyes. "Something the grandfather told you?"

"No. I never met the grandfather, but my editor knew him well."

Jack reached into his trouser pocket and pulled out the small silver framed photograph of Sara. He slid it across the counter. "Do you recognise her Tinus?"

Tinus fished around in his shirt pocket and found his battered reading glasses. He peered at the photograph. "Jeez, I need new glasses, can't see *fokkol* with these." He took them off and threw them on the

294

bar. Jack reached over for them and polished them with the hem of his shirt.

"Try them now Tinus, it helps to clean them now and again."

Tinus grinned at him, perched his glasses on his nose, and stared down at the photo.

"This is the English woman. Yes, I'm sure. She had blonde hair, attractive, walked around with her nose in the air. Wouldn't have helped her in prison though. I wonder what happened to her after she'd served her sentence."

Jack retrieved his photograph and slipped it back in his pocket. "According to the British newspapers, she went back to England, lived there for a while then committed suicide."

Tinus looked genuinely shocked. "*Ag*, that's a bad story Jack. But her son must be grown up by now? Maybe he will have a happier life back in this place called England. God willing."

Jack finished the last dregs of his drink. "Yes, I'm sure Ben will be alright. He's the only survivor of the family now. See you around Tinus."

Jack made his way to the door of the pub and turned around briefly. Tinus was watching him.

He had thrown a few nuggets of information at the big Afrikaner. Enough, he hoped, to pique the interest of Piet Joubert. Tinus would without doubt relay the conversation to him.

It had been Joubert's case and what detective wasn't interested in his prime suspect's life when she left prison? He would surely be interested in Ben and how he had turned out?

Chapter Seventy-Two
Joseph

Jack had maybe another day before Piet Joubert would be back in town after the visit to his sister. He decided to go back to Sara's old house.

Looking for Beauty, the nanny, would be a hopeless task unless Joubert had more information about her. As Tinus had said she might not even be a South African, she could have come from any of the surrounding countries, Malawi, Botswana, Zambia, or Zimbabwe, crossing the border illegally looking for work as many hundreds had done over the years.

If she had been in the country without the right paperwork why would she have scraped the letters ZA on the wall of her small house? Even if she had been a South African it would be rather an odd thing to do?

He wanted to take another look at her place and the scratching on the wall.

The day was mercifully overcast a respite from the brutal summer sun. He parked on the dirt track. The river looked dark green and moody today, he watched it briefly before heading for Beauty's small house.

It was gloomy inside with no sun to brighten the place through the gaping holes in the thatched roof. Creepers searched hungrily for places to attach themselves to, in the corner the wind had formed a vortex of dried leaves and broken branches.

Jack hunkered down and examined the wall again. There were the letters ZA. The Z was partially hidden by a tenacious vine covered in sharp thorns. Jack looked around for something he could use to prise it from the stone wall. He rummaged around in the pile of leaves, carefully watching for snakes and spiders, until he found a sturdy stick. He was no slouch when it came to danger in human form, but snakes and spiders made his skin crawl with fear, even though he had only seen them on television. He'd rather face a known killer brandishing an axe.

A watery sun broke through the clouds, throwing some light into the gloomy interior. He could feel the sweat running down his neck and back as he worked at the vine. It wouldn't budge. He went outside and found a sharp rock. A thorn jabbed his thumb and he swore as he sucked at the blood. Wrapping his handkerchief around it he gave the vine one final angry blow and watched as it released its grasp and fell to the dusty floor. He sat down abruptly.

EZA

He laughed. So much for Tinus's story of a patriotic local. There it was right in front of his eyes. The writer of the letter. He tapped the stick on the floor. Maybe Eza was Beauty's lover? Her husband? That would make sense.

He sensed a presence behind him. He had heard no footsteps, saw no shadows of anyone. He stood up and turned around, wiping his sweaty hands on his trousers.

A short wiry man, with skin the colour of strong tea, was standing watching him. Jack felt a brief flash of pure fear pass through him, not helped by the half-naked man's hand holding a quiver of short arrows with sharp shiny tips and speckled feathers.

He had nothing to protect himself with, only the rock near his feet. He should never have come alone. Crime was well known in this country, he had been warned to be on guard, not walk in dark places on his own, keep to lighted areas preferably travelling in pairs, and here he was in a gloomy broken house, miles from anywhere with a ferocious looking man holding a fistful of sharp looking spears, probably loaded with deadly poison.

The dark man's eyes were hard and hostile, they shifted slightly to the writing on the wall then back to Jack.

The man turned without a word, and beckoned Jack to follow him. He walked down the short track until he reached the banks of the river then indicated, with his arrows, Jack should sit on the tree stump.

Jack immediately did as he was told, fear still coursing through his veins. Was he going to kill him with one of those deadly spears and throw his body in the ever-hungry river?

He straightened his shoulders. He had been in tighter corners than this with dangerous criminals. He had done nothing wrong. He smiled shakily at the man with the arrows.

"Sorry, I thought the place was deserted, I wanted to take a look around." He prayed the dark man, with the hard-unfriendly eyes, would speak at least a little English. My name's Jack. What's your name, my friend?"

The man hunkered down, carefully placing his arrows in the dirt next to his foot. "My name is Joseph. This is my land. You must not be here. You have been here three times now. I have been watching."

Relieved the man spoke English, although not well, Jack allowed himself another shaky smile. "I meant no harm. I'm looking for someone."

"There is no-one here. This is my land, given to my father by the big white chief Miles from the place with the flat mountain. I have papers; these papers will give the land to me when the white chief dies."

Jack stood up quickly, and held out his hand, startling Joseph, who lunged instinctively for his spears. "You are the cousin of Eza yes?"

Joseph's face was impassive. He ignored Jack's outstretched hand. "I am the cousin of Eza. My father was the Chief of the village. How are you knowing these things?"

Jack saw the opportunity and took it with his years of experience. "I've been looking for you Joseph. That's why I've been coming here. Chief Miles is dead. This land is now yours. This is why I have been searching for you."

Joseph nodded his head slowly. "Then I thank you for this Mr Yak. But now you have told me this news you must go."

"You speak English well Joseph?"

"I was working on a hunting farm. I am a tracker. This is where I learned this language. Now you must leave this place."

"You must be able to drive if you work on a hunting farm. Do you have a car Joseph?" he asked casually.

A faint smile crossed the tracker's face, revealing two missing front teeth. "What good is a car for a tracker such as I? My feet are free and fast, these feet have no need of papers and fuel. They take me where I need to go when I look down and need them."

Jack scuffed the dirt at his feet. He needed more information. "Joseph before I go, I need you to help me. I have brought you the news that this land is now yours, and where I come from this is rewarded. It's not money I need. I need to find Eza. Chief Miles asked me to do this for him.

"The Chief wanted Eza to find his daughter Sara. She is missing somewhere in the Eastern Cape."

298

He reached for the photograph in his pocket and held it out to Joseph. "This is his daughter Sara. Do you know her?"

Joseph stared at the photograph then looked up at Jack, his face once again impassive. "I do not know this woman. Eza is not here, he does not know this woman. Eza has never been here. His village was many days walk from this place. He has returned to the land of his ancestors."

That may well be, thought Jack to himself, but it didn't mean he was dead did it?

Jack tried once more. "This place where we are now is where a child went missing. Eza wrote to Chief Miles. He said you, Joseph, saw what happened. Is this true?"

Like a grieving widow, a thick veil dropped over Joseph's face.

Jack tried again. "Joseph, tell me this. Why is Eza's name on the wall, if he has never been here?"

Joseph picked up his arrows. "What you are telling me is not the truth. Eza cannot write these English words." He stared at Jack, then with not another word he turned and loped off, melting into the thick reeds, trees and bushes along the river bank.

Jack stared after him. Joseph had appeared from no-where and now he was gone, taking his secrets with him.

*****

Joseph hurried through the long grasses. He prayed to his Gods he would never see Mr Yak again. Although the white man had brought him good news, and for this he was thankful. But he was much afraid for his cousin Eza.

Eza had come to this place where the child had gone missing. *Eish,* why had his cousin come here and left his name on the wall of the broken house? This was a foolish thing to do.

If Mr Yak went to the police, they would come looking for Eza. Then they would come looking for him to find the truth. If this should happen, he would not be able to build on his land.

He would have to hide in one of the many caves high in the hills. With no-one to tell the police the truth, they would leave him alone. They would not be able to find him. Then when it was safe he, Joseph, could come back and claim his land.

He would get word to his cousin and warn him. He would also have to let Eza know his wife, Mirium, was soon to leave him.

It had been many years since he had been back to his village, many years since he had seen his sister Mirium.

It had been safer that way.

Chapter Seventy-Three
Eza's Wife

Jack returned to his hotel in Willow Drift, his mind sifting through his conversation with Joseph. Finding him had been more than he could have hoped for. Now he had to find Eza. Joseph had said he had gone to his ancestors but, in Jack's mind, it didn't mean he was dead.

Maybe if he could find out Eza's surname the grumpy detective might be able to help. Maybe he would know Joseph if he had worked as a tracker on a game farm. Jack knew the wily detective had the blood of a policeman coursing through his veins, retired or not, he would have his contacts.

He showered and changed into long trousers and a long-sleeved shirt. The mosquitoes seemed to be attracted to the blood of an Englishman if last night was anything to go by.

He wandered into the bar and perched on one of the stools. Business men in suits took up three of the tables, otherwise the place was empty. A woman, behind the bar, in her fifties, with a red slash of lipstick and scarlet fingernails to match, was opening a bottle of wine and smiled at him, her mascara as thick as spider's legs. Silver bangles rattled on her plump arm.

"Be with you in a moment, sir." She whipped out a tray, plunged the bottle into an ice bucket, lifted the flap of the bar and deposited the wine on one of the guest's tables.

"Now, what can I get you? It's Mr Taylor isn't it? I'm Jean."

He smiled at her. "Yes. A beer please. Judging by the cars outside it looks as though you have a few guests staying tonight?"

"Indeed, we do. One of our locals died on Friday. Her funeral is being held tomorrow. Mirium Klassens. She made the most beautiful quilts. She spent her remaining years in our little care home here in town."

Suddenly the bar was plunged into darkness. Jean reached for the matches and ever-present candles, as did all the other patrons. She rolled her eyes. "I used to think candle light was romantic, but Eskom, our electricity suppliers, soon put paid to that. Dinner by candlelight takes on a whole new meaning now."

The growl of an engine enveloped the room. Jack looked around startled. Jean laughed. "That's the generator. Guests get a bit cross when they can't use their hairdryers and things, and they fully expect some light and a hot dinner!"

Jean slid another beer across the counter to him. "Mirium, the quilt makers children have already checked in...oh, excuse me Mr Taylor, there are some guests at the front desk. I'll be right back."

Five minutes later she was back taking up her position behind the bar. "Such a lovely couple the Templetons, the couple who just checked in. They used to live here in town before they returned to the UK. Diana used to teach a few of the local children, the poorer ones from the township, who couldn't afford the school fees."

Jack scratched at a mosquito bite on his wrist. "So, this English couple have come all the way over here for, what was her name again? Mirium?"

Jean nodded. "Mirium Klassens, yes."

"Long way to come for a funeral, but kind of nice. Did she work for them?"

"Oh no! But it's rather a good story and I gather you like stories Mr Taylor, being a journalist."

Jack smiled. "Call me Jack. There are definitely no secrets in this town are there Jean. But you're right I do like a good story."

Jean glanced around the bar, no-one seemed to needing her at the moment. "Apparently Diana Templeton was wandering around the market and saw those beautiful quilts I was telling you about. Mirium was sitting there with her two children. They lived in a village miles and miles away in the bush.

"Diana knew the children wouldn't have been to any sort of school and decided she wanted to help them. Over the years not only did she educate them, and pay the school fees, they came to live with her.

"Then, if that wasn't enough, when the kid's parents couldn't survive anymore in their village, she let them stay in a cottage in the grounds of their house. It's why the Templetons have flown over for the funeral."

302

Jack smiled. "A nice story. What happened to her husband? The children's father? You left that bit out. They must have had a father?"

"Yes, of course they had a father! But no one knows what happened to him. One minute he was living in the cottage with his wife and the next thing he was gone. Hasn't been seen since."

"Bit of a slap in the face for the Templetons after they'd been kind and generous to the family wasn't it?"

Jean shook her head. "These people, well ... they're not like us Jack. They're nomadic, some more than others. Having lived in the bush all his life I expect he missed it. Willow Drift would have been like a foreign city to him."

The bar started to fill up and Jean was busy. He nursed his beer and thought about his day. He would order room service, email Harry, and bring him up to date, then send a brief note to Doctor O'Hara, Ted, the loud Australian journalist, and Alex Patterson in Kenya, letting them know he was still searching for Sara, then he'd have an early night.

Chapter Seventy-Four
Eza

Eza was too late to say goodbye to his wife.

He stood in the shadows of the trees in the cemetery and watched as Mirium's coffin was lowered into the hard-baked earth. He saw his children, Kia and Jabu; Jabu with his arms around his little sister. The tears found their way into the corners of his mouth and he let them dry there.

The Templetons stood straight and tall and he felt a moment of guilt for running away from their cottage without telling them why. There were other strangers around the grave but he did not know them.

The priest's long white dress, with the big silver necklace, was moving like the wind in the grasses. Then he closed his book with the golden pages and the red tongue.

Eish, this is not where his wife should be lying, with the Jesus people, she should be with her own people in the hills of the sleeping lion.

The people in the dark clothes filed out of the cemetery, and he briefly glimpsed the faces of his children again. But they did not see him hidden there.

The sun was beginning to set, soon it would be dark and Eza would be able to say his own private goodbye to Mirium.

*****

Jack had spent the afternoon exploring the town, taking photographs of the magnificent church at its centre and getting a sense of the town where Sara Saunders had done her shopping. It was much bigger than he had first thought. He looked up at the sky, dusk was on its way, a fine veil of rain was sweeping down from the hills. He had one more stop to make.

304

The cemetery with the given moody light would make for some excellent atmospheric shots. He wandered around the headstones and found one fresh grave, and guessed this was the final resting place of the woman called Mirium Klassens, the quilt maker the barmaid had talked about the night before.

*****

Eza watched as the white man strode through the gates of the cemetery. He had heard from his cousin about the Englishman who was asking questions and who Joseph had met down by the river. This must be the man with the wild hair from the place across the sea.

He melted back into the shadows and watched as the man walked around the graves taking his photographs. He frowned when the man stopped at Mirium's, and took more photographs.

Then with one last look around, the man with the camera left and the cemetery was once again, still and silent.

*****

Jack headed towards his car and put his cameras on the passenger seat. Then he stopped. Damn one of the lens caps was missing, he must have dropped it, he picked up the camera. It would be a bitch to find with the fading light. He trotted back to the cemetery then stopped dead in his tracks.

A slight dark man was hunkered down next to the newly dug grave, his hands stroking the fresh earth. He was poorly dressed, his hair tightly curled to his head like a cap. He was talking softy in a strange lilting language peppered with clicks, his tears mingling with the fine mist reflecting the last of the light on his face.

Jack held his breath, then raised his camera. It would make a magnificent shot. Not wishing to intrude on the man's private grief, Jack turned and went back to his car.

*****

Jack showered and changed and decided to sit out on the veranda of the hotel gardens and enjoy the evening and a cold beer. The night skies were clear and he looked up admiring the magnificent stars above, happy to have no other guests chattering away nearby.

A waiter padded over to him and he ordered his drink. He had stopped briefly at the pub on his way out of town but the grumpy detective was no-where to be seen.

The waiter returned with his drink and poured it carefully. Jack thanked him and took a full mouthful. Lamps in the garden were suddenly illuminated diminishing the brightness of the stars above.

His eyes caught a movement to his left. A tall girl wearing a simple, but beautifully cut, shirt and dark jeans made her way to a table at the end of the veranda. Her gold hooped earrings caught the light of the candle as she sat down. Her braids were dark against her white shirt and cascaded down her back. He heard the soft clicks of the beads intertwined in her hair. She crossed her legs and the gold of her sandals glinted briefly.

The waiter brought her a glass of white wine and she turned her face briefly to thank him. Jack's breath caught in his throat. She was one of the most beautiful girls he had ever seen in his life and he had seen a few. The wine stood untouched on the table as the girl stared out into the dark night.

He watched as she stretched out a slim hand for the glass then withdrew it. Alarmed Jack watched as she put her face in her hands, her shoulders shuddering, the thin braids falling over her face.

He hesitated briefly then patted his pocket for his handkerchief before approaching the distraught girl. He knelt down next to her chair. "Hey, is there anything I can do to help?"

She shook her head the tears spilling through her fingers. "Please go away!"

He tried again. "Here take this." She put her hands down and he nearly forgot his name. Her eyes were the colour of fresh mint, her mouth full and sensuous. She was breath-taking, even the tears couldn't detract from her beauty, if anything they enhanced it.

She accepted his handkerchief and dabbed at her eyes. "Thank you," she whispered, handing it back. "Sorry, I didn't mean to sound so rude."

Jack reached for her wine glass and handed it to her. "Take a sip of this, it'll make you feel better."

She took a tremulous sip and handed the glass back to him. Tears once again filled her eyes.

"My name's Jack. I'm staying here. Look, would it help if I joined you. Talking about a problem sometimes helps and I'm a good listener with impeccable credentials. But if you want to be alone…"

306

The girl took a deep breath. "I'm Kia. It's been a tough day." She gestured to the chair opposite. "It's the least I can do for being so rude to you."

Jack almost sprinted to get his drink but managed to contain himself. He patted down his hair which immediately sprang up again.

He re-joined her and tried not to stare. "Do you live here in Willow Drift?"

Her beads clicked as she shook her head. "No. I live in Cape Town. But I know this area well. I went to school not far from here, as did my brother Jabu. We're here because my mother died. It was her funeral today."

Jack handed her his handkerchief again as her eyes filled with tears, like a green vase filling with water. "I'm sorry. It must have been a difficult day for you both."

He thought back to the story Jean had told him the night before. So, this was one of the two children the English couple had brought up and educated.

His thoughts went immediately to the cemetery he had visited only hours before. The fresh grave and the dark man kneeling next to it. Someone who had not joined the family group for the funeral. Who was he?

Kia sniffed, then wiped her eyes with the back of her hands, and took a sip of her wine. "So, what are you doing in this backwater of a town. Sorry, I didn't catch your name. Jack? You're English I think?"

"Yes. I'm here on a sort of holiday. Doing a bit of research for a book. There's a lot of history in this part of the country." Jack didn't think it was the right time or place to tell the girl he was a journalist.

"So, what do you do in Cape Town Kia?"

"I work for a lifestyle magazine. I'm going back to Cape Town tomorrow. She looked up. "Ah! here comes my brother Jabu."

A tall man emerged from the shadows and put his hand on her shoulder. "There you are. I've been looking everywhere for you."

She introduced him to Jack and they shook hands. "Nice to meet you Jabu, sorry it's under such sad circumstances."

Kia turned to her brother, a soft smile playing on her lips. "Come and sit Jabu. It's beautiful out here under the stars."

Jabu smiled at his sister. "You seem to forget I spend every night under the stars. A taste of life in town is what I need. The Templetons have booked a table for dinner at one of the restaurants in town. Ready to go?"

"Sure." Kia stood up and turned to Jack. "We're leaving early in the morning, but it was nice to meet you."

Jack held out his hand. "Perhaps next time we meet it will be under happier circumstances. I'll be back in Cape Town at some point. Maybe you could show me around?"

Kia reached into her bag and withdrew a small card. She smiled at the Englishman. "I'll return your handkerchief, nicely cleaned and ironed."

Jabu led her away, she turned briefly and lifted her hand. Then they were gone.

Jack sat down and as he picked up his beer, he noticed the small turquoise bead on the floor next to the chair Kia had been sitting in. He picked it up and rolled it between his fingers. It must have come loose from her hair. He tucked it into his pocket, then looked at her business card. *Kia Klassens.*

Jabu, her brother, was a good-looking young man with eyes the colour of wild honey, like a lot of young men these days he had shaved his head, but it suited him. On both of his coffee coloured wrists, and his upper arms, he wore cuffs of copper beads and around his throat a necklace made of tiny turquoise beads.

Brother and sister were a matching pair when it came to the turquoise beads but as far as Jack was concerned this was the only resemblance. Both siblings had the high cheekbones of the Griqua people and certainly their eyes were a different colour, a different shape – and there was something else he couldn't quite put his finger on.

But it was the sister who had captured his imagination. He rubbed his hands together. He would definitely look her up when he returned to Cape Town.

He finished his drink and wandered back to the bar. Jean was busy polishing glasses. "Hello Jack. How was your day? Beer?"

Jack nodded and leaned on the bar. "Have you lived here long Jean?"

She laughed. "It feels like forever, but actually it's been nearly ten years. I wanted to move out of Johannesburg and heard about this place. Came to visit and never left!"

"Have you heard of the game lodge called Bushman's Way?"

"Of course. Very swish, it brought a lot of tourists into this neck of the woods. But it's been closed for ages. The indigenous people claimed the land it was built on belonged to them, the government moved in and returned the land to them, but the lodge, of course, the

308

business, didn't belong to them. They tried to do a deal with the owners but it didn't work out so now it just sits there. Why do you ask?"

"No particular reason. I wanted to speak to the guy who used to manage it, but I understand he's gone to Australia. He was a sort of a friend of a friend of mine in Cape Town. I said I'd look him up."

Jean thought for a moment. "All lodge owners, tour operators and hoteliers belong to an association. Everyone in the tourism industry belongs to it. So, whoever owned the lodge would have been a member, especially as it was so swish, unlike some of the places sprouting up all over the country who don't belong to anything. It would be a good place to start to find your friend."

*****

Back in his room Jack phoned Ted Ford. Already anticipating his booming Australian voice, he held the phone well clear of his ear.

"Hey Ted. Jack here. I need your help?"

He explained what he needed. "Give me an hour or two tomorrow morning Jack. I'll have a name and number for you. I know the guys who run the association. Shouldn't be difficult. How's it going out there in the sticks mate? Have you managed to get talking to the detective Joubert yet?

"I don't think the old detective is feeling too friendly and fuzzy towards me. He's a grumpy bugger. Sussed me out as a journalist before I finished checking into the hotel. No flies on him. But I'm not giving up."

*****

Jacks phone chirped early the next morning. He picked it up and held it away from his ear.

"Morning Ted. Any luck?"

"Of course! The manager's name was Paul Weston. He was the one who kicked all us journos out when we were trying to follow the story of the missing kid. He left the lodge when it closed down. Went to live in Australia."

Jack swore. "Christ, how the hell am I going to find him there amongst all the thousands of other South Africans who emigrated there?"

Ted's booming laugh made Jack wince and he held the phone further away. "No worries, mate. That's my turf after all. Here's Weston's phone number. You should be able to get him now with the time difference. He lives in Perth, more South Africans there than here!

"That's another dinner you owe me Jack!"

Jack grinned down the phone. "Thanks Ted. I already have one dinner date, hopefully, with a beautiful woman, but I'm sure I can squeeze you in somewhere. See you when I get back."

Chapter Seventy-Five

Jack checked the time difference and dialled the number Ted had given him.

"Paul Weston here."

Jack took a deep breath. "Paul, my name is Jack Taylor. I'm staying in a town called Willow Drift, I think you know it?"

"Yes." Paul said cautiously. "Why do you ask? Who are you?"

"I'm a journalist, I work for *The Telegraph* in London. It's about Sara Saunders, there's been a development in the story and I need your help?"

"Mr Taylor, you're talking about something that happened twenty years ago, I'm not sure I can help you with anything. Is this why you're in South Africa?"

"Yes. There's now some doubt whether Sara Saunders was responsible for what happened to her child. I'm not sure if you know but Sara apparently committed suicide after she served her sentence?"

There was a slight pause, and Paul's tone softened. "I'm really sorry to hear that. I liked her; she often came to the lodge. What do want to know about her?"

"No-one seems to know who the father of the child was, the one who went missing. From what I can gather Sara rarely went to town so it's unlikely the father lived there. It would have been noticed. The only other place she apparently went to was your lodge. I need to know if she met someone there?"

"Look, Mr Taylor, Jack. The lodge has bad memories for me. No doubt you've been out there and seen the state of it? I don't want to be caught up in all of this again. I'll help you if I can, but on the understanding my name won't be mentioned?"

"You have my word Paul."

"Sara was very friendly with one of the volunteers who worked at the lodge. He was there for six months helping us out with a wildlife

311

project. I turned a blind eye to it all. It's not easy living out in the bush on your own. He was supposed to spend a year with us but cut it short and went back to Europe.

"I knew from his documents he was married but it was none of my business. Having said that Sara could have had other boyfriends. I didn't know her that well."

Jack scribbled some notes on his pad. "Do you remember his surname or where he came from in Europe?"

There was a pause, the line cut out briefly, then Paul was back. "Adrien. But I can't remember where he came from. He could be anywhere in Europe now. Can't remember his surname."

"One more question, Paul. I'm thinking there was something wrong with the child, either physically or mentally. No-one ever saw him. Do you think perhaps she did what she did out of compassion for a child who possibly had no future?"

There was another slight pause at the end of the phone. "I never saw Charlie. She didn't bring the children to the lodge, only Ben after Charlie disappeared. It's possible the child did have something wrong with it. I simply don't know."

"Thanks, Paul. I appreciate your help. Oh, by the way, I went out to your lodge. Deserted, of course, looking bereft and neglected. Perhaps Australia was a good move. I hope you've settled there?"

He could hear the longing in Paul's voice. "I'm not sure if it was the right move. I miss my country. But, no good looking back. Good luck with your search Jack."

"Oh, one more question, before you go? As I said the lodge is completely deserted now except for an elderly African guy, he seems to be the guard. He was the one who let me take a look around, for a small fee of course! I was wondering where his food came from. It's a hell of a long way out of town. I did see a battered old car parked under a tree though. Do you think he drives into town for supplies?"

Paul gave an abrupt laugh. "I doubt it. More likely some government lackey brings him monthly supplies. I doubt the government would supply a lowly guard with a car. I know there were no vehicles left there when we auctioned everything off."

312

Chapter Seventy-Six

Jack parked outside the Settler's Way. The sun was beginning to set, a dust storm was blowing in and threw the buildings of the town into soft relief.

He made his way to the bar and looked around.

"Hey, Englishman, is the wind blowing outside?"

He turned and saw ex Detective Joubert grinning at him, his battered baseball cap on the bar next to his glass.

Jack ordered his beer and slid onto the empty stool next to the detective. "Detective Joubert," he said shortly, "I can do nothing about my hair, it does what it wants, like the hair that sprouts from your ears.

"My grandmother was South African; she met my grandfather in England. She was a doctor, as he was. So, I have the same blood running through my veins as you, and yes, I am an Englishman as you call me, but I would appreciate it if you'd call me Jack. I have as much right to be in this country as you do. Okay?"

Piet Joubert waved a hand dismissively. "Whatever. Call me Piet.

Jack leaned over and shook the detective's hand. "I have more information on your case, Piet. I think you'll be interested. Let's call a truce here and pool our information? I have something I think you'll be interested in?"

"You're still a journalist, *Jack*. I don't like them, they muddy the water when we're trying to our jobs, or, rather, when we were trying to do our jobs. The Press are powerful; twisting and turning the information from a case. It was hard to work with when it involved an English woman and her child."

Jack took a sip of his beer. "I'm here because Sir Miles, the father of Sara Saunders, was an old friend of my editor. He received a letter which had been written some years ago, which cast doubt on whether Sara Saunders killed her child. As you no doubt know she supposedly committed suicide a year or so ago."

313

Piet was watching him intently. "Sir Miles didn't believe this was the case. He thought his daughter was still alive and back in South Africa, he wanted to know the identity of the writer of the letter. His name was Eza. Eza said Sara didn't kill her child. I need your help Piet?"

Piet Joubert looked into the depths of his glass. He knew this day would finally come. "*Ag*, Jack what do you want to know? Show me this letter."

Jack pulled it out of his shirt pocket and handed it to the detective. Piet stroked the stubble on his chin as he carefully read the contents, then read it again. He nodded and handed it back to Jack.

"This is not the place to discuss this. I have an office in town, meet me there tomorrow, and let's see what may come of this?"

He handed Jack his card. "There were things about this case which didn't stack up. It bothered me then and it bothers me now."

Jack looked at him innocently. "Don't suppose you have a copy of the file on the case, do you?"

Piet scowled at him. "I have a copy of the file. It's a cold case. Something I think you specialise in Jack Taylor?"

"In case you're not sure of my motives Piet." He reached into his pocket and withdrew the silver framed photograph of Sara Saunders. "You remember her, right?"

Piet studied the photo, the years tumbled back. "Oh yes, I remember her, of course I do. But the letter has no date. It could have been written by anyone, someone maybe looking for money? I don't remember anyone by the name of Eza, or Joseph come to that. Come and see me tomorrow and let's find out what other information you have found out and not told me about, hey?"

He rammed his baseball cap down on his head and stomped out of the bar.

Chapter Seventy-Seven

The next morning Jack drove through town, checking the address on Piet's card, and made a left down a short side road. Piet's office was an old run-down cottage, three short steps led up to the front door. Either side two drooping geranium plants made a valiant effort to brighten the place up, and failed. A small sign announced the office of *Streamline Security.*

Jack tapped on the door, pushed it open, and went in. Piet was sitting at a battered wooden desk sipping from a chipped brown mug. A pile of untidy files stood to one side, covered with a fine film of dust, the edges rustled as the orbit of a slow-moving fan moved over them. A small laptop computer was open in front of him.

Piet nodded at him and gestured with his mug that Jack should take a seat.

"Morning Jack. Shove the cat off before you sit on it. She has a bad temper, like my ex-wife. But unlike my ex-wife, the bloody thing insists on hanging around here."

Jack nudged the cat but hastily pulled back his hand when she hissed and spat at him.

Piet threw a magazine at it and the cat beat a hasty retreat, its tail thrashing angrily as it left the office. Jack sat down on what was possibly the most uncomfortable chair in all of South Africa.

"So, what does Streamline Security get up to in town Piet?"

"Not much to tell the truth. Bit of detective work, unfaithful wives and husbands. A lot of house owners sign up with us, we call it neighbourhood watch here. We set up the security for their homes. There's not a lot of crime in town, but we do get marauding gangs passing through, chancing their luck. The local police like having us around, helps their work load to have a few extra pairs of eyes out there. With all the technology around now, the locals are quick to tell us if someone shifty is hanging around."

He drained his mug of coffee and pushed it to one side. "Now, what else have you to tell me about the Saunders case I don't already know? Apart from the letter from this Eza person?"

"Not much more." He brought Piet up to date on what he had found out so far. "Sir Miles died recently with his questions unanswered. I have some questions though. The one that bothers me the most is no-one involved in your case ever saw the child before it went missing. Every shred of evidence was apparently destroyed in the fire. There's no photos, no papers to prove the child even existed."

Piet pushed a file across the table and stood up, he opened the window and perched on the sill, in the distance a dog barked mournfully, followed by another one further up the road.

"It's true there were no photographs of the child, everything was destroyed in the fires. Personal papers, birth certificates, passports, nothing was left. You must remember Jack, the country was going through a massive upheaval twenty years ago, there was a different kind of power struggle going on, tribe against tribe, black against white, everyone trying to grab a slice of the golden pie that was now the new governments.

"We were dealing with the daughter of a former British Ambassador, neither the British nor the South African government wanted to become embroiled in another political hot potato. In many ways our hands were tied. The media were given no information to feed on. For once we needed the media. We needed them to stir the story up and perhaps other witnesses may have come forward.

"But with little evidence to go on, and the fact that Sara Saunders was under the influence of a hypnotic drug the afternoon Charlie disappeared…" he lifted his shoulders.

Piet returned to his chair. "There was a witness who saw Sara take the child down to the river. It was never made public."

Jack jerked forward in his chair. "A witness! Who was it? Joseph?"

Piet shook his head. "Her son. Ben. He said he watched his mother carrying the child down to the river. She came back alone. He ran inside and hid in the cupboard scared she might get rid of him as well. Then, according to Ben, she went back to her bedroom and slept. It's all in there." He nodded towards the cover of the faded red file.

"Christ! No wonder Ben is so screwed up." He told Piet about meeting him at his grandfather's funeral.

"But why didn't Ben call out to his mother, or follow her?"

"Who knows? He wouldn't answer that question. Maybe he sensed something wasn't right and was too scared to call out or follow them."

Piet shrugged. "But let's go back to the letter from Eza. If he is telling the truth, then there was clearly someone else who saw what happened. This Joseph he mentions could have seen something or perhaps he saw someone else with the child."

Jack frowned. "If someone else had seen the child left by the river, or thrown into the river why didn't they try and rescue it?"

"That particular river is extremely dangerous; the child would have been swept away in minutes. Whoever saw what happened must have been hiding somewhere, some distance away. Probably knew he would be too late to save the kid, or maybe he couldn't swim. I have no answers to that Jack."

"But why didn't he come forward when the investigation was under way?"

"Jack you have to understand these people. They are brought up to be afraid of the police, afraid of anyone in authority. Perhaps this person was scared he may be accused. We searched all the villages in the area, in case the child had somehow survived, the four nearest ones were miles and miles away from Sara's house. Everyone was accounted for. We came up with nothing. The body was never found."

Jack stood up and paced the small room. "Do you think Sara was guilty Piet?"

Piet shook his head. "Despite all the evidence? No. Her shock and terror for the child was genuine. But, and there is a but, it's possible she did it whilst under the influence of the drug. I have no answer for that either, my friend. But one thing I do know Jack, Sara Saunders knew more than she was telling me, a lot more."

Jack ran his hand through his hair, and rubbed the back of his neck. "I think Sir Miles is, or rather was, right. I think Sara Saunders is back in South Africa. But the big question is why? Why would she come back to a place with such terrible memories? What does she hope to find or achieve?

"Sara has a close friend, a Doctor Karen O'Hara. Karen told me Sara was suicidal. I met with her, talked to her, and eventually she told me how she had helped her. Sara promised to keep in touch with Karen, but she didn't. She simply disappeared."

Piet shrugged. "I can tell you one thing Jack. I've checked back over the time frame you gave me. Sara Saunders never entered South

Africa. I still have contacts all over the country, I used them. She's not here.

"You think she didn't commit suicide in England or Europe as the plan suggested, Jack? But perhaps she did."

Jack picked up the file. "May I borrow this Piet?"

Piet nodded. "I tried to find your tracker Joseph, I know the hunting farms around here, it wasn't difficult. He seems to have disappeared off the face of the earth after your brief encounter with him. Probably scared stiff you'll drag him into the whole thing again. We won't find him. Trust me, I know these people. He's a tracker, he knows his craft, he would be able to melt into the landscape with no difficulty at all."

Jack scooped up the file and stood up. "It's the child that bothers me Piet. No-one ever saw it. The body was never found. But supposing, just supposing whilst everyone was looking for a white child, they should have been looking for a mixed-race child? Maybe the child didn't die, maybe it was kidnapped or rescued. A mixed-race child could easily blend in with the local landscape?"

Piet narrowed his eyes. "I thought about that but dismissed it as impossible. In the mid-nineties the country was different. A white woman with an African boyfriend would have been social suicide. Sara would have been shunned wherever she went, it would have been noticed and talked about in town. If she had any kind of boyfriend, her son would have said something."

Jack raised his eyebrows. "But it would explain why there were no photographs of Charlie wouldn't it? Why no-one ever saw him?"

"Nice try Jack but it's not possible. Now I have to get on. Let me have the file back when you've finished with it. Shouldn't take long, we had bugger all to work with at the time."

Chapter Seventy-Eight

Jack settled himself onto the sofa outside the coffee shop. He ordered a large black coffee and a toasted egg and bacon sandwich, then started reading through Piet's case file.

An hour later he brushed some crumbs off his trousers and closed the file. He was no closer to the truth, or finding anything new than he was before he started reading. Except for the one witness – Ben.

The waiter came and cleared the debris of his breakfast. Jack thanked him and asked for the bill, he paid and left, the file under his arm. He made his way to his car and looked at the number plate.

A young man walking his dog smiled at him and stopped.

"Have you lost your car?"

Jack laughed. "No. I'm intrigued with all the different number plates. I live in the UK and ours are quite different."

The young man wound the leash around his hand. "It's easy to tell where a person comes from by their plates. See, yours has EC at the end, that's the Eastern Cape, anything with a GP is from Johannesburg. CA is Cape Town and so on."

The man's dog was pulling at its leash eager to continue his walk. "Enjoy your stay," the young man called cheerfully over his shoulder.

Jack popped open the door of the car and sat with the windows and door open, it was like an oven inside. He pulled out his phone and scrolled through the photographs he had taken during his stay.

He found the one he was looking for. The car half hidden in the derelict game lodge. He enlarged it until he could see the number plate.

CA 46521.

Now what, he mused, was a car registered in Cape Town doing parked at a derelict game lodge? Paul Weston had said there was nothing left there. The car couldn't belong to the guard, if it had it would have an Eastern Cape registration.

Oblivious to the heat in the car he slammed the door. There was only one way to find out. He switched on the air conditioning then turned the car in the direction of the game lodge, and put his foot down.

In the distance he could see the thatched roof of the lodge. He approached slowly, trying not to kick up too much dust to give his approach any warning, wondering how he would persuade the guard to let him in again. More money should do it.

He parked a little way from the front gates and walked towards the guard hut. There was no sign of life at all. He peered through the dusty window and saw the guard was asleep, three empty bottles of beer at the foot of his chair.

Jack hesitated. Well it wasn't exactly breaking and entering was it? He slipped through the guard's small gate and made his way to the lodge. Fifteen minutes later he was staring at the blank spot where the car had been parked.

The curtains were still drawn at the windows of the small room he had noticed before. Looking carefully around he knocked on the door and when there was no response, he tried the handle and the door opened.

When his eyes had adjusted to the darkened room, he saw a typical stripped hotel room, in the corner was a small easel with a half-finished canvas. Leaning against the built-in wardrobe door was a small suitcase, on top of it a child's blue shoe, with a ragged hole in the sole.

He went back to the easel and studied the painting in progress. A child standing next to a river...

A single bed with a sagging mattress was covered with a thin bedspread. A threadbare rabbit propped up on a single pillow. The dressing table provided a small space for boxes and tins of food and a gas lamp. In the bathroom the shelves held shampoo, conditioner and some sort of body lotion. He doubted the guard used any of the products, or was an artist with obvious talent.

A small framed painting was propped against the shampoo bottle. Jack picked it up. A child next to a lake, an elephant in the background. He turned it over *The Lost Child*. He stared at it for some time, then placed it back against the bottle.

A toothbrush and paste lay next to a hairbrush. He knew without any doubt he had found the elusive Sara Saunders. He knew where she would be with the car.

He strode back to the guard house and prayed the guard would still be asleep. He was.

320

He slipped through the side gate and made his way back to his car and turned it in the direction of the river.

On the way to Sara's old house he tried to work out what he would say to her, how she might react when she saw him.

He nosed his way down the small track and stopped, turning off the engine. There was no sign of the car and no sign of Sara Saunders.

Disappointed he made his way to the river and sat on the old tree stump. It was possible she hadn't come to the river, maybe she had driven to one of the sleepy little towns to buy provisions from one of the service stations with a shop, after all she had to get supplies and petrol from somewhere and no doubt beer for the guard.

He sat there for an hour hoping she might still come, but she didn't.

He pulled her photograph in the silver frame from his pocket. He went back to the car and retrieved a plastic bank bag where he kept small change for tipping petrol attendants. Emptying it out he placed the photograph inside and sealed it.

Going back to the tree stump he wedged it firmly in between one of the dried roots.

Satisfied he went back to the car and reversed down the track then headed back to Willow Drift.

Although the grumpy detective had assured him Sara Saunders was not in the country Jack now knew he was wrong. She could have come to the country by ship, maybe using a different passport, then bought a car in Cape Town and made her way back to her old home.

She must have persuaded the guard at the game lodge to let her use one of the rooms, maybe he had worked there for many years and remembered her from her visits there. Otherwise money, in his opinion, opened a lot of doors. But what was she hoping to achieve hidden out in the bush there?

What was Sara waiting for?

Chapter Seventy-Nine

Jack let himself into his room at the hotel and sat at the small table going through his notes and photographs feeling the prickle and heat of excitement at the back of his neck as he put the pieces of his puzzle together.

He researched passenger ships from Europe and the UK that had called at Cape Town from November to February. He found what he was looking for. A passenger ship, out of Marseilles, had reported a missing male passenger. He almost missed the next bit. A female passenger had also gone missing, but the shipping line had assured the media that the woman had changed her mind about disembarking in Port Elizabeth and left the ship in Cape Town.

Jack nodded to himself. It was not unheard of for passengers who had one or two glasses too many, to fall overboard. Passengers often changed their mind about where they wanted to embark…

Thoughtfully he closed his laptop, had a quick shower, changed into long trousers and a long-sleeved shirt, his private war against mosquitoes, and made his way down to the outside veranda.

He ordered a beer and looked around. A middle-aged couple were sitting in the shadows, a lone businessman sat tapping at his computer, his suit jacket hanging over his chair.

The waiter returned with his beer and a tray full of lit lamps which he carefully placed on each table in anticipation of a power cut.

The lamp brought the faces of the couple into sharp relief. He recognised them as the English couple, Jean had pointed out, who had come over for the funeral, the couple who had educated the lovely Kia and her brother Jabu. The Templetons.

He stood up and approached their table. "Sorry to interrupt, my name's Jack Taylor. I met Kia and Jabu when they were here for their mother's funeral. I wanted to say what a great job you both did. Kia told me about you."

Startled, Diana took his proffered hand. "I'm Diana Templeton, this is my husband Norman." Jack shook his hand. "Would you like to join us Jack or are you expecting someone?"

He shook his head. "Thank you. I've had enough of my own company. Let me fetch my beer."

Norman tamped down the tobacco in his pipe, set it alight and took some short puffs until clouds of smoke enveloped his face. He gave a deep sigh of contentment. "So, Jack, what are you doing here in this little town of ours. Bit off the beaten path for a tourist I would think?"

Jack put his glass down on the table next to his phone. "Yes, I suppose it is, but I like the history and architecture of these small towns. The people are friendly and you learn a lot more about life here than you would speaking to someone in one of the cities. Did you like living here?"

Diana laughed. "Loved it! Then we went back to the UK and found it hard to fit in after all our years here and in Kenya. We decided to stay on a couple of days, after the funeral, to see if we could settle back here again. Things have changed quite a bit; we're still thinking about it. It would be lovely to be near Kia and Jabu again, especially now they've lost their mother."

Jack picked up his phone. "What happened to the children's father?"

Diana shrugged her shoulders, a small frown formed between her eyes. It annoyed her how young people today were always staring at their phones. Bad manners, she thought. But she continued.

"Their father was different. He had San blood running through his veins. He was only happy when he was out in the bush. He found it hard to settle here in town, when they left their village. He was a quiet, thoughtful, man. One day he was here, and the next he was gone. It hurt the children, but Mirium seemed to understand the ways of his people, she accepted it."

Jack took a sip of his beer. "Where do you think he went?"

"I've no idea. He would have heard about Mirium's death. The San people seem to know things before they happen. It's uncanny."

Norman puffed away on his pipe, saying nothing. But he was watching Jack carefully.

"So, he didn't come to the funeral then?"

"No. Perhaps it was too much for him. Too much explaining as to why he left without saying goodbye."

Jack scrolled through the photos on his phone. "I went to the cemetery after the funeral. The light was perfect. There was a fine rain sweeping across the town. I saw a man kneeling next to Mirium's grave."

He found the shot he was looking for. "I think this might have been the father of the children?"

Norman and Diana leaned forward, both of them reaching for their glasses and putting them on.

"Can you make it a bit bigger Jack?"

Jack enlarged it and handed the phone to Diana. "Oh, my goodness Norman. It's Eza!"

Jack's stomach flipped over as he tried to sound indifferent. "Eza? Is he the father of Kia and Jabu?"

Norman tapped his pipe into the ashtray. "Yes, Eza is their father."

Jack tampered down his excitement. "So, where do you think he lives now. It can't be too far away if he made it to the funeral?"

Diana plucked a moth out of her drink and flicked it into the dark night. "Maybe he went back to his village. He was happy there, although I think it must be deserted by now."

Jack smiled at them both. "Will you tell Kia and Jabu he visited their mother's grave?"

Diana looked at Norman, then looked down at her hands. "I think some things are best left as they are, don't you Norman?"

Norman nodded. But Jack was not finished. "I know it's a lot to ask but I really would like to see this village where Eza lived, where the children were brought up. I've never been to a genuine African village. Whereabouts is it?"

Diana looked at him. "You'll never find it. It doesn't even have a name. But we'll take you there if you like? There's probably nothing left of it."

She paused and took a sip of her drink. "When Eza and Mirium came to live in our cottage he brought a little three-legged stool with him. When we left here, we took it with us.

"When Mirium died, I brought it back with us. I thought the children might like to have it. It's not heavy, but beautifully carved. The children didn't want it. Kia regarded it as pagan, she said it wouldn't fit with her style of living in Cape Town. Jabu works at a game lodge, he wanted us to keep it, as a gift in remembrance of his father."

Diana glanced at her husband. "Perhaps we should take it back to Eza's village, where it belongs? Maybe if he visits his old home, he

324

might like to see it there. He used to sit out under the stars on it, and smoke his funny little pipe when he stayed with us. It would be something for him to remember?"

They agreed to meet in the morning and make the journey back to Eza's village where Diana's life with the children began.

*****

Diana stood at the window of their hotel room, watching the lights of the small town. Norman was propped up in bed watching her. "Diana, come back to bed. You knew this day would come, we discussed it. Jabu needs to know the truth, they both do."

She turned and looked at her husband. The steady hand on the tiller of her life, as it had always been. "I can't do it, Norman, why blow their lives apart now? We were in Kenya when all this happened. We did nothing wrong!"

Norman patted the pillow next to his. "No, we did nothing wrong. We just got caught up in the whole thing."

Diana lay down on the bed and he put his arms around her. "Leave it, my dear, it will sort itself out. Jabu and Kia are moving on with their lives, as we wanted them to. Don't take away what we've given them by dropping a bomb on them."

"But Norman, what about the mother? A child should never be taken away from its mother, no matter what the circumstances. She would have spent years tormenting herself with what really happened? I can't bear to think about it and I don't think I can live with it anymore. It's all wrong."

Norman rubbed her back, something he knew always soothed her. "Maybe, my dear, fate will take a hand. This Jack Taylor is, I think, more than he appears to be. We know nothing about him but I have a feeling he knows more than he's telling us. He's tough, inquisitive and highly intelligent. Not your average tourist travelling through the dusty towns of South Africa taking pictures of old buildings and chatting to the locals."

Diana pulled the duvet over them. "It's the mother who breaks my heart. She has to be told. We don't even know where she is, or if she's alive Norman?"

"I have the feeling that Jack Taylor will find the truth. Let him bring it all together, my dear. Let it go, my dear, let it go."

He reached over and turned off the light.

Chapter Eighty
The Mother

Sara carried her bags from the car and pushed open the door to her room. Instinctively she knew someone had been inside and it wasn't the guard Matthew. He would have said something. She knew, from him, someone had come to the lodge a few days ago to take a look around, purportedly looking for an old friend. But this time someone had gained access to her room.

She dropped her shopping on the floor and sat down heavily on the thin mattress on the bed. She had waited and waited for the person who had pierced her child's shoe and left it for her to find. Waiting hour after hour down by the river. She had seen no-one.

She ran back to her car and turned it towards the river. Someone was getting close.

The river today was churning and angry, brown and muddy. She made her way down to its banks and sat, once again, on the old tree stump.

She waved a fly from her face and her hand brushed against something stiff wedged in the stump's roots. She wrested the plastic bag from the deep roots of the tree, and stared at the photograph of herself. The photograph which had always stood in the drawing room of her father's house.

Instead of feeling fear, that someone was getting closer, she felt relief. Someone out there knew who she was and where she was hiding. This someone was somehow connected to her family, had had access to her home in Dorset and taken the photograph in its silver frame. Someone who must have met her father there, and he had given them the photograph.

She held the frame to her lips. Was her father finally, after all this time, reaching out to her, wanting to help her. Perhaps loving her at last?

Now she would wait for two people who might finally give her the answers to the questions she had tormented herself with.

The person who had left the shoe and the person who had left the framed photograph.

For the first time since that terrible day she felt perhaps someone was out there who believed her. Who wanted to help her?

She stroked the threadbare rabbit and watched the torrid water sweep by.

All she could do was wait and hope.

Chapter Eighty-One

Jack, Norman and Diana set off on their journey to the old deserted village where the story had begun. Diana, Jack noticed, was unusually quiet. She sat in the back seat of the car with her arms around the carved three-legged chair, saying little, only giving vague directions to the village she had visited long ago.

Jack pulled up and turned off the ignition. "Is this it, Diana?"

"Yes." She looked around despondently. "There's nothing left here as you can see."

There was nothing left. A faint shadow indicating the round circle of a hut, with only dusty thorn bushes and ghostly outlines left, of what might have been the dwellings these people had lived in.

Diana, holding the three -legged stool close to her chest, walked through the dust. She stopped and carefully slotted the two wooden slats together to assemble the chair. She placed it next to the stones where once the family had lived.

The memories tumbled back in her mind. And the one particular memory she would never be able to erase from her mind.

Norman, seeing his wife close to tears, called a halt to it all. "Look Jack, I think we should go back to town now. Diana's upset. There's nothing left as you can see."

Jack drove back to the hotel sensing the uneasy atmosphere in the car. He parked the car and opened the door for Diana.

"Maybe it wasn't such a good idea to go to the village," he said to her. "I'm sorry, it seems to have upset you.

"Perhaps you'll let me take you out for dinner this evening?"

Norman took his wife's hand and smiled. "Sounds splendid Jack. Thank you. Let's meet in the bar at, say, seven?"

Jack went back to his room and spread his map out on the bed. Eza's village, he reckoned, was a good forty miles from Sara's old house. That was one hell of a walk. But Eza must have done it at some point and left his name on the broken wall of Beauty's house. Joseph didn't have a car and it was highly unlikely Eza had one. He would have to find a different angle.

If the child had been taken, someone on foot could have evaded the police searches. Someone who knew the land, the bush and all its secret hiding places.

There was only one person who would be able to give him the answers he was looking for.

Eza.

*****

Diana seemed to have cheered up considerably as they dined at the hotel. Afterwards they took their coffee out onto the veranda and Norman went through his pipe lighting ritual, then sat back in his chair.

"Excellent meal, Jack. We don't get steak like that from our local supermarket in the UK!"

He looked steadily at Jack. "You're not a tourist, are you?" he said somewhat abruptly. "You're a journalist."

Jack swallowed his too hot coffee and spluttered. He wiped the drops off his shirt with his handkerchief. "Is it obvious? I thought I was doing a good job as a tourist." He ran his hand through his hair and gave them a sheepish grin. "What gave the game away?"

Norman squinted through the smoke of his pipe. "Mr Google gave the game away. Although I pretty much guessed when I met you. But you're not any old journalist. You specialise in cold cases and by all accounts you're pretty good at it. So, what are you chasing this time out here in the middle of no-where?"

Jack took a deep breath. "It's true, I am a journalist and I do specialise in cold cases."

He frowned. "I know how the system works in the UK, I know what to look for, who to contact when I want to speak to a convicted murderer in prison, or follow up on DNA. I have a nose for sniffing out long ago witnesses and putting a story together."

He scratched at a mosquito bite through the leg of his trousers. "But here it's complicated. The complexities of African languages, their cultures, their taboos. It's a completely different world but I'm starting to understand it…"

They were both watching him warily. "Maybe you can help me? It's something that happened over twenty years ago. A child went missing…"

Unexpectedly Diana stood up and reached for her bag. "I think I'll call it a night. I have a headache after the hot dusty drive. Please excuse me Jack. Thank you for dinner."

Norman also stood up. "Early night for both of us Jack. I think I'll join Diana."

Jack stared after them wondering what had brought the evening to such an abrupt ending. Probably finding out he had been a little economic with the truth when he said he was a tourist. Well, he was a tourist in many ways, but finding out he was a journalist and what sort of work he did had definitely spooked them. Perhaps in the morning they could resume their conversation.

There were things he still needed to know and his gut told him the Templetons knew more than they were letting on about Eza and his family.

The next morning, he had breakfast, then hung around waiting for them to appear.

After an hour he gave up. He went to reception to ask if they would ring their room.

The receptionist looked at him with a bright smile. "The Templetons? No, they checked out early this morning."

He had been right. The Templetons, nice as they were, had left the hotel in haste, taking with them information they clearly didn't want to share with him. Being a journalist had for some reason frightened them off. It wouldn't be the first time it had happened to him he thought wryly.

*****

Eza pulled the soft skin cape around his shoulders. He'd watched the Templetons and the white man with his wild hair place his chair outside his old home. He wondered who the white man was. He had seen him before. But what did he want now?

Eza sensed Joseph before he saw him. It was getting dark and Eza had built a small fire. Joseph materialised from the dark shadows and squatted down next to him.

The two men gazed at the fire saying nothing. Then Joseph cleared his throat and looked at his cousin.

330

"I saw the people bring your stool back to the village Eza."

Eza blew on the embers of the fire and watched the flames lick the dry wood. "I am frightened of these people Eza. The man with the wild hair, he is looking for you. He comes from the family across the water. He will not return until he finds what he seeks."

Eza said nothing as he reached in his pouch for his familiar pipe. "I have come now to say goodbye, Eza. There is much trouble coming and I do not wish to go to prison for something I have not done.

"You will be left alone. The only one who knows the truth of what happened. The mother of the child has had much punishment, she grieves for her child, for this I have seen down at the river. You must make your peace with her Eza?"

Eza nodded and sucked on his pipe. He looked at his cousin. "It is the police who I am also being afraid of Joseph. I took the child and hid it from them, from the mother. This they will punish me for even after many rainy seasons. They will lock me away and I will die of darkness in a cage. I will never be able to run free through the desert and grasses again."

Joseph stood up. He squeezed his cousin's bony shoulder. "It is true this might happen. The white man, Mr Yak. I think he is a good person. It would be wise to tell him your story. We do not know the ways of these people and how they think. But I am thinking Mr Yak will help you. I will go now Eza. You must do what is right, say what is in your heart. When you have done this, I will be able to return and claim the land the Chief Miles gave to my father. Until then I must hide."

Eza looked down at his hardened dusty feet. "How must this be done Joseph? I do not speak the language of the man who is looking for me. For many years I have carried this secret about the child. This secret cannot be told by another person it must stay with us?"

Joseph frowned. His cousin was right. "When you have decided what you will do you will get word to me. I will come with you to meet with Mr Yak."

Within seconds he had melted into the night again, leaving Eza with the second biggest decision he would ever have to make in his life.

Chapter Eighty-Two

Jack went back to his room and opened his laptop. Harry, in London, would be waiting for an update and Karen, Sara's friend, would be anxious to know how his search was going.

He sent both of them an email then pulled out his map again. Ten minutes later he made a phone call.

Opening the drawer of the small desk he found the hotel's letterheads and envelopes.

Dear Sara

My name is Jack Taylor and I am staying at a place called The Drop Inn, in Willow Drift. I am hoping by now you will have found the photograph I left for you down by the river near your old house.

I mean you no harm and will reveal to no-one where you are staying. I am a journalist, as you were. My editor, Harry, was an old friend of your father's. Your father recently received a letter from someone who told him you did not kill your child Charlie. Sir Miles asked Harry to send someone out to South Africa and find out the truth. Harry sent me.

I spoke to your friend Karen who admitted, but only to me, she had helped you fabricate your death by suicide, but not why. However, she has heard nothing from you and believes you might finally have carried out this threat.

There is a small town a half hour drive from Willow Drift called Whittle. I found a secluded guest house, on the internet, and have taken the liberty of checking you in there. Your room is paid for.

The Guest House is called Kelder. It is doubtful Maria, the owner, will ask for any identification. Just give her my name. I left my card with them which has my phone number.

I want to help you find the truth Sara. You can't hide out there in the bush forever.

I think the above should prove I am not just a journalist chasing a story. Your father worried about you and asked for our help.

But it is with great sadness I must tell you your father died before I had the chance to meet him at North End house. He left a letter for me which I must show you.

I hope you will trust me enough to go to the guest house and call me?

Sincerely, Jack.

He sealed the letter in an envelope, he would have to call in at the stationery shop he had seen in town and get a sealed plastic sleeve before he once more made his way to the river.

*****

Sara parked the car and leaned her head on the steering wheel. The hopes she had had about the little blue shoe and the person who had left the photograph were beginning to fade.

Soon she would have to make some kind of decision. The thought of another cold sink of water to wash herself in, provided by the large plastic can she filled up in one of the many small towns, the flickering light at night and the hopelessness of her situation were beginning to take their toll on her mind and body. She had no-where else to go and her money was beginning to dwindle.

Nothing was going to bring Charlie back and she had to accept it. She glanced at her handbag with all its solutions.

Today would be her last visit to the river. The river would go on, but she knew she couldn't.

Sara sat on the old tree stump. "I've come to say goodbye, Charlie, but maybe hello as well," she whispered. The light breeze feathered the leaves on the trees, the now placid river gurgled and hissed as it passed her by. A flock of noisy starlings burst from a tree, calling to each other. Then there was silence again.

She reached for her bag. Wedged between the old roots of the tree, she saw the plastic sleeve with an envelope inside. Putting her bag aside she quickly lifted it up.

Tearing open the envelope she read the letter, then read it again. She put it on her lap and lowered her head, as she wept at the news of her father's death.

With shaking hands, she read the letter once again. This Jack Taylor knew enough about her and her family to convince her he was genuine. She had nothing to lose and she desperately wanted to read the letter he had told her about. He wanted to help her, and God she needed someone to help her.

Snatching up her bag, and the plastic sleeve she ran back to her car and headed back to the lodge. The guard lifted his hand in greeting then bent to unlock the padlock to let her through.

Sara beckoned him over. "Leave the gates open. I'll only be a few minutes. I have to go somewhere."

He nodded and went back to the gates. Twenty minutes later Sara was back. She climbed out of the car and went towards him, taking both his hands in hers. "I must say goodbye now. Thank you for letting me stay here, for looking after me. I would have been lost without you."

The guard looked at the ghost woman from long ago, and frowned. "You are not coming back Missus?"

"No. It's time for me to go now." She fumbled in her bag and brought out a generous handful of notes. "This is to thank you for your kindness. I won't forget how you helped me."

He looked down at the money she had given him. "Enough for two small goats and some beer," he said smiling at her. "Go well, Missus."

Then with a wave of her hand she was gone, leaving a cloud of dust hanging in the still air.

Chapter Eighty-Three

Jack made his way through the bar and spotted Tinus in his usual spot.

"Hey, Jack!" He shook Jack's hand and he winced. "How's the detective work going? What have you discovered in our sleepy little town?"

Jack massaged his hand and ordered a beer. "Nothing much. All roads seem to have led to nowhere. Where's Piet tonight?"

"*Ag,* he's gone off to see his sister again. Not sure when he'll be back.

"You'll be moving on then Jack?"

"Yes, in a day or two. Hopefully Piet will be back by then. I need to return his file."

Tinus put his great paw of a hand around his glass, dwarfing it.

"You can always leave it under his office door. That horrible bloody thing he calls a cat might chow it up, but I'm sure Piet will have another copy somewhere."

Tinus stood up. "Well, I'm off. Hope to see you around before you go. Come and say goodbye, hey!"

He slapped Jack on the back, nearly knocking him off his stool. Jack wiped the beer off the front of his shirt and glanced at his phone.

No missed calls, no messages.

But he knew Sara would take the bait. He would have to be patient. He picked up the phone and scrolled through the numbers.

Maria, the lady who owned the guest house answered. "No, we haven't seen your friend yet. As soon as she arrives, I'll ask her to call you."

Jack realised he hadn't eaten anything since breakfast and he was hungry. He paid for his drink and despite his wet shirt and the smell of beer on it, he drove to the steak house he had often passed.

The smell of steaks cooking made his mouth water. The smiling waiter led him to his table. He ordered a rump steak with a side order of chips and fried onions.

Trying not to glance at his phone every few minutes he looked around the crowded restaurant. Waiters threaded their way through the tables with plates piled high, the chefs calling cheerfully to each other in the open plan kitchen, as they slapped steaks down on the red-hot grills.

Jack was becoming used to the South African way of life. The smiling waiter placed his order in front of him. Jack had eaten out in many restaurants and was more used to surly waiters. Maybe it was the UK weather that depressed them and robbed them of a smile or two.

He took a hungry bite of his steak and closed his eyes. A feast for the senses. The meat was perfectly cooked and melted in his mouth. He took a sip of his wine and glanced at the menu and the prices. Yup. He could definitely live in this country.

He glanced again at his phone then polished off the rest of his meal, enjoying every mouthful.

He paid the bill, left a generous tip, then made his way back to his car.

*****

Jack spent the morning typing up his report for Harry. He wondered how co-operative Sara would be after all she had been through.

He ordered a sandwich from room service then lay on his bed thinking. He had pretty much put the story together, but some of it was pure speculation, theories. Somehow, he had to find Eza. He was key to everything. But where was he?

His chirping phone brought him back to the present. He felt the beat of his heart quicken as he recognised the number of the guest house.

Sara.

"Jack? It's Sara. I'm at the guest house. How soon can you get here?"

Jack shoved his feet into his shoes. "I'm on my way. I should be there in about half an hour."

As he grabbed his keys there was a knock on his door. He threw the door open. A member of the staff, the hotel logo on his shirt, smiled shyly at him.

336

"Mr Yak?"

Jack frowned. "Mr Yak? My name is Jack Taylor as the hotel knows. What can I do for you, I'm in a bit of a hurry?"

The young man looked anxious as he glanced up and down the empty corridor. "I am Batu. I am a gardener here in the hotel."

Jack raised his eyebrows. "So, what does a gardener in the hotel want with me. There are no plants in my room? Look, I really am in a hurry."

Batu lowered his voice and Jack leaned forward. "I come with a message for you Mr Yak? From one of my people who wishes to meet with you?"

"Yes? Who wishes to meet with me, it will have to be later, as I said I'm in a hurry?"

"His name is Eza, sir."

Jack thought his heart might stop there and then. His head jerked up. "Eza? Where is he?"

Batu looked down at his shoes. "I will be in trouble with the manager for coming here to your room. Eza has told me it is important for him to meet with you. But he cannot come here. He does not speak English and wishes to bring his cousin Joseph who speaks your language, as you know, to meet with you as well?"

Jack looked at his watch. Eza could wait, but Sara could not. "Batu, please tell Eza and Joseph I want to meet with them, but it can't be now. I'll come and look for you tomorrow?"

Batu nodded. "It would be best to meet somewhere else, not here at the hotel. I ask you please not to speak to the manager about me coming here?"

Jack smiled at him. "Thank you for bringing me this message. I'll speak to no-one. I'll find you in the gardens when I return from my meeting. Tell Eza and Joseph they mustn't be afraid. I'm their friend. I'll meet them wherever they want. Thank you Batu."

Jack ran down the stairs. Eza? Joseph? Sara? My God the whole thing was finally coming together. He was nearly there.

Chapter Eighty-Four

Maria, the owner of the guest house, was waiting for him. "Sara's out in the garden. May I bring you a bottle of wine?"

Jack glanced at his watch. It was a bit early but why not? "Thank you, Maria. Which way to the garden?"

He made his way through the small garden. A woman was lying on a chaise lounge, a towel wrapped around her head, a light cotton dressing gown loosely tied around her waist. She seemed to be sleeping.

He looked down on her. Sara did not resemble the woman in the photograph he had carried so many miles, but she was still quite beautiful. Older of course, but with no make-up she looked younger.

"Sara?" he whispered.

Her eyes flew open as she sat up, hastily pulling the gown around her. The towel around her head came loose and her hair tumbled around her shoulders.

"Jack? Of course, you're Jack!" She held out her hand to him. "Thank you…"

Maria set down the bottle of wine, leaning in a cocoon of ice cubes, and two glasses. Then she left.

Jack poured them both a glass of wine, then leaned back in his chair as he looked at the woman sitting in front of him; the woman he had come so far to find. She was watching him warily.

He didn't waste any words. "Sara. I need you to trust me. I know we are both journalists, and you were particularly good by all accounts. You went to places where most of us would never have considered going. I know you're tough. But you don't have to be tough with me.

"This is not a war story we're covering. But it is your own war. A personal war is far more difficult. I want to help you."

The sun caught the light in her newly washed hair as she leaned forward to take a sip of her wine. She didn't waste any words either.

"My life is over Jack. There's only so much a person can take."

She twisted her hands in her lap. "I need to see the letter sent to my father? Someone else saw what happened that day?"

Jack passed her the letter and watched as she read it, then read it again.

"Who is this person called Eza, Jack? Who is Joseph?" she whispered unsteadily; her face drained of all colour.

Jack told her how he had met Joseph down at the river and the land her father had left to the old Chief, his father. Then Joseph had disappeared.

"I want to hear your side of the story Sara."

"And what will you do with it?" she said sadly. "Build up a big story and then publish it? I've caused enough trouble for my family, Jack."

He leaned forward, his hands on his knees. "Sara, you have no family anymore. Only Ben, and surely, he would want to know the truth? Don't you owe him that much after all he went through? You could clear your name with my story. You could go back to London and re-build your life with your son?

"I went to your father's memorial service. I met Ben. He wasn't in a good state. He's a deeply troubled young man, he needs help. Your son needs help."

"I don't want to go back to London!" she shouted at him, her voice raw and unexpected.

Her reaction astonished him. He had expected her to be elated with the contents of the letter. It proved she had possibly not been responsible for the death of her child. She could go back home and re-build her relationship with Ben. Knowing the truth, he would surely want her back in his life? He was her son for God's sake. He had told the police he saw his mother carry the child down to the river and return alone. But he had been a young boy, hysterical with grief…

Then it hit him.

He recalled Piet Joubert saying he felt Sara was holding something back, not telling the truth.

Jack leaned forward. "You've known all along haven't you Sara?" he said quietly.

She nodded, looking down at her clenched fists.

"Tell me what happened that day, Sara…"

Chapter Eighty-Five
Sara's Story

"The shock of finding Charlie had gone missing still has the capacity to bring me to my knees. It will never abate. In prison I had all the time in the world to try and remember every detail of that day and what followed.

"Yes, of course, I was in a dreadful state when we searched for Charlie, then the fires came and destroyed everything. Not only my father's house but me as well."

Sara pulled the belt of her gown tighter around her waist. "Ben had always been difficult. He would scream and cry as a baby, his face red and blotchy as he drummed his little feet on the floor in fury. I often wondered how his small body could hold so much rage, so much anger?"

She took a sip of her wine and pushed her hair back from her eyes.

"Simon, my husband at the time, couldn't handle Ben at all and he would take off as often as he could trawling the streets of Cape Town in search of more pleasant things to do with his time. Women as it turned out."

She rubbed the backs of her hands. "He was having sex in the back of a taxi unaware the driver didn't always have his eyes on the road ahead. He managed to take some photos of the activity going on in the back seat. He sold them to one of the local newspapers for a large sum of money.

"Simon left the country in disgrace. My father had a lot of power in those days. I never heard from Simon again. He didn't attempt to get in touch with Ben again either. Too much for even him to handle."

Sara reached for her shawl and wrapped it around her shivering shoulders. "Ben and I came here, to my father's cottage, far away from everyone. Where you left the photograph.

340

"Ben seemed to calm down a bit out there in the bush. He still had his tantrums, a violent unpredictable temper, but they gradually receded under Beauty's watchful eyes.

"On one of my visits to Bushman's Way where I sold my jewellery, I met Adrien. He was doing voluntary work with the animals at the lodge, game counting, helping with injured animals caught in snares, elephant calves who had lost their mother's to poachers, and anything else he could help with."

A small smile lifted her mouth slightly. "We were attracted to one another which resulted in me making more visits to the lodge than I normally would. Adrien had his own quarters and we would steal away there for a few precious hours. Paul, the lodge manager, turned a blind eye to it. He knew how lonely life could get out in the bush.

"The affair lasted for four months before Adrien had to return to his home in Europe. By then I knew I was pregnant. When I told him, he admitted he was married. I pondered the future and realised there wasn't one with him."

Sara rubbed her eyes. "I decided to keep the baby. Beauty helped with the birth. From the moment I laid eyes on Charlie I was smitten.

"Ben, of course, had noticed my body was changing shape but when I told him he would soon have a little brother or sister he became excited.

"I was already home schooling him even though there was a lot of pressure from my father to have him put in a boarding school where he would have the discipline he needed, and boys of his own age to play with. I think he saw that there was something wrong with Ben and I believe that's why he didn't fight to get custody of him when I went to prison."

Jack sat quietly, his glass of wine forgotten, letting Sara talk.

"A million times I've wished Beauty had not taken off to see her mother. But she did and on that terrible day our lives were torn apart. I never saw Beauty again. It was almost as though she sensed something. I think she went back to her mother in Swaziland, and stayed there."

She twisted the fringe of her shawl. "During my time as a journalist, a war correspondent, I saw things no human being should ever have to witness. But it was nothing compared to losing your child.

"Ben had been beside himself when he couldn't find Charlie. It had been a stormy afternoon and I was plagued by one of my relentless headaches. I'd taken a nap leaving the children to play inside. I must have slept for hours and woke up feeling groggy, the headache still pounding.

Her voice broke. "Charlie was gone…

Jack waited as she brought her emotions under control. "Go on Sara?"

"The next morning, after a hideous night with my thoughts and Ben's constant crying and screaming, Paul came back with his staff. But there was no trace of Charlie.

"Then came the terrifying fires and with the fires came the Press. In all the confusion that followed they managed to get one fact completely wrong. I was beyond it all. I didn't care. It didn't matter, Jack.

"The police arrived with their dogs and helicopters two days later. A Detective Joubert came to the lodge and questioned me, and Ben.

"Under the mattress in my room at the lodge the police had found Charlie's little tee shirt, blotched with old blood. In the bathroom they had found various pills I took for my headaches and also some Rohypnol left over from my days covering wars.

"Then Ben told the police he had watched me take Charlie down to the river…"

She sat up struggling to hold herself together. "I was arrested. Ben was taken away from me and put in a foster home."

She buried her face in her hands then dropped them in her lap. She lifted her head looked unsteadily at Jack.

"You see, Jack, we lie about what we love. To ourselves and to others. But mostly to ourselves. Life isn't about what you get, but what is taken from you, it's only then you know what love truly is. When it's suddenly snatched away from you.

"Before Paul took us to the game lodge, Ben had insisted on going back inside the house to find some toy he wanted to give to Charlie. He had always loved collecting and hoarding things, which he kept in a secret tin box under his bed, no-one was allowed to touch it.

"Once when Charlie fell over, I had told Beauty to throw out Charlie's tee shirt and not bother to try and get the blood out of it. Ben had obviously retrieved it and hidden it in his tin box along with the Rohypnol and other pills he must have stolen, at some point, from the bathroom cabinet.

"I think when he insisted on going back to get Charlie's toy, he grabbed the tee shirt from his tin box along with the pills."

Jack leaned over and refilled her glass. He had been right.

"At first, amidst all the chaos, I asked myself a thousand times if it was possible. Had I taken Charlie down to the river in a hypnotic state? Had I taken the wrong pill by mistake? Had Ben swapped some of the pills around at some point? It seemed impossible. But I couldn't be absolutely sure."

She reached for her wine with tremulous hands, spilling it over her gown.

"When I returned to the UK, I went to my father's house and met my son again. The meeting was an unmitigated disaster. He hated me."

The setting sun threw her face into a shadow, softening the deep lines of grief on her face. Distractedly she patted at the wet mark on her gown with a tissue.

"There was only one person I could turn to. Karen. I told her I was frightened of Ben, scared of the man he had become. He'd always been a difficult and vicious child and I thought he would harm me after the last violent encounter at my flat in London."

She looked at him defiantly. "I wanted to go back to South Africa. I didn't want to see Ben again. I wanted him to think I was dead. He was out of control – I was scared of him. Ben pushed Charlie in the river. He killed Charlie."

Sara rubbed her arms and pulled the shawl tightly around her body. "Karen seemed to understand. I'd never told her about Ben and the river, but somehow, I think she guessed. It's why she agreed to help me. She had met Ben and realised he had serious psychological problems.

"I was finally free of Ben and could go back to the child I had really loved. No mother should ever have to say this, but I never loved Ben. I didn't even like him. There was something terribly wrong with him and I sensed it from the moment he was born. I tried to love him but I couldn't. I didn't.

"It was one of the reasons I didn't get the children any pets, dogs or cats. You see, I did a lot of research on Ben. I knew he was dangerous. I can hardly bring myself to say this, but he showed all the symptoms of a, of a," she struggled to get the word out.

Jack moved uncomfortably in his chair choosing his next words with great care. "He had a serious personality disorder? Is that what you're saying? Psychopathic tendencies? Look, don't be frightened to admit it. In my line of work, I've met many seriously disturbed people. It's what I do. I go looking for them, in or out of prison, to solve a cold case. Nothing you say will shock me. Trust me, I have seen the very worst in a human being, the façade, and what lies beneath, whether an adult or a child."

Sara blinked her eyes rapidly, waving his words away with her hand. "Yes, that's what I'm saying Jack. Experts in that particular field, according to my research, agreed that some symptoms were less destructive and with the right treatment and supervision someone like Ben could lead a relatively harmless life.

"He was a cruel boy, violent. He enjoyed hurting things, living things. He lied and he was manipulative. Apart from a couple of incidents with Charlie, bumps, cuts and bruises, I didn't think Charlie was ever in any real danger."

"Beauty had a child, when she first came to work for me. Her child, Abby, was just a baby and she carried her around on her back, like most African mothers. When Abby started to walk, she wanted to play with Ben. Then one day Beauty went back to her mother's house. She came back without Abby.

"I was puzzled at first, then I understood. Beauty had left Abby with her mother. She never explained anything to me, but I knew she was well aware of how unpredictable, how cruel Ben could be, she was frightened for the safety of her own child. I think she was also frightened of Ben."

Sara stared at Jack. "You see, his mind was wired differently that's all. These sorts of people don't have the normal feelings of remorse, sadness or regret, or a conscience. They can go years without inflicting any pain on anyone. Everything I had read up and researched, told me one thing. He was dangerous, a ticking time bomb – it was just a matter of time…I still think that.

"Sometimes I would wake up in the middle of the night, sensing someone in my bedroom. He would be standing there, next to my bed, staring at me, his face expressionless, then he would turn and go back to his room, without saying a word. It seems ridiculous to be frightened of your own child, but I was frightened of him and the emptiness in his eyes."

Sara looked unseeingly around the small garden. "I knew, at some point I would have to get him the psychiatric care and treatment he needed, and I wouldn't find it anywhere in the bush. But I left it too late…I kept putting it off, hoping he would get better. But he didn't."

"But why didn't you say anything about this to anyone Sara? You had opportunities after Charlie went missing, when Joubert questioned you, then at the trial. I don't understand why you put yourself through

344

all of that and then went to prison for something you didn't do. It doesn't make sense."

"I didn't have the guts to tell the truth about Ben. As his mother, I couldn't do it, even though I knew Ben was guilty. Ben told Joubert he saw me carry Charlie down to the river then return alone.

"How would it have looked if I had turned the story around and blamed Ben? I would have looked even more guilty in Joubert's eyes, especially after they found the pills and shirt Ben had hidden under the mattress in my room.

"So, in the end it was all my fault, I didn't take enough care of Charlie. I was guilty, I deserved to be punished."

Her eyes came back to Jack. "After the incident in my London flat I knew I was in danger. I knew Ben was capable of anything. That's why I went into the care home, I was safe from him there, surrounded by people, and eventually I came back here. I didn't want him to find me. I was truly terrified of him. I still am."

The shadows lengthened across the garden. Maria arrived with a lamp and two blankets which she draped over the back of Jack's chair, then retreated.

Jack stood up and wrapped one of the blankets around Sara's thin shoulders, then he returned to his seat, anxious to hear more.

"On the trip to Cape Town I finally found some peace in my life, until the passenger called Emile recognised me. If he had told the Captain my true identity, the plans Karen and I had made would all have been for nothing. Karen would be in deep trouble for lying to the police and worse still…

"Ben would know I was still alive, I thought he might come looking for me. He would know where to find me. He would kill again.

"I couldn't let it happen, but I wasn't going to give into blackmail. There was a struggle, Emile tripped on a coil of rope, lost his balance, and the next thing he was gone."

She rubbed her face, wiping away the wetness. "I disembarked in Cape Town and disappeared. I found refuge with dear Edward and when he died, I took his car and drove back to the Eastern Cape. I was going to take my own life in the place where Charlie died."

Jack had not interrupted her as she told her story, he felt nothing but compassion for this woman sitting in front of him. This woman who had been torn apart and had gone to prison for trying to protect the son she had never loved; a child with extremely serious mental problems.

345

Prison would have become a haven for her – she would have been safe there. Away from her son.

"Was there a reason why no-one ever saw Charlie, Sara? Was there something wrong with him?"

She wiped away more tears from her swollen red rimmed eyes, adding another tissue to the small pile next to her. "No Jack, there was nothing wrong with Charlie. It was the one thing everyone managed to get wrong, the police, the Press – everyone. As I said I was too shattered to care. It didn't matter.

"You see Jack, Charlie was quite perfect. Yes. Charlotte, my beloved daughter, was beautiful. I loved her more than anything in the world."

Chapter Eighty-Six

Jack drove slowly back to his hotel in Willow Drift. He had stayed another two hours talking to Sara, then seeing she had reached a point of emotional exhaustion he had taken her back to her room and left her to sleep. Promising to return the next day.

As Harry had told him, before he had set out on this journey, some spectacular stories had come out of Africa and this one, he thought, was up there with the best.

The most startling revelation was the fact Charlie was a girl! He hadn't seen that coming.

Charlotte.

Even Ben had not revealed this fact. From what he could gather from Piet's case file, the child had gone into a screaming rage if the name Charlie was ever mentioned. From rage he had gone to refusing to even talk about his sibling.

He checked the time. Tomorrow he would go and look for the gardener, Batu. He would have gone home by now.

Eza was finally, tantalisingly, within his grasp. He hadn't said anything to Sara, preferring to find out the facts first before he presented them to her.

His gut feeling told him Eza was the key to everything.

Chapter Eighty-Seven

Early the next morning Jack found Batu clipping the hedges of a bougainvillea bush at the end of the garden.

"Morning Batu."

Batu wiped the sweat from his face with his sleeve, and placed the shears carefully on the ground. "Good Morning Mr Yak."

"I need to meet with Eza and Joseph, as soon as possible? I'll say nothing to anyone, especially the police. They have nothing to fear, you must tell them that okay?"

Batu looked at him warily, then gave Jack a tentative smile. "They have been some days waiting for you at the river. Joseph said you would know where this place is and come to them there. But not with the police."

Jack raced back to his room to collect his car keys. He backed out of the parking area and put his foot down. Heading once more for the river where Ben had killed his sister.

*****

Joseph and Eza saw the cloud of dust in the distance. Joseph hunkered down next to his spears.

"He is coming Eza."

*****

Jack turned off the engine and took a deep breath. He opened the car door and slid out, then walked down to the river. He was ready. The two men were waiting for him and stood up as he came towards them.

He shook Joseph's hand then turned towards the thin man he had last seen at the graveside. "Hello Eza." He held out his hand and Eza took it, cupping his other hand under his elbow, as a mark of respect.

348

"I see you," he said softly, then hunkered down next to Joseph who was waiting to translate.

Jack waited; letting Eza speak when he was ready. "This child you seek, the child of Mama Sara, she is safe. For it was I, Eza, who saved the little one." Joseph translated for Jack.

Jack sucked in his breath, finding it hard to breath. "She's alive?" he whispered. "Where is she?"

Eza nodded. "I found the girl child in the river and took her back to my village for I did not know where she had come from or who she belonged to. I was much afraid the child had been pushed into the hungry mouth of the river. That the girl child's life was in danger."

Joseph took up the story. "When the Chief Miles gave my father the land, I came many times to look at it with wonder. It was at these times I saw the children. The boy was cruel like no brother should be. He should have looked after the little sister. But he hit her many times, sometimes throwing stones and sticks at her. He was stronger than his baby sister and pushed her to the ground many times, sometimes he is tying her to a tree and leaving her there. This child cried many tears with her brother."

"In his head there was something wrong. This child was very much frightened of her big brother. Perhaps it is so she had not enough words to tell her mother."

"It was one afternoon, during the big storm, when I saw the boy take the little one down to the river. He is pulling her and hitting her before kicking her in the water with much strength. High in the trees I could hear her crying as the river took her away. I was too far away to catch her. When I came to the river the little one was gone." He looked at Eza and nodded to him to continue with the story.

"I found the little one at the side of the river. Around her arm was a strange toy, fat with air. This I am thinking saved her life, for she must have travelled far to the spot where she was found by me."

Jack looked at Eza, who was now looking more than frightened. "No, Eza. You saved the child's life. If the child had been returned to the mother, the brother would have hurt her again and you, Eza, would have not been able to save her."

Eza picked at a scab on his calloused foot. "What is the name of this child Mr Yak?"

"Her name is Charlotte. But they called her Charlie."

Eza frowned and looked into the distance. "When this child first came to us, she was much crying in the arms of my wife Mirium. Many times, she said this word *"lot,"* we did not understand this word. It was her name she was saying then?"

Hardened though he was to the ways of the world, and the people in it, Jack felt a lump in his throat. He swiped his sleeve across his eyes. Little Charlie must have been terrified being surrounded by these faces she didn't know, crying for her mother, utterly bewildered.

He cleared his throat. "Where is Charlie Eza? What happened to her?"

"The child is safe."

"But where is she Eza? What did you do with her? Where is she now?"

Eza looked uncomfortable. "We kept her as our own. The daughter we came to love, we gave her the name Kia, which in our language means water. Where she was found."

Kia?

Jack chased the story, his mind racing with disbelief. "How did you hide the child in your village when the police came looking? How did Kia live there so long and go to school without anyone seeing she was white?"

Eza shrugged. "At first she was not so white. She was the colour of a child who spends much time in the sun. But to be sure my wife used leaves and herbs to darken her skin. This was how we hid her amongst us. When the police came to the village my wife and I were hiding in the bush with the small one, for she was not dark enough then. When it was safe, we returned to the village where Kia became one of us."

Eza looked at Jack anxiously. "One time when Kia came home from the teacher's small school to be with us, she was angry her eyes filled with many tears."

Eza looked beseechingly at Joseph who picked up the story Eza had told him so many years ago.

"Kia asked why her skin was becoming lighter. She hadn't been home for some time and Mirium had not been able to cover her skin with the dark paste.

"Kia would not allow Mirium do it again. The next time she came back to the village she was dark again. In a shop she had found something to make her skin dark, and this she was using so she would be the same as the other children in the teacher's small class. But she wasn't the same as the other children, and this she did not understand, it made her frightened and angry."

350

Jack's mind probed the possibilities. Mirium had probably braided the child's hair from an early age, this, with the further darkening of her skin, was how they had disguised and hidden Charlie.

He looked at Eza. "Did you ever tell Kia how she ended up with you?"

Eza shook his head. "Kia was much loved by us, we wanted to keep her. I knew as she was growing, no good would come of telling her. Her blood brother was a dangerous person. We could not give her back. One more thing Mr Yak. I am not telling the truth to the Templetons when they needed papers for the children to go to the big school. I am telling them Jabu was older than Kia, so they would not guess who she might be, from stories from the past."

To his surprise he saw tears welling in the eyes of the old man. "Another thing, Mr Yak. I have been troubled all these rainy seasons by the mother. Kia's blood mother. For going to prison and thinking her child was dead. My heart is heavy for what I did. But what can I do, when the mother is no longer here in this place?"

Jack patted Eza's shoulder, his mind still reeling with shock. "The mother of Charlie, um, Kia, is here now. She is waiting for you. I think it was you who put the child's shoe here for her to find?"

Eza nodded. "It was I who did this. It was my thinking that one day the mother of little Kia might come back to the place where this child was lost, to remember her."

Jack stood up, he needed to get back before dark. Sara would be wondering where he was and why he hadn't called her.

Eza also stood. He shrugged his soft cape around his shoulders. "Will the police come now and take me away?" The fear was palpable in his voice and face.

Once more Jack patted his shoulder. "No. The police will not need to know about this, or anyone else. You're safe. But I'd like you to do something for me. To put something right with Charlotte's, um, Kia's, mother?

"She will not be angry with you Eza. You saved her child's life. I want you to meet her. She will forgive you and you will be free of your heavy heart.

"I will bring her here tomorrow, to the river. You'll wait for us?"

Eza nodded. "I will be here waiting for the mother of Kia. For the mother of the child I came to love as my own."

Chapter Eighty-Eight

As soon as he found a signal on his phone, he called Sara at the guest house, explaining he would see her tomorrow. This was something he could not tell her over the phone. She had to meet Eza, to fully understand the truth as it was now. Sara would have questions to which he had no answers. Only Eza would be able to answer them.

"There's someone I want you to meet Sara. I found Eza. I've arranged for us to meet at the river tomorrow. Will you come?"

"What! Yes, of course I will. How on earth did you find him?"

"He found me, Sara. He's quite shy and doesn't speak English, but his cousin, Joseph, will be with him and will translate for us.

"I'll pick you up at nine. Eza was the one who left Charlotte's shoe for you to find. But I want him to tell you his story. For once in my life I don't think it's my story to tell."

*****

Sara put the phone down. Picking up the little rabbit she held it close to her breast, and whispered her daughter's name, over and over. Finally, she would learn the truth about what happened down at the river.

*****

The following morning Jack collected Sara from the guest house and they drove back, once more, to the river. Sara said nothing, as she clasped, and unclasped, the little rabbit in her hands. Jack reached over and stilled her hands, as they neared their destination.

"This might turn out to be one of the most defining moments of your life Sara. I'm not sure how you are going to react to Eza's story. It's taken a lot of courage for him to agree to meet you?"

Sara looked down at the rabbit and squeezed Jack's hand. "The truth is all I have now, Jack. Nothing more can hurt me. No matter what he tells me."

Eza and Joseph were waiting for them.

*****

Eza stood up as she walked towards him, her face showing nothing at all. "I see you," he said softly, "the mother of the child who was lost."

Jack put his arm around Sara as she lowered herself onto the old tree stump which had become as familiar to her as her father's favourite chair far away in England. Jack saw in her body language how she was preparing herself for the final, brutal, truth about what really happened to her little girl. How she had died on that terrible day so many years ago.

"Eza," she said, her voice shaking. "Tell me about my child? Tell me what happened to her?"

Eza and Joseph hunkered down in front of her, Joseph ready to translate.

Eza squeezed his eyes shut then opened them, looking up at her. "I have caused you much pain, but always I thought of you. Every time I looked at Kia, I thought of you and your tears, falling like rain. I thought of you locked away for something you did not do. It was the brother who hit and threw the small girl in the river, this Joseph saw."

Joseph nodded. "It is true, this is what I saw."

Eza pulled a small thorn from his big toe. "A small baby will forget its birth mother, but this small girl cried much for you. We are thinking she did not forget her birth mother. This child knew she was not one of us. But she knew no others. Mirium loved this child as her own, as I did."

She stood up, wildly reaching out her hand, as she turned to Jack; her eyes crazy with hope. "Jack! She's alive, is that what he's saying? The child called Kia, is it Charlie?"

"Yes Sara. She's alive. Charlie is alive. Eza saved your daughter's life, he rescued her from the river."

353

Sara turned around unsteadily. Taking a deep breath, she reached for Eza's trembling calloused hands. "Where is my daughter Eza?" she asked urgently. "Where is she?"

"Kia is living in this place with the flat mountain. My son Jabu will know where to find her."

Tears ran unchecked down her cheeks as she held Eza's hands tightly. "I would like to meet her mother, to thank her for the love she gave to Charlotte, to Kia?"

Eza looked at her steadily, no longer afraid of any consequences. "Kia's mother has gone from this place, perhaps it is so that she is with her own daughter now, and her first husband, who she lost to the fever many rainy seasons ago. Kia filled the lonely place in her heart, but we both knew one day this child we loved, Kia, would have to be returned to her mother, this was you, mama."

Jack swiped his eyes with his sleeve, not sure if it was the light rain falling now, the humidity from the heat around him, or the sheer charged atmosphere of the scene playing out in front of him.

"Was my daughter happy, growing up Eza?" Sara asked softly.

"Yes, mama, she grew to be a fine young woman with much knowledge of reading and writing. This was a gift to her from the teacher in the town and her husband."

"Diana and Norman Templeton," Jack murmured to her.

He stood up, seeing how emotional and agitated Eza was becoming. "We should go now, Sara…?"

Sara once again turned to the gentle shepherd. "Don't be afraid Eza. Nothing will happen to you," she glanced at Jack. "Thank you Eza, thank you for the love and care you gave to her. I will never forget you. You did nothing wrong. You were a good and loving father to her. You should be proud of what you did, proud of your daughter. You will be in Kia's heart and mind for the rest of her life, which she owes to you, and only you."

Eza looked at Jack, his eyes full of tears. "Mr Yak?"

"You're a good man Eza. No harm will come to you."

"Kia must stay away from her blood brother, Mr Yak. He is dangerous. Who will watch over her and keep her from danger, when I am not here?"

Jack glanced at Sara. "I will watch over her Eza. No harm will come to her, this I promise you."

Eza and Joseph rose up as one, Joseph picked up his spears and went ahead.

354

Eza reached out his hand and briefly touched Sara's cheek before following Joseph.

Before they reached the bend in the river Eza stopped and looked back. A lonely figure silhouetted in the fading distance, the river moving swiftly next to him, the river which had given the lonely shepherd the gift of love.

After a few moments he raised his arm in farewell.

Then he was gone.

Chapter Eighty-Nine

Jack pulled up outside of the guest house. Sara had shown no emotion on the drive back. She hadn't said a word to him. She seemed completely stunned and overwhelmed. The truth about Ben now shockingly confirmed.

Jack turned in his seat. "Would you like me to come inside with you Sara? I don't think you should be on your own right now, later maybe, but I would like to be with you if that's alright?"

"Yes, Jack, I would like that."

He followed her into the tiny reception area and out into the garden. "Talk to me Sara?"

She slumped into a chair, her hand on her throat. "I don't know what to say Jack? For over twenty years I thought Charlie was dead. But my daughter won't even know who I am, despite what Eza told us.

"She's as lost to me now as she was then. How do I deal with that? I can't even get my head around she's alive. I should be feeling something? Yes, I'm feeling something. Utter joy Charlie is alive. But she won't remember me now. I don't know what to do next."

Jack pulled his phone out. "Would you like to see her?"

"See her? How can I see her?"

Jack scrolled through his photographs and found the one he had taken of Kia on the veranda of the hotel.

"Here she is Sara."

Sara looked at him astonished. "How did you get this photograph?"

"It's a long story. But take a look at your daughter. This is Charlie."

Sara took his phone and stared at it with disbelief. "This can't be her surely?"

356

"Yes, Sara. This is your daughter. It's not a clear shot because the light was poor and I was sitting a couple of tables away from her. But it's Charlie. I spoke to her."

Sara stared at the phone. "This is all a terrible mistake! Is this part of your big story Jack?" He saw the undiluted fury on her face, "because if it is I don't much like it! It's sick, Jack! Sick! How dare you!

"How much did you pay Eza and Joseph to tell their ridiculous story. How could you use everyone to get *your* damn story!"

Snatching up her bag she ran towards her room, stumbling and tripping over her own feet.

Jack waited a while. It was a huge amount of information Sara had to work her way through, she was highly emotional, overwrought. He waited ten minutes and then knocked on the door of her room.

"Sara? Let me come in. You can't go through this on your own. I told you I want to help you?"

He pushed open the door and saw her sitting on the bed, holding the rabbit. Her face white and pinched.

"Oh God, Jack. I'm sorry for shouting at you. Such a shock, I'm sure it's all a big mistake. Maybe you've been taken in by all of this as well."

"Of course, it's all a huge shock, but it's the truth Sara! It's not my story, it's not your story. This is Charlie's story. Eza's story. Every word is true."

He flopped down into a chair. "I need to tell you the whole story, right from the moment I arrived in Willow Drift. I need to tell you about my conversation down at the river with Eza and Joseph, before you met them. How Mirium managed to hide Charlie. Then you'll understand everything.

"It's an absolute miracle Sara, but the girl in the photo is Charlotte – you've found your daughter."

*****

The next morning Jack showered and dressed, then drove back to the guest house. He knocked tentively on Sara's door. Sara was sitting up in bed still dressed in the clothes she was wearing yesterday.

Sara plucked at the edge of the bedspread. "I'm sorry about last night, it was a shock to see the photograph. I expected her to look quite different…"

"Yes, I could see it was a shock; not what you expected at all. Mirium darkened her skin and braided her hair like the other young girls in the village, as I told you last night."

Sara nodded.

"I met Eza's other child, Jabu. He looks like his parents. When you put both children together it's obvious, they're not related. But apart? One wouldn't even question if Charlotte was anything other than a Griqua child. If she un-braided her hair she would look like any other girl with Mediterranean blood in her veins.

"The oil Joseph talked about was obviously self-tanning lotion. Poor Charlie must have been frightened and confused as her skin lightened, she had no-one to turn to, no-one to answer her questions, so she chose to keep up the façade. But I'm guessing as she grew older, she realised she wasn't a Griqua girl after all."

"Poor baby," whispered Sara, her eyes brimming, "and I wasn't there for her. How lost she must have felt. I can hardly bear to think about what she went through."

Jack smoothed his hair down. "Charlie was well educated and practically adopted by Diana and Norman Templeton. You need to meet them one day, although they live in the UK – not a place you want to go back to, which I understand. But they'd be able to tell you a lot about Charlie, her life at the teacher's house, Diana's house, what she was like as a girl growing up. It will help you build a picture of your daughter.

"I met them when they came over for Mirium's funeral. Charlie was lucky to have so much love in her young life, Eza and Mirium, Jabu, and the Templetons who loved them both, especially the girl they knew as Kia."

Sara smiled up at him. "I'd love to meet anyone who knew my daughter as a child. You're right, it will help me build a picture of all the years that were lost to me. My poor child how terribly confused she must have been, wondering who she really was. But she was loved. She had all the love I wanted to give her, but couldn't."

Jack patted his pocket and pulled out the turquoise bead he had found next to Kia's chair. "This came loose from one of her braids."

Sara held her hand out stared at the bead. The first thing she had belonging to her long-lost daughter. She gripped it tight, rolling it through her fingers, fighting back the tears.

Jack stood up. "I have to go back to Willow Drift. You need some time alone to think about what you're going to do next."

358

He kissed her on the forehead and quietly closed the door behind him.

He started his car and let the engine idle as he punched a number into his phone. "Piet? It's me Jack. I need to see you. Are you back in town?"

"Yup, I'm at the office, waiting for you. I'll be here all morning."

The bad-tempered cat was sitting in the only available chair and Jack waited until Piet had thrown a newspaper at it before he sat down. The cat hissed and spat at him then sat on the window sill, staring at him vehemently through half closed eyes.

"So, Jack how is your investigation going? Find anything new? You look bloody pleased with yourself for some reason."

Jack grinned at him. "I found Sara Saunders, the writer of the letter Eza, and his cousin Joseph. Not bad for an Englishman, hey!"

Piet Joubert narrowed his eyes, trying to supress a grin. "I thought you might find Sara. I've been busy with a little research myself. You're right she is in the country and I know how she managed to get in under the immigration radar. How about we trade stories?"

"I'll tell you the whole story but I need your word none of it will be repeated to anyone?"

"That's a lot to ask, my friend. Your new found friend, Sara, could be in a lot of trouble with the authorities."

"Do I have your word Piet? I don't have to tell you anything. Sara and I could disappear in the dead of the night and be gone before you know it. Taking our story with us?"

Piet drummed his fingers on the edge of his desk. "I doubt that. If you sneeze in this town, I'll know about it. But, yes, I give you my word this will remain between the two of us. I don't have any obligation to the authorities anymore. Fire away Jack. I'm more than intrigued now. Tell me what we missed, and you found?"

Chapter Ninety

Two hours later Jack sat back in his uncomfortable chair his shirt sticking to his back with the heat of the office. Piet's eyes hadn't waivered from his face and he hadn't interrupted Jack at any point.

Now he stood up, opened the window and turned on the overhead fan. The papers on his desk fluttered as the air moved around the stuffy room. He perched on the window sill, next to the bad-tempered cat who hissed at him before disappearing into the garden. Piet ignored him, and stared out into the derelict front garden. His mind going back over the case. He shook his head and came back to his desk.

"There's something else isn't there Jack?"

Jack tried not to sound too smug. "I found the missing child Piet."

The colour drained from Piet's shocked face; he took a moment to compose himself. "What! Where?"

"Right here, in Willow Drift. Her real name is Charlotte. They called her Charlie."

"Charlie." Piet murmured, savouring the name. "Charlotte. That was the one thing that always bothered me from the word go."

He seemed to be talking to himself, his thoughts miles away, across the years. "At the time, what mattered was that a toddler had gone missing. The Press got hold of the wrong end of the stick and assumed Charlie was a boy. Easy mistake to make especially when the mother didn't correct anyone. She only ever called the child Charlie. I knew she was holding something back, not quite telling the truth, never saying *he* or *she*. Only Charlie."

He was silent for a few minutes, before turning back to Jack. "It's hard for me to accept that no-one picked up we were looking for a girl not a boy. Okay Charlie is a boy's name, but even so, it was a big mistake on our part, with that old dog called hindsight."

360

"Not really Piet. Sara, any mother come to that, would have been out of her mind when her child went missing. Charlie's name would have been foremost on her mind, on her lips, her child, her baby was gone. It's probably hard now to recall the conversation of a hysterical mother under those circumstances.

"Then, of course, she closed down, shut down, when the child wasn't found. As I told you, she realised the Press and the Police had got it wrong, but in her fractured and broken mind it didn't matter, to her there was no point in clarifying the situation. Her baby had gone."

The ex-detective looked uncomfortable. "No. I know you're trying to make me feel better about this, but it was a big mistake on our part." He shrugged his shoulders philosophically. "But, boy or girl, the child was never found, until you came along that is.

"You've done a great job," he said begrudgingly.

He eyed Jack's phone. "Don't suppose you have a recent photograph of the once missing, now found, child? You said you met her here, but then, of course, you didn't know who she was, right?"

"Right. But, yes, I do have a photograph, not a good one…"

Jack scrolled through his phone then handed it over to Piet. "There she is. Charlie. But she was brought up with the name, Kia."

Piet studied the image intently. "Well. I'll be damned. Not only were we looking for a little white boy, we got that wrong as well. This child was clearly not white, no wonder we couldn't find her in any of the villages!"

"Ah, but she is white Piet. Mirium darkened Kia's skin and braided her hair, so she would blend in with the rest of the children in the village. The Chief of the village told Eza and Mirium to take Charlie and hide out in the bush, he knew the police would mount a search. Only the Chief and his two brothers, the Elders, none of the villagers, knew about the child. When Eza, Mirium and Charlie came back the search was long over. They told the villagers they had found the baby next to its dead mother out in the bush, and brought it back with them."

Piet nodded his head slowly, as he stared at the photograph again. "Well I'll be damned!" he repeated. "I'm pretty sure, over the years, I've seen this child around town. Hard to miss hey? This Charlie is a beauty, isn't she?"

Jack tried to keep a neutral expression on his face. "Yes, quite pretty, I suppose."

Piet handed back the phone and grinned. "I suspect you find her more than slightly pretty Jack?"

He clasped his hands behind his head and leaned back in his chair. "The question is what are you going to do next? There will be no witnesses. Well Joseph saw what happened, and Eza definitely knows what happened. But I'll bet my paltry pension you'll never see either of them again.

"Even if you could find them, they're hardly likely to board a plane and stand up in a court of law in England, or here, and tell the judge what happened are they? How can this seriously deranged Ben be charged with attempted murder? Sounds to me like he needs to be locked up one way or another, for everyone's sake."

Jack wiped a bead of sweat from the side of his face, then picked a piece of cat fur off his finger. "Sara would have to accuse him. She won't do that. She doesn't want to see him again under any circumstances. He's too dangerous and she knows it."

"That may be, but perhaps Charlie might want to meet her dangerous English brother once she finds out she has one. How is Sara going to deal with that little problem?

"Charlie won't remember what happened to her, Jack, she was too young. But Ben most certainly will. Might even try it again especially if there's a bloody great property involved and he thinks he's going to inherit it! He doesn't sound like the sharing type from what you've told me about him."

Jack rubbed his eyes feeling emotionally exhausted. "I haven't discussed any of this with Sara yet.

"You're right Piet, it's going to be a minefield, but Charlie needs to know the truth about how she ended up where she did."

Piet drummed his fingers on his desk again. "Another small thing Jack. Sara by all accounts committed suicide. Okay, her body was never found so she could walk back into her old life and say she went on holiday to South Africa, decided not to kill herself.

"Trouble is she's in the country illegally, on a false passport."

He looked at Jack with innocent eyes. "Funny story I picked up recently. A cruise ship from France docked in Cape Town in November – minus one passenger, a Frenchman called Emile Beaumont. By all accounts he fell overboard.

"He was a scumbag of note. Cruising the waters of the world looking for wealthy women to blackmail. The French police had been looking for him for a long time, but out there on the high seas he was difficult to track.

"So, passenger Emile Beaumont was no great loss to anyone. He had a grubby past with women, did some dirty deals in the underbelly of the world of art. Someone would have taken him out eventually and saved the French courts a whole bunch of money."

Piet waved a fly away from his face. "Apparently on the same cruise ship another passenger, also mysteriously disappeared, her name was Annabel Courtney. Strange, hey, Jack?"

He smiled. "Easy to get another passport in a different name in a seedy place like Marseilles; place is full of crooks apparently."

Jack tried to keep his face neutral.

Piet laughed. "As I told you once, we might live in the bloody sticks, but we Afrikaners are not stupid. But let's leave it there shall we? If you're going to tell me a story Jack, make sure you don't leave anything out okay?"

Jack lifted his palms in a gesture of acceptance. "I'm trying to protect Sara, Piet."

Jack's eye caught a movement at the window. The cat was back. It glared at him then jumped down and made its way towards his chair.

"Tell you what Piet," Jack said standing up hastily. "Let me buy you lunch before your bloody cat decides to sit on my lap and chew off half my hand. Has it got a name?"

"*Ja. Voetsak.*"

Jack's brow furrowed. "There's a lot of stray dogs in town, they all seem to be called that. Is it a popular name?"

Piet roared with laughter. "It means *fok* off – that's why it's so popular."

He rammed his hat on his head. "Come on then. I know the most expensive restaurant in town. Let's go."

He shook his head. "Charlotte eh! I think I can close my case now and stop trying to work out who did what to whom and where. It's up to the victims in the case to unravel the rest of it and come to some sort of, what do you call it in English? Ah, closure, that's the word I was looking for."

Jack rolled down his window as Piet got into his car. "Long way off of that Piet…"

Chapter Ninety-One

It was late afternoon when Jack parked outside the guest house in Whittle. He made his way down the short path to where he knew he would find Sara.

She was lying back on a swing chair, wearing a long white dress with colourful beading at the neck and waist, looking remarkably composed and in control.

"Hello Jack. I've had the whole day to think about things and despite the fact I know the road I've chosen is going to be difficult, I feel it's the right road to take. I want to see my daughter. I *need* to see Charlotte, I'm desperate to see her."

Jack smiled at her. "You know Sara, we're quite similar. I'm the detective journalist but you are definitely the warrior journalist. You've never been afraid of the truth and confronting it. How would you like to do this? What's your plan?"

"I'm going to need you, Jack. I have to go to Cape Town. Will you come with me?"

"Of course, I will! It'll be the climax of my story, wouldn't miss it for anything."

He pulled out his phone and pulled up the web site he was looking for. "There's a flight at one tomorrow. We could book that?"

He glanced at her and smiled. "What name shall I use for your reservation?"

Sara smiled. "Either one, I'm covered on both. Don't book the return flight though. I've no idea how this is all going to work out. How long it might take."

He tapped his phone with his credit card details. "Done."

He handed her Kia's business card. "Here are your daughter's contact details. How are you planning to make the first approach?"

"I was hoping you might help me with that Jack. You've met her…" her voice faltered as she stared at the card. "I don't know how to approach it."

Jack glanced at his watch. "I think I should phone her tonight and tell her I'll be in Cape Town tomorrow. She's expecting me to get in touch anyway. I promised her dinner and she promised me a clean, well pressed, handkerchief. I'll tell her there's someone I want her to meet. Let's take it from there?"

He paused. "I told you I met Norman and Diana Templeton at the hotel when they came over for Mirium's funeral?"

Sara nodded.

"It might make things easier when you meet Charlie if you know more about her? I have their telephone number in the UK, I managed to get it from Jean who runs the bar. I think we should give them a ring."

He tapped his phone on the side of his hand. "I think it will mean something to them if you talk to them. They seemed nervous when they found out I was a journalist. I think they know more than they told me. Will you talk to them?"

Sara nodded her head rapidly. "Yes, I'd love to talk to them, but it means you'll have to tell them the whole story Jack. Are you comfortable with that, seeing as you said they seemed nervous about something?"

He grinned at her. "It's what I do Sara. No stone left unturned." He scrolled through to the number in the phone, and waited for the call to connect.

"Diana Templeton speaking?"

Jack took a deep breath. "Diana? It's Jack Taylor, I think you might remember me?"

There was a slight silence at the end of the phone. "Yes, Jack, of course I remember you. You're the journalist."

"Yes, that's me. Look, the story I was working on has developed into something quite extraordinary. I think it's important that you hear me out?

"Forgive me for saying this, but I felt you knew a lot more about the story I was chasing, that's why you left the hotel without saying goodbye?"

He heard the hardness, the fear, in her voice. "I have nothing to say to you Jack. I don't know what story you're talking about. I'm afraid I can't help you."

Jack frowned into the phone; he wasn't making any progress with Diana Templeton, she sounded frightened. He would have to play his trump card, with no holds barred. He would have to be brutal.

"Diana, twenty odd years ago a toddler called Charlie Saunders went missing here, and was never found. That child was Kia. Kia was brought up by Eza and Mirium. Eza told me the whole story, how he rescued the child from the river and kept her as his own."

There was silence at the end of the phone. "Hello? Diana? Are you still there?"

"Norman Templeton here, Jack. What is this all about? My wife seems to be in a bit of a state, wait, hold on."

Jack could hear a muffled conversation, then Diana came back on the line.

"I've lived with this story for too long Jack," her voice sounded steady now. "It's time for the truth to come out, whatever the consequences for Norman and I might be.

"We did nothing wrong, but seemed to get caught up in something which was none of our doing, well, until the children came into our lives.

"Yes, we had heard all the stories of the missing toddler, I understood it was a boy, but it was years and years before our time, before we came to live in Willow Drift."

He heard her take a deep breath, clearly composing herself. "When I took Kia in as my pupil, I assumed she was a little village girl, a Griqua child. She had the same skin tone, high cheek bones and green eyes. I had no reason to think otherwise.

"She had her own room at our house with its own shower. One day I went to tell her the good news that we were going to enrol her in a private school, but first I wanted to be sure it was what she wanted.

"I interrupted her as she was taking a shower, she didn't see me standing at the bedroom door when she stepped out. I saw immediately that, how can I put this? I could see she wasn't the same colour all over. I was shocked, absolutely shocked."

Jack heard the sound of what seemed like a chair being dragged up to the phone.

"But it was too late Jack. Kia had already been accepted into the school and there was no turning back for me. As it turned out she didn't want to be a boarder, I think she realised living in close proximity to the other girls would soon reveal what she was trying to hide.

"Whatever had happened in her past was exactly that, it was the past. It was her precious future I held in my hands. I knew she would need papers, identity papers, birth certificate etc. I felt once I got those from Eza, I would know I was wrong about the child.

"However, Eza didn't have any papers for either of the children. He didn't even know when they were born, but I suspected he was hiding something.

"I wrestled with all these thoughts, as did Norman, and we decided to say nothing. Those two children had a lot of potential, especially Kia, how could I ruin all her chances for a good future by digging up the past, whatever it was?

"I realised Kia was using tanning cream to keep her skin dark. In the back of my mind I thought about the story of the missing child. The more I thought about it, I knew it was possible."

There was another short silence and Jack could hear Norman murmuring in the background.

"How could I ruin Kia's life, when her future looked so bright? I knew a lot of people would get hurt, especially Eza and Mirium. How did the child end up with them? Had Eza stolen her? Was that why he always seemed so quiet and morose? There were so many questions. Eza and Mirium loved their children, especially Kia, they were good people, not bad people. So, we didn't say anything to anyone."

Jack heard her blow her nose noisily, before she sniffed, and continued. "But it was the child's mother who kept me awake at nights. I couldn't imagine what she had been through over the years. It was my biggest regret and it still bothers me to this day. Kia's mother needed to know the truth and I had no way of helping her. I knew nothing about her, her name, or where she lived.

"But even if I had I wouldn't have had the courage. I could have found out the mother's name from the police, of course, but then I would have to tell them what I suspected. Eza and Mirium would have been arrested. No, I just couldn't do it. I wanted to keep Kia too."

Jack heard her crying softly.

"Kia's real name is Charlotte, Diana, she was the little girl who went missing all those years ago. I met with Eza recently and he told me the whole story, how he had found her, and why he kept her. He saved her life.

"Her mother is here with me now. Her name is Sara. Let's put this whole thing right. You did a wonderful job with Kia and Jabu, and indeed you gave them the opportunities they enjoy now. But Sara needs to know the truth, she needs to know all about her daughter before she finally meets her in Cape Town.

"Will you help her Diana?"

"Yes, of course I will! But perhaps you would give me half an hour or so to pull myself together before I talk to her Jack?"

Half an hour later Jack rang the number again, passed his phone to Sara and slipped out of the room.

*****

Jack scrolled through the numbers on his phone, then hit the number and held his breath.

Kia picked up sounding breathless. "Hi, Kia. It's me, Jack Taylor?"

He could hear the smile in her voice. "Well hello Jack Taylor! Had enough of taking dusty photographs of old buildings?"

"Yes! I'm heading for Cape Town tomorrow. Should arrive in the afternoon. There's someone I'd like you to meet, she's coming with me. Her name's Sara."

There was a moment's silence. "Sara? Don't tell me you've met someone in a place like Willow Drift and want to show her the bright lights of Cape Town! It was supposed to be me showing you around – remember?"

"Sara is special. I want you to meet her," he said stubbornly.

Kia sighed. "There I was thinking we were going to have a romantic dinner together, and you want to pitch up with another woman. Look, I'm busy tomorrow night, I'm meeting up with my best friend Josh. So, give me a ring when you get here and we can arrange for a place to meet for dinner the following evening, with your new special friend. I'll bring Josh, so I don't feel left out!"

Jack hesitated. "Any chance we could meet during the day, without your friend Josh?"

"Why are you being so mysterious Jack! Look, give me a ring the day after tomorrow, we'll take it from there?"

Jack felt a spasm of disappointment about this mate of hers called Josh. It was too much to hope for that she didn't have a man in her life.

*****

Kia put the phone down, disappointed. She had been looking forward to seeing Jack again and now he was bringing some other woman with him.

Maybe she shouldn't waste her time – but she was intrigued. She'd been attracted to Jack when she met him in Willow Drift, even though the circumstances had been difficult. He had been kind to her, and even though he was probably a few years older than her. She had found herself thinking about him for weeks after they had met.

Why on earth would he bother to contact her now when he obviously had another woman in his life, someone *special* he had said?

Kia looked out of her office window, watching the clouds tumbling over the edge of Table Mountain, heavy clouds, the colour of bruises, threatened rain. She felt her heart sink. Despite loving her job and living in Cape Town she felt unbearably lonely. A feeling she had known all her life, a feeling of not belonging to anything or anyone.

Tears pricked her eyes as she tidied her desk and thought about another long evening ahead in her flat, having dinner alone again.

Chapter Ninety-Two

Sara and Jack waited in the gardens of the hotel they were staying in.

Kia was due to arrive any minute.

Sara had chosen The Vineyard in one of the Cape Town suburbs; she knew it well. It was old and gracious. The gardens with their elderly oak trees and tables spread around the grounds. Her eyes were trained on the wide doors leading into the gardens, where her daughter would step through. Back into her life.

She was nervous, her knuckles white against the wicker arms of her chair.

Kia stepped down into the gardens and looked around for Jack. He stood up and waved her over. She looked dazzling, her short simple turquoise dress matching the beads in her hair, cascading down her back, and the delicate straps of her shoes.

He kissed her on both cheeks and took her hand, not letting go of it, leading her to the woman sitting in the chair, a wide smile on his face.

"Kia, this my friend Sara, she's been looking forward to meeting you."

Smiling, Kia shook Sara's hand and sat down, surprised the woman was so much older than Jack, and she was having a job extricating her hand from this woman called Sara. "Hi Sara."

"Charlotte?" Sara whispered. Unable to take her eyes off her daughter.

Kia looked at Jack and raised an eyebrow in question. This Sara woman had an odd look on her face, she seemed lost for words. No, she looked shocked, white faced, unwell. Something was wrong with her. What had she just called her?

Kia felt distinctly uneasy, after all she had only met Jack once. Who was he anyway, she knew absolutely nothing about him?

She smiled nervously. "No, my name's Kia. Why are you staring at me like that Sara?"

She turned to Jack a bewildered look on her face. "What's this all about Jack, something's going on here. Why did you want me to meet Sara?"

"It was Sara who wanted to meet you Kia. It's important to her."

"Why? Why does she want to meet me?" She turned back and looked more closely at Sara's face then she frowned. "Wait a minute. I've seen you before somewhere?"

Sara's eyes flooded with bright tears. "You remember me then? Is it possible you remember me – you were so young, just a baby…"?

Jack leaned forward, looking unsure as to what was coming next.

Kia rummaged in her bag for her phone. "Remember you? No, I don't remember you from anywhere. But I *have* seen you before." She bent her head and scrolled through her phone until she came to the photographs she was looking for.

Her eyes traversed Sara's stricken face, then back to the photographs on her phone.

Jack watched them both fascinated; wondering where the story was going next.

"Yes. This is you isn't it? Taken by Snowdon?"

The colour drained from Sara's face as she took the phone from Kia, reaching for her glasses. "Yes, this is me. Taken on my eighteenth birthday. But where did you get this from?"

"My friend Josh and I went on a photo shoot for Sotheby's in the UK. The owner of the house, it was called North End, wanted to put it on the market. He wanted to sell it?"

Sara's hand went to her throat as she took a deep shuddering breath. "Did you meet the owner?"

"Unfortunately, we did. He was extremely unpleasant to say the least. His name was Ben Courtney. He accused us of stealing a silver framed photograph. Searched all our equipment, then threw us out of the house."

Jack winced. "I actually took the photograph from the house. But in the scheme of things not important now, easily forgiven, I hope?" he muttered, to no-one in particular.

Kia's hand flew to her mouth. "Oh God, I'm sorry. You must be this Ben's sister? No that can't be right. His mother then?"

She shook her head before Sara could answer. "No, that can't be right either," she frowned. "He told us his mother was dead."

She looked at the woman sitting opposite her a wary expression on her face. "Who exactly are you Sara and why did you want to meet me?"

Sara looked at Jack helplessly. He nodded at her encouragingly.

"Ben is my son. It's a long story Kia, but one you need to hear. I came back here to South Africa, to the Eastern Cape where you were brought up."

Kia stared at her; her eyes locked onto Sara's face. "How do you know I was brought up there," she glanced at Jack accusingly. "You told her, right?"

Jack shook his head. "No, she already knew. Let Sara tell you her story."

Sara took a deep breath. "I came back here because I wanted to go to the place where my daughter disappeared over twenty years ago. Her body was never found. Her name was Charlotte. We called her Charlie."

Kia interrupted her. "You asked me if I remembered you. Why would I remember you?" Now her mind was racing. "Surely you don't think I'm your daughter Charlotte? That's ridiculous! But that's what you just called me right?"

Sara reached for the letter in her bag. "You were brought up by Eza and Mirium, right?"

Kia's body went rigid, her eyes wary and distrusting. "Yes, they were my parents. But how do you know all this about me?"

With panic written all over her face she looked at Jack. "What the hell is going on here Jack? I don't like this. I don't like it one bit. I don't even know you. Who exactly are you? What were you really doing in Willow Drift?"

"I'm a journalist Kia. I came here to look for you, to find out what happened to you." He nodded towards Sara.

Sara was holding out the letter Eza had written.

Kia looked at Jack her eyes wide with shock. Sara straightened her back and took a deep controlling breath. "Read it Kia, it will help you understand who you really are. The letter was written to my father, your grandfather, it's from Eza."

Kia snatched the letter. "That's not possible! Eza didn't speak English, he couldn't write," she said wildly.

Sara nodded at the letter. "Please read it. It's possible someone wrote it for him, but it's definitely from him."

372

The young girl read the letter, then read it again. She looked at Sara and slowly nodded her head, tears filling her dark green eyes.

"You think this child who disappeared? You think it was me?" she whispered.

"Yes Charlotte, I'm your mother. A simple DNA test will prove it without any doubt."

Kia squeezed her eyes shut trying to blot out the image of Ben Courtney and the terrible fear that had streaked through her body when she met him, the fleeting images of water and a storm, the rushing sounds in her ears.

"Ben is my brother?" She shuddered. "*He* pushed me into the river, didn't he?" The letter trembled in her hands. "I had terrible nightmares as a child, I was always frightened of water."

Sara nodded. "But he didn't pay the price for it. I did. Ben told the police he had watched me carry you down to the river, and came back without you. I went to prison."

Kia leaned across the table and impulsively took her hand. "I'm sorry Sara. I don't know what else to say."

Sara looked down at her daughter's hand and turned it over in her own. Remembering the tiny hand she had held a lifetime ago.

Jack beckoned to a hovering waiter. "I'm going to order a bottle of something. I think we could all do with a drink."

The waiter returned with a chilled bottle of wine and poured them all a glass.

Kia sipped her wine and watched the woman sitting opposite her. It was true she didn't remember her, but somewhere deep down she felt something tugging at her, long ago memories, all the questions no-one had given her any answers to. Her years of knowing she was different, and didn't fit in the world she was growing up in.

"*Lot, Mama, Lot,*" a whisper of something long ago, travelled down the years. A word that had stayed with her.

She turned to Jack. "So, that's why you were in Willow Drift then Jack? Who are you working for?"

"I work for an English newspaper; I specialise in cold cases. I came here to South Africa, firstly to try and find Sara, your mother, and to find out what exactly happened to a child who disappeared over twenty years ago. That child was you. Your grandfather wanted to know the truth."

Jack told her about his search for Sara, his meeting with Eza and Joseph and the final meeting when he had brought Sara to meet the man who had saved her life. Eza.

Sara put her glass down. "As a child, Eza told us you were happy. You learned their language and their ways, but when you went off to school with the Templetons, he felt you were unhappy, sometimes angry, as though you knew you didn't belong in their world either. Is this what happened?"

Sara leaned towards her daughter. "I've spoken to Diana. I think she always knew you were more than the little girl from the village."

Kia closed her eyes briefly. "Yes. Young children play together, they don't see any difference in each other. I knew there was something different about me. But who was I going to turn to? Who could I talk to?

"You see Mama, Mirium, always rubbed leaves and herbs on my skin, she told me it would keep my skin soft and safe from the sun. Every time I went home to the village, she would use this paste and I stayed brown.

"One day I noticed my skin was getting lighter and I didn't understand why. I must have known something wasn't right. I had a Griqua name, I spoke the language, I looked like a Griqua girl.

"I bought tanning lotion from the pharmacy and every day I used it to stay brown, even to this day I use it. It's more of a habit now, that tanned look white people always covet. Makes you look young, sexy and healthy!"

She looked at Sara and frowned. "When Jabu, my brother, and I had to register to go to school I think we both realised something was wrong. I was there when Jabu was born but Eza told the Templetons, and the officials, Jabu was born before me. We both knew they were not telling the truth to the Templetons. But we didn't understand why.

"I loved Eza and Mirium. But I felt no deep connection to them. I think as I grew older, I knew I didn't belong. But if I didn't belong to them who did I belong to?"

Sara's eyes filled with tears. "Oh, darling…"

"Jabu was definitely his father's son. He loved the bush and the animals, and he loved me. But I know he wondered why we looked different."

A large white cat with a red collar sauntered across the grounds of the hotel, Kia watched him disappear into the hotel. "I need to go and see Jabu. He needs to know the truth about me now."

374

She gave a small smile. "He'll always be my brother. He watched over me as I grew up, nothing will change how we feel about each other."

She looked back at Jack and Sara. "Where is Eza now?"

Jack willingly reached for her hand. "He's gone Kia. He's gone back to a world he knows and understands, where he'll be happy with the simple life he has always understood. A life before he rescued you from the river. You have to let him go. He gave you your life, you must let him live what's left of his now."

Kia nodded, her eyes once more filling with tears, as she remembered the gentle shepherd who had only ever shown her love, even though he had known she was not his.

Jack glanced at his watch, and rose from his chair. "I'm going to take a shower. I'll see you in the restaurant at seven."

Kia stood up and put her arms around Jack. He felt the softness of her, the smell of lemons and wild honey in her hair. "Thank you, Jack," she whispered against his chest. "Thank you for finding me."

He held her away from him, cupping her face in his hands, lost in the wetness of her green eyes. "No, Kia, thank *you* for finding me. Now, go sit with your mother."

Dusk was falling, shadows dancing across the grounds, the sky blood red promising another hot day tomorrow. He looked back before entering the hotel.

It brought a lump to his throat. Sara was leaning forward talking to Kia. The shadows of the past lengthened, the sun dipped, then was gone.

Mother and daughter silhouetted beneath the darkening skies.

Chapter Ninety-Three

A month later, Jack pulled into the driveway of North End house, and turned off the engine. Sara had stayed behind in London, with her friend Karen.

"Are you sure you'll be alright Kia? I can come in with you if you like?"

She shook her head as she buttoned up her coat. "Knowing you're waiting in the car will give me the courage I need."

"I'll be waiting for you Kia. I've been waiting a long time…"

Kia took a deep breath and opened the car door. He watched her slight figure as she made her way to the front door of North End house. Then she hesitated, turned around, panic written all over her lovely face, and looked at the waiting car. Jack gave her the thumbs up sign.

She lifted her hand and pressed the doorbell. The door was wrenched open and Kia stamped down her terror as she confronted her brother.

He looked at her angrily. "What the hell are you doing back here?"

"Hello Ben. Remember me? I'm your little sister Charlie. Charlotte."

She watched the colour drain from his face as he squinted at her, his eyes dark, cold and unfocused.

"Don't talk rubbish. I know exactly who you are. You're the girl with a name like a furniture shop. I told you before, and I'm telling you again. Get off my property before I call the police. I don't want you stealing anything else from my house."

"Oh, I don't think so Ben. You see this isn't exactly your property." She pushed past him and found herself in the large kitchen she remembered.

She unbuttoned her coat and turned around to face him, suddenly confident with her own truth. "Sara, our mother, isn't dead as you had obviously hoped. So, legally the house and its contents belong to her.

She's drawn up a new Will and left everything to me. I have to say you were a little hasty with putting the house on the market. It really wasn't yours to sell was it?"

The colour had returned to Ben's face as he stared at her.

"You're talking rubbish. You're not my sister, I mean, look at you! Impossible. Besides my sister is dead."

"No, Ben Courtney, not impossible. But you're right in a way. I'm not your sister, I'm actually your half-sister. Under this rather dark skin of mine I'm nearly as white as you are. My father was Italian you see. You always wanted to know who he was didn't you?"

She opened the glass fronted door of the glass cabinet and withdrew one of the four-hundred-year-old wine glasses.

Ben watched transfixed as she went to the fridge and helped herself to a bottle of wine. She poured herself a glass and took a sip.

*****

"So, this is what Sara, my mother, and I have decided to do. This house will indeed stay on the market. Neither of us want to live in it.

"I think you might remember grandfather's lawyer James Storm? Well he'll be here first thing tomorrow morning, with some of his staff, to make an inventory of the contents of the house. From now on everything will go through him. He will have power of attorney to sell the house, the contents, and the land."

Kia smiled at him triumphantly. "It should give you enough time to pack your bags and find somewhere else to live. As I said he'll be here at ten with a locksmith in tow.

"Oh, and don't try to make off with the family silver. Grandfather gave James a list of the contents. He'll be checking nothing has been taken. I shall take what I want, including the Snowdon portrait. Sara will have what she wants, and we'll have it all shipped back to South Africa. The rest will be auctioned off.

"The money from the house, the land and the auction will go a long way towards buying mother and I a beautiful home in the Cape, where we have decided to live.

"You're finished Ben. As you hoped you had finished me off when you threw me in the river. It's too late to accuse you of that now. Too much time has passed. You need professional help, but that's up to you. You're on your own now."

377

Charlotte buttoned up her coat and wrapped her scarf around her neck and took a final sip of her wine. "Well, that's all I have to say to you Ben Courtney. You sure as hell won't be seeing me again or Sara. She doesn't want to see you; can you believe that? Your own mother doesn't want to see you?"

A chair toppled over as Ben lunged at her. She dropped her glass in terror, and four hundred years of history shattered around her shoes.

"I wouldn't do that if I were you," a deep voice said quietly.

Jack was standing at the door. "You can't harm her anymore. Don't even think about it because this time there will be a witness. Just as there was a witness who saw you push Kia into that river in the Eastern Cape. Come on, my darling."

Putting a protective arm around her shaking body, he led her back to the car. The door of the old house slammed violently behind them, cutting off the howl of rage that came from within.

Jack held her until she stopped shaking. "It's alright, Kia, I've got you now, nothing, and no-one, will ever hurt you again. I'll take care of you, I promise. I made the same promise to Eza."

*****

Few people took much notice of the small article which appeared in *The Telegraph* a few days later, only the locals in the village.

The police had issued a statement about an accident in which a man had lost his life. The driver of the Range Rover had been driving under the influence of alcohol at high speed. The vehicle had hit a culvert on the curve of a country road in Dorchester and plunged into the flood swollen river.

The body of the driver had been found some miles away. It was thought he may have tried to swim to the banks of the river but had been overcome by the swiftly flowing water and the amount of alcohol in his bloodstream.

The victim has been identified as Mr Ben Courtney. Son and heir to North End House. Grandson of Sir Miles Courtney.

The verdict: Accidental drowning whilst under the influence of alcohol.

Poetic justice indeed.

*****

378

Down at the village pub, gossip was rife. Polly, the landlady, wiped down the bar counter discussing the situation with the locals.

"It seems to me that some houses are cursed. I'm afraid, given the history of it, North End house falls into that category. Poor Sir Miles, he would be heartbroken to know it will now pass to complete strangers. It's the end of the line for his family name, now that Ben has gone."

"I wonder what they'll do with all the contents?" one of the patrons asked. "With older people downsizing these days, it will probably be bought by a young couple, they won't want all those old relics that made up the sum of Sir Miles life."

Polly pushed a glass of wine across the counter to one of her customers.

"Auctioned off I suppose, and that will be the end of the Courtney family – the end of an era. All very sad I must say."

Chapter Ninety-Four

Harry leaned back in his chair and hooked his thumbs through his navy-blue braces. "Excellent work Jack, excellent! Another cracking story. I think we'll run it as a series in the Sunday supplement. Should keep our readers on the edge of their chairs. A child who went missing twenty odd years ago and now found. Pity about no book though."

Jack looked down at his tanned hands, enhanced by the whiteness of his shirt. "No book Harry. Sara was quite adamant about that. Too many people were involved and enough damage has been done."

Jack looked out of the window and although the April sun was shining brightly, in London, his mind went back to a different kind of sun in a country far away, and the characters he had met in a place called Willow Drift, a place he wanted to return to, with Kia. It was their story too.

He turned back to Harry. "I'm handing in my resignation Harry. I've had a taste of another kind of life and I like it. I'm going back to South Africa with Kia."

Harry grinned broadly at him. "Only Kia? What about Sara?"

Jack ran his fingers through his hair. "Sara is going back too…"

"Methinks you haven't only fallen in love with the African sun have you Jack?"

Jack shifted in his chair looking uncomfortable. Then he grinned. "No."

"Well I'll tell you what. I'm not going to accept your resignation. I don't want to lose you. You can be my man in Africa, as Alex was before he resigned and went to live at Mbabati. What do you think? We can work out a contract with the legal chaps."

Jack leapt out of his chair and pumped Harry's hand. "Thanks Harry it sounds good to me! We were hoping you'd suggest that."

He glanced at his watch then reached for his jacket. "Have to go, someone's waiting for me. By the way how's Maggie?"

"Maggie is fine, she's put everyone in their place including the wife and me. She's a real fur shedder though. The wife has given up wearing black. Good luck Jack. I'll get your contract drawn up. You'll need to sign it before you leave our damp little country. Go on, off you go, I assume Kia is waiting for you?"

*****

Jack took the steps down from the office two at a time. Kia was waiting for him.

"What did Harry say?" she asked anxiously. "Did he agree?"

Jack lifted her up and swung her around, her braids flew around his neck.

"He said yes, Kia. I'll be working out of Cape Town."

She kept her arms around his neck and hugged him, a big grin spreading across her lovely face.

Jack disentangled himself from her embrace and put her down. He cupped her face with his hands and looked into the big green eyes he had come to love, and wanted to spend the rest of his life with.

"He said yes, Kia. But what will you say now?"

She kissed him on the mouth. "I say yes, Jack. Yes, yes, yes!"

The pedestrians made their way around the couple forming an oasis on the pavement. The beautiful young women with beads in her hair and the attractive man with his wild untamed hair. There was envy in their glances.

Karen and Sara watched the couple, walking hand in hand towards them.

Karen turned to Sara and hugged her. "Looks like some good news is finally coming your way Sara."

Sara swallowed the lump in her throat as she watched her daughter walking down the long road back to her. Holding the hand of the man who had found everything he was looking for, with the added bonus of the love of her daughter. The lost child he had been so determined to find the truth about.

Kia, who had known the love of the shepherd, his wife and Jabu, had finally found someone of her own, someone she would love for the rest of her life.

But she would never forget the touch, and love, of the gentle shepherd, who had saved her life.

Eza.

*****

If you enjoyed reading this book and would like to share that enjoyment with others, then please take the time to visit the place where you made your purchase and write a review.

Reviews are a great way to spread the word about worthy authors and will help them be rewarded for their hard work.

You can also visit Samantha's Author Page on Amazon to find out more about her life and passions.

Also by Samantha Ford:

The Zanzibar Affair

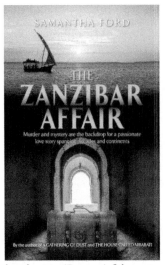

A letter found in an old chest on the island of Zanzibar finally reveals the secret of Kate Hope's glamorous, but anguished past, and the reason for her sudden and unexplained disappearance.

Ten year's previously Kate's lover and business partner, Adam Hamilton, tormented by a terrifying secret he is willing to risk everything for, brutally ends his relationship with Kate.

A woman is found murdered in a remote part of Kenya bringing Tom Fletcher back to East Africa to unravel the web of mystery and intrigue surrounding Kate, the woman he loves but has not seen for over twenty years.

In Zanzibar, Tom meets Kate's daughter Molly. With her help he pieces together the last years of her mother's life and his extraordinary connection to it.

A page turning novel of love, passion, betrayal and death, with an unforgettable cast of characters, set against the spectacular backdrop of East and Southern Africa, New York and France.

Amazon Reviews

"This book will keep you guessing; that's a good thing. I could barely put it down and one night dreamed about it so much I woke up and read more. It's unbearably sad in some places and wonderfully happy in others. Fantastic!"

"This book takes you on a safari round Africa. It is a compelling story with so many twists. It is beautifully and hauntingly told. The details and descriptions made me feel the heat, smell the ocean and slap the mosquitoes. Thank you."

"I loved The Zanzibar affair. I felt I was there sensing the smells, the sea and the warmth of Africa. The way she weaves the characters into the story is quite fascinating, leaving the reader spellbound and wondering where it's going to end. Always with an unexpected twist. A fabulous storyline and book which I could hardly put down. Highly recommended."

The House Called Mbabati

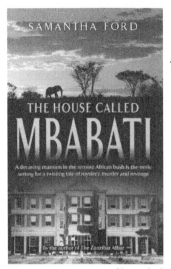

The Mother Superior crossed herself quickly. "May God have mercy on you, and forgive you both," she murmured as she locked the diary and faded letters in the drawer.

Deep in the heart of the East African bush stands a deserted mansion. Boarded up, on the top floor, is a magnificent Steinway Concert Grand, shrouded in decades of dust.

In an antique shop in London, an elderly nun recognises an old photograph of the mansion; she knows it well.

Seven thousand miles away, in Cape Town, a woman lies dying; she whispers one word to journalist Alex Patterson – Mbabati.

Sensing a good story, and intrigued with what he has discovered, Alex heads for East Africa in search of the old abandoned house. He is unprepared for what he discovers there; the hidden home of a once famous classical pianist whose career came to a shattering end; a grave with a blank headstone and an old retainer called Luke - the only one left alive who knows the true story about two sisters who disappeared without trace over twenty years ago.

Alex unravels a story which has fascinated the media and the police for decades. A twisting tale of love, passion, betrayal and murder; and the unbreakable bond between two extraordinary sisters who were prepared to sacrifice everything to hide the truth.

Mbabati is set against the magnificent and enduring landscape of the African bush - where nothing is ever quite as it seems.

Amazon Reviews

"It is a long time since I have been so absorbed by a novel about Africa. Reading it, I vacillated between willing it to last longer as I was enjoying it so much, and wanting to get through it to reveal the outcome. There can be no greater praise for this novel than its endorsement by the late John Gordon Davis, to whom the novel is dedicated. Anyone who has read any of JGD's novels, in particular his classic 'Hold My

Hand I'm Dying' will understand that Samantha Ford's novel is in the same league."

"What a wonderful story where you have a stormy love affair set in the heart of Africa. It twists and turns as the plot unfolds and you will surely shed a tear or two along the way. For those who have been on an African safari you will not put this book down. Such intelligent and beautiful writing."

"The book is captivating from beginning to end. It takes you on a riveting journey where the story develops and keeps you guessing. Loved it! Didn't want it to end!"

A Gathering of Dust

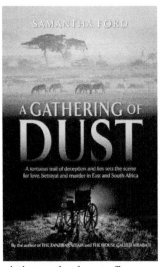

Through the mists of a remote and dangerous part of the South African coastline, a fisherman stumbles upon an abandoned car and an overturned wheelchair.

Thousands of miles away in London, an unidentified woman lies in a coma. When she recovers she has no memory of her past or where she comes from. As fragments of her memory begin to return, the woman has to confront the facts about herself as they begin to unfold. A disastrous love affair in the African bush: a missing husband: and a sinister shadowy figure who knows exactly who she is and where she comes from.

Tension builds as images and secrets begin to resurface from her lost past – rekindled memories that plunge her back into a world she finds she would rather not remember.

Set against the magnificent backdrop of East and Southern Africa. A Gathering of Dust is a fast-paced story of love, betrayal and murder scattered along a trail of deception and lies, with a single impossible truth, and an unthinkable ending.

Amazon Reviews

"What a writer this author is! So cleverly written and with twists and turns you never see coming. I am an avid reader and this authors books are the best I have read in a long time. Her books have everything, mystery, murder, romance, intrigue, suspense etc etc. Well worth a read."

"My husband knows when I am reading this author's books that there is little that will get my nose out of them. Her descriptives of even the simplest things create such a vivid picture. She has made me fall in love with Africa and her story lines are captivating and intelligently

thought out. I never want to finish one of her books only because I don't want them to end."

"Superb. Absolutely brilliant. I simply couldn't stop reading, turned TV off and just read and read, even ignoring my hubby. Can't wait to read the next book!!!"

"A gripping read, with many gut-wrenching twists and turns. I had trouble putting the book down to eat, sleep or work! Fabulous."

Printed in Great Britain
by Amazon

18390273R00233